CAMP
ZERO

CAMP ZERO

— A NOVEL —

MICHELLE MIN STERLING

ATRIA BOOKS

NEW YORK LONDON TORONTO SYDNEY NEW DELHI

ATRIA
BOOKS

An Imprint of Simon & Schuster, Inc.
1230 Avenue of the Americas
New York, NY 10020

First Atria Books hardcover edition April 2023

ATRIA BOOKS and colophon are trademarks of Simon & Schuster, Inc.

For information about special discounts for bulk purchases, please contact Simon & Schuster Special Sales at 1-866-506-1949 or business@simonandschuster.com.

The Simon & Schuster Speakers Bureau can bring authors to your live event. For more information or to book an event, contact the Simon & Schuster Speakers Bureau at 1-866-248-3049 or visit our website at www.simonspeakers.com.

Interior design by Jill Putorti

Manufactured in the United States of America

1 3 5 7 9 10 8 6 4 2

Library of Congress Cataloging-in-Publication Data
Names: Sterling, Michelle Min, 1982– author. | Hallak, Natalie, 1993– other.
Title: Camp zero : a novel / Michelle Min Sterling.
Description: First Atria Books hardcover edition. | New York : Atria Books, 2023. | Summary: "In a near-future northern settlement, the fate of a young woman intertwines with those of a college professor and a collective of women soldiers in this mesmerizing and transportive novel in the vein of Station Eleven and The Power."—Provided by publisher.
Identifiers: LCCN 2022040932 (print) | LCCN 2022040933 (ebook) | ISBN 9781668007563 (hardcover) | ISBN 9781668007570 (trade paperback) | ISBN 9781668007587 (ebook)
Classification: LCC PS3619.T47754 C36 2023 (print) | LCC PS3619.T47754 (ebook) | DDC 892.8—dc23/eng/20220826
LC record available at https://lccn.loc.gov/2022040932
LC ebook record available at https://lccn.loc.gov/2022040933

ISBN 978-1-6680-0756-3
ISBN 978-1-6680-0758-7 (ebook)

For A & A

CAMP
ZERO

CHAPTER ONE

ROSE

The Blooms receive their new names on the shortest day of the year. Six women in total. All strangers. They stand in an empty parking lot and wait to be checked in. Snow has scrubbed the landscape clean, capped the roof of the run-down mall that is one of the few buildings still standing on this frozen stretch of highway.

The Bloom last in line pauses to appreciate the freeze. It's colder in the North than she expected, and the snow is more delicate. She takes off a glove and watches a flake vanish in the palm of her hand. She's never seen snow before, and the snowflake feels refreshing on her skin, like a cool cloth pressed to a feverish forehead.

When she reaches the entrance to the mall, her new Madam introduces herself as Judith. She is nothing like the Bloom's previous Madam, who drifted around in a linen caftan and calfskin sandals. Judith wears a fur-lined parka, black snow pants, and a pair of steel-toe boots, as if she was hired to demolish the dilapidated mall they're standing in front of.

Judith reads off a clipboard. "Your name will be Rose."

"Rose," she repeats. A cloying, sentimental name. Like a grandmother who keeps apple pies in the deep-freeze. She had expected one of the pseudonyms shared among the "Asian Girls" in the Loop where she used to work: Jade, Mei, Lotus. It never mattered that the names were cliché, or that she is as white as she is Korean. Back in the Floating City, ethnicity was a ready-made brand.

Judith lowers her voice. "I wanted to let you girls choose your names for yourself. But Meyer likes things his way."

"Is Meyer my client?" Rose asks, careful to sound casual.

"He doesn't want us to use that word here, Rose. Think of him as your collaborator." Judith opens the front door of the mall and Rose follows inside. "Welcome to the Millennium Mall."

The Blooms' quarters are at the back of the mall in a department store that has long since been pillaged. Metal clothing racks are scattered in jumbled piles, and the beauty counters' mirrors are mottled. Rose can smell the faintest trace of artificial gardenia as she rolls her suitcase past a perfume display, where an ad of a woman's glowing face pressed against the bristly cheek of a male model still remains. Her mother never wore perfume and hadn't allowed Rose to either. She wanted them to smell as they actually did, like the saltwater breeze of the peninsula.

"When did the mall close?" Rose asks.

"Fifteen years ago," Judith says. "It was the first place to shutter when the rigs stopped drilling."

Judith leads Rose to the former furniture section where the Blooms' lodgings have been built out of plywood along an echoing corridor. Each room's entrance is framed by light, and Rose can hear the sounds of the other Blooms unpacking behind the closed doors.

Judith opens Rose's door and deposits her single suitcase on a mahogany four-poster bed. A bear pelt is splayed across the floor, and a rickety plastic chandelier is bolted to the ceiling. A vanity mirror with a small, upholstered stool in front of it is against the wall. The room reeks of damp pleather.

Damien, her former client who set her up with this job, warned her that the camp would be spare, but he said nothing about squatting in a derelict shopping mall. It's too late to give Damien shit now. Rose won't speak with him again until her assignment is complete. All she has is her contact in camp, who Damien promised would reach out when the moment is right. She wonders if Judith might be her contact, but then decides this clipboard-wielding woman is too straightforward for that level of deception.

"Water is heated to tepid," Judith says, and shows Rose the "sanitizing schedule" tacked to her bedroom door. Judith explains that the Blooms are expected to share the mall's washroom, where a nozzle attached to one of the sink's faucets functions as a makeshift shower. "We run on oil and have to conserve energy to maintain our supply."

"Oil isn't illegal here?" Rose asks in surprise. In the Floating City, oil usage is treated with the same moral outrage as murder.

"Nothing is illegal in camp," Judith says. "That's why we live off-grid. We're lucky enough to make our own rules here."

Rose wonders if the rules of the camp are like the rules of the Floating City, created to benefit those who made them. If this is the case, then she doubts Judith is the one who made the rules. Judith strikes her as a middle manager, a local hire paid to oversee the Blooms, whose influence in camp is confined to the domestic arrangements of the bedrooms. But Judith is technically Rose's boss, so she will have to adopt the blasé disinterest of a jaded escort to keep her new Madam from becoming suspicious of her. Even if Judith only runs the Blooms' side of camp, she still holds some form of power, which is more than Rose can openly say for herself.

Judith tells Rose to unload her suitcase on the bedspread. Rose dumps the contents into a pile: two slips, a bodycon cocktail dress, a black silk dress, a silk robe, linen pajamas, a merino wool sweater, two pairs of pants, a few blouses, socks, lingerie sets, back-seam stockings, shiny heels, calfskin boots, hair ties, and cosmetics. Judith is quiet and focused as she inspects each item.

"What are you looking for?" Rose asks.

"Sharp edges. And drugs." Judith flicks on the jet-black lace lamp on the nightstand, illuminating a stack of books. "We keep a clean house here. Only booze and cigarettes allowed."

Judith runs her fingers along the seams of Rose's clothing, rifling through the cosmetic bag, opening the lipsticks and powder. Rose feels an impulse to snatch her clothes away from her. She picks up one of the books on the nightstand instead, a hardcover titled *Building in Ruins*, with a photo of a young, bearded, solemn-looking man printed inside the dust jacket. His shirtsleeves are rolled to his elbows, and he appears to be standing in a parched acre of desert next to a modernist house.

"'An indispensable manifesto on finding silver linings in annihilation,'" Rose reads from the back cover. "Is it any good?"

"Oh, you like to read?" Judith sounds surprised. "You're welcome to find out for yourself. That's Meyer's first book, published right after he graduated from architecture school. You'll find all of his writings here." Judith taps another book titled *Utopia after the Anthropocene*. "He likes to keep us educated."

For a moment, Rose doesn't care about the mildewy smell in the room, or that a panel in the ceiling is caving in, or even that her new Madam assumes she's illiterate. Meyer's books are here for her to read. A small victory, but an essential one. Reading what Meyer thinks and feels will be the first step to gaining his trust. Everything Damien promised her depends on this.

"The room is very . . ." Rose searches for the right word. "Cozy."

Judith looks at her and then laughs. "That's bullshit and you know it. It smells like a dead animal in here. But we have to make do with what we have. Let me show you the kitchen."

Judith leads Rose down a dark hallway into a room that smells of fresh paint and industrial glue. The kitchen is nothing like the polished dining rooms of the Loop where she used to dine with clients. This kitchen looks like it was once the department store's staff break room, complete with a microwave, an electric two-burner stove, and a fridge that hums in the corner. A white plastic table, the kind left to mildew in a backyard, is positioned in the corner of the room next to a stack of patio chairs.

The camp's kitchen may not have a wine cellar, but at least it has natural light. Rose steps toward the floor-to-ceiling window and watches the snow softly falling on the trees. This view will be her refuge.

"The snow is so pure you can eat it with a spoon," Judith says.

Rose is impressed. Even in the Floating City, the water is filtered. Or is it ozonated? She can't recall. She touches behind her left ear to check which it is, but Judith interrupts her by gesturing to one of the chairs.

"I'm going to recite a short statement and need your verbal consent if you agree," Judith says.

Rose sits down at the table and nods.

"AKA Rose, do you agree to undergo Flick extraction for a period of three months?" Judith looks at her digital wristwatch. "Commencing at 1:12 p.m., December 21, 2049?"

Rose knows she has no choice. "Yes."

"Can you lean toward me?" Judith unzips a leather bag and snaps a latex glove on each hand.

Rose pushes her hair over one shoulder. "Will it hurt?"

"No more than it did going in." Judith ties Rose's hair with an elastic band and presses behind Rose's left ear until she finds the telltale bump. "You were one of the first to get implanted, weren't you?"

"How can you tell?"

"Your Flick is first-generation, which makes it easier to locate."

Rose had been five years old when she received her Flick. Before it became common practice to implant at birth, every child received a Flick before starting kindergarten. *One Child—One Flick.* A school nurse had scanned Rose's eyes and fingerprints, then imprinted her facial data with a flash photo. The nurse asked Rose to wave at the implantation robot with its smiling face and two disquietingly unblinking eyes. The robot waved back before making three tiny punctures along the crown of Rose's head as it weaved the electrode threads through the synapses of her brain. When the two-millimeter opening was cut behind her left ear, Rose felt a tiny implosion of pressure. A single tear had rolled down her cheek as the robot nested the iridescent chip into the incision.

Now Judith presses again, harder this time. "There you are." She marks the spot with a pen. "Count to three. This will only be a pinch."

Rose closes her eyes as Judith uncaps the metal plunger and presses firmly. A sucking sound, mounting pressure, and then a precise *pop.*

"You're all done, Rose." Judith uses pin droppers to place the Flick into a test tube.

"Can I see it?" Rose asks after Judith seals the tube.

Judith shrugs and hands the test tube to her. "It's yours."

Rose has never seen her Flick, even though it has been in her body for over twenty years. Hers is bulkier than the ones now routinely implanted. It is about the same size as the nail on her pinky finger, and almost translucent, but when she tilts the tube from side to side, the Flick shimmers in the colors of bioluminescence—coral, green, topaz.

"Do you feel different?" Judith asks.

Rose looks at the top left corner of the room. She blinks. Once. Twice. Nothing. No feed appears. Think of something dead. No, something beyond dead. Think of something extinct.

The last story Rose saw on her Flick involved Samson the tiger at the Bronx Zoo dying of heatstroke. A headline as feed-worthy as one of the last living tigers on Earth would usually trigger a proliferating cascade of stories—the encyclopedia entry on tigers in captivity; vintage footage of baby tigers rolling around in dirt; a biologist lecturing on the challenges of raising big cats in a warming climate; tiger stripes; tiger ice cream; stuffed tigers; humans in tiger suits. Rose focuses and thinks again: tiger. But still her feed does not appear.

Instead, she remembers the tiger she once saw at the Franklin Park Zoo in Boston, back when the zoo was still open and the resident tiger alive. Her mother had taken her to celebrate her sixth birthday, a rare break from their life on the peninsula. The memory is grainy, but she can see it more clearly if she closes her eyes: her mother, unfathomably young, eating an overpriced ice cream cone while seated on a blisteringly hot steel bench. She passes the ice cream to Rose and holds a napkin under her daughter's chin while she licks. Once the cone is consumed, she picks Rose up to see the animal behind bars, a happiness swelling between them that blooms into her mother tongue.

"Horangi," her mother says, and points at the tiger.

Rose dangles there for a moment in her mother's arms, trying to catch the attention of the lusciously striped animal by repeating the Korean word. She falters on the second syllable and feels her cheeks flush with embarrassment. The tiger doesn't care about her poor pronunciation. He sits perfectly still like he has been frozen in amber, blinking only when a fly settles into his eye's dark crease.

A dusty memory conjured from the ether. Damien had warned her that without her Flick, memories might surface unexpectedly, but she hadn't anticipated how near they'd feel again. She closes her eyes, and her mother is still there, laughing in a way Rose had forgotten.

"I can't access my feed," Rose says, and hands back the Flick.

Judith places the tube in the wooden box. "You'll get used to it. Meyer wants the Blooms to be pure and uncorrupted by technology."

Rose touches behind her ear instinctively. Nothing remains except for the blue dot of ink.

During their first morning in camp, the Blooms gather for breakfast in the kitchen wearing heels and shimmery powder, their cheeks and lips shining under the fluorescent light. It is still pitch-dark outside. They sit elegantly at the plastic table, but without their Flicks to hold their attention, their fingers tap the table or absently fidget with the bangles at their wrists, the delicate string of gold around their necks. Their eyes flicker to the corners of the room out of habit, but their feed doesn't appear to amuse them. Instead, they look at each other.

Judith tells them they are the first Blooms in camp and should feel proud to be chosen.

"We considered many girls," Judith says as she pins a name tag above each of their hearts. "Only you six were selected."

They quickly learn their new names: Iris, Jasmine, Violet, Fleur, Rose, and Willow. Pretty names. Prom queen names. Rose takes careful note of each Bloom as she introduces herself.

The one named Iris smells of perfumed figs. Her voice is low and sultry, and when she smiles at each Bloom, the lines around her eyes crinkle for a moment before disappearing. Her red hair is styled into a stiff chignon, and she wears a white silk blouse with a pussy bow. At Avalon's club in the Loop, mature hostesses like Iris were instructed to learn the holy trinity—politics, travel, golf—topics older clients of a certain provenance liked to discuss over dinner before retiring to their suite for the evening.

Jasmine's hair is cut into a blunt bob, and she has the long, delicate hands of someone who is adept at playing piano or flower arranging. She is what Avalon would call "a classic beauty," with clear eyes, clear skin, a lovely neck. She is also a type Rose has seen in the Loop before: the blue-blooded whore with the New England pedigree, educated at one of the last elite women's colleges, where she learned the cool manners and erudite references of Boston's business class. A girl who looks at ease in a designer jacket and pearls, who knows her way around a salad fork, and is conversational in three languages. Girlfriend experience. Travel companion. Vacations on private yachts and dune-swept islands guarded by well-paid thugs in cheap suits.

Violet is from New Orleans, and her roots in the region run deep. She tells the Blooms that her Creole father was a musician and taught her to play half a dozen instruments. Later, she received a partial scholarship to attend a renowned music college in New York, but she soon ran out of money when her funding disappeared with budget cuts. After dropping out of school, she worked to pay rent, playing gigs at small clubs and seeing clients on the side in the condo she shared with four other independents. She wears a red jumpsuit, and her hair is in long braids.

Fleur is self-consciously blond and justifies this fact by saying she is from California. She lived in a coastal town north of San Francisco before the town was evacuated during a wildfire and, after, packed all her belongings into her car and fled inland. She found work in the Blue Lady Lodge, one of the last legal brothels still running in the desert of Nevada, where she was relieved to discover that the land was barren and treeless. When she wasn't servicing military men and gamblers, she was creating sculptures out of colorful glass and clay. She wants to make more art after this job and hopes to open her first exhibition in a defunct gas station on the outskirts of Las Vegas, where she'll install her sculptures next to the long-derelict oil pumps. Fleur wears a shibori-dyed caftan, the bangles on her wrists clinking as she fiddles with the name tag on her chest.

The Bloom called Willow is the only one dressed casually. A slinky girl with a shaved head, she wears stained overalls and a white T-shirt, and has the trim, responsive body of a kickboxer. Unlike the rest of the Blooms, she offers no explanation as to where she is from, or why she is here. Instead, she pages her way through a novel while chewing on a fingernail, until Judith calls on her to introduce herself. Willow looks up to take the Blooms in for a calculated second, says her name, and then immediately returns to her book.

Judith turns toward Rose. "Rose joins us from the Floating City." The Blooms suddenly eye her with a mix of respect and suspicion.

Rose has dressed like a vigilant secretary on her first day of work to show the other Blooms that she means business. She wears patent leather pumps and back-seam stockings, a short black silk dress cinched at her waist, and lipstick the color of dried blood.

Violet says to Rose, "Do you know how lucky you are to have worked there?"

"Yeah, why did you leave?" Jasmine asks.

"I was looking for a change of pace, that's all," Rose says, noticing that Judith is watching her.

Fleur closes her eyes for a moment and smiles. "I get it. Totally. You wanted to see if life really is better up north."

Willow sets her book down on the table and runs a hand over her buzzed hair. She looks directly at Rose. "And is it?"

Rose can still sense Judith's attention on her, which makes her answer carefully. "Of course it is."

"That's right, Rose. We are all so lucky to be in the North," Judith says, and smiles benevolently at the Blooms. "But we also have to protect ourselves up here. That's why certain rules must be followed while we're living together."

Judith tells the Blooms that they will take two walks every day. Once in the morning after breakfast when the first rays of light spill over camp, and once in the afternoon as the sun sets. Wind, snow, ice, sleet—none of it matters. They will walk, Judith says, regardless of the weather. Other than their daily walks, they will be confined inside the mall. Their rooms, the kitchen, and the unused spaces of the department store are free for their use. But they should never wander unescorted into the farther reaches of the mall, or outside, where the stretch of highway winds north.

Rose already knows what it's like to stay indoors when the temperatures flare into triple-digit streaks during the summer months. She spent weeks in the cool climes of central air as the asphalt steamed in the intense heat. Staying indoors won't be a problem for her. It's who she is inside with that matters.

"You must never cross the highway," Judith continues. "Right now, the Diggers are in that warehouse, desperate for anything that will take their minds off their circumstances."

"Diggers?" Iris asks.

"Yes, Diggers. They're the men hired to work at the construction site," Judith says.

"We can take care of ourselves. We *know* men," Violet chimes in.

"You don't know these kinds of men," Judith replies. "The only thing they're good for is digging holes in the earth." She softens her voice. "Not like your clients, of course. They're real gentlemen." Judith looks out the window at the falling snow. "It must be a relief to feel the cold."

A few of Rose's clients in the Loop had taken vacations in the Arctic Circle, where they paid the equivalent of her yearly salary to drift in a luxury cruise ship among the melting icebergs. "A lost world," one client had said as he showed Rose image after image of blue ice. "Someday, seeing an iceberg will be more impossible than visiting the moon."

The prophesizing about *how* and *what* and, most important, *who* will survive was a common topic among Rose's clients. They often discussed how they planned to hold on to their wealth in periods of crisis. Offshore banks. Offshore cities. Temperamental government bonds cashed into gold. Divestment of all fossil fuels into clean-energy portfolios, with a healthy percentage devoted to data surveillance and cybernetics research.

Rose wonders if Meyer feels differently than her former clients. If he's anything like Damien told her, then he still naïvely believes in a better future. And this is what Rose can use to her advantage: his belief that he can save the world, not merely cash in on its destruction.

After a breakfast of boiled oats, Judith leads the Blooms to the entrance of the mall and shows them where their long, fur-lined parkas and knee-high snow boots are stored. Each jacket has a flower embroidered in colorful thread—a blood-red bud for Rose; a nest of dark blue for Violet; a cluster of white blossoms for Jasmine; a pink spray for Fleur; purple-and-yellow petals for Iris. Unlike the rest of the Blooms, whose flowers are depicted as cut from the plant they grew on, Willow's jacket features an entire tree with long, drowsy branches that reach to the intricate root system. Silver flowers blossom on each branch. Rose once saw a similar depiction of the willow tree in the cemetery on the peninsula where her father was buried, carved on the slate tombstones of the Puritans who settled New England centuries ago. A symbol of death, but also of rebirth.

The Blooms take their designated parkas and suit up for the outdoors. When they step outside, the morning sun is rising. It is crisp, bright, and freezing today. Rose inhales deeply. The air is so refreshing that it demands to be sealed in little silver cylinders and shipped to the south, where it would be as prized as a trunk filled with rations during a famine.

Rose chooses not to pair off with a Bloom and walks by herself in the snow-filled lot, along the edge of the metal fence that marks the boundary of their new home. She notices a locked gate in the center of the fence with an intercom to buzz people in or out. Judith's rules aren't the only obstacle keeping the Blooms inside.

Rose turns to watch the Blooms walk laps around the frozen parking lot. She wonders if they feel flattered to be part of a hand-selected crew. Curated. It's a word that emerges unbidden. It's true. They are curated.

The mature redhead. The refined WASP. The athletic Black girl. The dreamy blond artist. The tough alt-girl. And Rose, fulfilling the coy Asian role. Who chose them? And why?

A hand taps her shoulder, and Rose turns to find Willow standing beside her. In her massive parka and fur-lined boots, she seems younger and rangier than she did in the kitchen.

"They're watching us," Willow says, and points.

Across the highway, a group of men dressed in identical snowsuits the color of mop water stand huddled outside a warehouse. Each has a spade resting over his shoulder.

"The Diggers?" Rose asks.

Willow nods. "Yes. Judith says they're filthy bastards."

Rose watches them jostle each other playfully. One pushes another forward, and he laughs and steps back. "They look harmless to me."

Willow laughs harshly. "How can you be so sure?"

Three of the Diggers begin to walk toward the middle of the highway. They joke loudly, egging each other on, until one finally ventures forward and knocks his spade against the metal fence. He shouts and waves. The Blooms stop in their tracks and look back. The Digger suddenly flips into a handstand and moves along the side of the fence, legs dangling in the air as his gloved hands make indentations in the snow.

The Digger flips back onto his feet and takes a deep bow. His face is flushed with blood, and his mouth flashes gold as he grins at the pretty women in their oversized down parkas.

Rose greets the man with a wave, and he bows again, clearly pleased to have succeeded in getting her attention.

Suddenly, a flash of movement on the highway. In the distance, six SUVs curl through the still landscape, each towing a sleek Airstream trailer that shimmers in the low winter sun. As they drive past the mall parking lot, Rose notices each hood has a small green flag emblazoned with a geodesic dome. She can't see anything through the tinted windows, but she knows their clients are in there.

Judith calls the Blooms by their new names, and before Rose follows, she turns back to see the SUVs drive past the workers' camps, north along the highway. Where they're going is a mystery, but Rose intends to find out.

Rose hurries back to the mall. She should get ready. The clients will drop by soon and she needs to ensure Meyer chooses her.

———

Back in her room, Rose sits on the bed and out of habit taps behind her left ear. She winces. The place where her Flick was extracted is still tender. Her clients often spoke in rhapsodic terms on how the mind grows "free" without the intrusion of the Flick, but like most of the other hostesses in the Loop, she preferred to be on-feed when she wasn't working. Now, she feels uneasy without the Flick, as if a part of her body has been plucked off. But her mind also feels clearer. Sharper.

She picks up one of Meyer's books off the nightstand and reads the introduction:

This book begins with a simple premise: What can we create out of destruction? Building in ruins is a strategy once utilized in postwar environments, in the debris of bombed cities, the carnage of the killing field. Humans have always created empires by drawing borders with blood. But the war we now fight is not as nations, but within our own countries and communities, and with the earth itself. We must begin to rebuild on land that has been destroyed by human folly: a former nuclear test site; a clear-cut forest; a devastated city post-storm; the excavated remains of oil extraction. Land needs people to tend and caretake, to build and dream. By bringing people to live among ruin, we may still have a chance to survive.

The last thing Damien told Rose before she left for camp was that Meyer would argue that survival is a trait inherent to human evolution. "But survival is always a choice," Damien had said as they sat at the rosewood table in his suite. He reached for her hand and squeezed his thumb against her pulse. "You can choose to live. Or you can choose to perish. What do you choose, my dear?"

"Life," Rose said. Her pulse throbbed under his thumb.

"Smart choice," Damien said. "Let me show what you'll get once you return."

Damien led Rose to the apartment he had reserved for her and her mother: a white cube with floor-to-ceiling windows that faced the gleaming Atlantic. "You'll be the first to see the sun rise," he said. "And you'll never have to think about the mainland again."

At the time, she could barely believe that this life would be theirs. Erase everything that came before. Start fresh. Start anew.

Rose sets down Meyer's book and looks out her bedroom window at the snow falling on the boughs of a pine tree. A small bird flits from branch to branch, refusing to settle in one place. She wonders what her mother will think of the Floating City with its gleaming malls and landscaped green spaces, the immense towers that look like they are in conversation with the heavens. But her mother may never want to see the ocean again, and this worries Rose. That what they've lost can't be solved by simply replacing it.

The bird suddenly flaps its wings and takes off. She watches it arc into the sky until it disappears.

CHAPTER TWO

GRANT

To Grant, the land looks empty. He sits in seat 1A of the Cessna with a plastic cup of top-shelf whiskey in one hand, a decimated bag of pretzel batons in the other. He stares out at his new country. The window is flecked with tiny snowflakes, the tundra dotted with evergreens. Granite mountains rise from glacier lakes as blue as robin's eggs. Or so he thinks. Grant has never seen a real robin's egg before. Birds in the Floating City tend to be of the inbred variety, kept in cages and released each spring. In a more whimsical period, he had perused photos of robin's eggs on his Flick, searching for the exact shade of Jane's eyes, and discovered "lost egg blue" was another name for the hue. He'd celebrated the poetry of the term then, felt it was a fitting tribute to his love for Jane. But now all he feels is lost.

There, he's done it again. One dark thought and he's back in the abyss. Just like that, all the hope summoned for the journey is snuffed out. *Think positive thoughts*, the therapist his father hired often said. *Create a better reality through self-actualization.*

Grant looks out the window again and tries to feel happy. Everything looks crisper here than in Boston, he concludes, and feels his mood lighten. Maybe it's the third whiskey or the fact that he's thousands of miles from his family and all that he's left behind. No, he thinks. All the shit he's finally escaped.

As the Cessna descends, he sees the land is not empty. Stretches of ice crystallize into structures. A blackened barn burned to the ground by a wildfire. A grain silo rusted red. An oil well frozen in a forward bend. The straight shot of highway is still without the movement of traffic. Nothing is in motion. In fact, nothing seems alive.

And then, in the distance, he sees the green lights of the landing strip. A tiny compound glows below him as the plane hits the ground. The Cessna shudders on a strip of tarmac and rolls to the end of a fallow field. Grant accidentally crushes the plastic cup in his hand as condensation streams across the window. He is the only passenger in the six-person plane, but like the good Walden boy he is, he waits for the seat belt light to blink off before he stands. He brushes pretzel crumbs from his pants, grabs his suitcase from the overhead compartment, and carefully knots a cashmere scarf around his neck.

He's almost there.

As Grant drags his suitcase across the frozen tarmac, he looks back to see the Cessna rolling down the runway and taking off again. There isn't a single returning passenger? That's surprising. He'd assumed that the beginning of the semester would be a busy time for travel. He watches until the plane is only a dot in the sky.

The terminal is, in fact, not a terminal but a former gas station with a derelict motel attached on one side. The charging station still has two gas pumps out front, and the red neon sign of the motel buzzes on and off: VACANCY. VACANCY. VACANCY.

He deposits his suitcase by the front door of the station and cleans his fogged glasses with the scarf before taking in the dim yellow room: the hot dogs lazily rotating next to the tub of ancient pickles; the worn tables and slashed vinyl chairs; the radio duct-taped to the counter, tuned to white noise. A handwritten sign is posted in the window and warns the wayward traveler:

This is Your FINAL Resting Place
All Northern Roads Uncared For

Only three people are in the station: two truckers with intimidating facial hair who wear wool hats with earflaps and lined bomber jackets, as well as a teenage girl cashier who avoids eye contact when Grant smiles and says hello. He can tell the men are taking in his canvas sneakers and thin corduroy jacket with suspicion, and he wishes he had packed something other than tweedy blazers, wrinkly button-up shirts, and the one pair of tasseled loafers his mother had given him, which he now realizes will make him look like a certified Ivy twat. No hats. Or gloves. Or the kind of footwear that allows a person to tread through five feet of snow. He'll have to buy an entire wardrobe of wool plaid when he reaches the campus.

"Excuse me. I was wondering if either of you could drive me to Dominion Lake?" Grant asks the men. He pats the pockets of his jacket and pulls out a wad of American bills from his wallet.

Both men break into a belly laugh that shows the gold glinting in their molars. So it's true what Grant's read: the men up here have safeguarded their earnings in their teeth.

"Dominion Lake?" one of them finally says, readjusting his hat and exposing the oil derrick tattoo on his forearm. "No roads up to Dominion." The second man looks away and warms his hands against a mug of pitch-black coffee.

"Yes there are." Grant rolls open a map on the table to show them. "Right here." He taps a body of water shaped like a kidney. "I'll pay you well if you take me there." He drops the money on the table.

"No roads up to Dominion," the first man repeats, and turns his head to indicate the conversation has reached its conclusion.

"I'm sure this is the route," Grant says with more desperation than he'd like.

The second man glances at the curling line and nods curtly. "Might have been an oil road once. But no one goes up there anymore."

"I'm actually headed to Dominion College," Grant says. "You must have heard about it. I know it's a big deal for the region."

The first man pauses and looks at Grant curiously. "Where you from, boy?"

"Boston," Grant says, but corrects himself. "Well, I was actually born in Cambridge in one of the Walden teaching hospitals." He's more than a little buzzed to be talking like this. Clearly, these men don't care about the geographic delineations of New England. "But my family is originally from Boston."

"Walden?" the second man asks. "Like the university?"

"Yes," Grant says. "I graduated earlier this year."

A look of disgust settles on the man's face. "You're one of those nation-dodgers, aren't you?"

Grant has never heard the term "nation-dodger" spoken aloud. He's only read it in op-eds describing Americans who buy up swaths of land in northern Canada, desperate for the country's cold climate and wide, un-populated spaces. It's intended to be disparaging, of course, but he won't let the men see he's annoyed.

"I'm not, I swear. I'm here to teach English at the college." Grant pushes the wad of bills toward him anyway. "Please. I'll triple the fee if you take me there."

The men stand from the table, leaving the bills untouched. The second man tips his hat and says, "Not everything in the North is for sale."

Grant helplessly watches the men leave, and then pockets the bills again. When the door closes behind them, he sits at the table and taps his Flick behind his left ear, waiting for his feed to focus. Nothing. He taps again. *Turn on for a second*, he pleads. Just long enough to check the GPS. But his feed does not appear, to ping him in place.

He calls out to the cashier, "Is the signal down for some reason? I can't turn on my Flick."

"We don't get a signal up here," she says.

"Ever?" he asks in disbelief.

"Nope. We're too far north."

Out of all the dialectics Grant learned at Walden, tuning out the Flick was the most radical. Like his classmates, the Flick was the first object that pierced his body. It had been with him since he was born, glowing with an invisible power that he found too common to question. Even as he sat in the seminar room discussing the week's readings off-feed, his Flick was there, woven behind his left ear, patiently waiting to be tapped back. And while he practiced abstinence from the Flick while in class, he often binged when he returned home. Its absence made its onslaught even sweeter, and he would feel something akin to arousal when his feed washed over him. Hearing that there's no signal makes him feel even more anxious.

The cashier shakes her head and redirects her attention to the radio on the counter. She scans through the white noise on the radio until a flash of pop music bleeds through and then quickly fades. "You can use the house phone if you want."

The ancient rotary phone is by the cash register, and when Grant picks it up, he's surprised by how heavy and warm the receiver is. He places the phone to his ear and can smell the oily stench of strange skin. It feels both intimate and awkward, like he's pressing his bare cheek to a stranger's underarm. He rubs the earpiece with the cuff of his jacket, then dials the number.

The phone rings three times before a man answers, "Meyer, here."

"Yes, hello. This is Grant Grimley. I'm the new hire—"

"Grant!" Meyer cuts in. "You were expected yesterday."

"Well, I can explain. I missed my connection in the city and had to hire a plane to take me as far north as I could get."

"And you're where now?"

Grant pauses to recall the name of the area, something blunt and menacing, like Viking. He looks around and sees the name printed on a vintage matchbook sitting in an ashtray beside the phone: WELCOME TO VANDAL! WHERE EVEN THE ROADS ARE PAVED WITH OIL.

"I'm stuck at the charging station in Vandal and can't find a ride up to campus." He looks up and sees the cashier's back turned to him, and quickly puts the matchbook in his pocket as a souvenir.

"Not a problem, Grant. I'll come down and get you tomorrow my-self." Meyer pauses, and then adds, "I'm looking forward to meeting you, Grant. I've heard such promising things."

"I'm looking forward, too. I can't wait to meet my students."

"We're all excited to meet you. Now, get a good night's sleep, and I'll see you tomorrow."

Grant hangs up and breathes a sigh of relief. By tomorrow, he'll be up at the campus, eating a hot meal from the buffet in the dining hall. He'll take a swim in the saltwater pool to relax his cramped muscles and check out the Twentieth Century Anglophone collection in the library. Just one more day of travel, and he'll finally be able to unpack his belongings in his new apartment. He hopes there is a place to write by a window, maybe even a comfortable reading chair he can sit in to look out at the falling snow.

A glimmer of lightness returns to Grant. The more he focuses on it, the more it sharpens and begins to feel like hope. He notices the cashier is reorganizing a jar filled with hot dog–shaped gummy candies. Grant gestures at the gummies. "Do you only sell hot dog–shaped food here?"

The cashier looks away while tightening her high ponytail.

"Hot dogs." He taps the container to get her attention. "They're every-where."

"Okay . . . if you say so." She rolls her eyes.

"Never mind. It was a joke." He pauses but gets no response. "I need a room for the night."

"Rooms are up top," she says, still not meeting his eyes. "And you pay me in cash right now."

"All I have is American." He pats the pockets of his jacket and puts the wad of bills on the counter.

She looks at him skeptically. "You don't have anything else?"

He tries to keep his voice even. "I was told you would accept American up here."

"Manager doesn't like it when Americans come up here and poke around. Says we're not to take your money anymore."

"Oh," he says. "And why is that?"

She looks at him with dead-eyed boredom, like his question deserves the most self-evident response. "We know what you're up to. Buying up land. Trying to get out of your own country." She shrugs, then leans forward and whispers, "Not that I blame you. But the manager makes the rules." She turns around and taps a handwritten sign tacked to the wall that he failed to notice before: NO YANKEE DOLLARS!!!

"Listen, I just need a place to rest for the night." Grant pushes the pile of bills toward her anyway. "Please. I'm desperate."

She holds one of the green bills up to the incandescent light like she's examining a fossil buried under the silt. "'In God We Trust,'" she reads aloud, and then looks at him with a smirk. "There's your first mistake."

Grant reaches into his jacket pocket and feels the reassuring shape of the gold coin. He'll only proffer it as a last-ditch effort. "It will be for one night, I promise."

She pushes the cash back to him. "Your money is no good here."

"Fine." He takes out the coin and places it on the counter. "I assume you accept gold?"

She grins, and he sees that she, too, has gold caps on her two front teeth. She whisks the coin into the cash register before handing him a room key. "Checkout is at eleven."

———

In the motel room, Grant lies on the bed, feeling depleted that he gave up the gold coin so early in his journey. The coin was something his father had given him as a child, stamped with the face of a foreign dictator who forcibly turned all of his country's currency into gold when the financial markets crashed. "Always keep a commodity in your back pocket," his father told him. "Even if it means carrying around the memory of a flawed man." Grant did as he was told and kept the coin as a reminder of the ethics of his family—first in celebration, then in defiance.

The coin doesn't matter anymore, he reassures himself, and sits up in the bed. No one here knows who his family is. It's partially why he accepted this job in the first place. The only way to escape being a Grimley is to move to a place where the name means nothing.

He still feels proud that he was hired on his own merit. No strings pulled by his father; no calls put through to an old business school pal. Grant's Walden education probably didn't hurt, but *he* had been the one who'd written the cover letter painstakingly describing why he wanted to "give back by teaching a different student than the Walden demographic." It was maybe a little obvious, but it was enough to get him a video interview, and from there he convinced the recruiter of his expansive knowledge teaching introductory English.

Bullshit, he thinks, and flops back on the bed. The truth is that he has no experience teaching and has woken up at three a.m. every day for the last two weeks stricken with deep and abiding feelings of inadequacy. All of those Canadian souls waiting to be educated. By him.

What does he have to teach them? Until recently, his life was marked by ease. He floated in a frictionless drift, buoyed by the fact that choices had been made for him before he even realized they were choices. Being painfully aware of his privilege didn't make it any better. He was raised in a family whose name was carved into the marble edifice of the country's first public library. Streets were named after them. Buildings of Learning. Towers of Finance. And now privatized cities are being built with their money.

"Being a Grimley means deflecting the envy of not being a Grimley," his father always said before launching into the long and storied legacy of their lineage. How the Grimleys made their fortune financing shipments of opium, rum, and slaves across the oceans. When their commodities became politically dubious, they switched to textiles, establishing cotton mills made famous for the durability of their garments and brutal working conditions. Following worker strikes, the mills shuttered and relocated overseas for cheaper labor, so the Grimleys reinvented themselves through real estate, carving up Back Bay and Beacon Hill, and investing the rest of their fortune in oil drilled in countries beset by war and dictatorships. When oil went bust, they diversified into green energy and off-grid cities, financing the first Floating City in Boston Harbor, and striking out into rare earth mineral mining. Their wealth was so deep and so internalized that his father never thought about it in terms of money—their family was simply part of American history.

His father is wrong. Even history can be rewritten. After Grant studied the French Revolution in a European History class, he wondered if the Grimley line would one day be remembered like a bloated artifact of aristocracy. All of their success, their influence, and their fortune had been made by squeezing capital from workers' labor. During his darker moments, he liked to imagine a takeover of the crystalline Floating City as a moving mob of bedraggled working-class heroes armed with axes and spades and rusted iron picks, scaling the stairs to his father's corner office. Grant always stopped his apocalyptic vision when they arrived at his father's door, pausing the bloodshed and shattered glass. Although Grant despised his father, he was still his own blood.

If he can't kill his father, even metaphorically, then all he can do is run away. He spreads the map on the polyester bedspread to plot his journey to the college. This must be Vandal. He circles the charging station, and over here—he draws a line up to the blue kidney—is Dominion Lake. Just a blue blotch connected by a faint line that crawls through the wilderness.

Grant walks to the bathroom to shave, but pauses when he sees himself in the mirror. His face is covered in coarse stubble, and he looks wild-eyed and unwashed. For the first time, he sees what he might look like as a different man.

"You'll always be a Grimley," his father had said before Grant left. "Running away won't change a thing."

He'll prove his father wrong. He decides not to shave and returns to the bed to climb under the sheets, stiff with cold. He closes his eyes. Sleep arrives as quickly as a curtain drawn closed.

The next morning, a silver Airstream trailer hitched to a black SUV is parked at the charging station. Grant is waiting inside the station when the vehicle's door swings open. A handsome, well-groomed man wearing a sheepskin jacket steps out of the SUV. His neatly combed hair is the same pure white as the snow. He walks toward the station with a light and lively step in a pair of shining boots. He whistles once, and a spry English pointer darts out of the vehicle, the dog's groomed coat a perfect accompaniment to the man's refinement.

Grant steps outside. "Meyer?" he asks tentatively.

"No, I'm your Canadian kidnapper." The man laughs. "Of course I'm Meyer. Now get over here before you freeze."

Grant follows Meyer back to the vehicle and climbs into the passenger seat. The dog jumps in and nestles in the back. A warbling saxophone and electric keyboard play from the speakers. The music sounds hot and arid, and deeply melancholic.

"Ethio jazz," Meyer says when Grant asks what the music is. "I have a fantastic collection of original vinyl that will arrive next semester."

"Where's home?" Grant asks.

"Los Angeles, mainly. At least that's where my storage unit is. I used to own a bungalow in Los Feliz, but I sold it once the temperature habitually hit 110." Meyer shakes his head. "Horrible what's happening in the South." Meyer opens his window an inch and breathes deeply. "That's why I love the North. Fresh air. Clean. Untainted. When was the last time you smelled air like this?"

"Last June," Grant says, and takes a deliberate breath of cool air. "When my professor celebrated his book publication by ordering a case of New Zealand air."

"Canadian air is different than Kiwi air. It's colder and drier. Less salt because we're so far inland," Meyer says. "We're in a subarctic climate, you see. Although 100 million years ago, this region used to be the ocean floor. If you dig far enough down, you can find the bodies of sea invertebrates trapped in their mineral graves. The locals used to mine the ammonite and turn it into jewelry."

"Why did they stop?" Grant looks out the window as the landscape slides by, rows of dead pine occasionally interrupted by a blackened homestead with the roof caved in. A charred hull of a car is visible in the rubble, and Grant tries not to imagine what it would feel like to be burned alive.

"Fossil fuel, of course. You can't power a car with a necklace." Meyer turns on the left-turn blinker even though they are the only vehicle on the road.

"But that's all stopped now after the oil ban?" Grant asks.

Meyer nods. "Yes, the rigs stopped drilling fifteen years ago. I'm impressed that you've been familiarizing yourself with the region. But I should expect no less from a Walden boy. You know, I was a student at Walden myself, back when college wasn't only for the lucky few."

Grant glances at Meyer's hands on the steering wheel. "Is that your class ring?"

"Class of '14. And you just graduated this year, didn't you?"

Grant tugs at his own ring, recalling how Jane used to gently toy with it when she couldn't fall asleep. "Class of '49. But I never felt comfortable with the weight of it."

"It's a nostalgic gesture, really. And the ring does open certain doors if one is willing." Meyer turns down the music. "What else did you learn about the region?"

"That this is Indigenous territory," Grant says, "but some of the First Nations were forced off their land by oil companies."

"That's correct, Grant." Meyer waves a hand at the trees. "Our footprint needs to be lighter now, more in tune with the natural world."

"Are the locals hostile? Some men at the station called me a nation-dodger and refused to take me north."

Meyer bristles. "The irony of occupation will never fail to amaze me. Those men are descended from the first settlers who stole this land from the First Nations, and yet they call *us* intruders. At least we purchased it fairly."

"But we are intruders, aren't we?"

Meyer shakes his head. "They'll soon see us as friends. The locals need jobs and a future. They'll take what they can get, even if it's from a group of Americans with intentions that go beyond the narrow scope of their understanding." He turns downs the music and looks at Grant, his voice softening again. "This country needs a vision that extends beyond the bounty of extraction. One day, they'll thank us for living here." Meyer points out the window. "See all that pipe?"

Grant notices the silver pipe for the first time running alongside the highway, a foot above the ground, snaking into the horizon and then disappearing into a dense crop of trees.

"At one point, you could have followed that pipe down to the US border," Meyer explains. "All of that is completely useless now." Meyer taps the steering wheel of the SUV. "This is electric, of course. We're trying to build a better future here. But anything visionary requires initial sacrifices. I'm afraid to say that we're behind schedule."

"What do you mean?"

"We just broke ground on the campus earlier this month."

"You mean the campus isn't open?"

"At the moment, the project is a work in progress. I know certain housing bonuses were promised when you accepted the job, which is why I want to be clear with you. This is real work, Grant, not the kind of hand-holding you've experienced in Walden. But that comes with certain limitations, too. Simple meals. Simple living. And I promise that once we're up and running, you'll be the first to move into housing."

Back in the Floating City, a glass office is waiting with GRANT P. GRIMLEY inscribed on the front door. Tower One. Top floor. Right next to his father's corner office. All it would take is a single plea, and by tomorrow a helicopter would appear, hovering in the sky. In forty-eight hours, he would be sitting in a leather swivel chair, staring out at the Atlantic frothing onto the boardwalk. His father would stand at the door and say in an apologetic tone, "Forget about Jane, Grant. Why don't you take a visit to the Loop instead?"

As Grant looks at the silver pipe, he knows his father will never find him here, off-grid with his Flick disconnected. The thought fills him with an exhilarating happiness. All alone. For the first time in his life. No notifications pinging him in place. No geo-tracker mapping his movements. No one in the world knows where he is except for Meyer.

Grant turns to Meyer. "I'm never going back south."

"Good," Meyer says. "I knew I could depend on you."

———————

The building Meyer drops Grant off at in Dominion Lake is a boxy warehouse that looks like it has been abandoned for at least a decade. It's the sort of soul-crushing generic structure that Grant always associated with the suburbs, and that seemed to undulate endlessly beyond Boston. Meyer promised the Foreman would meet him inside, so he drags his suitcase across the packed snow to the warehouse's entrance. The windows are covered in the local newspaper, beige and wrinkled from the sun. An advertisement for the sale on pork chops at the Stop N Save. An article fretting about the plummeting gas prices. Another about the oil ban. He knocks his knuckles against the glass window and waits.

No answer.

He knocks again.

Nothing.

He rubs his hands together and hops from foot to foot to get his blood flowing. His fingers feel stiff, and he wonders how long it might take before frostbite settles in. He's read that when people die from exposure in the North, they're often discovered the following spring, perfectly preserved in a snowbank. Or their bodies are never found at all.

The door suddenly swings open, mercifully disrupting his macabre thoughts. A massive man in a bear-fur jacket with a long red beard stands at the entrance.

"Grant, my boy!" the Foreman says. "I was in the back and didn't hear you. We just got our oil delivery, and I was refilling the generator." He points to a semitruck covered in a blanket of snow in the parking lot.

"Oil isn't contraband?" Grant asks, and follows the Foreman inside. A line of bunks is clustered at the far edge of the building. The air reeks of burnt meat.

"We've only just met. You think I'd give away my secrets already?" The Foreman ushers Grant farther into the warehouse. "Just kidding, son." He slaps Grant on the shoulder. "You should see your face! Scared you, did I? Oil is the only resource this wretched region can offer. There's barrels of the stuff sitting in warehouses all over the North." The Foreman shouts to a man working at a steel table at the edge of the warehouse. "We've got a green one, Flin. First time in camp. We'll have to break him in tonight."

The man called Flin looks up and greets Grant with the twitch of a butcher's knife. He wears a bloodied smock and smokes a cigarette while rooting in the purple guts of a splayed animal.

"What do you have there?" the Foreman asks, and gestures at the butchered meat.

"Something one of the Diggers dragged off the road," Flin says.

"I hope it's not a fucking marmot again." The Foreman turns to Grant. "Sometimes the wildlife can get so degraded that it's hard to tell what it once was."

Flin doesn't look up and continues carving out the carcass. "This is good meat if you stew it long enough," he says under his breath. He pulls something out of the animal's body and drops a slimy coil on the table. "I'll use that for tomorrow's lunch."

Grant stares with horror at the glossy intestine. "You're going to eat that?"

"Hell yes, boy. Need to get our vitamins now that we're entering the deep freeze. You'll get used to chewing your food with a little extra vigor." The Foreman smacks his lips with appreciation. "Meals are served over there." He points to a set of long wooden tables flanked by benches. "And the Diggers crash over there." He points to the bunks at the back of the warehouse.

"The Diggers?" Grant asks.

"I like a pet name for my men. It's easier to communicate their utility." The Foreman grins, flashing two jagged rows of gold-capped teeth. Unlike the men in Vandal, who only had a faint gleam at the backs of their mouths, the Foreman's mouth is completely filled with gold. "Here, I'll show you." He leads Grant to the far side of the warehouse where a few dozen bunks are pushed up against the wall. A name is carved into the post of each bed: SWIFTY, WOLFE, FINGER, DIAMOND . . . "And you'll be bunking at the back. Come with me, and we'll get you settled."

Grant's room is at the back of the warehouse, down a narrow hall that smells faintly of dog food. The Foreman kicks open a wooden door with ASSISTANT MANAGER scrawled in black marker across the front.

"This was one of the manager's offices, back when the warehouse used to sell animal feed." The Foreman knocks his knuckles against a metal filing cabinet that appears to be rusted shut.

Grant takes in his new room with dismay. The ashen wall-to-wall carpet is streaked with an ambiguous brown stain, and a desk is pushed up against the wall to make space for a single bed and a stool. A lightbulb dangles from the ceiling, illuminating an outdated horse trailer calendar from 2034, still pinned to the wall. "I'm expected to sleep here?"

"A fancy boy, are you? I suspected as much since you're Meyer's hire. The Diggers would commit a minor crime to have a room with a door. But if you'd like, I can set you up in one of their bunks."

Grant sets the suitcase on the ground and tries to smile. "No, this is fine. Meyer already briefed me about the delay on the campus."

"That's more like it!" The Foreman steps toward the door, and then says, "And I'll try to find you a proper jacket and boots. We don't have a lot in camp, but what we do have, I can usually get."

Grant thanks the Foreman as he leaves, and then sets to work unpacking his belongings. His clothes, a few books, and the mementos of Jane he always keeps close by: a rabbit's foot on a key chain; a photo of her squinting into the sun; and a long, handwritten letter from her, its pages soft and creased from rereading.

He looks at the calendar on the wall. All of the days are crossed out except for September 1, 2034. This must have been the last day the warehouse was open, just weeks before the oil ban began. How long did it take for the region to empty out? Was it a gradual evacuation, or a sudden exodus?

Jane was born in a town like Dominion Lake, a place where the anti-abortion parade was the second most attended event after the yearly rodeo. She hated her hometown and never spoke in detail about the devastation the wildfires left, but Grant had seen images on his Flick: thousands of acres of blackened forest, entire counties reduced to ash. Only once did she describe to Grant the way the heat felt, like a hot hand clasping her throat, and that from a young age she'd grown accustomed to combing ash out of her hair. But many of the details of her childhood went undiscussed. Grant assumed the reason she had moved so far east was to put that life behind her.

Looking at the calendar fills him with a wave of sadness so strong he turns off the light and lies on the edge of the bed in complete darkness. It's the only way he feels close to Jane again. Him and her in their studio, cooking a vegetarian stir-fry and then retreating to the futon mattress to read in bed. Sweet and sweaty evenings, the humidity so thick that even the walls seemed to perspire as the mercury crept above one hundred. During the state-mandated blackouts, they ate crackers and tinned fish, drank whiskey with cold tea, read by flickering candlelight. Grant preferred not to think of the fact that suicide rates were highest during the blackouts. With Jane, safely tucked away in their studio, the threat of annihilation felt distant.

He closes his eyes and can almost feel her leaning into him, her neck glistening with sweat, wearing that peachy vintage slip with the frayed hem. One strap has slipped off her shoulder, so he tugs the other strap off and pulls the slip to her waist. She kisses the sweat off his neck, and moves to his chest, his stomach, the indent of his left hip.

"You know exactly how to touch me," he says.

Her voice sounds far away, as if she's trapped at the end of a tunnel. "That's because I know you."

He opens his eyes in a cold room in Canada. Now he knows. Love isn't a one-act play written by a precocious undergraduate. Love is raw and rank, and stinks of the rot that splits this world in two. It's lineage and duty. It's family. It's blood. It's too big and messy to fit within the tidy confines of their studio. He should never have tried to keep it there.

Outside, a bell sounds, and the warehouse doors clang open. Grant flicks the fluorescent lighting back on and leaves his room to find dozens of men dressed in snow pants and parkas streaming into the building. They leave their parkas heaped on their bunks and begin to form a line next to a long table.

Flin brings out a steaming pot and starts ladling brown mush into bowls. Each man takes a bowl and sits down at one of the tables.

"Grant!" the Foreman calls out from the feed line. "Get in line! It's cat stew night."

"Cat stew?" Grant asks. He feels his stomach turn.

"Flin is serving up stewed lynx," the Foreman explains. "It's like a chewier rabbit."

The Foreman tells Grant that Flin is from an island out east, a town so far out you need a car, a boat, and another car to get there. He's a cheery lad who likes to strum a ukulele and sing his own songs depicting camp life. But when he's drunk, he tends to blubber and grow morose, longing for a life back home when the icebergs drifted by every March, blank and indifferent to the crowds of tourists who once gathered in the harbor.

The line inches forward and Grant peers into a wide trough of food. The cat stew is brown and oily, with bits of gristle and what look like bones.

Flin ladles the stew into a bowl and tops it with mashed potatoes.

"You've never seen anything like it," Flin suddenly says to Grant. "Those icebergs were like huge fucking sculptures created by God. "

"Flin can't hold his drink, which is a shame," the Foreman says to Grant as they find their way to a seat. A few Diggers wordlessly make room for them at a table. "I told Meyer the most important thing isn't whether these men are good, or bad, or even human. Just find out who can drink real liquor." The Foreman sloshes whiskey into an aluminum mug for Grant.

Grant takes a sip of the whiskey. It tastes like burning tires. He tentatively eats a spoonful of the stew and is relieved to find that it's delicious. He hadn't realized how hungry he was, and quickly downs the entire bowl. When he is finished, he wipes his mouth with a napkin and asks the Foreman, "Are you from Dominion Lake?"

The Foreman pounds a fist on the table, making the mugs jitter. "God, no." He leans forward and whispers to Grant, "The Diggers are from this shithole, but I've done my time elsewhere. I became a man in the mines in the Pilbara. Learned how to work without light and sleep during the day. Fucked up my whole internal clock. Sometimes I have dreams with my eyes still open."

No one glances up from their bowl except for a man sitting at their table who wears suspenders over a button-up shirt, and a silk handkerchief folded neatly in his breast pocket. He pulls a pack of cigarettes from his breast pocket and lights one with a match. "What do you dream about?" the man asks, and leans across the table to drop the match into the Foreman's mug.

"None of your damn business," the Foreman says, and fishes the match out with a finger. He turns back to Grant and says, "Don't mind him. He's just the Barber. Most of the time, I ignore the damn fool."

Grant looks at the Barber again with interest but can't catch his eye.

The Foreman takes a shot of whiskey and seems to buck up. "Like I was saying, more than tinned meat, or dust in the chest, or losing hair in strange places, it was that dreaming that taught me to grow up. Get a grip on myself. Figure out what's real and what's not."

"Did you choose correctly?" Grant asks.

The Foreman laughs and slaps Grant on the shoulder. "Does this feel real to you?"

He reaches out and fills Grant's mug to the brim. Grant drains the whiskey and relaxes as the alcohol blossoms in his chest. Complacency is closer to inebriation than he realized. Maybe it will be fine here after all.

"Are the students eating later in the evening?" Grant asks.

"All heads are accounted for," the Foreman says.

"Meaning?"

"What you see is what you get."

"The Diggers are my students? I thought they were just the construction workers."

"They work out on the site, but Meyer expects you to teach them when they're back in camp."

Grant observes the Diggers with renewed interest. The male-only room reminds him of when he attended an all-boys boarding school with other students exiled from their parents' mansions. Grant finds it difficult to imagine the Diggers as boys. Thick cords of muscle ripple as they chew and grunt and swallow. Most are heavily tattooed, with long beards, some tinged with gravy. Many are at least six feet tall, with hands strong enough to crush a small dog.

The Foreman nods and gestures with a knife at the men. "We promised the authorities that we'd hire locals first before recruiting talent abroad. Most of the Diggers were unemployed before camp. Their fathers used to work up here, back when the oil rigs were still running, so they've heard stories of what camp can do to a man."

Grant sets down his spoon. "And what is that exactly?"

The Foreman pours more whiskey. "Drink up, Grant. Better not to ask too many questions on your first day in camp."

WHITE ALICE

The helicopters dropped us off in White Alice on the first day of our mission. We had never seen images of the climate research station and imagined an expansive complex engineered with state-of-the-art technology, announcing to anyone who dared to tread close that the US military was in command. But when we arrived, we were underwhelmed. The station looked like an unassuming middle school. A cluster of convertible buildings, constructed of dun-colored aluminum, were raised above the permafrost by struts. A darkened greenhouse was connected by a corridor, and in the distance, the gigantic shield of the radar looked like a frozen white moon.

Already the sliver of summer had waned. Snow was expected next week, so we quickly moved boxes of supplies, gear, and weapons to the entrance of the station. We had been briefed by our sergeant that summer is an abbreviated season in the Far North and exposes the land for what it is: craggy rocks, mossy patches, bald spots of vegetation, and sinking mulch. But the land was eerily still. No rippling trees; no vehicles shining down the highway; no bodies walking, running, talking. The land moved, of course, but not in a way we recognized as our own.

After we unpacked, we stood in a line outside the station and saluted the helicopters ascending into the sky. When they disappeared, we crowbarred open the front door and stepped inside our new home.

"Hello," we called out. A thick and silent darkness greeted us. We started the oil generator, turned on the fluorescent lights, and got to work.

Six months had passed since the last mission, and the station bore the marks of its former inhabitants. In the bathroom we found a rusted razor in the sink, still flecked with coarse, dark hair; a lump of green soap in the shower; and a barely used stick of sports deodorant. In the sleeping quarters, pieces of women's bodies torn out of glossy magazines were taped to the walls above the bunks. The beds were unmade, and the lank sheets smelled of men—sweat and semen and the feverish visions of a night without end. What did the previous missions dream of in White Alice? Did the men ever imagine that a brigade of women would one day arrive to take their place?

"Some of the best men I've known have seen things in the North," our sergeant warned us in home base. "Unspeakable things that seem real even though they're not." He looked at us and smiled. "Luckily, women are less complicated than men. You have less to conceal."

Our sergeant expected us to view his comment as a compliment, and initially, we were flattered. We were the first all-women mission dispatched to White Alice and we proudly accepted our superiors' honorifics and declarations of emancipation. We had been trained not to ask questions, and to believe in the greater good of our cause. Our squad consisted of a botanist, a biologist, a cartographer, an engineer, a geographer, a meteorologist, a programmer, and a security specialist all highly trained and briefed on the station's history. Since the 1950s, White Alice was one of dozens of radar stations built in the Far North of Canada as a "distant early warning" to detect Soviet bombers and missiles launched over the Arctic Circle into American cities. But after the Cold War ended, and no bombers or missiles were detected, White Alice remained in operation as a climate research station. Our job was to continue the station's research, which had taken on vast significance, both militarily and meteorologically. China and Russia, as well as our Arctic Allies, were all desperate for a foothold in the North. Vast riches of minerals lay below the frozen surface, and massive glacial melt had prepared the future for a sustained Arctic shipping route.

"Our collective future lies in securing the North," our sergeant told us. "And your job is to monitor our presence here and prepare for the future."

When we arrived, we did what women are expected to do. We cleaned. We stripped the bed linens for laundering. We scrubbed and mopped the floors. The bunkrooms, the bathroom, the exercise room, the library, the meteorological equipment, and finally the communications room, where we dusted off the equipment and flicked the radar on, transmitting a signal back to home base that we had arrived and were well.

We worked through the station in pairs, speaking very little until we arrived in the kitchen, which, mercifully, had a skylight punched in the roof. Our sergeant had promised stockpiles of specialty items—real olive oil, decent whiskey, and black truffles planted in the station's greenhouse—but all we found were military-grade supplies. Cans of vegetables, tinned meat, bags of dried lentils and powdered potatoes. The biologist took stock of what had been left in the storeroom and confirmed that we had just enough supplies to last us two years. The rest of us stood in the kitchen and blinked at one another in the sudden light.

"So, this is it," the engineer said, and looked around the room. We followed her gaze, first to the worn kitchen counters, and then to the long hallway with its flickering fluorescence, and then down to our own hands rubbed raw from scrubbing. Already we had lost our sense of time.

We nodded in agreement. This was it. Or, to be more precise, this would be it. Our collective lives condensed into five thousand square feet—625 feet per soul. It was a moment where things could have soured. Perhaps there had been a similar moment when the men of the previous missions finally began to understand the challenge before them. That all their training and expertise and education would be contained to this cinder block in the Canadian north, thousands of miles from anyone who would salute their eminent positions.

A small moment can have large consequences. We felt it in the kitchen as we stood with one another and thought, *Is this truly our home?*

All of us were inexperienced in surviving in the Far North. We had spent our careers in climate-controlled labs and research facilities, far from the heat of combat, and had never lived in isolation before. Our sergeant knew we needed someone to watch over us. Someone who would keep us in line and report back to home base if anyone experienced the "psychological aberrations" common in isolated communities.

That person was Sal, our security specialist, who had been tasked with leading the mission and maintaining our stockpile of weapons and artillery. Sal arrived in White Alice like someone with a grudge: steely-eyed, mouth set, hair in a tight knot at the base of her skull. We were immediately intimidated by her but respected her intensity and background. Prior to White Alice, she was stationed on the southern border and had committed acts our sergeant was not given the clearance to speak aloud. He simply assured us that Sal had the experience and instinct to keep us safe.

Sal broke the warping silence and gestured to a door in the kitchen. "This must lead to the greenhouse," she said, and led us through the elevated walkway to investigate.

The greenhouse wasn't dark like it looked from the helicopters. It was filled with plants and trees that nearly blocked out all the light. After a half-year of neglect, the plants looked dead, the leaves parched and yellowed, crackling under our feet.

The botanist shone her flashlight on a rectangular glass box set atop a table. The box flashed bright in the light.

"Look," she said. We gathered around the box. It was filled with dirt and connected to a tube that fed into a smaller box where a green, leafy plant grew.

"It must be irrigated," the botanist said, inspecting the plant with her flashlight. "Somehow the vegetation is still alive."

We crowded around the table, desperate to see a plant that could somehow survive in the North. Only then did we notice the glass tube was filled with insects.

"Bugs," the programmer said.

"Drones," the biologist corrected, and flicked her flashlight at the tube. "They're bringing food to their queen."

Thousands of tiny brown specks lumbered through the glass tube, each clutching a shred of leaf. Without ceasing, they moved in a uniform line while another track of ants weaved their way back to the plant to gather more leaves. We watched the drones work in silence, until Sal finally spoke. "They're all women, you know."

The biologist looked up at her and nodded. "That's right. The worker drones are all sisters, as are the soldiers and colony cleaners." She smiled and said, "They're the daughters of the queen."

"And the father?" the botanist asked.

The biologist shrugged. "The males are basically sperm-carriers. They fly in and mate with the queen, and then die within two weeks." She looked around the greenhouse. "There must be males somewhere close by. Otherwise the colony couldn't possibly have survived this long." She paused for a moment before saying, "Unless they're raider ants. They're the only ant species who can produce offspring through parthenogenesis."

"Parthenogenesis?" Sal asked.

"Asexual reproduction," the biologist explained. "It's a rare occurrence where female ants self-reproduce their offspring and give birth to a female brood."

"Fascinating." Sal tapped her finger against the glass box as the ants continued their ceaseless work. She looked up at us, and her normally stern face suddenly looked light and at ease. "They've figured it out."

It was the first time we saw her smile.

———

The short summer ended, and our new version of winter began. As the temperature plummeted and the land froze, we drove the snowmobiles deeper into the drifts. There, we found a world less motionless than the one we had first encountered. We discovered variations in the ice and snow—different textures, shapes, and depths—and began to understand that the landscape had a beauty of its own. The North Star became our compass, brighter and more constant than the compasses we brought with us. Even the direction of the ice, frozen in peaks whenever the wind moved, showed us where the North lay.

At first it was terrifying to feel so exposed when we walked out into the freeze. None of the simulations in home base prepared us for the ice's pure crystalline quality, sharp like glass and just as reflective. How shadows were shaped differently in the North, our own and each other's, and how even a familiar face could change.

Creating a schedule and sticking to it gave definition to the darkening days. Each of us was trained for a particular routine, and we found a comfortable rhythm moving through our duties.

The botanist visited the seed vault, located a mile from the station, which contained the seeds of thousands of plants and vegetables from every continent in the world. She deforested the greenhouse, leaving the ant colony intact, and planted a sampling of seeds. Within a month, the first seedlings nudged their green heads through the dirt.

The biologist set to work collecting samples in the permafrost around the station and tracking the migration patterns of the arctic fox and caribou.

The engineer inspected the meteorological and communications equipment, repairing any compromises to the system, and filled the generators with our stockpile of oil to ensure the station remained heated and operational.

The meteorologist studied the climate models last charted by the previous mission, while the programmer logged the encrypted data and sent daily reports back to home base.

The cartographer worked in the library, poring over maps of the region, while the geographer studied the previous Cold War missions in White Alice and learned about the Indigenous communities who populated the North.

While our work was focused on maintaining the station for climate surveillance, Sal's job was protecting us. She monitored the perimeter of the station every morning and evening. At night, she methodically took stock of our arsenal of weapons. She cleaned the assault rifles and polished the knives engraved with our initials in the handles. She ensured our bulletproof vests and fatigues were neatly lined up by the front door to the station, and our boots and helmets gleamed. Only at midnight did she clock off duty and sleep the five hours she allowed herself each night. At five a.m., she conducted her morning patrol.

What was Sal preparing for? It had been decades since the end of the Cold War. We hadn't been briefed on the possibility of an enemy invasion and were told no one lived near the station or had any cause to visit us during our mission. Yet, Sal continued her daily patrols as if combat was always imminent, and soon became fixated on training us with her same focus. She led us through chin-ups, squats, weight training, and calisthenics until our necks and backs were slicked with sweat, our hearts racing. Daily runs through the snow. Jumping jacks in the greenhouse. Skipping rope in the library. Shadowboxing down the walkways of the station. Under her watch, our bodies grew stronger and more responsive to one another, soldered into well-oiled machines.

As the months passed, we grew closer in other ways as well. Some of us started to sleep together in the bunkroom, sharing a single bed and an army-issue sleeping bag when the lights went out, or bunking by the bookshelf in the library for extra privacy. We took showers together, applied lotion to each other's feet, or snuck off into the greenhouse to kiss by the flowering pear tree. We cooked together in the kitchen and blasted the boom box with anthemic '80s cassette tapes left behind by the Cold War missions. We cussed. We laughed uproariously. We sang songs in the dark. We shared each other's clothes and danced late into the night on Saturdays, drinking the rationed liquor we brought out on weekends.

The shortest day of the year passed, marking our sixth month in the station. By then, we rarely thought of our lives back in the US. Our apartments and our personal possessions that we once ascribed so much value to. Our families, our debts, even our country that we had once pledged to protect.

Was this all it takes to be happy? we wondered.

Our work. Our home. Each other.

CHAPTER THREE

ROSE

In the Blooms' camp kitchen, Rose places two slices of frozen bread in the toaster. It will take some time to readjust to how she used to live back home on the peninsula. "Paucity" was the word Damien used to describe the limited resources most people had to contend with. Rose knew paucity before she learned the word for it. But she didn't call it that. She called it living.

Rose and her mother had lived on the peninsula in a manner that was inconceivable to Damien. They ate margarine, not cultured butter. They drank powdered milk, not champagne. A sack of rice was rationed to last a full season, served with soy sauce and sesame seeds, and whatever meat or fish was on sale at the Bi-Rite. Fruits and vegetables were bought on discount. Occasionally, a guest left an inch of tequila in a bottle in one of the cottages, and Rose's mother would drink it on ice, her cheeks flushing red as she laughed into a cupped hand. The rare jolts of alcohol loosened her, and it was only then that Rose could imagine her as a young woman, skin shining, hair long and loose. This is what she must have looked like in South Korea when her father met her. What she was like before she became a mother.

Rose's mother had met her American father while he was teaching English to rich kids in Seoul's Gangnam District. She once admitted to Rose, in a rare moment of emotional indulgence, that as a young girl she dreamed of becoming an artist. It was a quiet dream, never spoken aloud until she met Rose's father. He was from a town north of Boston and had taken out an enormous student loan to attend a private liberal arts college that taught him just enough to speak with confidence about art and poetry. She found his soul-searching charming, so unlike the Korean boys she had dated who expected that a proper Korean woman would inevitably set her interests aside for the higher purpose of family and children. She dated the American for a few months—sharing kimchi pajeon and icy bottles of beer in the basement restaurant down the street from her work; watching subtitled art-house films on the big blue screen; walking under the neon lights of the shopping district at night, feeling a thrill when other Koreans scrutinized her standing beside the large American man with his tight jeans and unkempt beard. For once, she felt different. Illicit. Special.

Everyone on the peninsula presumed it was the promise of a better life that led her to America. The well-trodden cliché was often trotted out. But Rose knew the real answer. Rose's mother moved because she had no choice.

When she found out she was pregnant with Rose, she knew her options were limited. At the time, she was making a meager salary at a doctor's office, filing paperwork and trying to save money for art school. She couldn't afford rent, so she lived with her parents and slept in the small room by the kitchen, where she kept her clothes folded in neat rows along the edge of the heated floor. Her mother was an evangelical Christian who claimed to love Jesus more than her own children and had pinned the white man's face, mid-crucifixion, to every wall. She had always felt secretly suspicious of the holy man, with his clear blue eyes and perfect droplets of blood, but she had been raised to turn to him if she ever had a question.

Will you forgive me if I leave with him? she asked the picture on her bedroom wall.

The man with his beautiful hair and shining, pious eyes said nothing.

"Will you forgive me if I get rid of it?" she asked her mother one evening as they prepared dinner.

Her mother continued chopping a daikon without pause. "You already know the answer."

When she could no longer hide her belly under a baggy sweater, she agreed to follow the American back to his small coastal town. She packed a bag with her paintbrushes and favorite collections of Korean poetry and borrowed the money for a one-way flight to Boston from a friend. As the plane descended into Logan Airport, she stared out the window at the white boats skimming across the bright Atlantic, as blue as Jesus's eyes, as clear as his gaze. A new country that wouldn't see her and her half-white child as maligned. A new life where she might speak her dreams aloud. Later, she would weep over her own naïveté. She never saw her family or Korea again.

Now when Rose thinks of her mother, the guilt takes the form of a rock in her stomach, small and discreet, but with the mass of a planet. Other times, the guilt is a cloud of fog, drifting and expanding in her chest, obscuring her heart and lungs, so that when she breathes, she feels like she's choking. Her birth and its effects are always there, a reminder that all actions have consequences that extend beyond their gravitational pull. Rose's mother never explicitly said she regretted the decision to leave everything she knew. She didn't have to. The evidence was undeniable, as rough and relentless as the waves that rolled onto the peninsula as she picked the guests' trash off the beach with her bare hands.

The toaster smokes. Rose gingerly extracts the slices and smears each burnt piece with the margarine and red jam left out on the counter. "Two slices of toast, half a tin of cocktail fruit" is listed on the Blooms' daily menu, tacked on the avocado-green fridge with a moose-shaped magnet. The breakfast tastes as good as it looks, like a strip of cardboard slathered in sweet blood. She eats while standing at the window and sees the same type of bird that she saw outside her room alight on the branch of a tree.

"It's a nuthatch," a voice says from behind her.

Rose turns around to see Willow leaning against the counter, wearing a pair of thermal underwear and a stained white cotton shirt. She stretches her arms above her head, yawns, and then says, "They nest in dead trees to survive the winter."

Willow reminds Rose of the tough girls on the peninsula who wore combat boots in the summer, girls who spat onto the sidewalk in front of the convenience store just to pass the time. Tough-as-nails girls who wore their older brother's broken-in jeans with a flannel shirt tucked in. Rose had always admired these girls. Their guts. Their certainty. How they seemed to know from a young age to leave the peninsula. Not like her. She stayed until the Atlantic seeped into her blood. Even years after she finally left, she still has dreams that it's not underwater. "How do you know that?"

"I grew up in the region and was raised to learn the migrations of wild birds." Willow takes a piece of toast from Rose's plate. "Do you mind? I'm starving."

"No, help yourself. I'm done." Rose watches her consume the toast in a few bites. "Are you looking forward to meeting your client?"

Earlier, Judith told the Blooms that their clients are expected to come by today. Rose already cleaned her room and selected the clothing and lingerie she'll wear.

Willow wipes a smudge of jam off her mouth with the cuff of her shirt. "No. I already know he's an asshole."

Rose is taken aback by her bluntness. "Who told you that?"

Willow's voice hardens. "No one. I just know. When I worked the energy circuit, all the men were assholes."

"Did you ever have trouble with raids?"

"Raids? Never. I learned to take care of myself from a young age."

"We never had raids in the Floating City either."

"Where is that exactly?"

Rose looks at her sharply. "You don't know?"

Willow shrugs. "Geography wasn't really my thing."

Either the girl is pretending to be stupid or she was raised by wolves. Not knowing where the Floating City is, is like not knowing that the sun is in the sky.

"It's an offshore city near Boston," Rose says. "I worked in a club there before this job."

Willow tilts her head. "What does it look like?"

"Like a glass globe floating on the ocean."

"I've never seen the ocean before." Willow's voice softens. "Maybe when I leave camp, I can finally see it for myself."

"Will you head south?"

Willow pours herself a cup of coffee. "Well, I'm supposed to go back home to my family. But I want to see if the world is as terrible as they say it is."

Despite Willow's casual toughness, there is a tender spot right under the surface. Rose wonders if she has any conception of the forces that shape their presence in Dominion Lake, or the men who truly hold the camp's power. Or is this job just another node on the energy circuit, a well-paid gig that will send Willow to the next northern town where she'll kneel in the snow for the right amount of money. Rose will have to keep an eye on her and see which it is.

Willow drinks a mouthful of coffee and then sets the mug on the table. "We should go. Judith wants us to walk the dogs."

Rose and Willow walk along the teal-and-mauve tiled floors of the west wing of the mall. Willow traces the beam of a flashlight along the ground, past a clothing shop where a pair of bejeweled stretch jeans hangs in the dusty window. Past the fishing and hunting store, where a pile of ominous red plaid jackets lies abandoned by the shuttered door. Around the corner from the phone kiosk with plastic cases left scattered on the counter—leopard print, pink sparkle, woodgrain, luxury marble.

Past the food court where a blackened neon sign still remains (WOK-EXPRESS!), with a pair of chopsticks holding an egg roll in the air. Past the Lotto Counter where an anthropomorphized lottery ticket gives a winning thumbs-up. All the way down a long, dark hallway, past a white metal bench bolted into the ground and a plastic ficus tree planted in fake dirt.

Finally, they reach an empty jewelry store inside the mall with a cupid-shaped doormat out front, a sign for two-for-one engagement and wedding rings in the window next to WE PAY $$$ FOR YOUR OLD GOLD.

Judith is waiting with a flashlight at the front of the store. When the Blooms approach, a pack of dogs runs toward her. Rose jumps back.

Damien had a cross-eyed Boston terrier to whom he fed edamame and filet mignon scraps, and who he occasionally brought around to the Loop when he wanted the hostesses to fawn over him. But she's never seen a pack of pit bulls before. Their eyes gleam red in the flashlight's beam as they bark and scratch at the metal gate.

"Shhh," Judith says. "It's all right, Annie. It's all right." She retrieves a biscuit from her pocket and tosses it to the ground. Annie hoovers it with one swipe of her tongue as three other dogs rub their rib cages against the gate, barking for their treat.

"Their names are Turnkey, Blake, Spider, and Annie," Judith says. "They even have certified papers." Judith unlocks the gate and pulls Annie out by her spiked collar, and then slips a harness over her shoulders. "You can pet her if you'd like. She's docile now that she's had her kibble."

Rose pets Annie tentatively. The pit bull's body is marbled with warm muscle, and her ears feel like the softest felt. "She won't hurt us?"

"As long as she trusts you, she's a complete sweetheart." Judith pulls a muzzle out from a bag and clips it around Annie's jaw, pulling it firmly over her mouth. "You should go on your walk now. And don't dawdle. Meyer will be by at noon."

The sun is a patch of red hanging low on the horizon when Rose, Willow, and Annie walk outside the mall. There has been fog in the mornings since they arrived, a fog so thick that it's like tracking the tail of a brush fire. They walk to the edge of the parking lot, passing a ditch on the other side of the metal fence filled with the detritus of a different decade—phone chargers, fast-food wrappers, batteries, a pair of boxer briefs with an emoji stamped on the fly poke out of the snow. Forgotten place markers of a period when things were tossed out of the windows of moving vehicles.

Across the highway, Rose notices the pipe. A stretch of silver tubing runs a foot above the ground, marked by a sign memorializing what this patch of earth was once used for: WARNING: OIL PIPELINE.

Somewhere, a truck crunches through snow. Annie pulls at her leash, yanking Willow toward the sound.

"Shhh, girl. Shhh," Willow says. "The Diggers must be heading to the site already. Judith tells me they're working overtime."

Everything is quiet again except for the sound of snow under their boots and Annie's snuffled breathing as she strains against her leash. The Blooms continue their morning circuit along the edge of the parking lot. Rose breathes in the fresh, icy air and focuses on the sounds of her boots crunching in the snow, the distant and plaintive honks of migrating geese.

When Rose had looked Dominion Lake up on her Flick, she saw a dot nestled in the Canadian north whose claim to fame had once been linked to oil. "A nothing place," Damien had said. "Only good for what is under the ground." He told her that the region had always been marked by extraction and profit. "And if we're lucky, we'll be part of the next wave."

Now, Rose sees something different. Dominion Lake reminds her of the peninsula with its strip malls and modest homes, the handwritten graffiti on the side of the Millennium, the rusted truck that sits abandoned off the side of the highway. It may be a town of little consequence to someone like Damien, but to her it's a real place where people once lived. They worked and raised their families here. And now they are gone.

A treacly sadness wells at the base of her throat, and she turns away from Willow as her eyes water. The feeling surprises her with its force and magnification. When she was in the Floating City and felt the sudden swell of unwanted emotion, she'd tap on her Flick to sink into the glittering escape of her feed. But here, in camp, she has nothing to lose herself in. All she has is this frozen place. The irony of her situation isn't lost on her. She worked so hard to get away from a town like this, and now she is right back where she started.

She blinks the tears away, and her vision clarifies.

When Rose rejoins Willow, Annie is bristling in the halter as a solitary figure approaches from a distance, her ears perking up to the sound of the stranger's boots in the snow.

As the figure draws closer to the gate, Rose sees a man in a navy peacoat, without a hat. His dark hair stands in stark contrast to the white of the falling snow. Even from a distance, Rose senses the man looking straight at her. He lifts his hand and smiles. She does the same. As he approaches, she sees he's in his late twenties, tall, a bit rakish, but still handsome.

He picks up the receiver of a phone hidden in a small wooden box and speaks quietly. The door buzzes open. He walks through the gate and then drops to one knee. "I've been waiting for you, sweetness." He takes off his gloves and holds his clenched fists out for the dog to sniff. The gesture is gentle and patient. "That's right, my girl. You know I have something special for you." He carefully pulls off the dog's muzzle and opens his left hand to reveal a brown biscuit. Annie trembles at the sight of it. She wags her tail and places her wet mouth in his open hand, ferreting for more treats. He strokes the dog's head, and then looks up at Rose. His green eyes are lined with a rim of copper, like a tiger's.

"I'm the Barber," he says, and takes Rose's gloved hand in his. "I cut hair on the Diggers' side of camp." Annie paws at the ground in front of him. "And I'm also lucky enough to take care of the dogs."

"They call me Rose," she says.

The Barber looks at her for a moment. "The name suits you." He nods toward Willow. "Unlike this one who should be named after an invasive species."

"Okay, that's enough." Willow laughs, and the sound echoes through the snowy lot.

"You all settled in there?" he asks.

"I am," Willow says. "In a room fit for a dirty queen. You should come and see it."

They talk for a few minutes about their living arrangements, while Rose stands back and listens. Their manner is familiar and intimate. Clearly, they know each other.

The Barber reaches into his pocket and then lobs a ball across the parking lot. Rose watches Annie streak across the snow, her coat glistening in the morning sun. The dog loves the fresh air as much as she does. If only she could be like an animal and inhabit the sheer happiness of a body rocketing through empty space, the sun on glossy fur, the knowledge that a meal and a bed awaits. She might even be jealous of the dogs if she didn't suspect their purpose to be more than playthings.

When Annie reaches the ball, she paws at the ground and starts barking.

"I'll get her." Willow jogs toward the dog.

The Barber turns and looks at the mall, a homogenous one-story building, similar to the countless malls that now stand abandoned in the suburban pockets outside the cities. The only distinguishing feature is the building's light coral color, a pink as soft and sweet as the inside of a newborn's ear.

"I used to hang around the Millennium as a teenager," the Barber says. "I'd smoke a joint with my friends by the dumpsters and then wander around inside, dreaming of all the ways I might leave this place."

"You're from here?" Rose asks, surprised.

He nods. "I was born in a little homestead on the other side of the lake. My father was born there, and his father's father. Our family has been here for generations. But I left when I was young and haven't been back in a decade."

A local. And not a local like those who stayed on the peninsula because they never imagined a different life. No, the Barber is her kind of local, an outsider who left, only to return.

"Why did you come back to Dominion Lake?"

"My father once told me that you never lose the scent of where you're from. Do you think I smell like blood and oil?"

She knows she shouldn't invite his attention, but she can't help herself. "Come closer."

He takes a step toward her. They're so close that she can smell the musk on his clean-shaven cheeks. She realizes now why he seems so familiar. He reminds her of the boys on the peninsula who keened to see beyond the perimeters of town. Who once daydreamed with her about their escape. She wonders if any of those boys made it off the peninsula alive.

"No," she says. "You smell like you."

He sounds amused. "How do you know?"

He leans toward her, but then Willow calls out, "Rose, let's head back. We need to get ready."

Rose turns quickly to walk back to the mall, but glances over her shoulder to see him still looking at her. She raises a hand in farewell, and he does the same. They stand there for a moment, two figures frozen in place. She turns again and keeps walking, knowing that she can't be distracted.

Meyer is waiting.

Rose used to enjoy the ritual of getting ready for a client, but here in camp, it brings her less pleasure. Still, she combs her hair into a sleek wave and dabs jasmine oil on her neck and elbows before moisturizing the bottoms of her feet with cream. She sits at the edge of the chair and inserts a small dollop of lube inside herself to mimic the wetness of arousal. Avalon taught her this tip, among others over the years. Use a second pseudonym if a client is desperate to know her real name. Always carry baby wipes in her purse and a variety of condoms in case the client pretends he's allergic to latex. Breathe a one-liner into a client's ear if he's struggling to relax, something suggestive yet obvious like, "You don't make this feel like work." At dinner, eat like a bird. Avoid the cheese. Never drink more than two glasses of wine. Triple your rate for staying the night.

When she had first arrived in the Loop, an armed security guard instructed her to wait next to a reflecting pool where orange and black koi swam in the clear green water. She sat on a bench and took in the elegance of the building. The Loop was designed to resemble an infinity loop, with curved siding and a lush sunken garden in the center of each oval. The building was made of sheer glass that dimmed and brightened depending on the sun's direction. In the foyer, a floating staircase led up to the second floor. The air smelled of cedar and sandalwood, and low-fi electronica emanated from a hidden speaker. The building felt exclusive in a way Rose had never experienced before, like stepping into the body of a machine—cold, functional, and sublime in its execution of perfect design.

She soon discovered that the Loop was stocked with the amenities the clients were accustomed to: coffee beans from Colombia; dark chocolate from Ghana; bottles of French champagne; charcuterie sliced from the fatty thighs of Iberian pigs. International delicacies plucked from the very best the globe could still offer, supplemented by the olive trees that grew in glass vitrines along the suspended walkways. Damien often sent Rose to fetch another bottle of champagne from the Loop's kitchen, but she never felt comfortable in the windowless room. The only light was the sterile fluorescent tubing, and the unblinking green eye of the security camera overhead. The kitchen felt cold, subterranean, nothing like the bright airiness of Damien's suite flooded in light. Only the clients' suites had the privilege of windows and the sun.

"Don't expect the North to be anything like the Loop," Damien had said before she left. "The camp is a real frontier, with the derangement of a man camp. When you're feeling down, just think about everything you'll get once the job is complete and you're back in the Floating City with your mother."

But now, sitting at the vanity, Rose feels the eerie sensation that it is the Loop that she has left behind, and Dominion Lake is the real world.

She leaves her room and waits with Willow in the atrium of the mall, next to the drained water fountain, where a shaft of sunlight filters through a massive domed skylight. The other Blooms are already with their clients in their rooms. Willow ties Annie up to a bench bolted to the ground and feeds her a handful of kibble. Then Willow sits at the edge of the fountain and takes out the pack of cigarettes. "Don't tell Judith."

Rose sits down next to her. "I won't if you give me a drag."

"Deal." Willow passes the cigarette to her.

The tobacco is stale and pungent, but Rose smokes it anyway. "Where did you get this?"

"The Barber found a carton in the EZ Gas and gave me a pack."

"Did you know him before camp?"

"I did. We grew up together. But I haven't seen him for a long time."

So that explains why Willow treated him like an ex-boyfriend she still holds a flame for. Rose wonders if there is still something between them.

Willow finishes smoking the cigarette and flicks the butt into the fountain. She stands and steps into the empty water fountain. "A dime!" she yells happily. She brandishes the coin and points to a gumball machine, still marked by the sticky hands of former children. "Do you want one?"

Judging by the vintage grime of the mall, the candy is at least a decade old. "I'm good," Rose says. "You go for it."

"Suit yourself." Willow liberates a blue gumball from the machine and pops it into her mouth before wandering over to the children's playground, where a motley crew of mechanical animal rides sit perched on a scraggly patch of synthetic grass—an ostrich, a badger, an elephant. Rose watches her blow a perfect blue bubble and then hop onto the elephant. Willow lets out a little hoot, then unzips her parka and tosses it onto the ostrich. Rose notices that she's changed into a slim-cut black jumpsuit with the sleeves cut off, revealing her toned arms. "Come on, Rose. Let's go for a ride."

Before Rose can answer, Judith suddenly emerges from behind a plastic ficus tree.

"Fuck, Judith. You scared me," Willow says. "How long have you been lurking there?"

"Get off the toy, Willow. Meyer just arrived and you look like a child." Judith quickly rubs a streak of blue bubblegum from her cheek.

Footsteps echo in the distance. Annie raises her head and growls softly.

"There, there. He's a friend." Judith touches the dog's ears softly. Annie wags her tail and settles.

The man who enters the mall wears leather work boots and a handsome sheepskin coat trimmed with golden fur. He walks slowly toward the fountain, looking around the mall with exacting scrutiny.

"Meyer," Judith says. "Welcome to our little nest."

He shakes her hand. "So, this is where they've stashed you? A little gloomy, don't you think? The Foreman told me that you'd be well taken care of."

Judith laughs. "Even you won't care about the décor once you've spent some time with our Blooms. They're all so eager to meet you. Especially Willow. She has a keen interest in architecture. Willow," Judith calls out. "Why don't you come here and tell Meyer yourself."

Willow steps forward. She smiles, and Rose can see her teeth are stained blue. "I have so many questions for you."

"Maybe another time, dear," Meyer says, and pats her on the shoulder dismissively. "I'm honestly exhausted from the journey. Is there anything to eat here?"

"I can cook something for you," Rose says quickly, and steps forward. "I was just about to have lunch myself."

"Well, if it's not too much trouble," Meyer says.

"Not at all," Rose says. "I'm happy to."

"Thank you, Judith," Meyer says. "I'll be fine with this one." He touches Rose gently on the shoulder.

In the kitchen, Rose dissolves a cube of bouillon in a pot of boiling water on the stove. She melts a knob of margarine with freeze-dried onions and a few shakes of garlic powder, and then sautés a cup of white rice in the savory fat. The broth is ladled in next, one cup at a time, until the rice absorbs the steaming liquid and thickens as she stirs a wooden spoon. She senses Meyer watching her as she cooks, and she wonders if he is the type of man who prefers a woman bent at the stove, cheeks flushed, steam rising. Or if this little episode of kitchen play is just fodder for what he really wants, her facedown on the bedspread as he loses himself in her body. She wipes her hands on a dishcloth and looks back at him, seated at the table. Cooking for him brings her no pleasure, but she smiles anyway.

"It smells delicious," he says, and then adds, "Thank you."

"It's not much," she says, and means it. Damien would never eat a meal composed entirely of pantry ingredients. He wanted his food to be so fresh that it was nearly alive.

"No, I mean it. I can't tell you what a hot meal means to me right now."

In the kitchen's light she sees his hair is lamb's white, but coarse like a horse's tail, with bits of black flecked on each side. He is older than his author photo on the dust jacket, his face now lined from years spent working under the sun, with a sharp crease between his eyebrows. But his eyes are the same—pale blue, nearly translucent.

When the rice is plump and glossy, she empties a packet of frozen peas into the pan and finishes the dish off with shelf-stable Parmesan and black pepper. She serves the rice in bowls, which she brings over to the table.

She watches Meyer eat his portion quickly. He is clearly ravenous, but he uses a fork and knife, tines pointed down, "in the continental style" as Avalon once taught her. When he is done, he dabs his mouth with a napkin, and then shakes his head. "You'll have to forgive me. I just realized I never asked your name."

"It's Rose," she says.

He nods, seemingly pleased. "A perfect name for a classic beauty. But I prefer the wild varieties to the English garden types. Do you know this region used to be called 'Wild Rose Country'?"

"I know so little about the North. When was it called that?"

"Back when the flowers still bloomed. I saw them years ago, right after the local economy opened to foreign investment. I was conducting my first land survey during a terrible drought. One day, I came across these bright pink flowers on a scraggly bush, inexplicably blooming. It had been months without rain, but somehow the flowers were still alive." He takes a sip of water and looks at her. "Those flowers were why I told Judith to call you the Blooms."

He is more sentimental than she imagined. She expected Meyer to be like Damien—distant, shrewd, calculating. Instead, she finds him to be warm, thoughtful, and curious. And most surprising, she finds herself touched by Meyer's story about the reason behind the Blooms' name.

"I wish I could see the roses," she says.

"Here, I'll try my best to show you." He withdraws a small notebook from the breast pocket of his khaki shirt and takes a stub of pencil from behind his ear. He quickly sketches a rose with five flat, ragged petals. "A wild rose's fragrance is so pure that it verges on rancid. You can keep it if you like." He rips out the sheet from his notebook and scribbles his signature in the bottom corner, transforming the drawing from an incidental sketch into artwork with value.

She takes the drawing and thanks him. "I'll put it up in my room." She touches his hand. "Would you like to see it for yourself?"

"Yes." He squeezes her hand. "I'd love to."

Meyer enters Rose's room and removes his boots at the door. He looks up at the ceiling with the missing panel. "I'll have to talk to Judith about this place. Are you sure you're comfortable here?"

She sits at the edge of the bed and can see herself reflected in the vanity mirror, arranged in a black silk dress. "You seem disappointed."

He shakes his head. "It's not you." He sits down next to her on the bed. "It's this room that causes some concern." He looks around again. "Does anything here belong to you?"

She takes his hand and places it on her thigh. "This." She moves his hand to the ridge of her collarbone. "And this."

"You have lovely skin." He withdraws his hand and pulls a flask from his sheepskin jacket and takes a slug before handing it to her.

She takes a small sip. Frontier liquor, probably fermented in a bathtub in a shack, mixed with last summer's juniper berries and a few handfuls of sugar. Liquor to lose yourself in, not to be leisurely enjoyed. The second sip is less harsh than the first and settles her nerves.

She points to the books on the bedside table. "I've read some of your work to pass the time."

"That's impressive of you. I'm glad you're taking this time to educate yourself." He takes another drink from the flask and finally seems to relax. "What did you learn?"

She tries to think of the most grandiose claim he made in his book, the one that struck her as being both wildly idealistic and terribly depressing, given the hindsight of history. "A better future is possible." She reaches over and picks up *Building in Ruins*. "I know this book is your first—"

His tone suddenly turns sharp. "You mean dated? Many of my inter-locuters have taken great pleasure in cutting down my youthful princi-ples. Especially after all that we've suffered through in the past decade."

There it is—the flash of menace Damien warned her about. She will act like the impressionable student to flatter him. "I don't think it's dated. What you wrote is very brave. And true." She opens his book to a passage she underlined and reads aloud, "'We must imagine a future of less. Less capital. Less resources. Less space. And we must accept that the survival of the human race depends on a radical reimagining. Use and destroy can no longer be our credo of living.'"

He waves a hand dismissively. "I was a young man back then. I had never truly suffered, so it was easy to string pretty sentences together."

"You don't believe this anymore?"

He takes a moment before he answers, "I still believe part of it. But with limitations. When I wrote that, I really did think that every individual had the right to breathe clean air and drink fresh water, to live free from personal injury, to pursue their personal passions and live according to their inner dictum. That's how deluded my thinking was—I thought of individual rights as aspirations. But the truth is, there are too many humans on this planet competing for the same resources. It's just not reasonable for us all to get what we want, when we want it, how we want it. Very few have the privilege of choice." He screws the cap on the flask and places it back in his jacket. "That's why we're here, isn't it? Just this morning, I saw geese flying north for the winter. Even they know north is our new direction."

She rubs a finger across Meyer's temple and feels his pulse beat inside his skull. "I want to build a better life, but I worry it's too late."

"It's never too late. If we band together, we can still create change." Meyer takes her face in his hands. "Thank you, Rose. You've reminded me of a version of myself that I thought I had left behind. And for that, I'm grateful. Can I come see you again?"

"Of course," she says. "Any time."

He kisses her on the head and wishes her a good night. After he leaves, she wraps the sheets tightly around her.

Meyer will not be a problem. She's certain of this now.

He is merely a man.

WHITE ALICE

Of course, it was sometimes boring and cantankerous to live and work with the same eight women in a climate research station in the Far North. Petty fights occasionally broke out over who was sleeping with whom, who had eaten the last tin of pickled herring, who had nodded off during their night watch. But it was surprisingly easy to be together, away from everything we knew. Like the ants that the biologist tended to in the glass-boxed colony, we moved through our duties with an intrinsic sense of purpose and well-being. And we felt the dimensions of time change as we adjusted to the long dark nights during the polar winter. We no longer saw each minute, each hour, each day as being part of the world we left behind. We lived on our own schedule.

After our first winter, Sal instructed the cartographer to complete a seasonal map of our area. Sal wanted to fix the winter season in place, arguing that it would be easier to live through the next winter if we had a record of our first. She told us it was common practice for the earliest explorers who first charted the North to name the frozen expanses in their own language.

"We should do the same," Sal said, and asked us to each take a turn naming the map's coordinates:

Dunce's Cap
The Bend

Deeper Waters

A Loss of Faith

Awkward Triangle

Beggar's Remorse

Maiden's Gown

A Frank Assessment of the Unknown

The cartographer charted the map. When she was finished, she unrolled it on the kitchen table for us to look at together.

"Why didn't you name our territory?" Sal asked when we gathered around the table.

The geographer looked at her with dismay and voiced the skepticism a few of us felt. "Our mission is to observe and record the climate. Not occupy the land."

"It's not an occupation if this is our home," Sal reasoned. "Write 'White Alice.'"

We had grown used to following Sal without question, so the cartographer did as she was told. We watched her mark the territory as *White Alice* on our map.

Was that all it took to make the station our home?

We all changed after living in White Alice, but Sal's transformation was the most profound. When she arrived, she called herself a patriot, loudly and proudly. But after a year of living in White Alice, she never spoke fondly of the country we vowed to serve. Instead, she was intent on disparaging the world we had left behind.

"What is it about men that makes them such deficient creatures?" Sal asked us one night after her evening patrol.

We were sitting at the table, about to eat dinner, and we looked at each other, thinking we already knew the answer. We were acutely aware of the destruction men inflicted on others and themselves. Some of us had experienced things that we had never discussed until we arrived in White

Alice—things that had been done to us, things that we had been forced to endure. It was partially the reason we had spent so many years studying and training in hard sciences, physics, engineering, computer programming, security, meteorology, the military. If we mastered the fields dominated by men, we reasoned, then we might insulate ourselves.

"Greed?" the geographer answered.

"No," Sal said. "Fear. Men are weak because they fear losing power."

We looked at each other and wondered if Sal was right.

"Maybe it will be different when we go back," the engineer offered. "Things may have changed."

"Not this," Sal said bitterly. "Men will do what they can to consolidate their power. We'll spend one more year here and then return to the same shit world we left behind."

We imagined what that future might look like. Reentry. Acclimation to the heat. Drought. Violent storms. The eerie haze of summer wildfires. Stockpiling water, canned rations, off-grid generators. Caretakers at war with our ravaged planet.

But we would be lying if we said we thought only of the threatened climate and the dominance of men. We all knew that White Alice was the apex of our careers. Some of us would work in the private sector, overseen by men who would belittle or take credit for our work. Others would remain in the military as evidence that women were finally seen as equals. It would be a full century before our reports and research were declassified, and by then, we would all be dead, long-buried or burned or whatever method we had chosen for our bodies' disposal (and we had chosen; our contracts demanded that we outline the grim details of what to do in all eventualities).

"We could find work in the same research facility," the biologist suggested. "Or work close to one another, so we can still see each other on weekends."

"Weekends?" Sal answered. "We'll be lucky if we cross paths in an airport. Classified squads are always split up after homecoming. We'll be assigned to different parts of the country, and we will never see each other again."

The finality in Sal's voice told us everything we needed to know. In one year's time, we would return to our separate lives until we met our separate deaths on our compromised planet. We would never see each other again.

"Will any of you have a child?" Sal asked.

"Of course not," the meteorologist said. "It would be unethical."

We all nodded in agreement. Not contributing to overpopulation was something we all shared as a moral philosophy.

"Back south it absolutely is," Sal said, "but I wonder if it would be different here." She pushed her chair back from the table, which was her signal that dinner was over. "Let's get into formation."

After each meal, Sal led us in drills through the snow. Three times a day we shouldered our weapons and wove in and out of an obstacle course made of oil drums and disused crates. We ran, jumped, and rolled, aiming our weapons at blind targets out on the ice. To preserve our ammunition, we shot rounds of blanks that snapped and echoed across the frozen tundra. Inside the station, Sal showed us how to care for our weapons, how to unsheathe a knife. And she instructed us to sleep an arm's length from anything that could be used as a cudgel.

What Sal did in her spare time when she wasn't patrolling the station or overseeing our drills was not entirely clear to any of us. She never partnered off with anyone, or even seemed interested in intimacy. Her desires were only attuned to protection and defense, as if the pursuit of pleasure would debilitate her control. Not once did she tell us what she loved or had left behind, or even why she had taken this position.

One evening, when the engineer was changing the linens on the bunks, she found a photo under Sal's bed of a baby with curly hair. When Sal was outside during her evening patrol, the engineer gathered us in the bunkroom.

"Sal had a son," the engineer said. She showed us the photo, and we all agreed. The baby was undeniably her child.

"He must have died," the cartographer said, "or she wouldn't be here."

Despite her bluntness, we knew the cartographer was right. The background checks had been extensive and rigorous. No one with living offspring was recruited for the mission, because they would have been considered a liability.

"How incredibly sad," the geographer said, and looked at the photo. "They have the same green eyes."

Broaching the subject with Sal seemed intrusive. The cartographer argued that Sal's silence on the issue and intense privacy was her domain to oversee. Part of what we loved about White Alice was how we could conduct our lives any way we wanted. If Sal preferred to keep parts of herself shrouded, then that was her decision.

But it would be incorrect to say we didn't think of her differently. She wasn't entirely like us, after all. She was a mother.

Now, her grave intensity had a new shape cast by this dark shadow. All of her grit, her sinew, her unwavering focus on protecting us, was framed by the fact that she had experienced such significant loss. How much of her son was with her now, we wondered, and how much was her fixation on training us part of a desire to annihilate her past? Many of us had experienced things that we wanted to forget, but nothing came close to the kind of loss she lived with daily.

Most important: Could we trust her to protect us, knowing that she had deceived us? Or should we take this knowledge as another indication of her seriousness of intent?

We chose to believe the latter—that her trauma was what had formed her, and what had turned her into such an uncompromising soldier. If Sal hadn't had the burden of the photo, then she would have been an entirely different person, unfit for the brutality she later showed.

How can you fault the fist when the heart spasms for air?

CHAPTER FOUR

GRANT

On his first day of teaching, Grant follows the Foreman to a room at the back of the warehouse and pulls a dangling cord on an exposed lightbulb, illuminating the concrete cube with a grayish light. A stack of folding chairs is pushed over to one corner, and a whiteboard is propped against the wall. The lightbulb flickers on and off while a generator heaves and shudders in another corner.

"This can't be right," Grant says. The room looks like a place where dead bodies are hidden and then happily forgotten. "Is this the boiler room?"

The Foreman slaps the generator like the rump of a horse. "This is our heart, our heat. In camp, this is what keeps us alive." He opens the side of the generator and siphons liquid from a red canister.

The smell awakens a long-buried memory. Their family's driver at the pump as Grant presses his face against the back-seat window. The smell of gas, thick and acrid in the air.

The Foreman sets the canister down. "I know what you're thinking, Grant. Don't worry. We'll upgrade to clean energy after the campus is more established."

Grant stares at the concrete walls of the boiler room. "This must be a mistake. I can't teach here."

The Foreman grins, his teeth flashing gold. Clearly, he's enjoying this. "You're free to teach in the great outdoors if you want. Might last only a few minutes before your fingers freeze off. Should I set you up outside?"

Grant forces a weak smile. He won't let the Foreman see he is irritated. It will only confirm what he clearly suspects—that Grant is an appendage, a superfluous rich boy who is only in the way. "This will be fine, thank you."

"You'll learn quickly to make do with what we have in camp. Now, you have a good class. I'll round up the Diggers."

After the Foreman leaves, Grant walks around the small room. This is insane, he thinks. Of course, he didn't expect Walden's tidy red-brick campus with its meandering footpaths and cast-iron lampposts. But he at least expected a window. He wishes he'd asked Meyer why the campus is delayed, and what the delay means for his employment, but he had been too overwhelmed by the wilderness, the weather, the journey, to ask many questions. He thinks of the Foreman's words. *Make do.* This is his only choice.

Grant unstacks the folding chairs in a circle and unpacks his books from his leather side bag. Someone has written PROF. GRIMLEY on the white-board under WRITING 101. Seeing his last name makes him feel a flash of anger. Even in this wretched boiler room, the shadow of his family is here.

Fifteen minutes later, only half of the Diggers amble into the room. They collapse into the folding chairs, pointedly avoiding eye contact with Grant, who tries to greet them each by name. The only Digger who looks perky enough to talk is Swifty. He sits at the front of the class with a piece of paper ripped from a ledger book and a pencil stub tucked behind his ear.

From the vantage point at the front of the classroom, Grant feels like he's seeing the Diggers for the first time. Last night they were his drinking companions, though not quite his equals. Now, standing at the front of the classroom, he wants to see them as students. But as he looks at Hattie chewing the stub of a pencil, Rabbit nodding off in his chair, and Wolfe rolling a cigarette on his knee, all he sees are strangers.

At Walden, Grant felt most at peace while sitting in the book-filled seminar room with a leafy view, an elegantly tatty Persian rug under the wooden chairs. A room where the line break in a poem was discussed with the veneration of a religious sect, despite the encroaching evidence of language's irrelevance. He loved opening the week's readings, photocopied on real paper, and reading a consciousness that existed in a pre-Flick world. All seminars were conducted strictly off-Flick, and any student suspected of tapping into their feed was ejected from the room. His professors believed that Walden students must be physically present in class because their studies existed above the mediocrity and ubiquity of the feed.

The path to a man's soul, Grant's professor once lectured, is in his pen, not in his Flick. If you want to learn who he is, what he longs for, what he desires, then ask him to write on a piece of paper. Grant thinks of this directive now as he hands out sheets of paper torn from his own notebook. This will be how he'll find a path forward. If he can get the Diggers to write, he'll finally be able to see who they really are.

"Welcome, everyone," Grant says. "I know that many of you may feel indifferent to me standing up here. Some of you might even be pissed off that you're being forced to sit in the boiler room. Whatever you're feeling, I want you to know that I, too, feel as you do. When I took this job, I didn't expect to be living like this, and I doubt any of you did, either. Now, I'm not asking for a lot from each of you. All I want is for you to write down on that piece of paper whatever you're thinking about. Good, bad, funny, scary, deeply personal or strikingly foreign. Whatever it is, get it down on the page without any judgment. Now, go." Grant retrieves a wooden egg from his leather side bag. He turns the egg clockwise and sets the timer ticking.

A few Diggers drag their pens across the blank page, while the others stare at the ceiling or chew on a nail. Grant is radiating cold sweat. Why should these men care about what he has to say about narrative subjectivities? To claim knowledge is to claim certainty, and he has never felt so uncertain before in his life.

The egg dings.

Grant clears his throat. "Would anyone like to share what they wrote?"

The class looks back blankly.

Hattie shifts in his chair.

Rabbit coughs.

"Please, anyone?" Grant hopes his voice doesn't sound too pleading.

Wolfe flicks open a cigarette pack. He lights up and exhales a cloud of smoke. Tipping back in his chair, he sends the pack around the room. Within a minute, the room is thick with fumes. The boiler shudders as it shifts into a different heating cycle.

"Where are you from, Wolfe?" Grant asks.

Wolfe exhales a stream of smoke and then answers, "Wolfe Creek."

"That's a shithole of a place," Swifty cuts in.

"I was born there, that's all," Wolfe says.

"What about you, Swifty?" Grant asks. "Where are you from?"

"Swift Falls," Swifty says with a trace of pride in his voice.

"Equally a shithole," Wolfe says, and then points a finger at all the Diggers. "You all know your town is no better or worse than mine."

Grant imagines the towns the Diggers are from: a gutted civic center, jumpy housewives in stained housecoats driving their ex-husbands' pickups, skinny kids in camo pants sitting on curbs. A place where everyone looks desperate enough to eat their own pets. "Do you ever think of home?" he asks the Diggers.

"More than I thought I would," Wolfe admits. The tenderness in Wolfe's voice takes Grant by surprise. "It may be a shithole, but it's *my* shithole."

The Diggers roar in response, and the sound of collective laughter makes Grant genuinely smile. Once the laughter subsides, Wolfe's manner turns serious again. "I can't wait to get back home."

"Everyone in Swift Falls wanted me to get them a job up here," Swifty adds. "But I don't trust this place."

"And why is that?" Grant asks.

"It's too easy to hide a body out here," Swifty says, and raps his knuckles against the side of his chair. The sound resonates and expands in the concrete room.

Wolfe looks around at the other Diggers in their gray coveralls, each absorbed by a cigarette or a sandwich. "No one here is worth murdering," he seems to suddenly decide.

Swifty laughs loudly and spits a fleck of crust across the room. "You make murder sound like a compliment."

Wolfe shrugs. "At least you know you're wanted for something."

A buzzer inside the warehouse sounds, announcing that the Diggers' shift is about to begin.

"We'll end class there today," Grant says. "You can hand back your responses on your way out."

The Diggers drop the papers on his chair and leave. When he is alone, Grant quickly sifts through their writing responses. Only a few have written an actual response, describing an argument they had with the Foreman, or a few sludgy curses flung at the Cook. Most of the pages are painfully empty, the white sheets as untouched as a remote slab of ice.

He looks over to see GRIMLEY scrawled on the whiteboard. What will it take for him to finally sever his name and cut ties from his family? He stands and erases his name from the whiteboard. It's a start, he thinks. But he'll have to do more.

––––––––

Grant's parents had met at Walden, as had his grandparents, and his great-grandparents. A Walden marriage had occurred in every generation in the Grimley family, stretching back to the period when the university was still separated by gender, and women occupied their own quad across the Square. When Grant learned he would be housed in the dormitories in the historic Yard, his father nodded with solemn approval. "A fine place to make a name for yourself. And," his father added, "to find a girl worthy of the Grimley line."

The irony, of course, was that his name had already been established. He learned when he arrived on campus that he'd received a special kind of dispensation. Brunch with the university president in the Arboretum; cocktail hour in the garden of the Divinity School; dinner in the Fireside Room in the Faculty Club. He often found himself cornered in a mahogany-paneled room wearing a too-hot wool blazer while balancing a liver-based canapé on a napkin, the oil paintings of former patrons looming like the ghosts of dead relatives above him. In fact, he would probably discover they were Grimleys if he had the ability to escape whatever conversation he had been pulled into. The line of questioning was always the same. Was he enjoying Walden? Had he declared his major? Surely, he wasn't considering literature as a concentration? And would he be kind enough to let his parents know that so-and-so wished them their very best? He assumed the conversations were a ruse to get closer to a connection to the Grimleys. And so he replied in a clipped tone, suppressing a rising fear that the trajectory of his life was already set.

His father was the one who encouraged him to accept the invitation from the Wild Boars, which arrived handwritten in ink and sealed with a red wax stamp of a boar. The Wild Boars were the most prominent Finals Club at Walden and held their notorious parties in a colonial-revival mansion at the edge of campus. The invitation meant the Wild Boars were considering him as a member, and the party was a trial run to see how he might fit into the club.

"Three former presidents have been Wild Boars, Grant," his father impressed upon him. "Dozens and dozens of high-impact CEOs. Endless senators and congressmen and diplomats. Grandad would be rolling in his grave if he knew you were planning to decline. This isn't an invitation. It's a summons."

As much as he wanted to, Grant could never say no to his father. So, he put on the suit he wore to Grandad's funeral and shaved the coarse mustache he'd grown after viewing a French New Wave cinema series. He wore a pair of tennis shoes and threw that week's readings into a tote bag (at least he could read in the corner if he felt awkward) and set off to the party.

When he arrived at the mansion, he found boys in pressed tuxedos pounding bottles of beer in the living room, the Victorian-era settees pushed against the wall, while their inebriated dates collapsed on the Persian rugs, high heels and miniskirts askew. Pop music blasted into the night. Someone handed him a bottle of bourbon, which he drank so quickly that his eyes watered and his throat burned. Now Grant understood. College wasn't about books and ideas and new directions. It was slow annihilation.

The bourbon settled in at precisely the same moment that someone mercifully put on an ancient goth playlist in the drawing room, and suddenly he was dancing in a way that made his limbs feel as if they were levitating. He didn't care that everyone was looking at him. Feeling drunk and elated, he danced vigorously for three and a half songs until the room started to constrict and he thought, for a terrifying moment, that he might vomit on the meze platter. After locating the fire escape, he hauled himself out the window, sucking in a lungful of air as he steadied himself on the metal railing. He could hear the Wild Boars and their dates laughing inside.

The fire escape was high enough to afford a clear view of Walden's campus. He could make out the pink sandstone of the English building, and the concrete monolith of the School of Design. He could see the Beaux-Arts library named after the alumni who drowned on the *Titanic,* and the Yard where the founding fathers of the college once grazed their cattle. There was the museum with his favorite artwork by a German Weimar painter encased behind bulletproof glass, and the faux Gothic dining hall where he ate under the black-taloned chandeliers. Even at this late hour, students scurried along the diagonal footpaths lit by yellow lamps. As Grant gazed at the campus, he felt an enveloping emptiness.

Nothing. He felt nothing at all. It didn't matter what he studied or who he hung out with, whether he became a Wild Boar or remained a peripheral weirdo. His destiny had been sealed the moment he was born. After graduation, he would join his father in the Floating City and work in the Grimley Tower, plotting the next resource their company would plunder.

"Don't kill yourself!" someone yelled through the open window. "Your dancing isn't *that* bad."

More hysterical laughter.

There was no way he would commit suicide over the Wild Boars. The club wasn't worth it. He started scaling the stairs until he reached the edge of the flattop roof.

A voice called out, "You're almost there."

He pulled himself onto the roof, and then stood, dusting the dirt off his pants. "Are you escaping the party too?"

A young woman sat on an overturned milk crate, trying to light a cigarette with a match. The wind blew, extinguishing the flame before the
tobacco caught fire. She cursed, and then held out a black bow tie. "I'm
actually working down there. Catering. Refiller of nacho bowl. Refresher
of shitty beer." She tried to light the cigarette again. This time the fire took,
and a small red cherry glowed in the dark. "But I'm on my break now.
Needed to escape the date rapists. Man, it's dank down there. You Wild
Boars should learn a thing or two about consent."

He tried to make her out in the murky light. Her voice carried a fierce-
ness that belied her small stature. She had somewhat elfin features: pale
skin, large blue eyes with dark hair tucked into the collar of an oversized
white button-up shirt. She seemed to be wearing tiny shorts or no pants
at all, and a pair of scuffed army boots without laces.

"I'm not a member," he said quickly. "I actually don't even know why
I'm here. I hate this place." There, he said it. The word *hate* sounded delicious in the muggy air.

She raised an eyebrow. "You know how lucky you are to be here, right?"

"That's what everyone keeps telling me. Are you a student?" he asked,
desperate to change the subject.

"No," she said bluntly. "I can't afford college." Her voice faltered for a
moment, and he could tell this fact bothered her. She turned away from
him and asked, "If you hate this place, why are you here?"

He realized he still had the bottle of bourbon in his jacket pocket and
reached down to take a swig, trying to appear indifferent. "I guess I was
just curious."

"About the Wild Boars?"

"No, not them." He felt embarrassed saying it aloud. "What a college
party is like."

"Is it what you hoped?"

"Everyone is so . . ."

"Wasted?" she offered.

"Glib." He took another drink from the bottle and wiped his mouth.
"They already know what they'll achieve."

She looked at him, her eyes suddenly growing intense. "What's it like knowing everything will be okay?"

"I don't know that." He passed her the bottle. "I don't fucking know anything."

"What are you studying at Walden, then?"

"Twentieth-century Anglophone Literature." He hoped he didn't sound like an elitist asshole.

She nodded. "Okay, so you're spending four years at the most exclusive university in the world literally studying something that barely exists. Physical books. Don't tell me that's a personal risk for you."

"It is! My father will be furious when he finds out."

"But he'll pay your tuition, won't he?"

He said nothing. She was right, of course. His educational expenses had been earmarked in his trust fund the moment he was born.

He passed her the bottle of bourbon. "Where are you from?"

She took a hearty slug. "A town you've never heard of."

"Try me."

She told him the name of the town in the West, population 327. "You know it?"

"No," he admitted, and then added, "It sounds quaint."

"Oh, it's great if you're into Jesus and your second cousin." She ground the cigarette under her boot and quickly said, "I'm actually not inbred."

He laughed. The moment of tension seemed to dissipate, so he found a milk crate and sat next to her. "I'm Grant," he said, intentionally leaving out his last name.

"Jane." She leaned toward him and placed a cool hand against his flushed face. "Let's get out of here."

"You're done with work?"

"I am now."

Jane snuck a bottle of red wine from the bar and met him on the street outside the party. They tipsily passed the wine back and forth as they walked by the Federal Revival houses and red-brick buildings. They passed a dormitory with bright white trim and a crimson flag that fluttered on the golden roof. Soft light glowed from each window. The building was modeled after the State House and looked fit for passing bills and resolutions, not housing college kids who decorated the windowsills with empty beer bottles and cans of aerosol deodorant.

"It's a beautiful campus," Jane said.

The sadness in her voice took Grant by surprise. "I thought you disliked it here."

"I do. But that doesn't take away from the fact that it's really nice. It's actually why I took the catering job in the first place. The only way I can enter Walden is by working here."

He'd only visited Walden on his Flick once and was surprised it was such a pathetic facsimile of the real campus. The red brick appeared wooden. The buildings slanted at odd angles, as if a child had drawn each structure. The students often repeated, so that he saw the same blond girl in a *W* sweatshirt sitting cross-legged beneath a leafless maple a dozen times. Nothing on the Flick captured the experience of walking the paths in the Yard, or up the granite stairs to the library. The simulation approximated reality, but it was lifeless and without feeling. After he logged off, he took pleasure in the crunch of maple leaves under his feet as he walked along the cobblestones and listened to the Russian bells chiming in the church's white tower. *This is real,* he tried to convince himself. *Everything on-feed is a facsimile.*

"Did you ever notice how there are no shadows on the Flick?" he asked Jane.

"Yeah," she said. "And no heat. I heard that the Walden on the Flick is purposely buggy, so that only real Walden students can experience the campus."

By then, they'd reached the footbridge that crossed the river to Boston. The lamppost cast a dim yellow light, engineered to evoke the Puritan-era nostalgia Walden was famous for.

Grant tipped the wine bottle over. Two red drops splattered to the ground. "We seem to be out of supplies."

"I've got some vodka in my freezer," Jane said. "I think it's cherry fla-vored. It was on a deep discount at the Russian grocer near my place."

There was nothing he wanted more than to drink sweet Russian liquor with her. "I love cherries."

"Me too," she said.

They were now standing in the center of the footbridge, right where the rowing team started its yearly regatta, and where Grant had met his father, months earlier, while the crowd cheered the eights racing by. He'd never understood the fierce devotion people had for sports, as if a sense of belonging could only be felt through shared victory. Standing there with Jane made all of Walden's rituals seem artificial—the team sports, the exclusive clubs, even the discussions in his literary seminars. None of it existed in the world Jane lived in. *Maybe Walden is the simulation*, he thought.

Jane leaned toward him and loosened his striped tie before clipping her bow tie to his collar. "It looks better on you."

"Thanks, I guess?" He threaded his fingers through hers like he'd wanted to on the roof. "Can I kiss you?"

She tilted her face to his. "Took you long enough."

The kiss was wetter and less controlled than Grant would have liked, but she didn't seem to mind. Jane tasted like wine and beeswax lip gloss, and when she slid her hand beneath his shirt, he could feel the ragged edge of her uneven fingernails.

Jane's studio was across the river in an industrial building that once housed the workers of a long-shuttered textile factory. It faced the turn-pike and consisted of one narrow room with a hot plate, and a small bath-room where she did all her dishes in the tub. A futon mattress, without a frame, was pushed into the corner of the room, and a folding card table with a stool and a chair was positioned against the front window. He'd never been in such a humble room before and tried to hide his surprise by examining the row of flowering cacti along the window ledge.

"Survival plants," she said, and set a mug of cherry vodka next to him. "I can neglect them and not feel guilty."

The cacti were small, prickly things, capped with neon-pink and orange flowers, vibrant and alive despite their defensive postures. Grant reached out to touch one of the cactus's spikes and felt a momentary prick.

"Careful," she said, and sat down next to him. "They hurt more than they look." She took his hand in hers.

A feeling hummed, sweet and low, in his chest, as he looked at her. The room glowed as the first hazy rays of sunlight crested over the turnpike. She pressed her thumb against the inside of his palm. The sun was now spilling its golden light across the studio's walls. The sounds of traffic filled the room and their shadows on the wall shifted as they kissed and undressed each other. When they fell onto the futon, it felt like falling into a warm cloud.

Finally. He kissed the space behind Jane's ear. Her Flick momentarily blinked on and off, as if to say: *I'm here.*

———

The Barber is spinning a gold coin on the table when Grant steps into the cafeteria for lunch. He's trying not to feel too disappointed by how terribly his first class went, and slumps down next to the Barber where two trays of sandwiches are left out on a table. NOT-TUNA is written on one of the trays, TUNA on the other. "Which kind is better?" he asks.

"Why not let the coin decide?" the Barber says. "Heads for not-tuna, and tails for tuna." The Barber flips the coin in the air and slaps a hand down on it after it lands. "Ah, it's heads. See?" He shows Grant the coin imprinted with the head of a dead queen.

"Not-tuna it is." Grant grabs a sandwich from the first tray. "I hope it's not lynx leftovers." He takes a bite and chews thoughtfully. "Are you sure this isn't tuna?" He opens the sandwich and looks at the pinkish filling. It tastes and smells exactly like the tinned tuna he and Jane would mix up with mayonnaise and chives and eat on crackers.

"Of course it's tuna," the Barber says. "It's always tuna. Flin saves the game for our evening meal."

Grant takes a suspicious whiff of the sandwich. "Then why offer a choice?"

"Because the sandwich always tastes better if you think you've chosen it." The Barber gestures toward the Diggers' bunks. "Every day I watch the Diggers come in for lunch and choose from one of those trays. They never complain that the sandwiches taste the same. They're satisfied with the illusion of a choice."

Grant puts the sandwich down on the table. "That is truly messed up. Does Meyer know about this?"

"I'm sure he does. It was probably his idea. Everything here is. What has Meyer told you about camp?"

"That construction is delayed, but he expects the campus will open soon."

"Does he now?" The Barber sounds amused. He taps the coin on the table. "You need to open your eyes, Grant, and look around you. There are no choices here. Meyer would never have flipped that coin."

"You mean he would have just chosen tuna?"

"No." The Barber pauses and then says, "He wouldn't have taken either of those sandwiches. He knows they taste like shit." He lights a cigarette, and then passes the pack over to Grant, who declines. "Any plans for New Year's?"

"None, to be honest."

"Well, there's a little party happening in the bowling alley down the street. You should come if you're free."

"Will Meyer be there? I need to talk to him about my classroom."

The Barber nods. "All the clients will be there. And the Blooms, too."

"The Blooms?"

"They're the women who work in the brothel across the highway."

Grant chooses his words carefully. "Are they willing participants?"

The Barber looks evenly at Grant. "Why do you ask?"

"It's just surprising that Meyer would condone sex work in a campus environment."

The Barber shakes his head. "Meyer has a lot of ideas, but he has a Bloom like all the other men who run the camp."

"Do you meet with one, as well?"

"No. I'm considered low-level, like the Diggers. I'm surprised you've been left out. You're more like us than I realized." The Barber grinds the cigarette butt under his boot. "Will I see you at the party?"

Grant shrugs. "Sure, it's not like I have a lot going on here."

"Good. I should get going." The Barber starts for the front door of the warehouse, then looks back and says, "Can you keep what I said between us?"

"About the tuna?"

"No. Meyer." The Barber opens the door and steps out into the blinding white light.

WHITE ALICE

Everything changed during our second winter. One evening, before dinner, the meteorologist was preparing her weekly report for home base. Before she sent it off, she noticed something odd. A small manila envelope labeled ABSOLUTE ZERO appeared on the computer's screen.

"Absolute zero" was a term used in the meteorology field to describe the lowest theoretical temperature possible on the thermodynamic scale. Absolute zero was equivalent to −459.67°F, a temperature so low that it was considered nearly impossible to reach. The meteorologist knew only another member of her profession would use such a term. She clicked on the folder and saw that it contained a single document. When she tried to open the document, a series of unintelligible numbers and symbols unspooled on the screen. It was clearly code.

For the meteorologist, not understanding the mysterious file felt like a personal failure, since it was clearly intended for her. She wondered if it contained interesting data sets. Her findings since arriving in the station confirmed what her colleagues already knew—the troposphere was warming, which meant the change wasn't limited to the Earth's surface. Large patches of sea ice had disappeared, and animals were searching longer for food, causing their migration patterns to become erratic and dangerous. The South already suffered through these ecological changes in the form of blistering summers, less precipitation, and significant periods of drought. The changes would only accelerate and continue. Wildfires, unprecedented storms, crop failure, and pervasive heat would render large sections of our country uninhabitable.

Perhaps this file was something different, she justified. A glimmer of hope for the future.

The meteorologist had been instructed to transmit all her findings to home base directly. Instead, she did something she knew was unauthorized. Instead of reporting the file, she asked the programmer to help her.

"We'll send everything later, once we know what it means," she promised the programmer. "Home base will never know otherwise."

The programmer had, admittedly, grown bored since arriving at White Alice. It wasn't clear what her functionality was beyond overseeing what was, in her estimation, the outdated computing software. Every day she booted up the computers and ran tests and scans to ensure the software and applications were healthy. And every night, she uploaded the day's data back to home base and into a backup hard drive. All the messages and signals we received through the radar were workmanlike and nonclassified. Dispatches from Russian icebreakers patrolling their marine borders. Chinese freights shipping containers over the Arctic Circle. Cruise ships filled with tourists snapping photos of icebergs.

A computer science freshman at a low-level technical college could have performed the same function, and the programmer often complained that she felt like her expertise was underutilized. The meteorologist's proposition, though undeniably wrong and liable for punitive action, was the first opportunity the programmer had to use her skills.

"Let's get started," the programmer said immediately, and began to work on breaking the code.

The rest of us had no idea what was happening. We merely assumed the two had forged some romantic bond and were spending the evenings pushed up against the consoles. They soon stopped coming to dinner altogether, and spent their entire evenings holed up in the communications room, eating crackers and jerky.

Sal found this amusing and rolled her eyes when someone noticed that, yet again, the meteorologist's and programmer's chairs were empty at the table. "You don't need to eat when you're in love."

We learned what had really transpired two weeks later, when the meteorologist and programmer emerged wild-eyed and underfed during the botanist's birthday party.

Yes, the two had grown close, but in an intellectual, near-spiritual manner, where their minds and thoughts had become bonded. They seemed like they had taken drugs together, and while the trip had been momentous, it had also gutted them by breaking down the laws of the universe into depressing nothingness. Or so the botanist said when they opened the kitchen door, looked at us with a holy oblivion in their eyes, and quickly closed the door again. The botanist had taken ayahuasca on a research trip in the Amazon. There, she had pursued a side interest ("purely for research purposes") in order to understand the ramifications of mind-expanding drugs.

"You'd better share whatever you're growing in that greenhouse," the geographer called to the botanist, which made us all laugh.

The botanist just smiled and downed a shot of vodka.

We like to think back on this moment because it's the last time things felt simple in our world. All of us around the table, drinking vodka chilled in a bucket filled with ice, laughing about the botanist secretly growing psychedelics.

The door opened again, and the meteorologist and programmer stepped out. Neither of them spoke as they took their places at the table.

Their uncharacteristically somber moods shifted the feeling in the room. The temperature seemed to drop, as if someone had flipped a switch. Our pulses quickened.

"Your meals are there," the engineer said, gesturing to two plates of food.

"We already ate," the meteorologist said with a thread of mania in her voice.

The programmer nodded aggressively. "Actually, we're thinking of going for a walk. Anyone care to join us?"

Sal laid down her fork and looked at them steadily. "You're going for a walk. Right now?"

"I could really use some fresh air," the programmer said with fake cheer. The programmer never willingly left the station unless it was for her mandatory night watch. We all knew this, but it was her tone that made us stand and start suiting up for the outdoors.

We pulled on our snow pants, parkas, gloves, hoods, and balaclavas. It was only −20 degrees, but we needed to be prepared. We stood in a line as Sal checked us up and down, nodding at each of us once she'd confirmed we were properly suited up. It was unprecedented for us to leave the station after we'd been drinking.

"Shouldn't one of us stay behind?" the cartographer asked. She never liked to leave her maps unattended.

"We're all going," Sal said. The edge in her voice told us everything we needed to know.

Outside, the winter sun had set many hours ago. It was pitch-black and windy, and as we stepped beyond the station, we patted our snowsuits for the extra flashlight, transmitter, and compass we always kept in our pockets. We pointed our primary flashlight at the snow and followed Sal as she led us around the periphery of the station, over to where the greenhouse dome rose above the ground.

"Is this far enough?" Sal yelled, her voice flapping away into the wind.

"No," the meteorologist yelled back. "We need to be out of sight of the station."

"Are you sure?" Sal yelled again.

"Affirmative," the meteorologist responded.

None of us had been to the moon, but as we followed Sal away from the station, we felt a galactic loneliness we'd never experienced before, like watching the curve of Earth blacken from view. Still, we kept trudging until the station was nothing but the center of a void. We felt breathless. Cut off. Untethered.

"We'll find our way back through orientation," Sal tried to reassure us. "We all know the coordinates."

We knew the coordinates better than our own names. Just the week before, the cartographer had spent an evening tattooing the orientation on our bodies with blue ink, a needle, and a flame. Even in the dark, we could feel the numbers prickle and glow on our skin. We huddled in a circle and gripped each other's arms.

"I discovered a report in code," the meteorologist finally said.

"Everything that is saved in our station is encrypted into code," the programmer explained, "which is why we didn't understand it at first. But once we were able to break the code, we accessed the file and understood everything perfectly."

"Was it a message from home base?" the biologist asked.

"No," the programmer said. "It was a warning from the previous mission."

We couldn't see her face, but the terror in her voice was clear.

The programmer explained that the last mission from White Alice had never returned back south. The squad was dropped off here, as we had been, with two years of supplies, tasked with their mission of climate surveillance. But as the days grew closer to the squad's return date, home base cut off contact and stopped responding to messages as the squad's supplies were quickly depleted. "They never heard from home base again."

"What happened?" we asked.

The programmer's voice quivered, so the meteorologist took over and told us that the men did their best with what they could—they tracked and hunted game across the tundra and tried to maintain their crops from the seeds in the vault. But their crops failed, and they eventually ran out of ammunition for hunting. By then it was winter, and the station was running low on oil for the generator, so they started burning scavenged branches and pieces of furniture to keep warm. Eventually, they ran out of food.

"And then?" Sal asked.

"They were starving," the meteorologist said, "and desperate." She paused for a long moment and her voice was uncharacteristically small when she spoke. "The last survivor was the mission's meteorologist. He had committed unspeakable acts in order to survive, but now that he was alone in the station, he had no will to live. So he left the encrypted file as a warning for the next mission and said that he planned to walk out into the tundra and never return."

The programmer's voice broke. "Don't you see? We're a living experiment. Home base will desert us, and we'll be forced to survive on our own."

We had arrived in White Alice with the best of intentions. To work peacefully with each other in respect for our environment. But the meteorologist's discovery presented a future as dark and cold as a distant planet. One day, we could be pitted against each other out of desperation.

Sal was the only one of us who didn't seem shocked. "The moment I stepped foot in the station, I knew this mission was compromised. Why do you think I trained each of you so intensely? Why do you think I never rested? I feared we would someday meet a decision like this." Then Sal said aloud what we had already begun to imagine. "Leave or be abandoned. The choice is still ours."

Sal always led us back to the station, but that night we didn't have to follow her. The sky was clear and crisp, and the North Star shone with an aching beauty. We thought of the coordinates pricked into our skin, guiding us back to the place where the axis of those numbers met. We walked in a line, our faces turned up to the brilliant light.

We would find a new home.

––––––––

The oldest records from the radar missions were archived in a series of rolodexes in the library, typed on cardstock with handwritten annotations. Certificate of Competency. Physical Examinations. Medical History. Assessment of Maturity. Psychiatric Rating Scale.

We gathered in the library and opened the rolodexes together, carefully sorting through the yellowed paper, as the cartographer unrolled the maps. For the most part, the soldiers who had been stationed before us bore the old-fashioned names of the previous midcentury. *Walt. Baxter. Alfie. Norman. Herb. Marcel. Rollie. Cecil.*

We imagined them as men with sharp crew cuts and polished boots, blond wives tending to their blond children in cul-de-sacs in the Midwest. Stars and stripes on the front stoop, a dog asleep in a patch of sun. Family men, though some still looked like boys in their military headshots, drafted into protecting our country from nuclear annihilation.

Name: Clint (last name REDACTED)

Hometown: Akron, OH

Age: 25

Health record: *Satisfactory*

Assessment of Maturity: *Well-adjusted*

Reasons for Wishing to Enlist: *Strong interest in aviation; father presently serving in armed forces; love of God and country.*

In one of the boxes of paper ephemera, the botanist found a poster torn at the edges and faded with age. She showed us the poster, and we found the sequence of events, outlining in step-by-step instructions what to do if the radar ever picked up on an incoming attack:

1. *SEND MESSAGE TO HOME BASE:* **WHITE ALICE IS HERE**
2. *TRACK COORDINATES OF ATTACK*
3. *DISPATCH COORDINATES TO HOME BASE; PENTAGON; CAPITOL*
4. *SHELTER IN PLACE AND AWAIT FURTHER INSTRUCTIONS*

"It wouldn't have worked," Sal said. "Even if the radar picked up on an attack, a ballistic missile would have reached the US in ten minutes."

"Why build the stations if it was futile?" the geographer asked.

"Men will build lies if it makes them feel safe," Sal responded. "Even a radar station that has no purpose."

"Here it is," the cartographer said, and motioned for us to join her at the drafting table. She unrolled a map that showed an aerial view of the region. "This is White Alice." She pointed to a red dot in the center of the map. We felt our purpose and significance shrink as we saw how small we were against the vastness of the North. "This is First Nations treaty territory," she said, and circled a large swath of land that included our station and the region to the south. "And over here is Dominion Lake." She pointed south at a blue dot on the map. "It's a two-day ride by snowmobile."

The geographer said Dominion Lake was wealthy from the extraction of oil buried within the region's mercurial sands. After the oil strike, thousands of workers arrived by the busload to the isolated region to claim their quick fortunes. They found work as administrators and foremen, pipe fitters and riggers, drivers and cleaners and cooks, and with their influx followed the sudden development of a new settlement. Townhouses with poorly insulated walls and leaky basements sprang up in cul-de-sacs, where bears occasionally wandered, drive-through restaurants lined the only highway, and primary schools and hockey rinks and office buildings were built for the newly appointed officials who created and bent laws. A church for the vigilant believers. A bowling alley for the elderly and young. A liquor depot and a strip club and a brothel for everyone else.

The geographer was certain there would be jobs for us, as well. "Boomtowns always need fresh talent," she said.

Sal leaned forward and kissed the geographer on the mouth, which made us all laugh.

We had never seen her so happy.

CHAPTER FIVE

ROSE

The shuttered bowling alley has a handwritten sign posted on the front door, CLOSED FOR MY OWN DAMN REASONS. The squat beige building still has its faded awning printed with an image of the waves of Dominion Lake lapping against a bowling alley, a few pins floating with the breeze. Inside, above the bowling shoe rental counter, three stags with glossy marble eyes are mounted on wooden plaques. The names of their hunters are carved into the wood: TERRENCE, BIG RICK, OLD MO.

Rose heaps her parka by the door with the rest of the Blooms. New Year's Eve. 2050. A year once used as a collective call to slow the warming of the earth. Yet no country has been able to fulfill their climate obligations, and now the second half of the century will be aimed at protection. What can be salvaged? Who will be saved?

The Floating City, perhaps. At least that's what Damien promised Rose. Even if global temperatures spike another degree, the Floating City has the green technology and economic backing for the city's children to see the future not as a dead end, or even a compromise, but an undulating road of shimmering possibility.

Right now, back south in the Loop, the toast will have just ended, and the hostesses will be leading their clients back to the suites. Rose can imagine Avalon walking by the koi pond, wearing her linen caftan, gold bangles clinking with each step. Round after round of fireworks light the sky on fire as the city's citizens wish each other another year of the wealth and prosperity they know will be theirs.

It pains Rose to think about. The pull of wanting to be there. The relief of finally getting away. The knowledge that if things do not go well in camp there will be nothing to even return to. She thinks of her mother sitting alone at the edge of a steel cot. No kin to speak of. No one who even knows her Korean name.

But it's still 2049 in camp, and the Blooms are growing weary. They've barely been in camp for two weeks, but their clients have been visiting them at all hours, driven by the animal need of a warm body next to theirs. Some are merely bored, and like how the Blooms are such "willing conversationalists," as Meyer remarked to Rose the other night. Others see the Millennium as a place to pass through, the Blooms as a notch on their belt.

When the Blooms are off for a night, they gather in the kitchen to talk shop about their clients and complain about the food. Rose stays silent during these conversations, preferring to listen rather than offer her thoughts. She feels cautious of giving away too much about herself and why she is really here. It's the same when she is with Meyer, who has implored her to tell him about her life back in the South.

And so she fabricated memories about where she lived and what she did before arriving in camp, what she longs for when she leaves. She unspooled a narrative that made Meyer comfortable and made him see her as a nonthreatening community college dropout now saddled with debt, who longs to have a family of her own one day. All of this is a lie, of course. She can't see the future clearly enough to imagine ever raising children, and college seems out of reach now. But Meyer doesn't seem to notice otherwise. He blithely believes her like he believes his building project in camp will happen.

Judith has done her best to insert her vision of a party into the neglected bowling alley. She spent a day methodically combing the dollar store in the Millennium, scavenging decorations to repurpose. Pink and red streamers are draped from the ceiling, and birthday balloons have been tied to the ceiling fans. A long dining table is set with a white plastic tablecloth and lit by tea light candles. Judith has even scattered glittery stars along the alleys and lugged a portable generator to power the ancient jukebox, which now pulses green and yellow and emits a sappy love song.

The kitschy decorations are in jarring contrast to the Blooms, who have all been told to dress their best. They wear slinky, backless dresses and high heels, and are surprised to see cocktails are already laid out on the bar counter. Clearly, tonight is special. They each take a drink and wait for their clients to arrive. Their beauty and poise seem wasted in this recreation center once used for children's birthdays, retirement parties, proms, the weekly practice of the local geriatric bowling league.

Judith greets each Bloom with a perfunctory kiss. She wears a plum satin dress that she's pilfered from one of the clothing stores in the mall. It's a new look for her, but not a terrible one, and she's worn makeup that softens her hawkish features. "Welcome, girls," she says. "I want you to enjoy yourselves tonight."

The front door swings open, and their clients arrive in a cloud of cold, tramping in ice and snow. Judith trots over to them and takes their coats, greeting each man like an old friend.

Unburdened by their winter layers, the men enter the room and head to their Bloom. Rose watches the men carefully, wondering if one of them is her contact. The camp's PR, Reilly, follows Iris down one of the bowling lanes, leaning into the corner near the gutter. Willow throws her head back in laughter while the Foreman draws her close. Tonight, she's worn a bright pink wig cut bluntly across the bangs, giving her face an impish quality. Fleur and Jasmine have already disappeared with the two security goons, Orson and Carter, and Waxman, the camp's chief financial officer, pulls Violet into the bathroom.

When Meyer reaches Rose, he smiles apologetically. "Don't mind them. This is their chance to show off." He kisses Rose's cheek. "You look appropriate for the occasion."

It's the first time Rose has seen Meyer without the sheepskin jacket. In a button-up shirt and dinner jacket, he looks polished and put together.

She pushes her sheaf of hair to the side and exposes the long plane of her neck. The Blooms have already told her who their clients are, but she asks Meyer anyway, "Are these your colleagues?"

"That's a flattering way to describe them." Meyer looks around at the bowling alley and shakes his head. "These are the men who are helping me get the project off the ground. I can't say I like them very much, but they get things done." He points to a young man in a tweed jacket and jeans, who stands by himself at the edge of the room without a Bloom. "That's my newest hire, Grant. A brilliant young man who is going to run the academic program once we're up and running." He waves at Grant, who visibly brightens and waves back. "And you know the Barber, of course. He's here to keep an eye on things." Rose looks back to see the Barber smoking a cigarette while standing sentinel at the door. He nods once, and she smiles in return.

Meyer reaches into his blazer pocket and retrieves a box. Inside, a gold locket necklace rests on white silk. "Happy New Year, Rose."

She pops open the box and sees a photo of an oasis embedded in the locket, a tiny palm tree bending over a blue blot of water.

"Remember," Meyer says, and gently clasps the gold chain around her neck. "There is always water in the desert."

"Thank you, Meyer. I love it." She kisses him on the cheek. "Any resolutions?"

"I always set a series of intentions, but this year I've decided on just one."

She senses his hesitation and squeezes his hand. "And?"

"To finally do good."

"That shouldn't be hard. You've already accomplished so much."

His tone suddenly turns sour. "I haven't. We should be much further along on the project, but here we are." He looks around again at the clients paired with their Blooms. "Moored in this terrible midcentury."

"Don't say that. You'll find a way forward."

"Thank you, Rose. I hope you're right." He kisses her again. "You always see the best side of me." He finishes his glass quickly. "Can you fetch me another drink?"

She takes his glass and finds her way to the bowling shoe rental corner that Judith has transformed into a makeshift bar and lined with a few bottles of whiskey.

As Rose inspects the labels, a voice says from behind her, "Meyer will like this one best."

She looks over to see the Barber is next to her. He reaches over and pulls out the stopper on a bottle of whiskey and pours it into Meyer's glass.

"Thanks," she says. "Can you pour me one, as well?"

"Of course." He makes a drink for Rose, then himself, and looks around the room. "I used to come here as a kid."

"To bowl?"

"No," he says. "To watch my grandfather drink with his buddies. I'd read a comic book and they'd shoot the shit right here, drinking rum and Cokes in plastic cups." He raises his glass to her. "Cheers to watching old men drink."

She laughs and clinks her glass against his. As she drinks, she looks up at the stag heads above the shoe racks. Their eyes are fixed on the far wall where a hand-painted mural of Dominion Lake, frozen in winter, remains.

She wonders if she can trust the Barber. Hired by Meyer without Damien's knowledge, and yet somehow friendly with Judith and the Blooms. A local who sees himself as an outsider; a hunter who is gentle with animals. She remembers how Annie's bristled fur softened when she heard his voice, how she trotted toward him like a friend instead of a threat. Maybe the animals know something that the humans don't.

She looks over him and says, "It doesn't feel right to be here."

He sets his glass down. "I know." He leans toward her and lowers his voice. "Not everyone is as happy about the camp as Meyer thinks."

She glances behind her quickly and sees that Meyer is deep in conversation with Judith. "Who? The Diggers?"

"I can't talk about it here. Maybe somewhere else. But not here."

"Where?" she asks.

"I'll try and think of something that might work." He reaches over and refills his glass, and for a moment his fingers brush against her hand. His face flushes as he looks away. "I should get back to my post." He nods toward Meyer and Judith. "Before they see us talking."

She watches the Barber walk away and resume his place by the door.

"Keep your eyes on the prize," Damien warned her. "Stay focused on Meyer and don't get caught in the periphery."

But perhaps life is lived on the periphery.

The New Year's Eve dinner is served at a long banquet table decorated with bunches of freshly cut holly in glass vases. Judith guides each Bloom to a place at the table, and seats Rose between Reilly and the Foreman. Rose notices that Willow is chatting to the new hire, Grant, who seems to have loosened up after the predinner cocktails. He leans into Willow as she whispers into his ear.

Iris's client, Reilly, is a short, rotund man with reddened cheeks who looks Rose up and down when she sits next to him. He's dressed formally for the evening in an ill-fitting blazer and a loosely knotted tie, his blond hair slicked to one side. Rose already knows from Damien that Reilly is a PR shill, hired by the camp to maintain a good image with the public. He was the one who sold the line of the "societal benefit" of the settlement to the local authorities. In the ranking of the clients, he is low-level. A well-paid pawn brought north with a suitcase of gold.

The Foreman, though, is different. He's the only man present at the table who has not changed out of his work clothes. Rose knows that he's been hired to oversee the Diggers and spends more time on-site than any of the other clients do. Up close, she takes note of his particular presence. His booming voice, his stained coveralls, his salty smell of sweat. At nearly six and a half feet tall, with a knotted red beard, the Foreman is more Viking than man, more stone than flesh.

"You're Meyer's Bloom," Reilly says to her after the first course is served, a potato soup that the Cook unceremoniously plonks down in front of them. "He's mentioned you a few times. I have a good thing going with Iris, but I'm open to other arrangements if you're willing."

"I don't think Meyer would like that," she says as a deflection.

"Of course he wouldn't. But we don't have to let him know." Reilly smiles a smug schoolboy smile intended to be disarming.

Rose tries to remember whether she is contractually bound to entertain the advances of the other clients. Judging by the way each Bloom leans into the man by her side, she is.

Thankfully, Judith stands and taps a knife against her wineglass, beaming in her plum splendor. "I've been informed that we broke ground on the prototype this morning. Meyer, can you say a few words?"

"I'd rather not, Judy," Meyer says. "Reilly is the natural public speaker."

"Speak, old seer!" Reilly yells. "We want to hear from our fearless leader!"

The clients all join in tapping their knives against glass. Meyer shakes his head, but the men keep urging him on.

Finally, he folds his cloth napkin on the table and stands. "You've experienced this northern country yourself—the space, the fresh air, the water and trees. You all know how increasingly rare these resources are, and how lucky we are to be here." He takes a sip of wine, and then continues, "This is the most ambitious project I've ever been a part of. And the most important. We once imagined fleeing here during times of political unrest, but what we're doing is much more altruistic than nation-dodging. We will build a new way of life here. A new home."

As he sits back down, the men break out into applause, cueing the Blooms to as well. On Judith's signal, the Cook clears the soup, and serves the main course. He sets a plate featuring a lump of brown meat garnished with dried herbs in front of Rose. She prods at the meat with a fork disappointedly. She takes a bite and tastes the deep iron of game.

"How are the Diggers?" Reilly asks the Foreman.

"Surprisingly resilient," the Foreman says.

"That's encouraging to hear." Reilly takes a swig of wine. "Any unforeseen problems?"

"A couple of curious minds, but nothing we can't handle."

"Good. I heard that the site is spectacular."

"We've discovered an utterly beautiful parcel."

"As beautiful as her?" Reilly asks, and pokes his steak knife in Rose's direction.

The Foreman places a heavy hand on the nape of Rose's neck. "It's even better. Less contaminated."

Reilly laughs and busies himself with slicing strips of bloodied meat. "She's listening, you know."

"Of course she is." The Foreman's fingers press on her neck. "But she knows what her role is here." He scrutinizes her with his pitted eyes the color of raw sapphire.

Her role. How she despises the way he is looking at her, forcing her into a tiny box. Peripheral whore. Irrelevant female. Pretty handpiece with a poor sense of humor. Why does she have to take herself so seriously? he's wondering. Why can't she just loosen up and have a little fun? Isn't that what she's being paid to do? She's heard it all before from the Loop, this kind of bemused pandering. A justification to define her based on her job.

She wants to tell him that he is wrong. That this place is wrong. That the decorations and altruistic speech can't change the fact they are sitting in a mildewy bowling alley lined with the heads of dead animals. That Dominion Lake is as dead as the taxidermy, and despite Meyer's high-minded dreams, it's never coming back alive.

But she doesn't say any of this to the two men. It would be stupid and risky. Instead, she smiles and excuses herself from the table, and then walks quickly to the bathroom.

The bathroom is mint tile. Three stalls. Someone's phone number is scribbled on a cracked mirror. Tea lights flicker on the counter. Rose applies a swipe of lipstick in the mirror.

The door opens, and the Foreman walks in. He kicks open a stall door, unzips, and then takes a long, luxurious piss. She caps her lipstick and quickly washes her hands, but before she can leave, he looms in front of her.

"Did our conversation bore you?" he asks.

She doesn't like how he's looking at her, but tries to keep her voice light. "I don't know what you mean."

"You seemed disinterested." He's so close now that she can smell the whiskey on his breath, the smell of rank meat. "What would you rather talk about? Clothes? Boys? What it's like to fuck Meyer?"

"Fuck you," she says, and turns away.

"Defiant little thing." He grins, revealing the gold caps on his teeth. "You may think you're better than me, but we have more in common than you realize." He leans in and sniffs her hair. "We're both Damien's bitches."

For a moment she has no words. So this is him. Her contact. She should have known that Damien would choose someone who would never put them together. The Foreman is the antithesis of the Loop's clients, the well-groomed men who kept their hair short and fingernails clean.

"Are you surprised?" he asks.

"Nothing Damien does surprises me."

"Good. Then you'll be prepared for a message he asked me to give you." He grabs her by the waist and pulls her close. "He wants you to know that he's watching over your mother. That he'll take good care of her as long as you do your part."

Her skin prickles. "And if I don't?"

He runs a finger down her spine. "You're a smart girl. I think you can figure it out." She tries to move again, but he has her pinned. "Damien wants an update, so I'll ask you again. What is it like fucking Meyer?"

She turns her face away from him and tries to keep her voice steady. "Meyer has no idea what Damien is after."

The Foreman nods. "Good. So he's still charging ahead with his asinine plan."

"For the time being. But he seems restless."

"Well, you'll have to keep him distracted." The Foreman places a hand on the inside of Rose's thigh. "It hasn't been easy dealing with Meyer, but he'll be gone soon, and you'll be back with your mother in the Floating City in no time."

She looks uneasily at his hand. "What will happen to Meyer?"

"He'll be sent back to the South, where he'll find some other cause to obsess over."

"And the rest of the workers?" she asks.

"You mean the Diggers? They'll find another hole to dig."

"I mean the Blooms."

"Those sluts are disposable. They're not like you, my dear. You're Damien's prize horse."

They are all alone. If she were to scream, would the Blooms hear her? She tries to push him off, but he squeezes her thigh. "I can see why Damien is so smitten."

The door swings open, and Willow walks in. The Foreman steps away from Rose and smiles broadly at Willow. "There's my girl. Were you looking for me?"

"I was," Willow says, and glances over at Rose. "Everything okay in here?"

Rose forces a smile. Better to play it light. To brush this terrible man away and pretend that he is nothing to her, when in fact, his cooperation means everything.

The Foreman splashes cold water on his cheeks and uses a hand towel to wipe his face dry. "I was just washing up. How's the party going?"

"Good," Willow says, and then turns to Rose. "Meyer is asking where you are."

"Well, you better go to him, Rose," the Foreman says. "He must be wondering where his little dog has run off to."

Rose pushes past the Foreman, and Willow follows. When they are outside the bathroom, Willow grabs Rose by the elbow. "Come with me. The rest of the Blooms are waiting outside."

"But what about Meyer?"

"He's getting wasted with the rest of the clients. Judith says we're done for the night and can go home."

The clients are clustered around the bar, drinking shots of whiskey. They're so drunk that they don't seem to notice, or care, that the Blooms are pulling their parkas and boots on by the door. Judith stands behind the bar and pours out rows of shots. The men drink, and she refills the shot glasses again. Only the recent hire, Grant, seems to notice and waves goodbye to Willow. She waves back, and then says to Rose, "I feel sorry for him."

"Why?" Rose asks. Nothing about the clean-cut young man makes her feel pity.

"He's completely cut ties from his family in the South." Willow pauses before saying, "And he thinks the North will save him."

Rose was born in a sun-bleached shack with a partial glimpse of the ocean. The cottage had two twin beds, covered in a polyester paisley bedspread, that were pushed together during the birth. Rose's grandmother, a tough and taciturn New Englander who grew her own vegetables and made her own gin, served as the midwife. She clipped the umbilical cord with a pair of gardening shears and swept the dark red placenta from the floor into a black trash bag, as though birth was as straightforward as a spring cleaning.

Rose's mother assumed she would stay in bed during the first three weeks that Korean mothers traditionally spent post-birth eating seaweed soup, nursing and bonding with their baby, and recovering from the physical trauma of delivery.

"Not working for three weeks is for the pampered and monied," her mother-in-law responded. "And staying in bed is bad for the bones."

When she could stand, she joined in preparing the cottages for the summer season that had been the lifeblood of her new family for over a century. She tied baby Rose on her back with one broad piece of quilted fabric. It was a throwback to the way her own mother had bundled her, and it brought her a surprising amount of comfort. Flashes of homesickness were rare, but when they arrived, they felt like a torrent of nausea. As much as she tried, she couldn't sweep away her past like a pile of dirt.

When Rose was a month old, her father's family began to call her mother Joy, stating that her Korean name was too troublesome to pronounce.

Her mother later told Rose that being called Joy was like shedding a layer of skin. The name sounded clean and fresh—a one-syllable wonder that made her think of a white sheet hanging on a line to dry. It was an identity to step into. A name to wear. Joy dressed in cotton shorts and sleeveless denim shirts and pulled her long black hair into a ponytail in the style of the women of the peninsula. When she walked, her ponytail swished over her shoulders with American cheerfulness and purpose. But the promise of her new name quickly faded.

"Women are expected to suffer," Rose's mother once told her, "because we're strong enough to bring life into this terrible world."

Rose never saw her mother take aspirin for a headache or heard her complain when she broke her arm falling down the stairs. She once told Rose that she didn't cry when Rose's father drowned in a boating accident when Rose was six months old. She didn't cry when she went to the shoreline and identified his waterlogged body, facedown on the sand, his cotton shirt ripped at the neck. He still looked like a stranger to her. She didn't cry when she watched the gravediggers lower a wooden box into a pit in the Puritan cemetery, or when the people of the peninsula took turns throwing flowers into the grave.

She only cried late that night, alone in the dark kitchen, while clutching Rose's sleeping body to her. She focused on her baby's breathing and spoke softly in Korean, knowing no one on the peninsula understood her mother tongue. As her tears streamed onto her baby's downy head, she made a series of promises:

You will live a better life.
You will not suffer.
You will leave this place behind.

After Rose's father died, the cottages were inherited by Rose's uncle, a libertarian small-game hunter who lived in New Hampshire and openly declared himself the favorite son. Her uncle told Joy that he wouldn't sell the cottages if she agreed to continue working for him in exchange for room and board. All the profits from the cottages would go directly to him, but she would be free to stay on the peninsula and raise her daughter. Knowing she didn't have a better option, Joy agreed.

From a young age, Rose and her mother worked side by side each summer season, cleaning the nine cottages. They scrubbed the black mold in the showers, swept the sand off the walkways, pulled clumps of hair out of drains. Bleach on their hands, sweat on their brows, mother and daughter worked methodically through the cottages, wiping and dusting the antique furniture and rugs.

The summer people equated the furnishings with a more innocent era when a hot summer was merely a hot summer and not symptomatic of the uncertain present. The guests were comforted by the hook rugs, the peeling vanity dressers, the creaky single beds and dented Formica tables, as if stepping into a cottage was retreating back into a simpler time. Rose's great-great-grandfather had named each cottage himself, anointing each structure with a meteorological name (*Breezy Sky, Little Storm, Salty Waves*), even though the weather now was more of a threat than a pleasure.

Rose and her mother continued to work for months and months with the summer sun high in the sky. Then the off-season arrived overnight: a downshift in the wind to a cooler temperature, the color of the ocean darkening with the shortening of each day. Winter was emptied of people and silent on the peninsula. Rose's days were spent at school, gray evenings filled with rain. On the weekends, she amused herself by reading the piles of books that were left in the storage shed out back. She read murder mysteries and crime thrillers abandoned by summer guests to yellow and turn soggy at the edges, but also some classics from her father's collection. *Moby Dick. Crime and Punishment. Wuthering Heights. Madame Bovary.* She loved the physical tangibility of the books, even their mildewy smell, and preferred to read propped up on a stack of neon-orange life jackets in the shed, rather than log on to her Flick. For this, she was often ostracized at school. Her feed was blank in comparison to everyone else's, but she didn't really care. The world inside the books was alive with possibility. In comparison, the Flick gathered what had been processed and collated by companies and brands, tastemakers and influencers, celebrities and their offspring and dogs. It had been decided how she should feel about the feed even before she saw it.

The books transported her to other centuries, other worlds, other minds. It was through reading that she learned the pleasure of being eclipsed by another consciousness, to crawl inside a character and experience the raw emotion of their life. And it was through reading that she first experienced romantic love. In some of the pulpier novels she read, men and women were drawn together by an otherworldly magnetism. Love and desire were depicted as fevered and irrational, not pragmatic and restrained. But when Rose looked around the peninsula, it seemed like people only stayed together for reasons other than romance: money, security, children, religion, habit, boredom. Love was never flight or freedom. Love was duty and obligation.

Rose's favorite part of her day was after dinner, when the dishes were washed and the counters wiped. She'd teach her mother the new vocabulary she had learned that day in school, and in exchange her mother would tell her stories of her life as a girl in Seoul. How she shopped in the wet markets where ajummas hawked razor clams so fresh they tasted of the saline of the Yellow Sea. How her father once drove her on the back of his motorbike, without a helmet, to the coast, where they waded out into the emerald-green seawater to harvest kelp. How she wandered the Itaewon district at night, listening to music on her headphones before meeting friends for galbi and soju.

The peninsula had only one mini mall and two fast-food drive-ins, plus the overpriced seafood shack that opened for tourists in the summer season. There was one electric bus that ran twice a day up and down the two-lane highway, but Rose and her mother never took it because there was nowhere to go.

As Rose grew older, she thought more often of Seoul, imagining less of a story told before bed and more of a living, breathing place. Would she ever leave this shred of coastline and see it for herself? She liked to imagine the banal parts of city life because they felt the most realistic. Going to the grocery store and buying a quart of milk and loaf of bread; wandering down a crowded street; walking up a subway station's stairs into sunlight. Living among strangers who didn't ridicule her mother's accented English or know of her father's tragic death. But she often felt that her life was tied to the peninsula and her mother, and whatever local boy she might one day marry.

"It's better to be alone than with someone who you never loved," her mother warned Rose when she turned sixteen.

The boys of the peninsula fell into two categories: complacent or despondent. The complacent ones were the boys Rose never liked. They were part of families like her father's, who had hacked a life out on the peninsula for centuries and liked to announce, when drunk, that they were descended directly from the first Puritans. These boys never questioned what lay beyond the narrow strip of land that jutted out into the ocean.

The despondent boys were punks and delinquents who vaped weed and kicked curbs by the mini mall. Rose found the despondent boys to be superior to the complacent ones. Not superior enough to imagine a life with, but good enough to roll around with. After her work for the day was done, she would sometimes sit with them in the dunes drinking warm cans of beer. Some of these boys were gentle with her, others less so. Regardless, they never felt entirely present as they made out, still linked to their Flick when they shimmied off their jeans. She never logged on, which made her seem old-fashioned, but she didn't care. She wanted to be as present as possible. It was only much later when she learned from Damien the true consequences of the Flick that she thought back to these moments and felt grateful she had remained off-feed.

It was out on the dunes that Rose noticed the house for the first time. It was a gray saltbox with sun-bleached clapboard windows and a slanted garret on the second floor. The blinds were always darkened, and the rotating cast of cars were never parked for more than an hour. Women in denim cut-offs and bikini tops often hung around out on the front porch during high season, smoking cigarettes and drinking cans of soda.

For Rose, the women were a source of fascination. Sometimes, when she was done with her shift, she would ride her bike to the edge of the property and sit behind a dune to watch the house. The women would sun themselves on the front porch, chatting and listening to music, greeting the men who streamed in and out of the front door at all hours.

Like the rest of the peninsula, the women were dependent on the weather. When the summer season ended, they shuttered the house, moved all the furniture into the storage shed, and then sandbagged the property. The women sang along to whatever beachy tune was on the stereo as they worked, their voices light and joyful, rolling out into the dunes. Where they went during the winter was of no concern to Rose—the only thing that mattered was that they could leave.

These women wielded a kind of power that she had never been exposed to. They were longed for, and desired, but they also seemed at ease in their bodies and in control of their destiny. Most important, they had chosen to work on the peninsula; it hadn't chosen them.

Rose had just celebrated her twenty-first birthday when she found her mother painting the steps of one of the cottages. Her mother was bent over as she worked, her expression dull and distant, which meant her Flick was tuned to a Korean soap. It seemed to Rose that all her mother had done with her life and limbs was clean the cottages for the pleasure of others. And yet she seemed to have accepted this fate without question and never imagined a better life. Not once had Rose heard her wonder what her life might be like if she left the peninsula—back to Korea, or south to Boston, or even another part of the world.

Her mother suddenly seemed to notice Rose standing there and tapped twice behind her ear. "Nice day," she said, and smiled. "You out with Jasper?"

Jasper was the most recent despondent boy Rose had been rolling around the dunes with. He was fine, if slightly tortured, prone to scribbling incomprehensible lyrics in a little black book that he carried with him everywhere.

"Yeah," Rose said, and wondered if her mother could see the sand in her hair.

Her mother squinted up at her. "Be careful who you grow close to. Some men are a mirror and others are a blade. When a man is a blade, you have to be careful."

"Why?"

Her mother paused for a moment, and then said, "He has something to defend."

"What was my dad?" Rose asked.

"Your father was a mirror. He saw what he wanted to see, not who I really was."

"Then why did you stay here? You could have gone to Korea or moved to another city."

Her mother reached up and touched Rose's hand. "I had to think of what would be best for you."

The apartment Rose grew up in was above the cottage's office, high enough that Rose could see the waves roll in. While the cottages had only partial glimpses of the ocean, their apartment afforded open views. Rose sat by the front window in the living room and listened to the shush and moan of the waves. She had once loved the sound of the ocean and watching the tide's retreat. Its consistency was something that she could depend on to always be there. The waves had been rolling into the peninsula even longer than her family had run the cottages, longer than the dead Puritans buried in the cemetery next to her father. But now she saw the ocean as a steady, advancing encroachment, shearing away at the coast. When Rose was long gone, the ocean would continue its indifferent wave.

That night, she saw the future with startling clarity. If she didn't leave the peninsula and find better paid work, then she would bury her mother next to a man neither of them knew. Her children would bury her, and their children would bury them. Each generation would bury the last, until the cemetery filled with the bodies of the dead.

She closed her eyes and tapped her Flick on.

Free College, she thought, and started scanning the generating results.

After she rejected the first round of "low-interest student loans!" she found a list of area colleges that offered free tuition. At the top of the list was the country's most elite institution, Walden University, which offered "need-blind" scholarships to students of "exceptional talent."

Rose had been a perfectly average student and never distinguished herself in school. She didn't play sports or join any clubs. She didn't debate and she didn't volunteer. When she wasn't cleaning the cottages, she was reading, and when she wasn't reading, she was cleaning the cottages. There was not a single thing she could bring to mind that made her exceptional.

She rejected the result and started scanning for others. She stopped searching when she saw:

Hiring workers in the Floating City! Great benefits, fair salary. Live and work in the most innovative research cluster in the world. Interested? Fill out a prescreening questionnaire and tell us why YOU deserve to be a part of our future.

Rose had first heard of the Floating City from a classmate in high school whose father had attempted to reach the island in a rubber dinghy. He'd lost his job in the seafood section of the local grocery store and had heard that if he could just get to the city, he might find well-paid work. But before he reached the shoreline, he was apprehended by the city's marine patrol and shipped back to the peninsula, where he was fined and banned from ever entering the city's territorial waters again. When Rose had asked her classmate why his father had made such a dangerous journey, he responded, "My dad told me that if you're lucky enough to find work there, you'll never have to worry about money again."

Rose immediately filled out an application and described her work experience maintaining the cottages:

I've spent my entire life working in a place that refuses to let go of the past. Every season, I've cleaned and prepared nine antique cottages for guests who are comforted by the relics of a bygone era. But I want a different life than the one I was born into. I want to see the future the Floating City is building.

When Rose received an invitation for an interview in the Floating City the following week, she was surprised and elated, but also deeply worried. Would her mother think she was abandoning her? Or feel jealous that Rose had finally found an exit? The guilt ballooned as she tried to formulate how she'd let her mother know of her plans. But it turned out, she didn't have to.

During dinner one night, her mother suddenly looked at Rose directly. "You're leaving, aren't you?"

Rose was taken aback. She had said nothing about the interview or her plans. "What do you mean?"

"It's okay." Her mother reached for her hand. "I saw that you packed up the books in the shed."

Rose nodded with relief and let it all tumble out. "I have an interview in the Floating City, but I promise I'll come back and visit you as soon as I can."

Her mother smiled and squeezed Rose's hand. "I'm so proud of you. You're finally doing what I was never brave enough to do. You're getting out of here."

On her way to the Floating City, Rose dragged her duffel bags packed with books and clothes to the station and bought a one-way ticket for the next train headed south. The train was nearly full, so she walked down the length of the car, and then the next, and the next, finally finding a free seat in the very last car. Every single passenger was logged on, their eyes jittering as their feed unfurled, their pupils reflexively flickering to her as she passed by, and then returning to the deep dream of their Flick.

She spent the three-hour journey with her face pressed against the pane, watching the pine trees and clapboard houses flash by. The small towns eventually gave way to the postindustrial ruin that announced Boston was near—defunct textile mills with smashed windows; stripped granite quarries; rivers swollen with plastic and sludge; piles of dismembered cars in the metal junkyard. People waited at the railway crossings as the train raced by, but even from inside the train, Rose could see that they too were on their Flicks. Millions and millions of people linked to their feeds, absorbing and reprocessing what their feed offered them. It made her feel deeply and inconsolably sad.

Boston, which had once been prized for its history and architecture, had transformed into a receptacle for the virtual plane. Gone were the parks, the public squares, the green spaces along the waterfront. Gone were the markets, the outdoor cafés, the public gardens. Now, Boston was a city of ghost kitchens and fast-food chains, emptied storefronts and darkened office towers. No one wanted to live in the present-tense city anymore when they could select and inhabit any historical period on their Flick. Hong Kong in 2000. New York in 1970. Florence in 1500.

The few people who walked its streets were guided by their Flicks. She selected a model of Boston, circa 1895. The Flick synthesized archival photographs and created a historically compressed scene. Suddenly, the people on the streets transformed into men in long jackets and hats, women in full dresses toting parasols. A screeching tram rushed past her. She smelled smoke and horseshit and could tell by the slippery cobblestones under her feet that a rainstorm had just passed. She followed a walking path lit by gas lamps to the Public Garden, where the cherry blossoms scattered pink petals over the pond. When she reached Boylston Street, she saw that the Boston Public Library was only a few blocks away.

She had learned about the Public Library in elementary school, when her teacher showed the class archival images of the ornate domed reading room and the rows of leather-bound books.

"The first public library in America," her teacher had said, and explained that in the pre-Flick era, it was common to visit a building that housed tens of thousands of books. "You could take any book off the shelf just to feel its pages, and then check it out to read at home."

"That would take forever!" a classmate exclaimed, and the kids broke out in laughter.

"It was slow, but that was the point. You were meant to spend time with these books. To get inside them." The teacher's tone was wistful,

which Rose recognized as the sentimental affectation older people sometimes assumed when they spoke of life before the Flick.

"What happened to the library?" Rose asked.

"After the books were uploaded to the Flick, there was no use for their
physical bodies. The rarest volumes were sent to the libraries at Walden,
and the rest were pulped to make room for the servers. Now the building
is a data center, but you can still walk by and see the original building."

When she reached Copley Square, she saw the library in the distance.
In 1895, it had just been completed, and as she walked closer, the marks
in the engraved marble edifice appeared fresh and stark. FREE TO ALL.
She stood at the edge of the sidewalk and read the names of the long-
dead philosophers and writers and composers. All presumed geniuses.
All men. She tapped her Flick off so she could see the building in its
present state.

The carved names were still there, but eroded and faint. Through the
windows she could make out the green glow of the servers, casting all
of Copley Square in an eerie hue. Her teacher had said that the books
and desks and lamps and chairs had been trashed to make room for the
servers, which were stacked in rows that numbered into the thousands.
"Each server holds the data of a thousand people. Millions of feeds are
now stored in that one reading room."

She looked up at the building, staring deep into the green glow. Was
she in there too? Everything that she searched for and thought, her interests and desires, her family and medical history, all of her memories
and inner thoughts, archived in a tiny black box? Even now, her feed was
pinning her geographical location in place, tracking her journey, assess-
ing her next steps. It had been with her like a second skin since she was
a child and would continue to be until she died. She wondered if this was
what experiencing your own mortality felt like—knowing that one day the
body you inhabit would be pulped and abandoned, while all of your data,
an entire life's worth, was left shining in the server.

What is a body, then? she wondered, and started walking east toward
the harbor. She felt like one of the sodden paperbacks she packed in her

duffel bag. Useless. Outdated. A book uploaded to the cloud for someone else's future.

When she arrived at the docks in the harbor, she looked out over the water. The Floating City rose up in glass spires. Citizens zipped up and down in elevators running along the shiny buildings as the sleek monorail curved past the massive greenhouses and abattoirs, the shopping plazas, the glistening apartment towers. If she hurried, she'd be right on time.

A crowd was already streaming into the subway station. She joined the line and took the subway three stops to the Third Sector, where the posting indicated the recruitment would take place. When she arrived in the glass lobby of Tower 3, she saw that the room was already packed with people jostling against each other to keep their place in line. An aerial map of the Floating City was projected against a wall.

"The Floating City is organized into four concentric sectors," a woman's calm, recorded voice piped over a loudspeaker. *"The most exterior circle— or what is known as the First Sector—is where our citizens shop in our vast interconnected malls, and where our greenhouses and solar panels stretch to the edge of the boardwalk. The Second Sector is where our engineers and entrepreneurs innovate in the city's glass spires, brainstorming projects that will solve the problems humanity will face tomorrow. The Third Sector is the entertainment district, where restaurants, bars, and cinemas offer socialization opportunities and a place to relax. And the Fourth Sector, at the very heart of the city, is the home of our exclusive club, the Loop."*

A slim silver circle glowed at the very center of the city. The projection faded to black, and then resumed again from the beginning.

Rose read the list of positions available on her application form. The list only included the menial jobs available for those without a college education:

Janitor
Nanny
Barista
Catering Service

Groundskeeper

Stockperson

Sanitation

Dishwasher

Server

Hostess

"What's a hostess?" Rose asked a recruiter standing by the door. The recruiter wore a crisp blazer with the central spire of the Floating City embroidered on the breast pocket.

He looked her up and down before responding, "All your questions will be answered in the orientation." He pointed to the double doors of an auditorium, where the theater's seats were already filling with hopeful workers.

"Welcome, welcome," a man wearing a cordless mic said to the crowd as Rose found a place in the back. "We'll be getting started soon." The man, dressed casually in jeans and a pair of sneakers, looked to be in his forties and radiated good health and impeccable hygiene. He checked the time on his smartwatch and began.

"You may be wondering why your Flicks aren't working right now. I remember feeling the same when I arrived: disoriented, anxious, confused, and maybe even a little angry. I can assure you this is not a technical error. In the Floating City, we've firewalled multiple havens like this one, so citizens and workers can truly disconnect. No job is too trivial here, and we want all of our workers to experience the same liberation as we do."

A screen lowered behind him on the stage, and an aerial view of the Floating City rotated in blue water. "So, why are we here now?" He paused for dramatic emphasis. "The Floating City in Boston Harbor was the first city built. Three more cities are currently in various stages of development off the coasts of New York City, Los Angeles, and San Francisco, modeled after what we've accomplished here. How did we do it? Well, we began with a simple proposition: How can we create a zero-carbon city that utilizes the latest cutting-edge technology while vastly improving governance?"

A cascade of stock images flashed across the screen: an underwater fish farm, solar panels, rotating wind turbines, greenhouses, clouds pinwheeling through blue sky. A glass tower, a woman standing in front of a boardroom, a screen glowing with code.

The recruiter grinned. "Who remembers oil?"

A scattering of hands rose in the room.

"Good, good, so we have a nice cross section of age. Many of us here remember what the world was like with fossil fuels."

The screen darkened as a solitary smokestack emitted a black stream of smoke. Brown water flowed from a faucet. A forest alive with flame, and then reduced to ash. Dead fish festering on a shore.

"Terrible, isn't it?" the recruiter said, shaking his head. "But we've managed to build a better world here than the one we left behind. And we hope as workers, you'll learn from our successes and bring this knowledge back to the mainland to rebuild your own communities."

The video went on to summarize the roles and responsibilities of each job. Rose's interest dimmed until the role of hostess appeared on the screen.

Hiring one (1) hostess for employment in the elite Loop Club. Hostess responsibilities include, but are not limited to: entertaining club members, providing sexual intimacy, and serving drinks and food. Hostesses must be a minimum of twenty-one years old, excellent conversationalists, in peak physical condition, and be available to work on nights and weekends.

Hostesses will receive a yearly salary, free room and board, health benefits, and a monthly stipend for incidentals (clothing, entertainment, travel). Hostesses must live on-site in the Loop and be comfortable accommodating a range of erotic interests and proclivities.

The woman next to Rose shook her head. "Damn. Those tech bros truly get everything."

Rose turned to the woman. "Is this legal?"

The woman shrugged. "I think they make their own rules here."

Rose knew her experience working in the cottages might land her a cleaning job, but she never wanted to feel the callouses flare on the insides of her hands as her skin prickled in the high-noon heat.

When the recruiter came to collect her application, Rose had selected only one job.

After Judith says they can leave the party, the Blooms head back to the Millennium Mall. Outside, they link arms and walk together down the highway. The dogs lead the way. Having had too little to eat and too much to drink, they stumble through the snow toward the Millennium. The air is crisp and cold on their cheeks. When Fleur lets out a howl to see how far it will echo, the rest of the Blooms join in, their voices rolling down the highway and then disappearing.

Later in the kitchen, the Blooms pick through the refrigerator. Fleur finds a tub of cream cheese and spreads it on saltines and makes up a platter of snacks. Violet pulls out a bottle of vodka from her parka and brandishes it in the air.

"Carter was so wasted that he said I could have this." The Blooms clap happily as Violet looks in the freezer. "But we seem to be out of ice."

Willow reaches for her parka and then grabs a butcher's knife from a drawer. "I'll be right back."

The Blooms sit slumped around the table, leaning into each other, their cheeks flushed from the cold, eyeliner slightly smudged.

"Look what Reilly gave me," Iris says. She opens a heart-shaped tin filled with truffles and passes it around the table.

"Damn, these are good," Violet says. She reaches in the tin for a second truffle, but Iris playfully smacks her hand away.

"Let's save them for another night," Iris says, and then adds, "Something to look forward to."

Violet shakes her head. "You're cruel, you know."

"I prefer restrained." Iris pushes the box to Rose. "Here, Rose. Try one."

Rose takes a truffle and involuntarily closes her eyes as she savors its taste. Orange rind, cognac, the bitter tang of pure cacao. An intensity of flavor that she occasionally experienced in the Loop when Damien wasn't undergoing "a purifying cleanse" and swearing off anything with sugar. Reilly may be an asshole, but at least he has good taste.

A door opens down the hall, and a set of footsteps approach. The Blooms suddenly grow quiet.

Willow steps into the kitchen clutching a chunk of blue ice. "Everything okay in here?"

"We thought you were Judith!" Violet said. She gestures to the door. "Close it behind you so we can start talking shit again."

Willow laughs and sets the ice in the sink and starts chiseling out shards. "Can someone find something to put these in?"

Jasmine rustles up six mugs from the cupboard and fills each one with ice. She passes them to Violet, who uncaps the vodka and pours a generous glug. The mugs circle the room, and the Blooms drink and eat the saltines quickly, chatting with each other about the night.

Rose listens quietly. She still finds the Blooms' banter intimidating. The easy way they are with each other feels foreign to her, so unlike the Loop, where the hostesses were in constant competition with each other for clients. "The market dictates what the market wants," Avalon once said to justify why the oldest hostess, Ginger, had been unceremoniously fired. A new crop of hostesses had just arrived in the Loop, and Ginger's clients had suddenly turned fickle as they gravitated toward the new hires.

At first, this cutthroat approach to the business seemed natural to Rose. As one of the newer hostesses, she benefited from the novelty of her presence. A new face. A new body. A new persona for the clients to project themselves onto. But she quickly grew uncomfortable with how the other hostesses only saw her as a threat that would cut into their business. Not a friend. Or a confidante. Merely competition.

When she established herself in the Loop with a client list that showcased some of the most powerful men in the Floating City, she, too, started to see the new hires as obstacles. She kept her distance from the hostesses, new and old, and told herself that no one could be trusted. And because of this, she formed no real friendships in the Loop that went be-yond a superficial level. There was no one she spent time with. No one to confide in. And no books to read other than the copies she'd brought with her from the peninsula. Only her Flick offered an escape.

"Do you know what card I pulled from my tarot this morning?" Fleur asks. Her voice turns serious. "The Fool. An omen of a new beginning."

"That makes sense," Jasmine whispers. "I heard a few of the clients talk-ing at the party. They say things are going to change around here very soon."

"What did they say?" Rose asks.

"Not much. Just that the camp is undergoing a crisis of some kind. Carter wouldn't say why, but I bet it has to do with money." Jasmine shrugs.

Iris is indignant. "They're already broke? I didn't come all this way to not get paid."

"No shit," Violet says. "The least they could do is get us some better food. The meal tonight was garbage."

"I can make us all something simple." Rose stands and starts searching in the pantry. She finds a can of tomatoes and a box of dried pasta and gets to work. Soon the kitchen fills with the smell of simmering tomato sauce.

The first meal of the new year is simple and comforting: tomato sauce on pasta, steaming and hot. The Blooms eat and talk, praising Rose for her cooking skills, Violet for her vodka-hustling, and Iris for her generous and sentimental client.

When the meal is done and the dirty dishes are piled in the sink, the Blooms drink and talk until it is so late that Rose feels like she could fall asleep in her seat. She puts her head down on the table and remembers the way the Barber's fingers grazed her hand. A subtle gesture that sur-prised her, not because he touched her, but because she wanted him to. She closes her eyes and imagines the Barber lying awake in bed right now, sensing her thoughts drift across camp to him.

She sits up and joins in conversation with the Blooms. The rest of the men from the party feel blissfully far away: Meyer, the Foreman, even the long reach of Damien. All she feels is the lightness and joy of being among the Blooms, how their laughter floats around the kitchen into one sound.

CHAPTER SIX

GRANT

Grant awakes fully clothed in the assistant manager's office. The first day of the New Year. He winces as he remembers what he consumed at the party last night—a few sugary cocktails, a bottle of wine, and then the death blow of Meyer's whiskey, tossed back as shots to bludgeon the strangeness of the party. He has a vague memory of collapsing on the bar of the bowling alley only to be dragged back to his room by the Barber, who seems to have pulled off Grant's boots and mercifully left a glass of water by his bed.

Grant drinks the water in one gulp. The night clarifies and comes into focus. The Bloom. Willow. She'd immediately latched on to him the moment he stepped into the bowling alley. At first he tried to keep his distance. He didn't want to give her the impression that he was only interested in sex, or "her work," which was the term he felt most comfortable using. But she was irrepressible, bringing him drinks and sitting next to him at dinner.

"Where will you go after this job?" she asked, and refilled his glass with wine.

"I'm not sure," he said. "But I'd like to stay in the North."

She seemed surprised. "Why? It's so lonely here."

"Exactly. I like the emptiness. If you saw how overpopulated the Northeast is, you'd understand."

"Will you miss your family?"

"No," he said bluntly. "I never want to see them again." He was taken aback by how certain he sounded, and wondered if his short time in camp had already hardened him. But was he really so sure? Or was he simply trying to impress Willow? Unlike Jane, who initially intimidated him by seeming tough and seasoned, Willow struck him as curious and naïve, and he liked how she seemed to think he was so worldly.

"So you'll stay in the North?" she asked.

"Hopefully." He swallowed a mouthful of wine. "If I can find a place to live. The campus isn't exactly what I imagined."

"It'll get better," she said, and leaned toward him. "I hope you'll stay." She pulled him to his feet. "Come and dance with me."

Soon, he was swaying with Willow by the jukebox to the 1950s doo-wop group that someone had put on, the syncopated harmonies of girls with piled beehives crooning about a love that will last until tomorrow. The song ended, and Willow put on a 1970s belter, and he suddenly felt the courage to pull her close as they danced on the parquet floor. The lazy disco ball rotated above them as her face glistened with diamonds of light. An hour passed without him thinking about Jane, and then another. The ripple of guilt blossomed into euphoria. This is why people drink, he thought, and extended his glass to Willow for a refill.

But now, back in the assistant manager's office, Grant's hangover has sharpened into a throbbing pain at each temple. He remembers Jane's low and soft voice, the lavender scent of her hair, how she slept with her cheek pressed against his back. How she put the kettle on for the French press and brought him a mug of coffee to bed. Sometimes he placed the mug on the floor and pulled her to him, her mouth tasting of the cruelty-free peppermint toothpaste she used, her skin warm from reading in the morning sun. An hour would pass in an instant, and they'd clamber out of the sheets, stinking of their sweat and sweet exertion.

He sits up in his bed, listening to the Diggers getting ready for work. The glassy-eyed pinto on the outdated horse calendar seems to mock him. *Do something, Grant. For fuck's sake, do something.* Still slightly drunk, he stands up out of bed and steadies himself by bracing the wall. He'll get some breakfast in him and try and sober up.

In the cafeteria, Wolfe is eating a bowl of oatmeal. He greets Grant with a curt wave and goes back to eating. Grant grabs a bowl for himself and joins the Digger at the table.

Wolfe looks him up and down. "Rough night?"

"I had a few too many." Grant jabs his spoon toward the door. "You know, New Year's and all."

"Who were you with?" Wolfe asks.

"Meyer," Grant says. "And the other men who run the camp." For some reason, he feels uncomfortable mentioning the Blooms.

"What about the Foreman?"

"He was there too."

Wolfe nods and continues eating. "Figures. The Foreman likes to pretend he's one of us, but we know he's cozy with management."

Grant starts to eat. The oatmeal has an unpleasant glue texture, but it is bland enough to settle his stomach. He looks up at the Digger. "And that bothers you?"

Wolfe pushes away his bowl and lights a cigarette. "If the Foreman was straight with us, then I wouldn't give a fuck if he's drinking with the bosses. But he's been lying to us since the day we arrived."

Grant sets down his spoon. "What do you mean?"

Wolfe ashes into his bowl. "Come out with us to the site today, and you can see for yourself."

For a moment, Grant feels the haze of his hangover lift. "When are you leaving?"

Wolfe picks up his tray and stands. "Right now."

———

Grant rides with the Diggers in a van an hour north of camp along a two-lane highway. He sits in the back seat squished between Wolfe and Swifty as Finger drives. The winter sun reflects off the packed snow in a bright white hue. Grant looks out the window and suddenly recalls the time his father took him to stand at the base of the Grimley Tower in the Floating City.

"Do you see how even the sun bends toward our building?" his father asked.

Grant looked up and saw what he meant. Sunlight shone off the glass panes of the tower, reflecting the passing clouds and bright blue of the September sky.

"Our job is to look around us and see how we can leave our mark. How we can take everything we see and remake it in our vision." His father patted young Grant on the shoulder. "One day, this tower and everything it looks on will be yours."

Grant's father's shrewd calculation of place had rubbed off whether Grant liked it or not. It was something Grant immediately noticed when he stepped into a new room or environment. What was lacking. What was less than it should be. He's tried to suppress this analysis since arriving in the North—the whole point of being in camp is how different it is from what he's left behind—but now that he is on his way to the Diggers' site, he feels the Grimley in him sharpen.

The camp is a disaster. Poorly run. Underfunded. Likely hemorrhaging money, which is why the Diggers are overworked. Meyer's plans have clearly gone awry. Grant can't pretend anymore that if he just waits another week, a new Nordic-style campus will suddenly spring out of the earth, complete with a library stocked with leftist periodicals, an espresso machine, and a wireless signal.

The van takes an abrupt left turn onto a back road that cuts through the black spruce, winding and bumpy, like someone shaved a strip from the land while drunk. The road ends at a deep pit that stretches out to a grove of snowcapped trees. They park next to a group of Diggers who are dragging logs to a pile of desiccated shrubs. In the distance, two Diggers work on felling trees, hacking the black spruce with hatchets.

Grant follows Wolfe and Swifty to the far side of the site. The chopping sounds of the hatchets are fainter here, and it's possible to focus on the solitude of the location. But Grant is shocked by how ravaged the land looks, like it's been chewed to death and then spat out. A pit has been blasted out of the ground, deeper than a ditch, wider than a swimming pool.

"There was jack shit when we arrived," Wolfe says. "No machinery. No loaders. No tractors. Nothing. Just two dozen spades lying in a heap on the ground."

"Remember when the Foreman told us to dig?" Swifty calls out. "And you said, 'Are you fucking kidding?'"

"I turned to the Foreman and said, 'What are we digging for?' And he shrugged and said, 'I just deliver orders.'"

Wolfe says the men had no choice but to shut up and dig. Each picked up a spade and made a dent in the ground, and by lunch they'd dug a shallow trench wide enough for three bodies. The next day they returned to the site and started the work from where they had left it. When the pit was deeper, they reinforced it with a wooden lagging and used a ladder to climb in and out. As they dug, they found surprises in the soil, mineral deposits and clay and rock. And at the bottom of the pit, a thick sediment oozed under their boots.

"I told the Foreman we can't build on this land." Wolfe picks up one of the spades and digs it into the ground, and then flings the sludge over his shoulder. "The foundation pit won't hold. He told me to shut up and keep digging."

"What do you mean it won't hold?" Grant asks.

"The ground is fucking mush. We can't build shit out here." Wolfe rests against the handle of the spade. He wipes a dirty glove over his forehead and points in the distance. "Foreman's early today. He must have heard you're here."

A vehicle has pulled into the clearing on the far side of the site. Grant recognizes the Foreman's truck by its red sheen, the only splotch of bright color in the dull gray terrain. The Foreman gets out of the truck and speaks with a Digger, who points at Grant.

The Foreman waves at Grant, and then makes his way across the site to greet him with a slap on the shoulder. "You should have told me you were coming. It's not very often that we have visitors."

"I know you're busy and I didn't want to bother you," Grant says. "And Wolfe was kind enough to take me here himself."

"I just would have liked to show you the lay of the land myself." The Foreman looks up at Wolfe, working with Swifty on the pit. "Good worker, Wolfe. But a little daft. Did he tell you anything about what we're doing out here?" The Foreman's tone is soft, almost jovial.

"Just that the foundation pits won't hold."

"That so?" Foreman pulls a blueprint out from his pocket and points a gloved finger at a series of geodesic domes nestled in the tundra. "Some of the Diggers, bless their stupid souls, don't have the engineering knowledge to understand what we're doing out here. They're not used to building in these kinds of conditions." He taps the plan. "We'll be erecting each structure above ground to take in temperature shifts. Meyer is hell-bent on ensuring that the buildings will last."

The Foreman shows Grant the blueprint. Each house has the rounded symmetry and clear glass of a fishbowl, with hexagonal windows domed under the sky. Nothing about the idyllic houses looks like the pocked landscape they're standing on.

"Meyer's calling these 'the prototypes.' We better build the rest of these fuckers before spring. Once the ice roads turn to slush, it will be a lot harder to deliver building materials by land."

"Why did you choose this particular site?" Grant watches the Diggers fling spadefuls of sludge as they deepen and widen a pit. "It seems like a challenging parcel of land for a campus."

"It's what we could get our hands on," the Foreman says. "A lot of the land up here is protected by Indigenous treaties, which means negotiating with the First Nations before we can build. And there is no fucking way we're going to do that."

"Why not?"

"Negotiating always leads to demands, which leads to lost profit." The

Foreman shakes his head. "We'll do what worked when I was in West Australia. Find a foothold in the region, claim it, and then push forward into more pristine territory once we're comfortably settled." He grins at Grant. "Better to be a mouse than a bear here."

"But Meyer's told me he's invested in land stewardship and partnering with Indigenous communities."

"Meyer knows nothing about getting ahold of land. Do you know how happy the local government was when we said we'd invest in their shit economy? They parceled up a chunk of this wretched oil land and practically begged us to take it." He points at the Diggers. "Most of those men were unemployed until they arrived in camp. They're making good change, too, which they'll send back home. Not that they're grateful for it. But none of that should be of concern to you, Grant. You clearly have other things on your mind. Did you have a good time with my Bloom last night?"

The Foreman's question takes Grant off guard. "Willow? She's very bright."

"Bright. That's a good one. Don't be a cunt, Grant. Willow is good for only one thing."

Cunt. The casual use of the word takes the breath out of Grant.

"She's more than that," Grant says firmly.

"You sound like Meyer." The Foreman parrots Meyer's precise diction, "The Blooms are such keen observers." He laughs bitterly. "But he continues to fuck, doesn't he? As if his dick is exempt from his own morality." The Foreman steps toward Grant. "Just because you're a Grimley doesn't mean you can get everything you want. In camp, we don't give a fuck who your daddy is."

Grant takes a step forward, his voice shaking. "Don't talk about my father like that."

The Foreman pushes lightly on Grant's chest and laughs. "Ah, don't be so serious. I was just fooling around with you. You'll have to develop a stronger spine in camp." He looks at his watch. His voice is relaxed now, light. "You must be freezing. Why don't you head back with the first crew?"

Grant takes a moment to calm himself, and then follows the crew to one of the idling vans. Before the Foreman rolls the van's door shut, the Foreman calls out, "And I wouldn't believe everything the Diggers tell you, Grant. Even simple men can have a complex agenda."

While the van drives away, Grant looks back to see the Foreman still watching.

WHITE ALICE

The days leading to our desertion followed a strict schedule. We woke up in the bunkroom at six a.m., ate our breakfast oats in the kitchen, and prepared for our departure. Sal had written detailed instructions in our logbooks the night before—how we'd caravan on the snowmobiles down south and set up camp by nightfall. A second day of travel would follow, and then we'd arrive in Dominion Lake. Back in civilization. Back among men. We wondered what a paved road would feel like under our boots, the smell of fried food in the air, the furtive looks of the oil workers. Would we want to stay there? Or would we push on to another region?

All we could do was prepare.

The engineer examined the snowmobiles to ensure they were in good working order for the journey to Dominion Lake.

The botanist took stock of what she had successfully grown and gathered the seeds to be planted in a new greenhouse.

The cartographer set to work finalizing the seasonal maps and making immaculately detailed copies of the region.

The geographer sorted through the library's catalogue and packed a few precious texts.

The meteorologist downloaded all the findings from her climate models and sent them to a colleague at Walden.

The biologist took samples in the melting permafrost and selected a sample of petri dishes to pack in a cryogenic suitcase.

The programmer's job was the most laborious. She wrote a code that would send timed dispatches with fabricated data sets to home base. Every week, a different message would be sent back south with the hope that home base would assume all continued to be well in the North.

Sal cleaned our weapons and took stock of our arsenal. Before we departed, she wanted to conduct one last patrol around the perimeter of the station.

When she stepped out of White Alice, she saw the black chopper bearing down on us. The helicopter was unmarked, without a flag or insignia, and after it landed on a ridge of ice, six figures jumped out.

Sal ran back into the station, shouting, "Get into formation!"

Sal had trained us for this, so we were ready. In the event of an invasion, she told us to disarm the first intruder, and then muscle anyone else into the freeze. Intruders would be unfamiliar with our environment, which we could leverage to our advantage.

We hid in the hallway that connected to the entrance of the station. But no one kicked in the front door. Instead, we heard a light knock, a pause, and then a soft voice called out, "Hello there?"

The man's voice was more formal and younger than we expected, like a college valedictorian greeting a crowd.

"On my count of five," Sal whispered.

A knock again, and then, "Everything cool in here?"

"1 . . . 2 . . . 3 . . ."

We lifted our weapons and set our sight lines on the door.

"Guy, step aside," a woman's voice rang out. Light, lively, tinged with a shred of annoyance that we all immediately recognized as a superior speaking to a speck of dust. A few of us put down our weapons, unnerved to hear a woman in charge.

Sal gestured for us to keep our weapons raised and she walked quickly to open the door. Her hand hovered above the hilt of her knife. When the door swung open, a woman stepped into the station and grinned at Sal.

"You look like shit," the woman said.

Sal dropped the knife and embraced the woman closely. "How the fuck did you get here?"

"I have my ways." The woman stepped into the station and looked around. "So this is it . . . the famed White Alice mission. I expected something more impressive."

For a moment, we saw White Alice through her eyes: the station's sparseness and utility stripped down to pure functionality, the greenish fluorescence, the worn furniture. The woman sniffed audibly, and a few of us felt a ripple of irritation. Who was she to judge how we lived?

"Smells about right." She called out to the squad waiting outside, "We're clear. Sal's invited us in."

On Sal's command, we set our weapons back in their holsters and joined the six-person squad in the dining room. They were dressed in civilian clothing, so we were surprised when Sal introduced the woman as the General. Her eyes shone as she assessed us, and we felt an instinctive compulsion to stand and salute her. A younger woman dressed in an aviation jacket played with a deck of cards at the table while the four men stood in a line.

"Dottie flew us in," the General said, and nodded at the pilot. "She always feels a little out of sorts unless she's in the sky." Dottie shuffled and cut, then shuffled and cut, drawing a card from the deck, examining it, and then returning it back to the pile.

None of us had met the General before, but we knew her career and legacy. She had led numerous battalions on foreign territory and was the only woman who had ever risen to the rank of five-star general. She was decorated with medals and distinctions that the most powerful hands on earth had pinned to her chest, and her reputation and career was often co-opted by conservative pundits to prove that all women, finally, had risen to the top. She remained agnostic in her political affiliation, pledging allegiance only to the flag.

We felt humbled to be seated at the same table as her, and yet deeply troubled by her presence. Clearly, home base had dispatched her to deal with us.

The other four men consisted of a small, nervy-looking kid with a shock of red hair who kept cleaning his glasses with a handkerchief, and a square-headed lump of a man with a buzz cut and a scar on his chin, who stripped down to his tank top when he sat down. He was clearly and proudly the muscle.

"Hot in here," he said to no one in particular, and flashed his unnervingly white teeth at us.

The third was a grave-looking man whose face naturally settled into a grimace. He spoke in a melancholic manner, in perfect, grammatically correct sentences, and wore his khaki shirt buttoned to the very top, as well as a wool cardigan. "I'm pleased to make your acquaintances," he said, and took our hands in his damp one.

The fourth man, and the final member of the squad, was the Valedictorian who had tentatively knocked on our door. He was blond and blue-eyed, handsome in a sunscreen-commercial kind of manner. When he smiled, it was like pure, brilliant sunlight. He spoke in deferential tones, apologizing for "busting in here like this." We assumed he didn't have much substance and took little interest in him until later.

The General explained why they were here. "Home base knows that you are planning to desert White Alice and flee into Canada."

Sal cut in. "Who told you?"

"I'm not at liberty to reveal. While home base is pleased to know you've formed a functional community up here, we're concerned that you've been given incomplete intelligence about the encrypted file you found from the last mission. Do you know anything about Winter-Over Syndrome?"

"Of course," the biologist said. "It's a condition caused by adapting to extreme cold and darkness. Symptoms include insomnia, irritation, and depression."

"Yes, the milder symptoms," the General said. "But in extreme cases, anger can turn into violence. Mild trances into dangerous delusions. Even a dear friend can appear like a monster. It's a well-documented phenomenon in the polar bases."

"We're familiar with the literature." The biologist cut in. "But no one here has experienced atypical symptoms since arriving in White Alice."

"Of course not," the General said. "You're flourishing here. Each of you are stronger than you were in home base, more self-possessed, in tune with your bodies and minds and each other."

We felt a glow of happiness spread through us. It felt good to be acknowledged by the General for what we had created.

"Winter-Over Syndrome only afflicts those who cannot find emotional satisfaction in isolation," the General continued. "Those who refuse to join in the cohesion of the group, who stake their claims and egos as individuals. The men of the last mission suffered because they refused to find harmony together. Up here, they discovered that the power they regularly enjoyed—and in fact, had never realized was a form of power— needed to be contextualized by the world they left behind. In White Alice, power possesses a different weight and shape."

"They went mad?" the engineer asked.

"Yes. And with a horrific conclusion. Two members of the squad killed each other during a violent delusion, and after, the mission was terminated and the remaining six were shipped back south for a military trial and psychological examination. The file you found was left by the meteorologist, who has since been diagnosed with extreme Polar T3 Syndrome. He claimed that the sun was speaking to him through the long winter nights, urging him to burn down the station while the men slept. Luckily, we shipped him out before he could act on his psychosis, but not soon enough to stop him from leaving an Easter egg for your crew."

We were silent for a moment as the General's words sunk in. So, the mission hadn't been compromised by home base after all. The men had merely lost their minds.

We looked at each other and felt a swell of pride. The General's explanation confirmed what we already believed. A group of men could never thrive under these conditions like we had.

"Now that you have a fuller picture of what happened, I'm here to offer you two options," the General said. "The first option is that Dottie will radio the two choppers who are standing by and you will have one hour to pack and prepare your belongings for departure. You'll be whisked back south for a full trial and prosecution for attempted desertion. Most of you will be ruled as minor accomplices and will receive the basic punishment for mutiny: ten years in the compost heap and travel privileges revoked for a lifetime. And you, dear Sal, who trained these good women to aim their weapons at your superiors will most likely receive the full term of life imprisonment, if you're lucky."

"And if I'm not lucky?" Sal asked.

"The Box awaits you."

We all felt an icy hand clamp our hearts.

We had once caravanned past the Box during training and saw the black metallic cube shining in the distance. It was a solitary confinement complex made up of small, pitted cubes that formed the ominous square, marooned out in the hottest part of the desert. Viewing the Box was a mandatory part of orientation in home base. We never saw the inside, but we knew even then that there were prisoners trapped alone in each cell without air-conditioning or insulation to keep out the elements. Our sergeant told us that being inside the Box was like living on a hot plate perpetually turned on. Depending on how the wind blew, sluices of the desert would creep in. Sand, of course, and prickly bits of cacti that still managed to survive without water, and creatures of the scaly reptilian variety who were impervious to human presence. Craggy lizards who stalked across the length of a prisoner's body; snakes who slithered and coiled through the open slats; and the infamous scorpions of the region, whose small, defensive postures belied their death blows. The Box was considered a legal loophole—create the conditions for a prisoner to receive a constitutional death sentence without having to hold the state accountable. Let nature do her nasty deed, however she saw fit. Heat, dehydration, scorpion, the mania of solitary confinement—who could say what ended a life? All we knew was that we never wanted to find ourselves there.

The General cleared her throat. "Can someone get me a glass of water? This altitude always dehydrates me."

Cardigan stood and moved around the kitchen, touching cabinets and opening the trash door without speaking. Eventually, the biologist showed him where we kept our supply of freshly filtered water. He nodded with thanks and decanted the General an ice-cold glass.

The General took a long, indulgent sip, then paused to appreciate the drink. "Absolutely phenomenal. It's reassuring to know water like this still exists."

"Long way to travel for a glass of water," Sal said.

"Is it? I think it's a reasonable distance for such an important commodity. We've traveled farther for less, haven't we?" The General shook her head. "Don't look at me like that, Sal. I thought you'd be happy to see me."

"You didn't present the second option," Sal said.

The General finished the glass of water and set it on the table. "The second option is home base will allow you to resume your duties in White Alice and continue maintaining the station. We expect an accurate transmission of data every week." She looked at the programmer knowingly. "In exchange, we'll supply you with food, fuel, and any supplies or gear that you require."

"And we're expected to trust that this will actually happen?" Sal said.

The General reached over and touched a hand on Sal's shoulder. "If it makes your decision any easier, all findings in White Alice point to the same outcome: irreversible warming. You should feel lucky to be living in this station. The North is our future now. All we can do is prepare." The General stood from the table and looked each of us in the eye. "I'll give you some time to decide."

We gathered in the greenhouse to talk. As we stood there waiting for someone to begin, the botanist noticed that a shrub was blooming white and yellow flowers.

"Strawberries," she said, and picked up a flower pot to show us. There, nestled under a bloom, was a tiny green strawberry, no bigger than a child's fingernail, flecked with white fuzz. "I wonder when they'll be ready for harvest?" she asked, and we all understood the sentiment in her question.

Would we be here to pick them?

The programmer must have been thinking the same thing because she was the first to speak. "Do we believe what the General said about the encrypted file?"

"That it's the work of a madman?" The meteorologist paused before answering, "Polar Syndrome can have devastating effects."

We nodded in agreement. Already, we were revising the narrative, rewriting our perspective so we could stay.

The geographer looked around at us. "Plus, if we return south, Sal will be sent to the Box, while the rest of us will be prosecuted."

The biologist nodded. "Most of us will never work in our fields again. And if we do, it will only be at the lowest levels possible—a janitor in a lab where we'll clean up the messes of those we once saw as our protégés."

She was right. We all knew it. No one spoke for a long while, until the botanist pointed at the ant colony and said, "Look."

We walked over to her. The queen was in the center of the colony, surrounded by her attendants. Numerous clear sacs contracted around her as she lay on her back in complete stillness. One of the sacs stretched, distended, and then puckered wildly, and suddenly a trail of baby ants spilled out into the dirt. They were tiny, glossy black things, with nearly invisible legs that revolved in the air, as some tumbled onto their backs. The queen's attendants gently moved toward them and started corralling them into small clusters, dripping a thick, white mucus onto their bellies and heads, which they gobbled up furiously.

"I knew it!" the biologist said. "Parthenogenesis. There's no way a male could have arrived here and mated with the queen." She crouched down and gently stroked the glass where the queen ant was being fed by her attendants.

"Life persists, even here," Sal said softly.

We were quiet for a few moments as we watched the ants move in synchronicity together. Everything they needed to live was in the station.

"If we stay, we do it on our own terms, not theirs." Sal looked at each of us. "They chose us for this mission because they think we're expendable. But what if we flip the script and create a new life for ourselves?"

We leaned forward and listened.

The General was relishing another glass of water when we walked back into the kitchen. "So, you've made your decision?"

"Yes," Sal said. "We'll stay."

The General looked curiously at us for a moment, and then nodded. "This is your final, binding decision?"

We all said yes and gave her our verbal and written affirmation.

After we signed our contracts, the General's mood visibly changed. She seemed lighter, more carefree. She accepted the shot of vodka that we served to the squad to celebrate our newly defined future.

"Bottoms up," she said, and took the shot like it was water. She pointed at the bottle to indicate a refill, which we quickly gave her.

The biologist had been tasked with ensuring that the men had plenty to drink. Only Muscle took more than two shots. Young Red could barely stomach his first. He had been having dizzy spells related to the altitude since arriving at the station, and his skin had turned sallow.

Cardigan inquired if we had an aperitif. The geographer found a bottle of gin stashed somewhere in the pantry. This seemed to perk Cardigan up, and he took small sips from a shot glass. The Valedictorian sat shyly in the corner, drinking the last six-pack we had in our supply.

Despite Dottie's clear desire to fly back that evening, we cooked the squad dinner and asked them to stay overnight.

"You'll be our last visitors for a long time," Sal said to the General.

Surprisingly, the General consented, but requested she receive her own room. "I don't bunk with my squad." Sal promised to set her up in the exercise room, where the meteorologist pulled in one of the cots and made it up with fresh sheets. Dottie was clearly irritated and refused to eat with us, taking her deck of cards and a plate of food back to the bunkroom to play solitaire.

After the General retired for the evening, someone brought out more vodka and we started to dance to the cassette player in the kitchen. Old tunes, high school tunes, drunk-in-the-night tunes, free-and-easy tunes.

Muscle was the first to join the dance floor, and in no time had the botanist and the biologist on each of his arms.

"Want a puff?" the botanist asked after he tried to sloppily twirl her toward him. It was true that she had been secretly cultivating the purple-green
buds of medicinal marijuana in the sunniest section of the greenhouse.

Muscle grinned and took a drag. "Bad girl," he said, and the botanist
had to clamp a hand on her mouth so she wouldn't laugh uncontrollably.

Young Red was the next to join when the programmer dragged him to
his feet.

"Let's talk code," she whispered into his ear, and showed him to the
communications room, where the meteorologist was waiting.

"Or we can talk about the weather," the meteorologist said shyly, and felt
a swell of relief when Young Red smiled, the color returning to his cheeks.

In the library, the cartographer spread out the seasonal maps for Cardigan to evaluate, while the geographer lectured him on the ice forma-
tions of the northern wind.

"Fascinating," Cardigan said, and pored over the maps. "I never thought
of seasons as having fixed coordinates."

The geographer looked at the cartographer and raised her eyebrows.
How would they proceed with this man? His tone was so formal and distant that it seemed more likely he would make love to a compass than
either one of them. A direct proposition was the only option.

"Excuse me," the geographer said. "Would you like to have sex?"

For a long moment, he didn't respond, and the geographer became
worried she would have to repeat her clinically phrased request. But then
he looked up at her, his face drawn and serious. "You mean in general? Or
at this precise moment?"

"At this precise moment," the cartographer said, and then added,
"with us."

For the first time that evening, the grimace on his face contorted into
a shy smile. "Why, certainly."

By then, the Valedictorian had been left in the kitchen with Sal and
the engineer. He had not moved from his place in the corner, now sipping

his third beer and tipping back in his chair lazily. His eyes had begun to droop, and he started to hum a familiar tune.

"What's that song?" the engineer asked, and pulled up a chair next to his. Sal watched from across the room. They were closer in age than their expertise suggested, though the engineer had grown accustomed to making herself appear older, to solidify respect.

"It's just something I have stuck in my head," he said. "It came to me when we were flying out of home base."

"It's beautiful," the engineer said, and by the tone of her voice, Sal could tell she meant it.

The Valedictorian smiled and shined his beam of sunlight on her. "You're too kind," he said. "And pretty."

The engineer reached forward to kiss him gently on each eyelid, clasping his heavy head in her hands.

Sal left them and walked down the hallways of the station. The light in the library was lit, as was the communications room. She could smell the skunky stench of the botanist's weed wafting from the greenhouse. In the dark of the exercise room, Sal felt her way to the cot, and climbed in with her clothes still on. The General rolled toward her.

"I knew I could count on you," the General said, and placed a warm hand on Sal's thigh.

Sal brushed aside the General's hair and searched for the place on her neck that always smelled of fuel. "This is my last chance to kiss the most powerful woman on earth."

"Hush now," the General said. "You know how I feel about flattery."

Sal pulled her shirt off and pressed into the General's body, both familiar and foreign, in the way a visit to a place you once loved always felt.

"You made the right decision," the General said. "Our nation thanks you."

"Now you hush," Sal said, and placed her mouth on the General's neck. "You know I how I feel about the nation as foreplay."

The General laughed, her voice open and clear, the sound ricocheting around the room like splinters of light.

Outside the station, the radar gently hummed.

CHAPTER SEVEN

ROSE

A storm swept through camp last night, and a thick layer of snow now lies outside the kitchen's window. It's been two weeks since the New Year's party. Two weeks of long evenings and short days as the Blooms rise to catch the first light. Two weeks of eating canned fruit and factory bread, boxed rice and instant mashed potatoes, dehydrated eggs and tinned meat. During meals with the Blooms, Rose dreams of the bounty of summer: fragrant tomatoes, gleaming cherries, dripping peaches. She imagines eating fresh fruit until her fingers are stained with their juices, lying in a grassy field as the sun sets low and golden on the horizon. In this perfect, green midsummer of the past, it is never too hot or too dry or too scorched to be outside. A summer that will never exist in her future.

This morning, Rose is the first Bloom in the kitchen. She gets to work on breakfast—setting out the preserves and margarine on the table, putting a pot of water to boil on the stove. Ever since the New Year's party, she's started to prepare meals for the Blooms more often. She likes the care extended through the preparation of food, how cooking doesn't require language or disclosure.

As she cooks, her mind wanders. Without the Flick, memories feel closer and more Technicolor than before, and she finds herself feeling comforted by their presence. She remembers the way her mother simmered oats in milk and served the oatmeal in shallow bowls dusted with brown sugar and cinnamon. They'd take the bowls out to the beach and sit with their toes in the sand, watching the tide roll in. It was a rare quiet moment when they were together, de-linked from their Flicks, before they dusted the sand off and began the day's work. Sometimes they talked, but often they sat in silence, as her mother stared at the hard blue edge of the Atlantic, her gaze distant and unreadable.

Willow appears in the kitchen, dressed in a pair of gray overalls and a cable-knit sweater, and plops down at the table.

"How was your night?" Willow asks, and helps herself to a cup of coffee.

"Fine." Rose sets a platter of toast on the table. "Meyer came by, but he didn't stay long." Meyer had, in fact, arrived at her room in a terrible mood. He said he was feeling down about how poorly the camp was progressing, and that they were nearly out of seed money. Rose had tried to cheer him up, but he left early, which was uncharacteristic of him. "What about you?"

"The Foreman kept me up all night." Willow pulls her feet up on the chair and drinks her coffee. "He was drunk and kind of belligerent. He kept on going on about how he's been mistreated in the camp, how hard it is for him to be here." She looks at Rose. "I've been meaning to ask you, did he say anything to you at the New Year's party?"

Rose keeps her back turned to Willow and continues cooking at the stove. "About what?"

"You seemed pretty upset when I found you two in the bathroom."

"We were just talking."

"You can tell me, Rose," Willow says. "I already know he's an asshole."

Rose brings a bowl of oatmeal to Willow. "He just wanted to know how we're doing in camp. If Judith is taking good care of us."

"Really? I honestly didn't think he gave a shit about us. What did you tell him?"

"I told him the truth. That we're looking out for each other. And that Judith can be a real pain in the ass sometimes. He agreed."

Willow laughs and digs into the oatmeal. "She means well, you know. It's just hard for her to express it."

"Does she? Because I feel like—" Rose stops short when she sees Judith walk in.

"Good morning, girls," Judith says. "I see you're up early." Judith is dressed less like a demolition expert today and more like a high school gym teacher. A pair of razor sunglasses are snagged in her hair, and she wears a microfiber sweatshirt and a pair of jogging pants with two stripes running up each side. The clothes match the vintage fashion still available on the Millennium's shelves.

Judith taps the spoon in Willow's hand. "Patience. Not everyone is seated."

Willow rolls her eyes, and then drinks her coffee until the rest of the Blooms finally stream into the kitchen, dressed in robes and slippers. When they are seated, Judith smiles broadly and pours a cup of black coffee into dainty porcelain teacups, each etched with one of the Blooms' signature flowers in delicate gold.

"A postcoital buffet," Judith says as she sets out plates of trembling, rehydrated eggs.

"Can we eat now?" Willow asks, and then says, "We're starving from all that *fuck-ing*." She draws the word out into two sharp syllables.

The Blooms can't help but laugh. They all agree that there is something strange about Judith. Is she their mother, their guardian, their caretaker? Surely not their Madam, the one who signs them up for an "episode of lovemaking," a turn of phrase she uses to describe a session with their clients. In the halls, in the bathroom, in the kitchen when she's not listening, the Blooms whisper to each other, "episode of lovemaking," to underscore the fact that Judith is not one of them.

"Yes, of course. Dig in." Judith takes a cup of coffee and leans against the counter, watching the Blooms as they eat. "Enjoy breakfast, girls. Meyer has informed me that our monthly delivery has been delayed."

Fleur looks up sharply. "Meaning? We're out of food?"

Judith shakes her head. "Not yet, but we should supplement our supplies just to be on the safe side." She looks at the Blooms. "I need someone to go out ice fishing with the Barber today. He'll show you what to do, but he needs help on the lake."

"I'll do it," Willow says immediately.

"I need you to walk the dogs, so I'd like you to stay," Judith says to Willow. She asks the rest of the Blooms, "Any other volunteers?"

Rose looks around the table and sees that the other Blooms are studiously avoiding Judith's gaze. *Wait another moment,* she thinks, *so they don't hear your excitement.* "If no one else wants to, then I can."

"Good." Judith nods. "It's decided. Rose will head out later today."

When Rose steps outside, the Barber is waiting by the entrance of the mall.

He sees her and smiles. "You're on fish duty?"

"None of the other Blooms were very keen."

"That's okay by me." He looks away and then says, "I probably shouldn't say this, but I was hoping it would be you."

She takes a step toward him. He's shaved today, and she can see a red nick on his chin where the razor faltered. A barber with an unsteady hand. She feels an impulse to touch the ridge of his chin where the red line glistens.

Instead, she keeps her hands to herself. "I wouldn't have volunteered if Meyer was fishing, but for you I'll make an exception."

"It's good to hear I'm an exception." He reaches for her hand and helps her step through the snow. "We'll swing by the ice fishing shack to get my gear. And then we'll head out to the lake."

They walk across the parking lot to the metal fence and wait for Judith to buzz them through the gate. On the other side, the tracks of the Diggers' vehicles mark the highway to Dominion Lake. The Barber sets the pace and Rose hurries to keep up, following the path his boots make as they lean into the wind and barrel forward. Their breath blows out in enormous white billows as they press on. Past the defunct recreation center with the giant hockey stick affixed above the entrance. Past the spray-painted gas station, the pumps long drained. Left at the weathered sign warning of bears in the area, complete with a diagram on how to recognize bear droppings ("scat," Rose learns, is the technical term for the animal's excrement). They follow the highway until it curves down to the village, tucked into the frozen banks of Dominion Lake.

When they reach the edge of the lake, the Barber points to a fishing shack on the ice, painted the color of a purplish bruise. "That's where we're headed. But first, put these on." He digs in his rucksack for a pair of ice cleats and shows her how to strap each one to her boots. She stands, feeling wobbly and uncertain.

"It's easy. Just follow me." The Barber steps out onto the ice first and starts walking, but then turns back to see Rose still waiting on the shoreline.

"It's completely frozen, right?" Rose calls out.

The Barber jumps in the air and lands on the ice with a thud. "Solid as the earth."

Rose nods and tentatively takes a step, and then another, until she's walking in pace with him. They walk for a few minutes without speaking, until they reach the shack.

The Barber pushes open the door and grabs two empty buckets, a fishing pole, and a tackle box. He hoists a long, serrated ice saw over one shoulder. It flashes silver in the bright sun when they step onto the ice.

"If we're lucky, we'll pull something in live today." He hands the tackle box and fishing pole to Rose, and they walk together toward the center of the lake until the snow-covered buildings of the village are faint splashes of color.

"This will do," the Barber says. He edges the saw into the ground, chiseling out chunks of ice until a hole appears. Rose leans over to see the black water ripple below and reaches a hand toward the hole. She hasn't seen a liquid body of water since leaving the Floating City and feels a desire to touch it.

"Careful," the Barber says. "You could lose a finger. Hypothermia sets in faster when you're wet." The Barber opens the tackle box and expertly threads a plastic neon minnow to a length of line attached to a rod. "There's not much to it. We'll drop the bait in and hope a pike swims by."

The Barber overturns the two plastic buckets, sits down on one, and lights a cigarette. Rose sits on the other, staring into the dark hole.

"You're the only person I've taken out here other than Meyer," the Barber says. "He said he loved fishing into the abyss."

Rose laughs. "Sounds like Meyer. Do you come out often with him?"

"I used to when he first hired me. But since the Walden kid showed up, he's been occupied with the camp. And with you, of course."

She can hear the bitterness in his voice. "How did you find out about this job?"

"I heard about Meyer's camp when I was working in a barbershop in Vandal and the Foreman came in for a haircut when he was visiting the region on business. Prospecting, he called it, and told me there was a growing foreign interest in the North."

"Were you surprised?"

"I was, but I tried not to show it. I asked him why anyone would be interested in the region since the oil industry had shuttered. And he laughed in my face and said that my head was stuck in the dirt. That I couldn't see what's under my feet."

The Barber tells Rose that he dragged the razor under the Foreman's jawline as he laughed. The razor jumped in his hand, nicking off a triangle of pink flesh. The Barber apologized and held a white cloth to the man's neck as it darkened with his blood.

"I knew then that something was happening here, so I packed up a bag and went back home."

The Barber headed north to his family's abandoned house and slept in his childhood bedroom with a loaded hunting rifle under the bed and waited for the new arrivals.

He finally saw them when he was out hunting one day and a semi-truck drove down the highway. He watched two men unload the truck and begin to move furniture and supplies into the deserted Millennium Mall. They wore brand-new parkas with the symbol of a geodesic dome stamped on their left sleeves, and they drove shiny electric SUVs he had never seen in the region before. He watched them for a week before introducing himself to their leader, Meyer, and he wasn't surprised to find out they were American.

Meyer said he was establishing a base camp in the mall to develop a parcel of land the Canadian government had auctioned off to foreign investors. He was looking to hire a local to teach him how to survive in the North and told the Barber that he would pay him handsomely if he did so.

The Barber accepted the job and led Meyer on surveys of the region, out past the oil patches and the dilapidated village into parts of the boreal forest. He taught Meyer how to shoot and hunt, how to skin a deer, how to chop wood for kindling.

"But I was studying Meyer, too. It had been a long time since anyone other than an oil company was interested in Dominion Lake, and I was right to be suspicious. Meyer told me that he planned to build an off-grid settlement shielded from the rising temperatures and economic chaos of the US, where Americans could immigrate to and forge a new life. He called it Camp Zero and said this camp is just the beginning. And that he wanted me right here by his side to help him. I knew then I could never trust him."

"Then why did you stay here and work?"

"Someone had to keep an eye on Meyer."

Rose is quiet for a moment as she thinks about what the Barber has said. A settlement. Not a campus. A Floating City in the North. "Do you think he's delusional?"

"It's hard to say. All I know is when the Walden kid arrived and construction started, Meyer treated me like a stranger. We stopped spending our days tracking hares or hunting for geese. I was simply a barber to him."

"Did that bother you?"

"No. I never had any pretenses as to what my job is here." He leans forward, unbuttons the cuff of his shirt, and carefully rolls it to his elbow. He takes her hand and places it on his forearm where a tattoo curls across his skin:

The barber was the only person trusted enough
to hold a razor to the emperor's throat

"When did you get this done?" she asks, and traces a finger along his arm.

"When I realized I was more than a barber." He quickly pulls his shirt-sleeve down and buttons the cuff again. "You asked me at the party who is unhappy at the camp, and I told you that I couldn't say then, and I can't say now."

"Why?" She looks around at the wide expanse of ice. "No one is here except us."

"I know. But I don't want to put you into a difficult position. It's better if you know as little as possible."

She reaches toward him and places her hand in his. "You can trust me." He avoids her gaze and looks away. "It's not you I'm worried about."

Rose looks at the circle of black water glinting in the sun. She chooses her words carefully. "You don't need to worry about Meyer. He's harmless."

The Barber looks at her sharply. "What did he tell you?"

"Nothing yet. But I can find out more. I'll ask him to take me out to the prototype and see how the settlement is progressing." She looks at the Barber carefully. "You just need to tell me one thing. Who are you working for?"

He pauses before answering, "I'm not beholden to any man."

"What about Willow? You two seem familiar."

"I knew her back in my Dominion Lake days, but we're just friends now. She's changed since coming to camp."

"She has?"

"Of course she has. Everyone changes here. You'll see."

The fishing line suddenly tightens, and the Barber grabs on to the rod. He reels in the line. "Here, Rose. Just reel it in, slow and steady."

Rose takes ahold of the rod and feels the fish straining at the line. The weight is more than she expected. She digs her heels into the packed snow and reels the fish up through the hole.

"A trout," the Barber says when the fish lands flapping on the ice. He sounds impressed, and Rose feels a swell of pride. The fish is enormous, nearly two feet long, flipping from side to side. "You're a natural," he says.

The Barber angles the ice axe and spears the trout between its black eyes. The fish spasms as blood sprays onto the ice. He leans forward and pulls the hook out of the trout's throat, tosses the body into the bucket, and then reels in the slack line. "We'll fillet back at my place and then bring it to the mall. But I think we can treat ourselves to a little fish fry first. Are you hungry?"

"Starving," Rose says. She hadn't realized how ravenous she was, and her mouth begins to salivate. She picks up the tackle box and follows the Barber back across the ice.

The Barber leads Rose through the abandoned village where small bungalows with warped roofs cluster around the edge of the lake, past the general store, the school, the post office. They turn left, then right, until they are standing in front of a pale-yellow building with a slanted roof and a steeple. On the stairs, they step over the plaster figure of a small child resting with her hands folded in her lap. The Barber opens a door painted with two white crosses.

Inside, the pews have been pushed aside to make room for a single bed, a dresser, and a desk, but the light remains undeniably devout. The stained-glass windows illuminate a succession of holy images: a white dove bearing a laurel leaf, a flaming sword piercing a sacred heart, a lamb with its eyes cast piously to heaven.

The Barber takes their parkas and drapes them on a pew. He unwinds his scarf, revealing a sparrow tattoo on his neck, and walks to a makeshift kitchen on a stage next to a preacher's pulpit.

Rose sits in the front pew and watches the Barber prepare the fish on a cutting board. He works quickly and efficiently, scaling the shiny body, and then slicing the belly open with a switchblade. The guts are dark red and glistening. After he fillets the white flesh, he dredges two pieces with flour and drops them in a pan shimmering with hot oil. Soon, the church fills with the smell of frying fish. He opens a jar of pickled vegetables floating in a dilly brine and serves them on a cracked porcelain plate.

They eat with their fingers, cutting the grease with bites of pickled vegetables, while seated at a table by the altar. The Barber opens a bottle of beer and pours two glasses for them to drink. The fish is perfectly fried, and Rose eats her portion quickly and chases it with the cold beer. Simple and satisfying, far better than the gravlax she ate with beluga caviar in Damien's suite, which he often fed to her with his fingers.

"I've never eaten fish this fresh before," she says. "It's delicious."

The Barber grins and tops her glass off with more beer. "I'm glad you like it. My dad didn't teach me much, but he did show me how to cook a fish."

"Where is your family now?"

"My dad died on the rigs, and my mom moved away when the oil industry collapsed. We've lost touch since. I haven't seen her in over ten years."

"I'm sorry," Rose says. "My father died as well."

The Barber looks at her and his face softens. "I know how hard that is."

"I was six months old when he drowned, so I never knew him. I used to think I'd never live near the ocean again. That I'd move inland, far away from any body of water. But that never happened. Even now, I'm living a mile from a lake. Why did you leave home?"

"I thought I could find a better life elsewhere."

"Did you?"

"Better? No. Everything I left still trailed me."

She nods. "My mother used to say that you can't push back the past, even if you want to."

"Sounds about right." He cleans the fish guts off the switchblade with a hand towel and presses it into her hand. "I want you to have this."

The switchblade feels smooth and cool against her skin. "I told you that you don't need to worry about Meyer."

"It's not Meyer I'm worried about."

She flicks the blade open until it flashes silver in the low light.

"Who taught you how to use a blade?" he asks, clearly impressed.

"My mother." Rose carefully puts the switchblade in her parka's pocket.

He reaches to touch her hand. "Can I see you again?"

She searches his face for anything that might betray him, but his expression is open, willing. Meeting him again is wildly off script. Illicit and liable to compromise her aims in camp. If she's caught by Judith, she'll immediately be sent back to the Loop, where Damien will tell her in excruciating detail how stupid she is. "After everything your poor mother has gone through," he'll say, and press an index finger to his temple. "You throw it all away for a common fuck?"

A common fuck. Damien only ever saw her desires as allocated to sex and money. He once said that she was incapable of real love because she only understood intimacy as a paid arrangement. "Consider yourself lucky," he said. "Love obscures reason." She smiled and said nothing, but inside she seethed.

Damien isn't here for her to prove him wrong. She squeezes the Barber's hand gently. "Meyer's always around, but if I know I'll be alone, I can put my lamp in the window. But what about the fence?"

"I know a way in that won't alert the dogs."

"Good. If my window's bright, it means I'm waiting for you."

"My new moon," the Barber says. He leans toward her and tucks a strand of hair behind her ear gently. A prickle of pleasure passes over her skin. "I'll come by your room and see if you're on the rise."

When she worked in the Loop, it was necessary to shield her life from a client, to keep the sharp particularities for herself, so that she could have something to look back on as her own.

With the Barber, she feels more open for the first time. But she knows that if she wants to keep him safe, she can never tell him why she's really here.

When Rose first arrived at the Loop for her hostess interview, she felt incredibly self-conscious in the old jeans and T-shirt she wore, no makeup or heels, just green rubber boots and unwashed hair. This was a mistake, she thought. She clearly didn't belong here. She rose from the bench, but the security guard was already walking toward her.

"Avalon likes what she sees," the guard said. "You can follow me upstairs."

"She saw me?" Rose asked, looking around. No one had entered the lobby since she arrived.

"She sees everything." The guard pointed to the glass ceiling where the green dot of a surveillance camera pulsed on and off steadily.

She followed the guard upstairs. The bedroom he left Rose in was small but elegantly appointed. A low teak bed, neatly made with cream linen sheets, was positioned against the wall. Two egg-shaped chairs were clustered in the corner next to a table set with champagne flutes and a bowl of prickly dark red fruit. Like the rest of the Loop, the floor was reflective white tile, the oval windows fashioned out of tinted glass. In the garden below, two women reclined nude on sun loungers in the shade. One of them languidly applied sunscreen to her shoulders, and then turned onto her stomach. They seemed to exhibit no shame in lying exposed for anyone in this building to see.

Suddenly, her clothes and boots, even the loose elastic in her hair, felt uncomfortable and heavy. She looked at herself in the mirror and saw a peninsula girl, dressed in utilitarian clothes, worn at the knees and elbows from work. A girl who never allowed herself to dwell on beauty in the real world, only the beauty she found in the pages of books. She thought of the women who worked in the garret house during the high season, how they seemed to have formed a bond with each other but didn't remain tethered to a place because they left when the season ended. She could take this job for a short period to see if she liked it, and then decide what she would do with her life.

She pulled the elastic out and smoothed her hair with a hand. People rarely remarked on her appearance, and she had always assumed it was because they thought her odd-looking. Her black hair, which she rarely combed or cut, was thick like her mother's, and her face was dotted with freckles. But she had her father's physical stature, tall and strong, with a tendency to hunch her shoulders to compensate for her height. Now she stood up straighter as she examined herself in the mirror. She pulled off her clothes and left them in a grayish pile on the marble floor. Already she felt lighter.

The room's closet was filled with gauzy dressing gowns, shimmery cocktail dresses, and sets of sheer lingerie. She touched a pale green gown. The material was cool and impossibly soft. She took the gown off the hanger and held it against her body as she stood, still wearing her plain cotton underwear and bra.

"You can try it on," a voice said from behind her.

Rose turned around and saw a handsome woman standing in the room. Avalon wore a slate-gray tunic that reached to her ankles, and her silver hair was twisted into a long braid. A set of golden bracelets clinked as she extended a hand. "Green will look good with your skin tone."

The way she said skin tone bothered Rose, but she tried not to show it. Instead, she slid the gown on and tied the silk belt at her waist.

"See, I was right. You look radiant." Avalon smiled. "What do you think of the Loop?"

"I've never been in a building like this," Rose said, and looked around. "Do all of the hostesses live in similar rooms?"

"Of course. Everyone in the Loop is treated as an equal." Avalon folded herself elegantly into one of the egg chairs. "Like the Loop itself, we try to be as transparent as possible as to what this job entails, and what it can do for you." Avalon gestured to the chair next to her. "Please, sit with me. Have a rambutan and a glass of champagne. You must be exhausted."

Rose sat down and watched Avalon expertly unpeel the prickly fruit. She handed the iridescent orb to Rose. The rambutan was sweet, almost creamy, and at its a center she tasted the bitter pith of the fruit's seed.

Avalon peeled off the gold foil around the opening of the champagne bottle. "We specialize in a boutique experience here in the Loop. Everything we source is of the finest quality—single-origin coffee beans, champagne from prominent producers, even the sheets on our beds are handspun with the highest thread count. We think these small, thoughtful choices mark a different kind of life—one focused on wellness, equity, and honoring the traditions of those who came before us."

"What kind of traditions?" Rose asked. On the peninsula, tradition was a word she associated with church or sports or drunken hazing rituals out on the dunes.

"The traditions of a world that no longer exists." Avalon examined the label on the champagne. "This is a millennium bottle. Year 2000. I remember that year clearly, even though I was just a child. It was the first time I ever truly thought about the end of the world." She popped the champagne and poured it into the flutes. "Nothing happened, of course, and the clocks moved forward at the stroke of midnight, so it was easy to forget the fear we felt. Looking back now, it's clear that the year 2000 was an early warning."

What Avalon said interested Rose. She had never heard anyone speak in such grandiose and vivid terms before. She took the flute of champagne and enjoyed how the bubbles delicately popped on her tongue. "And who visits the Loop?"

"Engineers and entrepreneurs, mostly," Avalon replied. "Long-term thinkers who are tackling the big questions head-on. Amos Rust often stops by. As does Damien Mitchell."

Rose set the flute down. "As in *the* Damien Mitchell? The one who invented the Flick?"

Avalon laughed. "So you have heard of him."

"Of course I have. What's he like?"

"Brilliant. And cunning." Avalon tipped the champagne back and sipped. "Creators are the ones who can best see the flaws in their designs. Parents are the same—they tend to notice a child's weaknesses first. While the Flick is good for many things, experiencing intimacy it is not. Here in the Loop, no one uses their Flick. When each hostess is with her client, she is completely and utterly *with* him. There is no flickering to and from the feed. Our clients expect that when they are here, our attention is focused entirely on them. Most girls keep a rotation of regulars and see a few clients a day. You're paid per client, not by the service, so it's really up to you as to how many clients you take on. Room and board are also covered, and you're given two days off a week. It's a very humane schedule, not anything like this line of work on the mainland. And it's perfectly legal, so no need to be concerned about raids or arrest. We maintain a security detail in-house, so you can be assured of your safety while on the job."

"And what do the Floating City citizens think of the Loop?" Rose asked.

"We are as much part of the city as they are. This is real work, and you're respected for it." Avalon smiled warmly. "Many girls are in your precise situation when they arrive in the Loop. They have certain conceptions of what we do. But you need to understand that we're cultivating more than sexual intimacy. We're offering a return to a physical bond that many people feel they have lost post-Flick. If you're interested in the job, I can offer you a test run. See if your talents are suited to this type of environment."

Rose tried to imagine what it would be like for a man to take possession of her body, and then leave. The relationship would be clear, delineated, not like the muddiness of dating a boy from back home. A transaction occurs in any relationship, Rose justified. Even her mother would agree with this fact. At least here she would have a lovely and clean room and a good salary to send back home. Maybe she could even save up enough money to take her mother to Seoul one day.

"I'm interested," Rose said.

Avalon reached for Rose's hand. "Good. We'll get you settled."

Her first client was a well-known Founder who'd made his first million marketing cold vacations. He had the muscled and evenly tanned body of someone who spent a lot of time in the gym, or sunbathing nude on the roof-deck of his penthouse. In his publicity shots, he stood with his fit arms folded over his sculpted chest, wearing a tight T-shirt and tailored slacks. He had a bombastic head of hair, which he took no small amount of pleasure in raking his fingers through.

He walked into the room like he owned it, immediately made a pot of sencha tea, and served it to Rose in a porcelain teapot and two dainty cups. After, he instructed her to take a bath, and leaned against the counter to watch her undress.

"Avalon always has the finest taste," he said as she dropped her clothes to the floor. "Half Japanese?"

"No, Korean." No one had ever asked her with such directness about her ethnicity before. Usually the question was cloaked with an inquiry as to where she was really from.

"Aha." He nodded. "I should have known. You have that typically Korean square jaw." He ran his fingers along the ridge of her jaw. "Don't ever get facial reconstruction surgery."

They didn't have sex. He wanted to get to know her body, he said. To understand all her sensitive points—her skin's innate frequencies, so that when they finally fucked, it would be "a symphonic experience." They drank tea by the window, took long, indulgent baths, and lay on the bed as he expertly applied shea butter all over her body.

"I want you to be so desperate for it," he said, "that at night when you close your eyes, all you dream of is me."

That would never happen, but she knew her job was to create the conditions in which he believed this possible. She gasped in pleasure when he touched her, wrote little notes of adoration that she tucked into his pocket, told him that she thought of him in the middle of the night.

"Good," he said, stroking her hair. "Keep it that way."

Soon, she began to wonder if her production of longing was in vain. He never seemed to want to have sex.

"What's the deal with him?" she finally asked one of the other hostesses.

"Who knows." She shrugged. "Eventually he'll get bored and move on to the next girl Avalon hires."

"I wish all the clients were like him," Rose said. "It's so easy."

"I guess," the hostess said, "but I prefer being with someone where the conditions are clear. Drink. Fuck. Shower. Done. With him, you have to continually stroke his ego."

After a while, Rose understood what the hostess meant. It was exhausting having to attend to his needs, to pretend that she thought only of him and that the purpose of her existence was to focus on his "essence." As predicted, the moment a new hostess was hired, he stopped coming by to see Rose. When she occasionally crossed paths with him in the foyer, his eyes glazed over her as if she were a stranger.

"Excellent work," Avalon said to her after. "You're very responsive. You see what a client wants, and mold yourself to his needs."

Avalon intended this to be a compliment, but Rose thought otherwise. To be malleable suggested a lack of definition. A lack of knowledge about one's purpose. Was she really that uncertain who she was?

A year passed. Then another. Some of her clients preferred her to be "docile like a real geisha." To avert her eyes when they spoke to her, to serve them tea on her knees. Others liked that her mixed race made her more "approachable." Playing to each client's tastes required skill and patience, and while there were aspects of the job she liked, she sometimes wondered if this would be the sum of her life. Pouring drinks. Servicing clients. Acting poised at dinner while nodding along to a mind-numbingly dull conversation about tax havens. Pretending that she absolutely loved it when a client went down on her for an hour. It was exhausting work, and while she was paid well for it, she often wondered to what extent she was interchangeable. If she were to suddenly leave the Loop, would anyone even notice her departure? Or would they immediately hire another half-Asian hostess to fill the space she'd left behind?

She spoke rarely of these questions with the other hostesses, who all seemed perfectly content to work in the Loop. Many of them loved the freedom and money their jobs provided. Most were just grateful to have a job. Others had their own families back on the mainland that they supported with their work. But for Rose, it felt like the work cleaved her heart in two—half of her was present on the job, while the other half was still searching.

She often wondered where this searching would lead her as she walked through the Floating City on her days off from work. A home, she hoped. A place to call her own. "Sanctuary" was the word often used to describe the Floating City. But *sanctuary* also suggested a moral imperative that the lives lived here were somehow better, more blessed than the lives lived elsewhere. No one in the Floating City thought of themselves as religious, yet the place had become a belief system unto itself, a way to justify its separateness from the mainland.

The design of the Floating City underlined the contradiction of sanctuary. When Rose walked through the cool glass plazas of the First Sector and saw families dining together in the helicopter-to-table restaurants, she wondered how many of them thought of the Loop glittering at the city's center. Or if they ever looked at her and assumed she was paid to unzip the trousers of their husbands or fathers. Did they ever think about the armored train that brought poorly paid workers from the mainland to compete in the weekly hire to see who would work the least per hour?

Rarely, she suspected, even though workers were everywhere. Unlike Rose, whose work was done in the private quarters of the Loop, most of the contingent labor in the Floating City was on display. Workers dug ditches, irrigated the greenhouses, slaughtered pigs and chickens in the abattoirs. They cleaned the windows of the glass towers, disinfected the elevators and conference rooms, plunged the toilets, and wiped the counters of the marble bathrooms. They nannied the city's children, worked the cash registers at the grocery store, filed dead skin and painted nails in the salons. Everything they did ensured the seamless life that the city was prized for. Flooding, fire, drought, riots, revolt, overpopulation—none of it ever touched the city shining in the ocean. And yet the city was still tethered to the mainland because it remained reliant on it for labor.

Once a month, Rose took the train to the peninsula to visit her mother, bearing gifts from the Floating City—an oozing round of raw milk cheese, a bottle of Porto, a bouquet of real tiger lilies. She'd set out the cheese as an appetizer, but what she really wanted was her mother's cooking. Her mother would have spent the day preparing for Rose's arrival—spicy tofu jjigae bubbling in a stone pot, a hunk of short rib stewed with soy sauce and boiled eggs, seafood pajeon cooked with long, green chives until golden and crispy, and half a dozen banchan: soybean sprouts, pickled cucumbers, dried anchovies, cubes of yellow daikon, two varieties of kimchi. The cheese would go uneaten while Rose and her mother feasted with a quiet intensity, only interrupting the silence to ask for a refill of water or rice or if the anchovies were too salty. After her mother poured them each a bowl of cold cinnamon punch for dessert, she would look up at Rose and ask her a question about life in the Floating City. "Are there really helicopters there?"

"Everywhere," Rose said. "They circle the city like flies around raw meat."

Her mother took a sip of the punch. "And what are they doing?"

"Delivering supplies, mostly. Sometimes citizens. Everything is delivered by air to the Floating City. Except for workers, of course." Rose laughed. "I take the train like everyone else."

"And they treat you well at the hotel?"

"Yes, they even said I might get promoted to manager one day."

"I'm proud of you for finally getting away. I always knew you would find a life better than mine."

Rose lifted the bowl to her lips and drank, the sweet, syrupy dessert the only cure for the bitterness she felt. "Your life isn't so bad."

Her mother laughed and called her by her Korean name. "Every year brings less and less guests."

Rose reached across the table for her mother's hand. "The regulars will book. They always do."

"The ones who are still alive. They're all getting older." Her mother refilled Rose's bowl. "Like me."

That night, Rose lay awake on the stiff mattress of her childhood bed and heard her mother call out in her sleep, as she often did when the night terrors set in. As usual, the sentences were in Korean, so Rose was never able to glean what the nightmares were about. If only she could understand her mother's native tongue, then she might know how to save her.

In the morning, Rose asked her mother how she'd slept.

Her mother responded, as she always did, "Like a baby. And you?"

Rose had dreamed of a dark tide rising, her face pushed into sand, the spray of salt and wind as she struggled to a distant shore. But she never told her mother her dreams, in the same way her mother never told Rose hers. The equilibrium of their relationship depended on a mutual deception that everything was perfectly fine.

"Very well," she said, and poured two mugs of coffee. She looked outside at the sun rising over the Atlantic. "Looks like another beautiful day."

Two years became five years, and Rose was growing tired of the Loop. The clients were often the same: inflated Founders who wanted their egos stroked, or depressed salarymen who paid her to feel desired. Few of the clients ever interested her in more complex terms, and the things she used to enjoy—cocktails in the sunken garden, conversation in the lounge room, breakfast in bed—began to feel formulaic and trite.

Avalon must have suspected Rose's waning interest in her work because she approached her one day with a proposition. Would she be interested in an exclusive arrangement? One client. One job.

"You'll receive a pay raise and move to a larger suite," Avalon said, "but it requires that you're on call twenty-four seven for the VIP."

"Who's the client?" Rose asked.

"Damien Mitchell," Avalon said. "Consider it a privilege to take him on as an exclusive."

Since Rose started working, she had often wondered if she would ever meet the Loop's most powerful client. Unlike her other clients, who had made their fortunes from tech stocks and real estate, the source of Damien's fortune was far more intimate. Whenever she tapped her Flick on, she felt strangely connected to its inventor, and she wondered if the millions of other users felt the same. Damien was the closest thing to an actual god in a society where religion held little sway, but he was also famously private. This would be an opportunity for her to find out who he really was, and how his power manifested.

Rose immediately agreed to the job, and Avalon tried her best to prepare her. She told Rose that Damien was meticulously clean to the point of obsession, dressing in a brand-new white pressed shirt each day, which he wore with drawstring linen pants. Rose would need to shower before she met him, scrubbing herself with a specific soap made from the volcanic clay of the Canary Islands. Anything that Damien put in front of her, she would consume—champagne, of course, but also the jackfruit and guava he ate during the day now that he had become a semi-fruitarian. At night, she would join him in devouring whatever slabs of meat he had chosen. He liked to gorge on duck pâté and offal after the sun set, washing the rich iron down with bottles of slightly chilled red wine from his biodynamic vineyard in the Veneto countryside. Whatever he put into his body, Rose was expected to imbibe as well.

Damien always took a private elevator into the Loop, which opened up into the walk-in fridge of the commercial kitchen. He liked to arrive into cool chaos, weaving through the hanging cuts of beef, the cases of wine, the rounds of cheese, sampling a vat of whipped cream with a precise index finger. He would grab a clutch of Napa Valley grapes, sucking on the purple orbs as he walked through the kitchen in a mad rush for the dinner service. Here, he would collect more delicacies: cantaloupe wrapped in prosciutto, Belgian-style frites with a dollop of remoulade, a hunk of cave-aged Gruyère. All the food would be sent on a platter to his personal suite, where the first bottle of champagne was already chilled, and where Rose would be waiting. Unlike the other clients, who visited the hostesses in their rooms, Damien had his own customized suite located at the intersection of the infinity loop, the precise place where the two ovals crossed, offering views into both sunken courtyards.

His suite was furnished in the same simple refinement as the Loop, but was much larger with its own wading pool, sauna, and mirrored cycling room. The living quarters featured a dining room, a kitchen, a bedroom, and a meditation room. Rose was instructed by Avalon to wait for Damien in the bedroom.

When the door to the bedroom slid open, Damien stepped into the room covered in sweat, rubbing his bare chest with a Turkish hand towel. Either he didn't see Rose, or chose not to see her, as he walked quickly to the en suite bathroom, where she could hear the faucet turning on.

"Are you coming?" his voice suddenly called out.

She stood from the bed and followed his voice to the bathroom, where he was already lathering himself in the walk-in shower. He nudged the door open with his foot.

She undressed quickly and stepped into the shower. He nodded when he saw her and transferred some of the lather from his body to hers. "I like to get as pure as possible before I meet anyone new." He indicated for her to raise her arms in the air and began to vigorously wash her armpits with the intensity of a pet groomer.

"Turn around," he instructed. She did as she was told and felt a brush with thick bristles scrub her back. He moved on to her ass, the backs of her legs, even the bottoms of her feet. By the time he had deemed her sufficiently clean, it felt like a layer of her skin had been scoured off.

When they stepped out of the shower's steam, she was able to get a better look at him. He was thinner than she expected, with the sinewy frame of someone who could sit in the upright lotus pose for extended periods of time. She had heard that he spent his brief vacation periods doing intensive meditation practice, subsisting only on tepid vegetarian soup in the Tibetan monastery, where he was the sole patron. Most surprisingly, he was not bald, like the photos of his famously gleaming head suggested, but, like a monk, his light hair was shaved to the skin. His eyes were the unnerving blue that he was famous for, and when he finally set them on her, she felt the uncanny sensation of being filmed. The robotic intelligence in him seemed inhuman—too calculating and shrewd for the delusions of the soul.

He passed her a towel and a pair of white linen pajamas and told her to get dressed. "We'll want to be comfortable tonight."

The room he led her to was painted a rich mahogany and covered in soft gold carpeting. In the center was a low rosewood table with two embroidered bolsters.

"Please," he said, and gestured to one of the bolsters. "Sit." She sat cross-legged, and he did the same. "I've already reviewed your feed, so we can mercifully skip past the useless chitchat. I know all about where you grew up, why you took this job, about your poor struggling immigrant mother and your hard life on the peninsula." He looked at her carefully. "I know you'll think I'm being disingenuous—your analytics point to a tendency to think the worst of people—but I'm not, at all. I find your background fascinating. Raised on the Flick, yet you chose to reject it. There aren't a lot of people like you."

"There are in the Loop," she said.

"Well, the Loop is in a different solar system than out there." He waved a hand toward the window. "And what I'm interested in is out there. But you've grown tired of this place, haven't you? I've noticed an uptake in your Flick use lately."

"I've been feeling a little bored here, to be honest."

"Yes, I can only imagine how dull it must be. Talking about *this* vintage of Sancerre, *that* cut of farmed calf. I've hired many of the clients here, and I know that they can be incredibly daft. They're not interested in pursuing a conversation about what goes on out there. All they care about is their stock portfolios and whether they'll be promoted. Did any of your clients ever ask what your life was like outside the Floating City?"

"Most of them claim it ruins the mood," Rose admitted.

"Of course they do," Damien said. "They still believe the world they live in will never end." He reached over the table and picked up her hand delicately. "What repels you about me?"

"Nothing, of course."

"Cut the ruse," he replied. "I can tell when you're lying."

She looked away, and then said, "You think you know everything about me."

"And why is that a problem for you?"

She picked at the cuff of her pajamas. The linen was cool and light to the touch. "I want to find out for myself who I am."

"Of course you do. Here, I want to show you something." He opened a small drawer in the rosewood table and set a black rectangle with a screen on the tabletop. "This was my last phone before the Flick." He picked it up and caressed the screen affectionately. "I remember this feeling well. So much of my life was spent tapping this screen, looking into it for the answer."

"Did you find it?"

"Of course not. That's why I devised the Flick. I thought for us to compete with machines, we would need to become part machine ourselves. But a soul is more than an algorithm. A soul exists beyond code and can never be replicated. A soul has no place in the world we live in now. I thought the Flick would allow us to dispense with the glitches of the soul. Plug into the mainframe and let the data guide us to our next epiphany."

"You were wrong, of course," Rose said. "I could have told you that."

Damien finally laughed. "Yes, but I made enough from the Flick that even the most pronounced existential angst should have been sufficiently quashed. And yet . . ." He paused and turned the phone off. "It turns out you can't create a soul, but you can suppress its desire and longing if you redirect it." He clapped his hands and the room suddenly plunged into darkness. "It's far easier to create darkness than it is to create light."

The phone throbbed with an eerie glow. They sat quietly in the darkness for a few minutes. Rose listened to his shallow breathing.

"Why are you telling me this?" she asked.

"There's power in the past," Damien said. "And you're going to help me unleash it."

CHAPTER EIGHT

GRANT

Ever since Grant visited the Diggers' site, the Foreman has been close by. During Grant's weekly class, as he attempts to rouse the Diggers into completing a writing prompt, the Foreman is stationed on a chair in the corner of the boiler room, watching his every move. At meals, the Foreman sits next to Grant, cracking foul jokes and plying him with more whiskey if he doesn't laugh hard enough. Whenever a Digger tries to speak with Grant, the Foreman immediately interrupts and orders the Digger away. It's clear the Foreman doesn't want Grant straying far, and Grant knows it's because of what he saw at the work site.

But what is that, exactly? Grant thinks again of the gaping pits at the site and Wolfe's comment that the ground is mush. Can he trust the Diggers to be straight with him? In class, they've continued to treat him with indifference at best. Perhaps the Foreman is right, and the Diggers don't fully understand the scope of Meyer's building project. Or perhaps the Diggers found out who his family is and are trying to manipulate Grant for their own means. Whatever it is, Grant feels anxious and worried. Who can he depend on in camp? He thinks of Willow and wonders if she might be someone he can turn to for answers.

He walks into the cafeteria for dinner to find the warehouse transformed. Someone has put tablecloths on the picnic benches and lowered the lights to a dim glow. Flin sets out a trough of roasted goose on the buffet table, along with scalloped potatoes and three bowls of mint jelly.

"What's the occasion?" Grant asks Flin as he takes a plate.

Flin shrugs. "The Foreman told me to make sure dinner tastes good."

The buzzer sounds, and the Diggers file into the warehouse from their shift. The Foreman greets them at the door, clapping each man on the shoulder and pointing to the buffet, where the table is laden with food. The Diggers excitedly heap the meal onto their plates and find a seat at a table.

Grant sits next to the Barber, who is inspecting the mint jelly suspiciously. He says to Grant, "We haven't had food like this since we arrived."

Grant crams a piece of goose into his mouth. It is fatty and delicious, and he quickly devours it. "Where did Flin find this?"

"Meyer must have had a good day of hunting," the Barber says.

The Foreman claps his hands at the front of the cafeteria. "Gather round, now," he announces. "You've all been working flat out at the site, so we're going to play a special game tonight. But first, I should tell you the prize." He pauses for a dramatic flourish. "One lucky dog wins an evening with any Bloom."

"And we can do whatever we please?" Rabbit calls out.

"Anything your dirty mind desires," the Foreman answers. The Diggers break out into loud cheering.

Grant turns to the Barber. "I thought the Blooms were for management?"

"They are." The Barber pauses a moment before saying, "The Foreman must be trying to distract us."

"From what?"

"I'm not sure. Wolfe told me that he took you out to the site. Did you notice anything strange when you were there?"

"Just that the work site was a mess. The men were digging these holes into the ground. The Foreman said they're building the foundations, but Wolfe said the pits won't hold."

The Barber lowers his voice. "I think they're searching for something."

The Foreman quiets down the Diggers. "All right, everyone. Listen up. The rules of the game are simple. Each player has one bet. If you bet wrong, you're out. The contenders move to the second heat, and we keep repeating heats until we're left with one winner."

"Will you play?" the Barber asks Grant.

"No, I'm fine," Grant says. "I feel a little uncomfortable about the prize."

"It's part of the Blooms' job," the Barber says. "Besides, don't you want to see Willow again? I can tell she liked meeting you at the party."

Grant sets his fork down. "She did?"

"Of course she did. She couldn't stop talking to you. You should play, Grant. This might be your only chance to see her again."

Diamond and Finger drag a large steel cage covered with a black curtain from the kitchen. The Foreman tears off the curtain and unlocks a small door. A scraggly bear cub crawls out of the cage, its back leg bandaged neatly with a splint. It reaches a wet nose up to the ceiling, sniffing, as it limps out. Grant has never seen a bear before and is taken aback by the animal's glossy eyes sunken into black fur. The cub curiously looks from side to side as it drags itself across the floor.

The Foreman reaches down and touches the cub's head. "Hungry little one," he says softly. He clips a leash to the cub's collar and leads the animal to where Flin has left three hunks of meat on three overturned boxes. Each box has a number written on its side.

The Foreman turns his attention toward the men. "Now, each piece of meat has been weighed and crafted by our team of experts to ensure a perfect match."

"Thatta boy, Flin!" Swifty yells, making the crowd erupt into laughter.

"Quiet now," the Foreman says. "The Beast has been fasting, preparing for this moment. Diamond, can you gather the bets?"

Diamond walks around the cafeteria handing out slips of paper. When he approaches Grant, he asks, "What number do you want?"

"I'm sorry?" Grant asks. His eyes are still fixed on the soft splendor of the cub. He has never been this close to a wild animal before.

Diamond points at the boxes. "Which piece do you think it'll eat?"

Grant flicks his gaze to the marbled meat. The pieces look exactly alike. "Three?"

Diamond nods and gives him a slip of paper with 3 written on it.

After the Foreman unclips its leash, the cub sniffs the meat sitting in dark pools of blood. The first round is decisively played. The cub overturns Box 3 in one quick movement and devours the meat while lying on its back.

"Number 3!" the Foreman yells as a group of Diggers whoop in delight. Grant waves his winning slip in the air. Against his better judgment, he feels a flush of excitement. Maybe the odds are in his favor, after all.

Diamond quickly goes around the room, checking numbers, and comes back with a fistful of paper. "We've got eight contenders."

The rest of the men ball up their slips of paper and toss them on the ground or at each other. One Digger lights a slip on fire and watches the flames blacken the paper into ash.

Grant joins the other winners. He is so close to the cub that he can smell the blood smeared on the bear's fur. Flin clears the rejected meat and places a skinned hare on each box. Each hare's fuzzy ears droop around its raw pink face.

When Grant is handed a shot of whiskey, he tosses it back and huddles with the winning Diggers. Diamond walks in the center of the circle and takes each man's new number.

"All guesses in, Diamond?" the Foreman asks.

Diamond nods.

The cub stalks toward the boxes, knocking aside Box 1 to snap the delicate body of the rabbit. Its meal is accompanied by the roar of the crowd.

Only three hands hold slips of paper in the air. Grant takes a second shot of whiskey in celebration.

Flin drags three potato sacks across the floor and pulls out three deer heads with the antlers still intact.

"This is good meat, too," Flin says to himself as he places them on the boxes. The heads have been sawed off at the neck to allow them to sit upright. Their eyes stare out at the men with the same glazed expression as the taxidermied stags Grant saw above the bar in the bowling alley.

"Now, you three, gather round," the Foreman says to the winning men. "You'll be drawing numbers to see which head is yours."

Diamond hands around a hard hat for each of the men to grab a slip of paper. Grant looks quickly at his number, and then at his chosen deer head as he tries to ascertain whether his is the most appetizing. Hattie and Rabbit are somber and focused.

"She can eat her fill now," the Foreman says as he releases the cub.

In the first and second rounds, the cub had moved with hesitation, and then with desire as it realized its hunger would soon be sated. This round is different. The cub bounds toward the boxes, dragging its splint leg behind, but then pauses when it sees what is on offer. The cub sits down on the ground and lazily bats Number 3 off its pedestal. All the Diggers in the cafeteria hold a cloud of smoke in their lungs, knowing the rules are clear: the cub has to eat the meat in order for it to be declared the winner.

"Flin shouldn't have served venison yesterday for dinner," the Barber says to Grant.

"And why is that?" Grant feels the leaden weight of booze in his gut.

"The bear is smart. She knows we've already eaten the best cuts."

The cub rolls on its side, knocking one of the heads to the ground, and starts to play with its antlers. After a few minutes, the Diggers begin to grow restless, and the Foreman clips the leash back to the cub's collar. "All right, all right," he says. "It looks like we'll have to try something else." He gestures for Flin again. "Bring out their hearts."

Flin places one of the slick dark organs on each of the boxes and mock-bows to the audience. The Foreman releases the cub, and within a minute it has eaten Number 1 and moves on to the second heart.

"And we have a winner!" The Foreman holds up Grant's arm as the bear finishes devouring the raw heart. Blood drips from its jowls as the Diggers cheer and clap Grant on the back in congratulations.

The Foreman whispers to Grant, "I know we parted on poor terms at the work site, but I think an evening with a Bloom will make everything better."

"Is this a bribe?" Grant asks.

"Consider it payment for being a good worker," the Foreman says.

Grant pulls away from the Foreman and searches the crowd for the Barber. He sees him slip through the front door of the warehouse.

Grant rushes outside to see if the Barber is still around but finds the frozen parking lot empty. His heart is hammering in his chest, and he feels both elated and uneasy that he won the game.

He looks up at the sky filled with the pink slashes of the setting sun. It's a beautiful evening, crisp and quiet. An evening for writing, for reading, for drinking a mug of tea with whiskey and nuzzling a loved one in bed. Not an evening for betting on the dismembered corpses of animals for a fleeting encounter with a woman.

Then he hears a solitary sharp whistle. The door to the mall across the highway opens, and a pack of dogs start running giant, erratic loops around the parking lot, the muscles in their sleek bodies rippling in the setting sun. A woman walks to the edge of the fence and calls out, "Grant?"

He recognizes her voice even though he can't see her face. "Willow!" he answers and rushes across the highway. As he approaches, a dog runs toward Grant, barking and snarling through the fence. Grant steps back as the dog rears up on its hind legs, toenails slashing at the metal bars. The dog's eyes are two black pits set in its lustrous head. Grant's blood rushes between his ears.

"It's all right, Annie," Willow says softly. "He's a friend." She touches Annie between the ears, and the dog settles at her feet. Her cheeks are flushed from the cold. "I was wondering when I'd see you again." She reaches a gloved hand through the fence. "Are you allowed to be here?"

"I think so." He glances back at the Diggers' warehouse to see if anyone has followed him. "I just won the game." He tells her about the game he played with the Diggers, and how an evening with one of the Blooms is the prize.

A flicker of irritation spreads across her face. "Do you think of me as a party favor?"

"Of course not. But this might be the only way I can see you again." He adds quickly, "Just to talk. Not for . . ." He trails off, searching for the right word—*sex* seems too clinical, *fucking* sounds too crass. ". . . intimacy." He thinks of Jane with a sudden ache. "I'm sorry I'm being so cryptic. It's been a while since I've been with someone, and I'm kind of a mess right now. I want to see you, but it might take some time before I can visit."

"It's okay. We can take it slow." She leans toward the fence. "I want to see you too."

The door to the mall opens, and the sharp whistle sounds again. The pit bulls stream toward the mall, flowing like a glistening river.

Willow looks over her shoulder at the mall. "I should go back in. Come and see me when you're ready to talk. There might be another route out of here."

She smiles at him and pops on her hood and starts to jog toward the mall. Grant stands at the fence and watches her dark silhouette move across the white landscape.

WHITE ALICE

Six weeks after the General visited us, we discovered that our gamble to stay in White Alice had paid off.

The engineer was pregnant.

With the excitement of the pregnancy came a flurry of preparation. What room would we turn into the nursery, who had the knowledge and the medical skills to midwife the delivery, how would our carefully overseen supplies of food and fuel need to be rationed to supplement the life of another human.

The library was deemed the best space for the nursery. It was the coziest room by virtue of the books that lined the walls and the mottled globe in the corner that lit up at night. The botanist cut down the birch trees in the greenhouse and built a crib with the engineer. The meteorologist collected an old army-green sleeping bag and sewed an impossibly tiny sleep sack. The programmer sutured a flashlight with a flap of birch bark for a night-light and connected two transistor radios as a baby monitor. The biologist researched newborn nutrition and planted root vegetables and leafy greens in the garden, while the cartographer and the geographer made a baby book with the unused ledgers of the previous missions.

As the General promised, new supplies from home base arrived the next month. We received customized weapons; new ATVs; military food rations; extra RAM for the computers; higher-powered microscopes; barrels of oil; and bags of high-grade fertilizer for the greenhouse. But we really wished for diapers, bottles, boxes of digestible cookies, onesies, and stuffed animal toys. We received none of these items, of course, since Sal told us it would be safer to keep our newest arrival a secret.

"They'll take the baby away from us," Sal said. "They won't see the station as a safe place to raise a child."

So we said nothing when the shuttle dropped a crate of supplies onto the ice next to the station.

Sal, who was the only one of us who had given birth, told us what we could expect during the birthing experience. She broke the process of labor down into three separate phases.

First, the initial contractions: the sudden tightening of the belly and uterus as it prepared for birth. Secondly, the water breaking, kick-starting the more aggressive contractions. This would hurt, she warned, and become more frequent in intensity. She called this phase "active labor," and emphasized it would be a form of work for us all. Our job would be to shepherd the birth, dipping cloths into buckets of water and pressing them to the forehead of the engineer, breathing in tandem, moving when needed. She said it would be good for the engineer to practice visualizations and imagine a physical place she could turn to when the sensations—and she always used the word "sensations," never "pain"—became too intense. "Think of this place as a refuge you can retreat to when the labor becomes overbearing."

Next, the active labor would transition into something more intense and grounded.

"You will feel a need to bear down," Sal said. "It will be like a rock inside of you is being pulled to the ground." Here it was important for us all to be present and alert, as this, Sal claimed, was the most primal stage of the labor. "We call this 'the Transition.'"

The last stage was when the baby would be pushed out. This could take twenty minutes, or seven hours, depending on the baby's positioning.

It was imperative that we all witness the moment the baby entered our world and became part of our brood.

"Women have been delivering babies in environments far less conducive than ours since the beginning of time," Sal assured us. "Everything will be fine."

Time was suddenly divided into trimesters, then days, and finally hours. The engineer's pregnancy remained true to form and progressed with a mechanical purposefulness. During labor, the engineer timed her contractions with a stopwatch and make a series of notations in her logbook. She seemed eerily lucid throughout the experience, talking to us in full sentences, and only buckling against the wall, or clenching our hands when a contraction roiled inside her.

Our daughter was born three weeks early. She was small and feisty with wide-open dark eyes.

"She looks like a raisin," the engineer remarked tearily, as she held the slimy bundle to her chest. Our baby screamed and screamed, her little fists making futile jabs in the air, and was only quiet when Sal popped her pinky into her tiny mouth.

"This one is a fighter," Sal said, laughing. The engineer slid the baby to her breast, and she began to eat greedily, making soft, animal snuffling noises. We stood around the engineer and watched in awe as our daughter's body became still as she nursed.

We named her after the Borealis and called her Aurora. When she was three months old, we lay her swaddled among the lettuce and herbs in the greenhouse and looked at her admiringly. The love in our hearts was vaster than the frozen tundra spanning beyond the station.

"It's like we grew her," Sal said with no small amount of pride.

At the time, we couldn't help but agree.

———

While our pre-child life had been marked by seasons and work, our life with a baby was fundamentally different. For the first time in our lives, we didn't control the clock—she did. Every developmental milestone represented another passage of time, but we didn't feel a sense of anxiety about the days slipping away. Instead, we gave in to the chaotic machinations of raising a tiny human.

Since most of us were not producing milk, we often walked around the station clasping our daughter to our chests to soothe her until she settled into the crook of our necks fast asleep. Our baby didn't show a preference for her "birth mother." Sal considered it a biological victory that her first word, *mama*, was spoken to all of us, regardless of genetic association. As long as she was fed and held, she was happy.

Aurora confirmed her disciplinary origins by bearing distinct personality and physical traits. She remained small and intense, with the fine motor skills of a technician in training. At a very young age, she was able to undo buttons, pull string, crack open the shell of a nut. Her fingers were deft and nimble and seemed to communicate a language of her own. Her favorite pastime was taking objects apart only to put them back together again. An old rotary phone, the busted transmitter of a radio, a length of cable found in the communications room. The physical world built by humans was her playground.

Aurora was optimistic and cheerful about our circumstances, never fussing or demanding something that wasn't hers. We owed this to the botanist's gentle disposition, and the fact that Aurora spent so much time in the greenhouse. There, she witnessed firsthand how hard work, patience, and care could turn an inert seed into a plant of wild beauty, and that transformation grew from the ground up, rooted in the deep terra of earth.

After the first ivory wedge jutted out from Aurora's bottom gums, the botanist harvested the bland root vegetables best for growing teeth and new digestion—turnips, carrots, sweet potatoes. We mashed the vegetables into silky purees and laughed as our baby slathered her first solids all over her face and the table, not worrying, for once, about wasting our precious food supply.

Aurora needed us, but we needed her, too. Sometimes one of us would crave a moment in the greenhouse, alone, without the scrutiny of the others. There, we would often find Aurora plopped down on the ground, raking the raspberry bushes with her chubby fingers. We would sit with her among the flowering fruit, leaning forward to kiss her sweet, broad face, streaked with dirt and berries. From the vantage point of child, soil, and plant, it was possible to forget we were surrounded by eons of unforgiving permafrost.

Our version of spring arrived again, and our daughter celebrated her first birthday. With the passing of a year, it felt like it was time to take her on a trip.

The engineer constructed a sleigh out of a plank of wood, wash bins, and a pair of cross-country skis. We bundled our daughter in a bunting sack sewn from the fur-lined hood of a parka and strapped her into the bin. She smiled when Sal dragged her outside, noticing the way her breath vaporized into cloudy plumes. When they hit a ridge of ice, the sleigh flipped over, and her round bundled body tumbled into a laughing heap. We dusted her off, plopped her back into the wash bin, and continued our journey to the seed vault.

The vault was located a mile from the station. The cartographer thought that examining the crates in deep storage would be a good way for our daughter to start learning about the regions of the world. All countries had contributed—even those in political standoffs and ongoing wars agreed to leave their agricultural legacy on the same shelf. By virtue of us being its guardians, we were allowed to use a small number of seedlings to maintain our own crop in the greenhouse.

We first took Aurora to the Asian section because it featured the most animals stamped on the sides of the crates: a tiger, a panda, an elephant. The cartographer pointed to a box shipped from Bengal, hand-stenciled with a tiger stalking in profile, its luscious fur painted in orange and black tempera.

"This is filled with lentils," the cartographer said, and lifted Aurora up first to inspect the crate. She set Aurora on top of a crate filled with rice seeds from Vietnam. Our daughter found a flattened cherry tomato somewhere deep in her coveralls, and plopped the reddish mush into her mouth, chewing.

"Baba?" Aurora asked, and pointed at the tiger on the side of the Bengali crates. Our daughter's knowledge of animals had been limited to the books in the library that featured Arctic mammals. The polar bear, the penguin, and the seal were the first animals she recognized and knew by name.

"No, that's not a polar bear. It's a tiger," the cartographer replied. She traced a finger along the animal's outline. "See, it has striped fur."

Aurora demanded to be picked up so she, too, could touch the tiger's stripes, laughing when one of us made a *rawr* sound and held our hands out like claws. Until then, we hadn't thought much of the animals we learned about as children from books—the tiger, the zebra, the hippopotamus, the rhinoceros. Would our daughter ever see them?

"Tiger, tigre, hǔ, тигр," the geographer dutifully repeated as she always did when teaching a new word. Aurora tried to sound out the words, and then toddled to the next aisle, where the engineer was certain a panda was stamped on the Chinese crates filled with dried soybeans.

It was there in the seed vault that we began to think differently about what we had chosen. To create a utopia requires a rigid set of values. We would live with deep respect and love for each other. We would maintain our home in the station. We would raise our daughter to know the morality we believed to be true. These three tenets felt correct. But what about everything else out there?

The world we had left behind, however spiteful and horrific, was still the world.

CHAPTER NINE

ROSE

In her room in the Millennium Mall, Rose looks at herself in the vanity mirror. She lines up a hairbrush, the gold necklace Meyer gave her, a tube of red lipstick, and the Barber's switchblade to impose her order over the deliberate, inherited space. This is mine, this is mine, this is mine, this is mine. Of course, nothing here is hers. This fact never used to bother her, but now it does. She puts on the necklace and fiddles with the Barber's switchblade. A quick flick of the wrist, and the blade flashes under the low light.

Rose can hear Judith making her final patrol down the hallway, the *click, click, click* of a dog's nails in sync with her own steps. A client calls out a greeting. She quickly hides the knife under her mattress.

The door to her bedroom opens. Meyer pushes his way into her room. "Where were you yesterday? I came by and couldn't find you."

She knows better than to mention her fishing trip with the Barber; it will only make him jealous.

"I was taking a walk in the mall," she says instead.

Meyer frowns. "I'd prefer if you'd stay in your room where I can find you. I don't like thinking of you wandering out there."

She can tell he's been drinking heavily. His words are slurred and un-characteristically sloppy. He blinks slowly and looks around the room as if he's surprised to find himself here. For a moment, it looks like he might topple over.

"Are you okay, Meyer? Do you need to lie down?" She takes him by the hand and leads him to the bed.

"I need a drink." He points at the dresser, to the bottle of whiskey.

She pours him a glass and brings it over to him. This close, she can tell he's spritzed himself with cologne to cover up the stench of booze. "How is your work going?"

"Terrible." He lies back on the bed and rubs his temples. "I need to secure more funding or everything will be ruined."

"Will that be hard?"

"It depends on who the investors are. In the past, I accepted funding from whoever could write me a check. But I'm not going to do that this time. I need an investor with a conscience and a vision. Someone who understands the importance of what we're doing here and won't try to corrupt the project for their own gain." He shakes his head. "I'm sorry, Rose. I just get angry when I realize how much more work there is to do."

He sits up in the bed and motions for her to join him. When she sits, he rests a hand on her thigh. "For this project, I don't want to compromise." A sadness passes over his face. "This will be my last large-scale project."

"Don't say that," Rose says. "You'll move on to something else."

"No, this is it. I'm not going back to the US. I'm staying right here." He looks at her and nods vigorously. "Yes. This is the only place for me now."

Damien never said anything about Meyer's plans to permanently relocate here. He'll be unhappy when he finds out. "Where will you live then?"

"On my campus, of course. Well, not my campus—it will have a proper name by then—but the one we'll build for our own."

"Our own?"

"Americans, of course. Once the campus is complete, we'll be less outnumbered by the locals. We'll start with a few hundred in the first season to staff the campus and create some kind of civic and academic culture. And then we'll work quickly to admit students. A thousand each year. And after the campus is established, it will be much easier to create an incentive for a larger population to settle here."

"Are you planning a city?"

"No cities. I'm done with urban architecture. This will be low-level, low-density housing, built in harmony with the natural surroundings. No structure will rise higher than two stories, and every home will have its own acre of land for hunting, fishing, gardening. We'll reconnect with nature here, not cover it in concrete and call it our own."

So, the Barber is right. Meyer believes he's establishing a settlement for well-intentioned Americans to stash their children and assets. A place to flee to and evade the problems of the South. She feels a surge of pity for him. He still thinks of himself as a good man, that his work in Dominion Lake is morally correct.

He looks away from her and then says, "And who knows, perhaps you'll still be up here and can be part of it all." He takes her hands. "I see something in you, Rose."

A certain kind of sentimental client, like Meyer, often made predictable proclamations to her like this. Rose will humor him. She leans forward and smiles. "And what's that?"

"You're watching everything. Observing. Processing. You're like me. You can see beyond the current realties of this camp. The inherent potential of this place." His voice sharpens as he says, "We might be the only ones."

"Will you show me what you're working on?" she asks, and then adds, "So I can see for myself."

His face breaks into a grin, and he pulls her into his lap. "I can take you out to the site tomorrow, if you'd like?"

"I'd love that," she says, and kisses him on the cheek.

He grunts happily and reaches for her. The fur of his jacket scratches her skin. She can feel a warming, a slow glow of desire drifting from him. He pulls her to the bed, and his breath quickens and matches the movements of her body.

"Your name," he whispers. "I want to know your real name."

She says the pseudonym she always uses to appease clients who want to know her "real name." And with that, he finishes, his face blotched with pleasure and shame. He kisses her and pulls her toward him in bed. "Good night, darling."

Soon, Meyer is gently snoring. Rose carefully extracts herself from his arms and sits up to watch him sleep in the dim light. His chest rises and falls, his face blank and peaceful. She places a hand on his chest where she can feel his heart thudding against her fingers.

She thinks of the tattoo on the Barber's forearm, and the suggestion of violence in the deft handling of a razor. To wield a weapon is to hold a certain form of power. Yet the barber never watched the emperor sleep at night, never saw his body grow still as his breathing slackened and his consciousness dropped into the doomed colony of his dreams.

But she has.

Rose's mother only used her drowned husband's pocketknife during holidays.

"So we can taste each one," her mother said while halving the truffles Rose had brought home from the Loop. The light was on in the kitchenette, and she had strung Christmas bulbs around the foot-high plastic pine. Rose watched as she prepared the oozing sweets and felt a swell of sadness. Somehow, her mother had grown old. She could see the change in her hair, which she had stopped dyeing recently and now cut into a silvery crop close to her scalp. Her eyebrows, too, were now silver, and she moved with a stiffness in her joints. She seemed at least a decade older than her actual age, and Rose knew it was from working relentlessly on the cottages. Since Rose moved to the Floating City, her mother refused to hire anyone to help her, claiming she couldn't afford the extra expense, even when Rose gave her the money to cover a second salary. Rose suspected her mother preferred to be alone and couldn't bear the idea of growing close to someone else.

They spent the Christmas holiday logged on to their Flicks when the news broke that followers of a doomsday cult had taken their own lives.

The cult had grown notorious for their on-feed incantations about the end of the world:

The End Is Already Here
Survival Is a Choice
Doomsday Commences

"This country," her mother said, and shook her head with sadness. "Everything is so broken."

Three months later, Hurricane Xavier hit the Northeast Coast. The Loop closed for the first time. Avalon gathered Rose and all the hostesses in the wine vault under the kitchen, where they sat in the damp dark for a full day, until the wind stopped howling. When they emerged, they found that the Loop's generator had seamlessly turned on. The storm had caused minimal damage to the city and only required light landscaping in the First Sector. The clients considered it a success—nature had showed its worst, and still the city persevered.

The mainland was a different story. Large portions of the coast had been devastated by the storm. Entire neighborhoods were underwater, brick chimneys sticking out of the surging tide. Streets filled with water to the second and third floors of buildings. The Charles River was choked with the wreckage of people's lives. Cars and bodies were dredged up on the shoreline just one block from Walden itself. The university had managed to barricade the historic Yard with a twenty-foot wall of sandbags. A child drowned in the back of a car, his father found floating facedown in the river. A family who escaped to the roof of their apartment building, only to die from dehydration. The gymnasium of a school, which had been deemed safe for refuge, filling with water as people tried to climb the walls.

The surge was so strong that it immediately enveloped the peninsula, the tide rolling over the boardwalk, the cottages, all the way to the marsh, where it finally pulled back, sucking everything with it. Most people had evacuated by then, but there were those who refused to leave, and stubbornly closed the curtains on the windows of their cottages to ride out the storm.

The watery deaths of sailors and fishermen were common lore in the local history Rose had heard as a child, narrated as a dignified end. When she walked through the cemetery to visit her father's grave, she read the gravestones of perished sailors:

RESTING WITH HIS ONE TRUE LOVE

MAY THE SEA BRINGETH WHAT IT TAKETH AWAY

DEEP IN THE WATERY SHADOWS, HIS SOUL LIES

But the stories never featured the deaths of women by the sea. Women waited at home and lit a candle in the window to remember their husbands or sons who had disappeared into the deep. Women were entrusted with memory. They carried the stories of the last generation to their own children. Women mourned and grieved what was lost, only to see the same mistakes and tragedies repeated in the next generation. Women were witnesses.

What did it feel like for her mother to pull open the curtain and see the dark surge of water advancing? A woman whose husband was taken by the sea, finally meeting its fury? Did it feel like extinction?

Her mother lost everything in the storm. The cottages. The furniture. Their electric hatchback, and the supplies in the shack out back. Only the foundations of the cottages remained. Everything her mother had sacrificed her life for had been swallowed by the sea.

Rose went to visit her mother in one of the Dispossession Estates as the rebuilding effort slowly began. She shared a room with three other families in the basement of the building, with a single rectangular window that opened out onto the sidewalk. From the perspective of her cot, she could see the feet of people walking by on the street.

Her mother sat on the cot, wearing the clothes of a six-foot man. She looked up when Rose walked in, and tried to smile. It was a dank little space, but clean enough and blessedly dry. Her corner of the room was comprised of all that she had managed to keep: a photo of Rose as a child and a book of Korean poetry. She'd been evacuated from the peninsula with these two possessions and the clothes on her body.

Rose sat down next to her. She seemed impossibly tiny in the oversize clothes.

Her mother reached for her and stroked the stray hairs around her forehead in the way she used to when Rose was a child. "How are you?"

How could Rose tell her that during the storm she feasted on Portuguese mackerel and water crackers, and drank Vinho Verde as the hostesses tipsily sung songs together in the dark until the generator flickered on? Or that Damien sent a magnum of champagne to her suite with an invitation for brunch the next morning?

"I brought food," Rose said, and placed the bag of nonperishables she'd taken from the Loop's kitchen on the cot. "And some clothes that should fit."

Her mother looked into the bag gratefully.

"I'm going to get you out of here," Rose promised.

"I'm fine, really," her mother said, and then looked at Rose with an inquisitiveness in her eyes. "Are you?"

"Of course," she said, and forced a smile.

The next morning, Meyer drives the SUV down the highway. There is just enough light on the road to see the camp sliding by. The cool air coming through the inch of open window reminds Rose of what it feels like to be in acceleration again. What it will feel like to leave this place behind.

Meyer looks at her and smiles. One of his hands rests on her lap as he steers the truck with the other. "It feels good to be on the move with you."

She tells him she agrees, listening to the soft hum of the vehicle as they drive down the little hill that dips toward the village.

When they approach the yellow church, Rose sees light shining through the stained-glass windows. The Barber is home. She imagines opening the passenger door and rolling into a snowbank, running across the street and through the church's front door. In five minutes, they could be back together.

But Meyer's hand is still on her leg, and he is speaking. "When we first arrived, I didn't immediately see this place's potential. Terrible suburban townhouses with aluminum siding, leaky basements, and moldy carpeting. Rows of housing constructed with the cheapest materials possible. A place built on quick expansion, not thoughtful, sustainable growth. But the land! My god, the land! Such possibility. Lumber. Wildlife. Ice and snow and the lake that still freezes."

The yellow church recedes in the rearview mirror as they drive away from the village, and suddenly they're skirting the lake itself. The sun is so bright that Rose shields her eyes as she gazes out at the frozen water. In the distance, a dome rises above the trees. It looks like an enormous golf ball nestled in the woods, but as they drive closer, she sees it is still only scaffolding.

"We've just installed the insulation. It should be ready for habitation by the spring." Meyer parks the SUV in front of the building. He rests a hand on her shoulder. "Come, I'll show you inside."

Rose gets out of the vehicle and follows him into the dome. He leads her through the small rooms, their utility marked out on the ground.

"Here is the kitchen and living quarters, and at the top of the spiral staircase is the hydroponic rooftop garden." Meyer pauses in his tour to speak fondly of the vegetables and fruits that he wants to grow there. "What is your favorite fruit?" he asks.

The way he poses the question is paternal and intimate, as if he is asking her to decorate her teenage bedroom. "Strawberries," Rose says without much thought.

He smiles. "I had a feeling you'd say that. That was my daughter's as well."

In the articles and interviews she's read on Meyer, he never once spoke of a family. She always imagined him alone, walking through the scorched desert, scouting for his next project to build. A man who doesn't require the love of another. A man who is satisfied by the execution of his work. But the image of Meyer as a laboring, solitary genius has clearly been cultivated. She feels a ripple of sympathy for his daughter, to be cut out of her father's story so easily.

"Where is your daughter now?" she asks.

"She's back south, working on the rebuilding effort. She doesn't think very kindly of the work I've done."

"And why's that?"

"I oversaw a project for the military when I was going through a difficult period in my career. It was co-opted into something that I had no intention of creating. I've since managed to distance myself from the thing. She's never forgiven me for it, and in some ways, I can't blame her. But I'm doing good work now that I can be proud of. My dream is that my daughter will come north and see what we're building."

She says nothing and follows him up the stairs as he continues his tour. Meyer's voice, normally steady and even, seems to lift to a higher octave with each stair they ascend. On the second floor, he shows her where the bedrooms will be, and indicates the dimensions of each room marked on the wooden floor. "A murphy bed pulls out of the wall here." He gestures at a space framed by an empty square. "And a small writing desk, here. The children's rooms are here and here." Suddenly he turns to her. "Can you see it, Rose?"

She stands in the bedroom and looks out the window at the snow in the trees. She sees nothing but an empty pit; the black eyes of the pit bulls; the dark, inky tattoo that curls across the Barber's forearm; a room with a view of the ocean, where her mother is reading a book of Korean poetry. An exit. An escape. Once she leaves camp, she'll never have to see Meyer again. Never wonder if he watches her while she sleeps. Never stand patiently as he pulls a brush through her wet hair after she showers. For now, her job is to tell him what he wants to hear.

"Yes," she says. "I can see it perfectly."

After Hurricane X, Damien and Rose shared a jackfruit that he ceremoniously split open on the rosewood table. He was in a sour mood and was taking it out on the pungent fruit, which he dismembered with his fingers.

"The problem," Damien suddenly said, "is that people have become too fixated on the present. When I invented the Flick, I argued for it in purely utopian terms: access, connectivity, productivity, revelation. The deep polarities and abiding differences in society would be resolved. People would finally be linked beyond citizenship, offering a new way to harmoniously coexist in their feeds. It was a ridiculously naïve proposition, but it was the only way to get the Flick on the market."

"What if you had sold it for what it actually is?" Rose asked.

"A data-harvesting surveillance tool?" His mood suddenly lightened, and he laughed. "That *is* an amusing consideration." He popped a yellow shred of jackfruit into his mouth, chewed thoughtfully, and then continued, "The at-birth implantations would never have become normalized, let alone the Flick itself. No, this had to be the way it happened. Freedom. Connectivity. Hope. It's easier to sell an optimistic idea than a damning one."

"I used to worry that the Flick made me feel less like myself," Rose said.

"And why is that?"

She paused for a long moment and then said, "I couldn't fully remember who I was or what I wanted."

"Lobotomized." Damien nodded. "That's a common reaction to overuse. The user feels a distinct sensation of disconnection. Specifically, the cerebral cortex that archives memory darkens with prolonged use. It literally begins to shut down. We've run tests to prove it."

"And you did what with these tests?"

"Absolutely nothing." He grinned and popped another piece of jackfruit into his mouth.

"Why perform the tests, then?"

He looked at her with irritation in his eyes. "You're smarter than this. Do you think I would continue to use something that endangered my brain? Or that I would allow you, or Avalon, or any of the clients who visit the Loop to risk erasure? We have solid evidence that the Flick erodes more memories with each year of use. By the time the first users are ready for retirement, all they'll retain is what they had for breakfast."

Could Damien sense the disgust she felt? Everyone she had grown up with in the peninsula had experienced significant loss after the storm—

loss of house, family, work, ambition. Now his Flick was causing them to lose their memories, too. Yet here he was, eating a tropical fruit that had been flown in overnight from a Malaysian rain forest. She was off-feed, so at least her emotions weren't being archived, her heart rate, her pulse racing with resentment. She looked at him and smiled, the coy girl smile she had learned to affect when it suited her. "And you never go on your feed?"

"I still have to go on for publicity events, specifically when we roll out an upgrade. But I never, ever go on for more than one hour, and after, I undergo an extensive psychological and biological cleanse to purge the feed from me. It takes at least a day to recuperate."

"Sounds exhausting," she said.

Damien looked at her sharply. "Is that a sarcasm spike? If only I could check your analytics."

"We're blissfully free from our Flicks in here, aren't we?" she said sweetly.

Damien went back to dissecting the jackfruit, which signaled that the time for talking was now over. This suited Rose. For him it was a break from her, but for her it was a chance to observe her client. He had grown used to talking with her, and with that came a looseness in his physical affect. She noticed smalls signs of insecurity: how he sucked in his stomach when he passed a window, how he never wanted to have sex with the lights on. And with this knowledge came a certain power. He wanted to appear in control and was becoming worried that he wasn't.

Damien cleared the jackfruit from the rosewood table.

"Do you know that there are people in this world who have no memory of their childhood?" he asked.

"It can't be that common," she said.

"Oh yes, more than you'd expect. A decent percentage of Flick users are online full-time. They have no interest in the past. All they care about is their present feed." He picked a piece of jackfruit from his teeth and flicked it over his shoulder. "They're not my target demographic, though, because they're too far gone. It's those who exist in the half-life I'm interested in. Users who sense that the life they once knew has progressively eroded through years of use and are desperate for contact with their authentic selves. This group represents the largest pool of users, and the ones who we're now engineering for. A future when people are so linked to their Flick, they will pay an astronomical amount to access the memories and sensations they hadn't realized they'd lost."

Rose was quiet for a moment. She recalled how her mother sometimes found it difficult to remember details from her childhood, and how she faltered when referring to someone's name. Even though Rose tried to encourage her otherwise, her mother spent most of her time on-feed. Was she a half-life user? Rose felt a flare of anger, imagining her mother's memories wiped blank so that the only record of her life would be what she had already told Rose. She kept her voice steady and asked, "Are you planning on helping them?"

"With limitations. My investors have determined it's an economically sound position to engineer an upgrade to the Flick. Or, as I like to think, a corrective. But 2.0 requires a tremendous amount of processing power. Ten times more than the current Flick. What do you know about rare earth minerals?"

"Not much, to be honest. Just that most of it is extracted in the East."

"That's correct. Everything we use to power the Flick is extracted from a vast mine in China, near the Gobi Desert." He shrugged. "But it's become politically inconvenient to work with the Chinese, and while I don't give a fuck about politics, I do care about the bottom dollar. The Chinese are threatening to shut down the mine if we don't offer them a piece of our technology, and I'm tired of playing their game." He placed a sheet of serrated metal on the rosewood table. "Dysprosium. The rare earth mineral we use to power the Flick, and what we'll need for 2.0."

She touched the mineral, and it disintegrated into a pile of ash. "Why are you telling me all of this?"

He tried to look sympathetic. "How has your mother been?"

"Not well. She's still in the Dispossession Estate and keeps threatening to move back to the peninsula."

"But there's nothing there anymore."

"That's what I told her, but she can't accept that everything is gone. Our home was her life."

"Have you considered moving her here?"

Rose laughed. "To the Loop? I think she's a little mature to work here."

"No, not to the Loop. But the First Sector might be a good place for her. Plenty of retirees with a strong sense of community."

Rose looked away from him with irritation. "You know I can't afford the First Sector."

"What if I set you up with a job?" he asked. "Short-term, highly paid, that would allow you to transfer your mother to the Floating City."

"I'm listening," she said, and leaned forward.

"There's a piece of land in the Canadian north I'm interested in. The first surveys suggest that it's rich in dysprosium. I want to send a larger team up there, but it's turning out to be more complicated than I anticipated. The region has a troubled history of oil extraction, and if the land is claimed for what's underneath, the locals will want it for themselves. But if it's for something more altruistic, say a college campus, they'll approve of an American camp."

"What do you want me to do?"

Damien laughed. "Live there and act like your lovely and effervescent self."

"That's it?"

"Well, there's more. The project depends on the uninformed cooperation of the head architect to justify our presence. I know Meyer well—he's the one who designed the Floating City. He's a brilliant man, but prone to gloomy periods that he claims are all a part of his process. Your job will be to spend time with him. Try to perk him up. Distract him from his apocalyptic pondering. And if he begins to sense his building project is not what it seems, then you're to alert your contact in camp immediately." Damien looked at Rose directly. "Meyer will grow to trust you, I'm certain of it. And maybe even depend on you. In exchange, you'll receive a condo in the First Sector with all-inclusive access to our facilities, plus a yearly allowance for your mother."

Rose knew condominiums in the First Sector were far more than she would ever make over her tenure working in the Loop. More than the price of college. More than a hundred round-trip flights to Seoul. The cost was so astronomical that it carried the illusion of fantasy.

"When you return, you'll be a legitimate citizen of the Floating City," Damien said. "Not just an employee. And your mother will have a path to citizenship through you."

Rose looked at the pile of ash on the table. She suspected that Damien already knew this wasn't even a decision. Gaining citizenship to the Floating City meant that she would never have to worry about the rising sea level again, never stare at the Atlantic and wonder if it would swallow her alive.

"I'll do it," she said.

"Good girl." Damien smiled. "Consider it a cold vacation."

CHAPTER TEN

ROSE

Since visiting the prototype, Meyer has dropped by Rose's room every night, often drunk and listless. She's done her best to cheer him up by letting him win at cards, pouring him glasses of whiskey, watching him pace back and forth like a caged tiger in her room. Sometimes he collapses on her bed, unzips his pants, grunts into her hair, and calls her by the pseudonym he still thinks is her real name; but most evenings he falls asleep with his boots on, and she spends the rest of the night thinking of the Barber. Is he down in the church, sleeping on a cold, hard pew? Or is he drinking at the Diggers' camp, playing cards to pass the time? Neither, she hopes. She likes to imagine him outside the mall, trudging through the snow past her room to see if the lamp is lit in her window. But it never is. Not as long as Meyer snores by her side.

Tonight, the wind lashes against the aluminum siding of the mall.

"Heavy snow this evening," Judith says to the Blooms as they eat their allotted mashed potato and slab of pink ham. "Your clients will not be visiting tonight." She brightens for a moment, and then says, "So, we're going on a field trip. I want each of you to grab a garbage bag and follow me."

Judith leads the Blooms through the mall to a fast fashion store at the far end of the food court. She uses a crowbar to jimmy open the sliding metal door.

Willow walks in first and uses a flashlight to find the power console for the lights. She flicks on a switch, and bright light flickers on overhead. The walls are neon pink, with faded posters of young models sitting cross-legged on the beach, squinting into the sun. They wear crop tops and low-rise jeans, chunky silver jewelry and baby barrettes, kicking out their white sneakers, or reaching their brightly manicured nails up to the blue sky.

"Help yourself, girls," Judith says. "If we don't take it, someone else will."

Stacks of neatly folded jeans line the low tables, and the clothing racks are filled with patterned hoodies, slinky tank tops, shift dresses, and miniskirts. Everything is coated in a layer of dust. Jasmine starts unbuttoning a denim jacket off a white faceless mannequin, while Violet rummages through the clear plastic bins in the checkout line. She finds five-packs of ankle socks and cotton underwear, swatches of eye shadow and pots of pearly lip gloss. Fleur starts picking through the denim and holds up a pair of slouchy jeans to her waist before stuffing them into her garbage bag. Iris joins her, and soon the two Blooms have sorted through the clothes into two piles—sequined crop tops, neon leggings, and dresses for work; and thick socks, thermal underwear, and outerwear for their daily walks outside.

Willow turns on the speaker system, and the store fills with sugary pop music. Rose watches from the entrance while the dogs trot through the store, sniffing for whatever the store smells of. Violet and Jasmine take turns trying on clothes in front of a full-length mirror, while Iris rifles through the cosmetics with Fleur. They sample lipstick colors on the inside of their wrists. Rose wants to join in and be free and loose with the Blooms, but she's made uneasy by the thought of who was last here, and why this has all been left behind.

Judith walks up to Rose. "Don't see anything you need?"

"Are you sure it's okay we're here?" Rose asks.

"Of course it is," Judith says. "You don't know how lucky we are to find an untouched store. It must have been overlooked somehow."

"How did you find it, then?"

"It's my job to know what this mall holds." Judith pushes Rose gently. "Go on, Rose. You've been so serious since you arrived in camp. Have some fun for once."

Rose goes to the back of the store, into the storage area where Willow is sorting through unopened boxes of stock. The room reeks of wet cardboard and rot, tinged with the animal scent of the eyeless rodent Willow pulls out of a box of polyester turtlenecks.

"Judith banished me back here," Rose says.

Willow laughs and hands her a box cutter. "Dig in."

Rose starts slicing open boxes while Willow reads the shipping labels aloud, "Vietnam. Sri Lanka. China." Willow calls out, "Have you ever been to China?"

"Never. This is my first time outside the US. Have you?"

Willow shakes her head. "No. I've never been outside of the region. But I plan to go somewhere after camp."

"Do you know where?"

"Somewhere hot. I want to feel the heat on my skin."

Rose stops slicing open a cardboard box. "Don't say that. People are literally dying from the heat. Do you know how many people want to be in the North?"

"I'm sick of everyone telling me that," Willow snaps. "Why can't I decide for myself where I'll go?"

"You're in a foul mood," Rose says. "What's going on with you?"

Willow opens a box of clothing and dumps it on the ground. "I'm just so tired of this." She gestures at the pile of hot-pink tank tops. "Digging through piles of garbage in search of a treasure. It's fucking depressing." She slumps down on the clothing and lights a cigarette from a pack she fishes out of her canvas jacket.

"We'll be out of here soon," Rose says. "And then you can head south if you really want to."

Willow doesn't say anything, and continues to sulk and smoke. Rose keeps working and pulls open a box of high-necked minidresses manufactured in India, shipped to this store during the micro-season before the oil market crashed. She puts a dress in a garbage bag and then looks up when she hears a rustling in the ceiling.

A pair of doves are nesting high on a storage shelf. She pauses to appreciate how the birds' heads are tucked into each other for warmth. And then she sees it, a spray-painted message on the ceiling:

WHITE ALICE IS HERE

The name is chilling in its simplicity. *White Alice*. Prim and melancholic, like the name of a girl with glossy hair who rides dressage through the moors of her father's estate.

"What is that?" she asks Willow, and points to the ceiling.

Willow stands and looks up at the ceiling. "It's still here. After all these years."

"What is?"

Willow stamps out the cigarette and turns to Rose. "When I was a kid, White Alice was a story parents told to keep kids from misbehaving. You better watch out or White Alice will come and get you, that kind of thing."

"If White Alice is a story, then who wrote that?"

"Drunk teens. Oil workers who were pissed they'd lost their jobs. When Dominion Lake emptied out, people would break into this mall and scavenge for supplies. By then, White Alice had become a myth, something people could blame for their problems."

"Did you believe it?"

"No," Willow says. "I was raised to never believe in ghost stories."

Rose hears Judith calling their names, and quickly fills her bag with a few more dresses. Before she leaves, she looks up at the ceiling one last time.

When Rose and Willow join the other Blooms at the front of the store, Judith is saying, "Good work, girls. Let's head back home and admire our haul."

After Rose returns from the mall, she goes to her room and looks out her window to see the wind has calmed. She waits an hour, and then opens the curtains and places the black-lace lamp in the window, hoping that tonight the Barber will finally stop by.

She reads one of Meyer's books in bed to pass the time.

Some say the Zero is a tool of absence. Erasure. The nil. The pit. The gaping chasm of nothing. But I would argue that the Zero is also the first. The first number. The first phase. The first step to harness the power of the negative and imagine a different existence. The Zero shows us redemption can be found in the ashes of what we have burned.

She feels restless and sets down the book to look at herself in the vanity mirror. Her skin is sallow, with dark circles under her eyes, and no amount of blush can bring the red to her cheeks. She's noticed the same in the other Blooms as well, the physical evidence of living in camp. It's not just the lack of sun or exercise or a proper diet. It's the feeling that the world continues to spin while they remain encased in ice.

After Judith's final patrol fades down the hallway, she hears a soft knock on the window. The Barber stands outside in the knee-deep snow, holding a kerosene lantern in one gloved hand. She slides open the window quickly. He hauls himself into her room, and the sweet sight of him makes her want to see him awash in sunlight, barefoot in the sand.

He dusts the snow off his boots and unbuttons his jacket. Underneath his peacoat, he's dressed handsomely in a white cotton shirt tucked into wool slacks. She feels her heart lift when he looks at her.

"I came by whenever I could to see if your light was on," he says, "but Meyer was always here."

"I know, he's been extra needy these past few weeks since he took me out to the prototype."

The Barber sits down on the edge of the bed and lights a cigarette. "So, he finally showed you. What do you think?"

"It's incomplete, but he says that he's not going to leave after it's done. I think he wants me to stay here with him."

He passes the cigarette to her and looks at her steadily. "Is that what you want?"

It takes her a moment to respond. "No, not with him. I want a place to call my own. Without feeling like I owe a favor. When I go back to the Floating City, I'll finally have that. My first home."

Something flickers over his face. "I envy you, Rose. You can see the future."

"And you can't?"

"My life ended the moment I left this town."

"Have you ever thought of moving out east?" She adds lightly, "There's lots of work in the Floating City."

He ashes the cigarette into the empty glass Meyer left on the nightstand. "Don't you need a visa to work there?"

"You do, but I'm going to become a citizen when I return." She tries to keep her voice casual, as if citizenship in the Floating City is as direct as walking in a straight line, when she knows it requires an act of God, or better yet, a well-connected and powerful client.

"What do you get when you're a citizen?" he asks.

"Protection from the elements, my Madam used to say. She meant clean air, green space, low taxes, but for me it's really about having a place to live. It's beautiful, too, floating on the ocean. You can look at the horizon and forget the mainland is right there."

"But it is right there, isn't it? All those people, trying to survive."

"Yes, of course they're still there. I was born on the mainland, so I know what that life is like. I just want something better."

"Don't we all? But all we do is run away. Create our own fiefdoms. Our own colonies. Cut a piece of the earth and call it our own."

She turns away from him. "You have no idea what I've gone through for this opportunity."

"I'm sorry, Rose. It's just that I've spent my entire life living as an outsider because I was misled to think it was the only way to survive. But is a place like the Floating City really the answer?"

She feels her anger soften. "I don't know," she says, "but it's the only option I have right now."

He reaches for her. They're so close now that she can smell the smoke in his hair. "Can I take you out one night? Away from here?"

"Like on a date?"

"We can call it that."

A date. The innocence of the word charms her. "But how?"

"Well, I happen to know Judith will be away next Friday night. I can pick you up and we'll head out from there?"

"I'd love to."

"Good." He smiles. "Meet me in the right-hand corner of the parking lot, just after midnight."

"I'll be there," she says, and then adds, "I can't wait."

"Me too." He stands from the bed. "I should go now. Judith is a light sleeper." He turns to her before he opens the window. "Next Friday. Midnight. Meet me by the north boundary of the fence."

She nods and watches him climb back into the night. When he's gone, she leans back on the bed and slowly exhales.

She picks up Meyer's book and continues reading.

Camp Zero is an acknowledgment of what we have done, and what is left. If we finally accept that the end doesn't exist in the faraway curve of another generation, but that it is here, right now, then we can imagine a different path forward.

Meyer is right. The men may run this camp, but the future is still hers to decide.

WHITE ALICE

We were sitting around the dinner table after our daughter had gone to sleep when one of us finally asked the question, "Can we continue pretending that the South does not exist?"

The threat of the future was on our minds. We had just celebrated Aurora's second birthday, a sweet evening spent watching her eat sugared raspberries that the botanist had painstakingly saved for the occasion. Now that she was two years old, she was sloughing off her baby mind and body and embracing the earnest questioning of a young child. Her conception of the world would be shaped by what we created. A room. A station. A military outpost marooned on a piece of frozen land. Yes, this could be her conception of reality. A safe space. A separate space. A place where she would be protected and loved and taken care of.

But how would we prepare her for the rest of the world?

Sometimes at night, when we drifted off to sleep, we remembered things from our past lives with a claustrophobic intensity:

- the desert sun as it sank pink and fat below the dusty shoulders of a mountain range
- dancing in a dark, crowded bar, a sweating beer in one hand, something loud and bass-y thumping on the speakers

- a painting in a museum of a woman's back that looked like she was carved out of marble
- sitting in a subway car, hurtling through a dark tunnel while millions of strangers walked aboveground
- the taste of chilis and citrus
- chocolate ice cream
- our mothers' faces, cast in morning light

The visitations from our past lives came to us at night. We could see that sun, hear that bass, taste that heat, and we would close our eyes tighter, hoping the images would stay a moment longer before burning away.

"What if we take Aurora south," the cartographer asked one night, "when she's old enough?"

Her question, while casually phrased, held a line of intensity through it. We had all thought it already—what would happen when our daughter reached puberty? Would we be able to justify keeping her with us when she noticed her body and desires changing?

Sal looked down at the table for a moment and breathed deeply before looking back up at us. "I didn't want to burden you with this unless I thought it was absolutely necessary."

We leaned forward, and there, at the table, she finally told us about her son.

One night, after working late, she came home to find her apartment dark. She unlocked the front door and flicked on the lights in the hall and called out to her husband. After hearing no response, she rushed to her son's bedroom to find his crib empty. She frantically searched every room in the apartment, but neither her husband nor her son could be found.

The call from the hospital simply stated that her husband and son had been admitted to the ER. When she arrived at the hospital, her husband was, in fact, sitting in the waiting room with a bandaged cut on his forehead. She rushed over to him, but she immediately knew something was wrong when he wouldn't look her in the eyes.

The report later stated that her husband had been drinking heavily and had run out of milk for their son's bottle. He was drunk enough to justify that it was acceptable to take their baby in the back of the car and drive to the grocery store. It was a short drive, he reasoned, and the baby wouldn't go to sleep without a warm bottle. It was dark and rainy, and he misjudged a left turn onto a side street and collided into oncoming traffic. A truck T-boned the car. Both the truck's driver and her husband climbed out of the wreckage unscathed, but the back of the car was totaled.

Her husband was a well-respected lawyer who defended affluent criminals on trial for tax evasion. During the trial, he adamantly denied responsibility for his son's death, and said that Sal was to blame for working late, yet again, and not leaving enough milk at home. Like his clients, he too was white, wealthy, and without a criminal record. He donated to charities, attended fundraising galas for well-liked senators, kept in shape by running half-marathons for medical research. He was handsome and educated and had developed a reputation as a methodical and clear thinker. Most crucially, he had attended law school at Walden, where many of the judges who sat on local and state courts were also Walden alumni. The favor of the system was his, he reasoned, and if he could prove that this had been a momentary lapse of judgment driven by a neglectful wife, then perhaps he would be spared the Box.

It turned out, the Box was the furthest punishment from the jury's verdict. As he suspected, his sympathetic face worked in his favor, particularly in contrast with Sal. The defense portrayed Sal as a negligent mother whose commitment to her job superseded her love of her family. Why else did she work such late nights and neglect to leave enough milk for her son? Why else had she driven her husband to drink? The defense argued that her husband feared that if she came home from work and found the baby still awake, she'd explode with anger at him and their child. What he did was merely a coping mechanism.

All of this was bullshit, of course. She had been the one who worked a series of temp jobs to pay the bills while her husband attended law school. And she had been the one who cared for their son during the first year of his life, watching her husband's career grow and evolve, while she re-mained stalled in place. But the jury didn't see this. All they saw was her rage. During Sal's testimony, she often deviated from the line of question-ing and spat epithets of hate at him. The electric shock she received when her son died had rewired her brain and her heart. Now she was aflame, and she didn't give a fuck whether she followed the script or not.

"When we were first married, I never suspected he was capable of such neglect," Sal said. "He seemed good, upright, even moral. He was gentle with animals and never raised his voice or spoke in harsh terms. And yet . . ."

Her voice trailed off, but we knew exactly what she was thinking. We knew it so intimately that we felt it in our bodies, our bones.

"You see," Sal said, "his face was his alibi. He was sentenced to man-slaughter and received a ten-year prison term with mandatory mental re-habilitation. Next year he'll walk free. Do you understand now why that world can never be redeemed?"

That night, during our evening drills, the rivulets of sweat that slicked our bodies felt like a baptism. We ran around the radar and looked up at the greenish haze of the northern lights that seemed to pulse with an alien premonition. At that precise moment, men had set their sights on other planets, hurling satellites into the reaches of space, scanning for their next destination to conquer.

Sal was right.

Even the vastness of the universe was still governed by the will of men.

CHAPTER ELEVEN

ROSE

At midnight, Rose walks down the hallway past the Blooms' silent rooms, carrying her parka and boots. The doorways are dark. Everyone is asleep, but still she treads lightly through the hallway. A single misstep could send the dogs streaking after her.

At the front door of the mall, she quickly pulls on her winter clothes, then pauses. It's not too late to slink back to her cold, dark room, spend the night rereading one of Meyer's books, fall asleep and dream of packing her suitcase with the meager possessions plucked from Damien's suite in the Loop. Staying in line and finishing the job she is being paid to do.

"I'll be back as soon as I can," she had told her mother. They were sitting side-by-side on her cot in the Dispossession Estates. The next day, Rose would leave for camp.

"Don't worry about me," her mother had said. "I'll be fine." She touched Rose's cheek with the back of her hand. "A mother should worry about her daughter, not the other way around."

"I know." Rose tried to smile. "I want you to have what you deserve."

"I have you. That's all I need. So try to take care of yourself," her mother said. "You only have this one life."

She thinks of her mother's words now as she steps outside the building. This one life. It takes a moment for her eyes to adjust as the outdoors fuzz into focus. It's a clear night. The moon is full and streaks the snowy lot with its cold blue light, allowing her to hazily divine the dark hedge of trees.

When she reaches the north boundary of the lot, the Barber is already waiting. He doesn't speak as he shows her where to shimmy through the narrow opening in the metal fence. On the other side, he takes her hand and leads her through the trees. When they arrive at a black snowmobile parked behind a dumpster, he finally asks, "You sure about this?"

She can feel her heart thrumming in her chest as she slides onto the seat behind him. "Yes. Let's go."

He starts the snowmobile, and it picks up speed as they weave in and out of the trees. The Millennium shrinks in the distance. She presses her cheek against his wool coat as the wind whips past their bodies. The wilderness streaks by her, the wind howling in her ears.

They drive for half an hour before the Barber turns onto a road barred by a wooden fence. He jumps off the snowmobile to unlatch the gate, moving with exaggerated steps in the deep snow, working quickly to tether the fence open. In the headlights, Rose can see his breath form soft white billows. His fingers fumble with the kerosene lamp until it glows yellow. He holds the lamp up and guides her through the snow to the front door of a small wooden house.

The house is a modest structure, with wooden walls and wide plank floors. It's at least a hundred years old, judging by the antique floral wallpaper peeling in the hallway. A well-worn rug lies in the foyer, and the air smells like the Barber: spruce, kindling, and smoke.

The Barber seems more at ease in this house than he did in the church. He takes off his jacket and hangs it on a peg. He's dressed formally this evening in a soft button-up shirt and a pair of suspenders. "I'll start a fire," he says, and brushes past her, so close that she can feel the coldness of the outdoors seep off his body.

She looks around the house as he tends to the fireplace in the front room. The hall is sparely decorated except for a group of framed photos on the wall, illuminated by the soft light of the lamp. The oldest image is a black-and-white photo of a family of twelve, posed around a wooden plow in a field. The men stand stiffly in coveralls with their hair matted to one side, their unsmiling sisters or wives sitting in the long grass with their hands folded over blotchy aprons, while the children cluster around.

She tracks the photos down the hallway as each generation morphs sharply into the next. Here the family wears horn-rimmed glasses and hoop skirts, grinning as they pose in front of a wing-tipped station wagon. Here the family wears bell-bottoms and crocheted shawls, their hair long and parted in the middle, the youngest mischievously flashing the peace sign. Here the family is in neon parkas, perched on snowmobiles, the expanse of the frosted forest behind them. A clear lineage. A family intact.

The only portrait that she's seen of her family was taken the month before her father drowned. In the photo, she is held by her mother as her father looms half a foot above them, grinning lopsidedly with one arm thrown over her mother's slender shoulders. Her mother looks shy, even nervous, her hair is pulled back into a ponytail, and she is wearing an ill-fitting paisley blouse with a Peter Pan collar, scavenged from her mother-in-law's attic. Her father wears a rumpled shirt with a grease stain on the breast pocket. His face is pure bliss. *Here is my wife and child. Here is what I have created.*

"You have your father's height," her mother often said, "but your face is mine."

It's true that she has her mother's black hair and coppery skin, her downturned mouth and sparse eyebrows, but the portrait proves that her eyes are her father's—a light hazel that burns orange in the sun.

Looking at the photos on the wall, Rose feels herself fracturing. She has no sense of her family's history, her mother's birth country, the language and culture that she never felt the right to claim as her own. Home existed within the boundary of her mother. When Rose is away from her, she feels rootless and free. But she also feels unbalanced, as if she can never find her true center.

The final photo in the hallway is the family at its most compact: a father, a mother, a boy. She recognizes the features that have repeated through the decades—a strong nose, wide-set eyes, and a flop of dark hair. The boy's features are the most pronounced. "It's you," she realizes with satisfaction. "This is you."

The Barber illuminates the boy's face with the lamp. "I was wondering if you'd notice. That was taken a day after my tenth birthday."

She looks around the hallway. "Is this the house you grew up in?"

"It is," he says, "but no one has lived here for a long time." He presses his finger against the face of the woman in the photo, who holds the boy's hand. "My mom's hands were always warm, even in the middle of winter." He pauses for a moment, and Rose can tell a memory is washing over him, a remnant long buried in the dirt. He touches her wrist gently and says, "I'll get us some drinks."

The Barber leads her down the hallway to the back of the house. The kitchen is neat and tidy, brightly painted in yellow with faded gingham curtains in the windows. The wooden floor has been covered with lino-leum, thinned and faded by the sink.

She watches him as he works, liking the care he takes as he unwraps a loaf of bread bundled in cloth and uncorks a bottle of whiskey. He hums a little as he cleans two glasses and pours an inch of whiskey into each. After, he cuts two thick slices of bread, and serves them on a wooden plat-ter with a hunk of cheese and slices of cured sausage.

They take the whiskey and food to the front parlor, a sparse room scrubbed clean, with lace curtains in the window. The Barber gestures for Rose to sit in one of the coral velvet armchairs. The smoke and crackle of the fire is warm and pleasing.

"My parents ate their meals in front of this fireplace," the Barber says, and sits down in the other armchair. "So that's why I prefer to sit here whenever I visit the house. In respect to how they lived out their last happy days."

He tells her that his parents had been born in Dominion Lake, as had his grandparents and great-grandparents, stretching back to the first set-tlers who moved north when news of the oil strike spread. He was raised to believe his life would extend forward in such a manner that he too would work on the rigs, making enough money to buy his own house and yard big enough to throw a few kids into. His children would grow older and eventually take his place out on the rigs, drilling the bounty they believed would never end. Decades and decades stretched forward, all bound together by oil, and his father promised him that his own children would receive all that lay under the soil. This was the lie he had been taught to believe by his father, who had been taught by his own father. Never question what you are born to do. Just keep your head down and work hard.

He was twelve when the oil ban was mandated. By sixteen, everyone he knew had been laid off from work, their houses foreclosed. He was too young to understand the politics of what made people lose their jobs and their homes. All he knew was that people were leaving Dominion Lake, especially anyone under the age of forty. The town's population had been halved and halved again, reflected in the customers who shopped for their groceries. No longer were they young riggers buying lotto tickets and a two-six of vodka with a hundred-dollar bill. Now the shoppers were elderly and feeble, plunking a loaf of white bread and a can of tuna on the conveyor belt. They, too, would soon be dead, and there would be nothing left in Dominion Lake. At eighteen, he decided to leave town.

It was only after he left Dominion Lake that he reflected more on what really happened. How his country had been created by taking from the land and the Indigenous peoples who lived there. That this desire for dominion was what established the colony as a fur-trading post, what later brought industry to its borders and powered the economy. A cold, sparsely populated country with the longest border on earth, rich with minerals, timber, and oil.

"I was wrong to think of myself as an outsider, as somehow different or better than my family," the Barber says. "My family has always profited off of the land's exploitation, and I have too. We needed energy, food, a plot of land to make a home. And we did what we needed to get it. Still, I was surprised when Meyer set up camp. Why would Americans want to come up here now? It's only since working in camp I've realized that he's just repeating what's already happened. He wants to make this place his own."

The Barber is only partially correct, but it's still too risky for Rose to tell him what the camp is really for. Instead, she looks around the room and asks, "How does it feel to be here now?"

"Eerie," he says. "Like I've stepped back in time, but no one is around to remind me why I left."

The fire spits red embers threatening to burn out. The Barber unsheathes the small hatchet attached to his leather belt and splits a branch of white birch for kindling. He tosses the pieces into the fire. They watch the flames catch the splintered wood. "Have you ever felt like the life you're living isn't yours?"

His question takes her by surprise. "What do you mean?"

"That what you're doing feels preordained."

She thinks for a moment. "No," she says. "Not exactly. But I do wonder if I'll ever get what I want."

He looks over at her. "What do you want?"

Whenever a client asked her this question, she usually responded with an answer that would please him—that she wanted new experiences and to meet interesting people like him. Whenever a hostess asked her, she said she wanted money and shelter. But the Barber isn't asking her *what* she desires. He's asking her to describe the shape of her desire.

What does it mean that she has forsaken love for so long? That she rejected it before it even arrived? She had sensed, once or twice, that a client was in love with her, or had decided that he wanted to be. The client felt that love was as simple as stating it. And if it wasn't so, then money and champagne and cold fruit platters and soiled sheets would create it. That love was an arrangement that could be crafted and planned, right down to the way one feels when they see their beloved walk into a room. That quickening of the pulse. A feeling of being outside of one's body. The room recedes and there is only that radiating person.

This is probably why her relationship with Damien worked so well. There were no expectations of love between them. At first, she thought he avoided love because he wanted to avoid despair. A messy breakup. A punitive divorce. But now, she realizes he wasn't so sentimental. He was calculating. Damien viewed love as a commodity, and if he didn't love anyone, then nothing could be taken from him.

"I want to love in return," she says. She feels her face flush with the unadorned truth of her admission. It sounds so quotidian. So obvious.

The Barber's voice softens. "But how can anyone love in a place like this?"

She stands and walks to the window to look out at the snowy field. In the window's reflection, she can see him looking at her. For a moment, his face looks like the boy in the photo. Soft. Searching.

"Because we have no other choice." She turns to him. "This is where we are." She reaches for his hand and says, "Show me upstairs."

———————

The second floor is a converted attic with a slanted roof and two tiny bedrooms separated by a narrow hallway. The Barber has to stoop through the doorframe to enter one of the rooms, a marine-blue bedroom with a hand-painted border of anchors, sloppily and lovingly created for a child far from the sea. With its porthole windows and slanted plank floors, the room feels like a ship moored on land. The Barber lights the candles in the room, sparely furnished with a single brass bed covered in a faded blue crocheted quilt, and a side table.

When Rose first met a new client in the Loop, she'd sit in one of the egg-shaped chairs in the far corner of the suite with her legs tucked under her. She liked the perspective of watching the client walk toward her, seeing how he held his body, how he moved, whether he seemed nervous or at ease. The way a man walked into a room told her everything she needed to know about who he was and what he wanted.

Here, in the bedroom, the Barber sits on the edge of the bed, and it is Rose who walks toward him. She stands over him and kisses him on one temple, then the other. He pulls her onto his lap as she slides each suspender off his shoulders. He leans back and keeps his eyes on her as she undresses him slowly and with great care. First the soft button-up shirt that reveals the curl of tattoos on his chest, then the tailored slacks, which he kicks to the floor. The cotton boxers come off next, and finally his long wool socks. When he is completely naked, he crawls into the bed. She undresses quickly and without any ceremony. All she wants is to feel his warm skin against hers.

Under the sudden coolness of the sheets, Rose feels her mind shearing from her body. She doesn't care that they've pushed the blanket off the bed and knocked the framed print of a gray whale off-center. She doesn't hear the branches of a tree rake the window, or the kitchen door slam open and shut with the wind. All she feels is the Barber, his voice low and loose when he tells her how good she feels. She pins him to the bed and buries her face in his neck, breathing in his scent of smoke and pine. He cries out her given name, *Rose.*

After, she sits up on the edge of the bed and pins her hair into a loose bun.

The Barber reaches for her and runs a finger down her spine.

"I'll remember this as an old man," he says.

She turns to him, fixing him in her memory, too—one arm folded over his head, a cigarette dangling between his fingers, looking at her with a word tattooed in cursive above his left nipple. She'll take this memory of him with her and return to it again and again in the future, until it is soft and shimmering at the edges. She places a hand on his heart. "Genesis?" she asks, reading the tattoo.

"The beginning of the world," he says, and taps the tattoo. "But I'm going to get it removed when I leave camp."

"Why?" she asks. "I like it."

"I want a different beginning than the one I took." He tugs at a strand of her hair that's fallen over her eye. "Don't you?"

She thinks about his question before responding. "I never thought of my life like that."

"Like what?"

"A road you can choose."

"Then choose me." He kisses her gently on the shoulder. "Stay here with me tonight."

"You know I can't."

"Forget about Meyer for once. Give me a chance, Rose."

She imagines the simple act of waking up before him with the sun filtering through the curtains. Turning over to see him caught in a dream of his own making as he reaches for her. It's an image so unassuming, but it still stuns her with its possibility. Maybe true love requires risk. A reckoning with the unknown.

"I want to sleep a full night with you," she says.

He runs a finger down her arm. "And I want to wake up next to you."

She smiles. "I'll stay."

"You're serious?"

"Yes. I just have to be back early before anyone wakes up."

He kisses her again. "That's no problem. I'm an early riser." He pulls her under the sheets, and she curls up with her head on his shoulder, her hand resting on his chest.

Genesis. A new beginning.

WHITE ALICE

Our next delivery from home base was the month after Aurora's second birthday. We set the date firmly in our minds and marked it on the calendar we kept in the communications room. In preparation, we told Aurora a story about a gigantic black dragonfly that had the power to create magical properties in the air. It could create anything it wanted—even another machine.

"Panda?" Aurora asked.

"It won't bring us a panda," we said, stroking her hair and kissing her on the cheeks. "The black dragonfly will only bring us what we need."

What we needed was oil. And lots of it. The generator had recently started to act erratic, like an irrational man, prone to fits and temperamental broodings. It demanded that we tread lightly and keep its oil supply steady. Every day we fed our depleting stockpile of oil into the generator's belly and looked up at the empty sky in the hopes that we might discern the helicopter's presence.

But the day of the black dragonfly's arrival came and went. As did the next day, and the next. The programmer sent a series of alarmed and increasingly agitated messages requesting confirmation of our delivery. One evening, she finally received a response.

"A tariff war between Canada and the US has compromised the supply chain," the programmer said. "American aircraft are now barred from entering Canadian airspace. Home base says they'll try to send supplies from Alaska, but that we are on our own for now."

"For how long?" Sal asked.

"They didn't give a timeline, just that we should do whatever it takes to survive."

The lack of direction in the message deeply troubled us. We requested further clarification but received none.

After one month without a response, the engineer confirmed that she had tapped open the last barrel of oil. Sal called an emergency meeting in the kitchen when our daughter had gone to sleep.

"We're fools to have trusted the General," the meteorologist said. "Home base has abandoned us."

"We don't know that for sure," the geographer suggested. "I think we should just sit tight and ride this out."

"No, we've been manipulated. We're on our own out here," the programmer replied.

We argued back and forth on what could justify the delay. Half of us believed there was an acceptable reason, while the other half felt it was intentional and sinister.

Sal was uncharacteristically quiet. The cartographer turned to her and asked, "What do you think?"

She paused for a long time before answering. "I honestly don't know. I vouched for the General, but the lack of communication from home base is alarming." We could hear the pain in her voice. She turned to the engineer. "How much oil do we have left?"

"A week's worth," the engineer said.

Sal nodded. "We have to act now."

We all knew it was too dangerous for our entire squad to leave the station with Aurora. Sal proposed that half of us should caravan down to Dominion Lake, retrieve oil and supplies, and make the return journey to White Alice. The other half would remain in the station with our daughter.

We took a vote and agreed that the botanist and the biologist should stay behind in the station to tend to the greenhouse and Aurora, while the programmer and the meteorologist maintained the communications room in case home base made contact. The cartographer, the geographer, the engineer, and Sal would set off for Dominion Lake the next day. We didn't discuss how risky it was to send the engineer on the mission instead of keeping her in the station with the generator. Instead, we preferred to think that sending the engineer south was a promise to the members of White Alice who remained: we would not fail.

That night, we sat for a long time in the dark to preserve energy, holding each other's hands around the kitchen table. Something passed between us this way—an electricity, a vibration, an awareness of the tick of the others' pulses. We closed our eyes and breathed together as one.

Before the four left, we each took a turn holding Aurora. She still believed that an insect machine would arrive. We couldn't bear to tell her that it might not, so we told her a story about a girl who could walk on ice and survive even in the coldest of winters. She listened carefully, tucked cozily into her bed in the library.

"About me?" Aurora asked before she drifted off to sleep.

We kissed her on the forehead.

"Stories are about everything," we said, weaving a false note of happiness in our voices.

CHAPTER TWELVE

ROSE

Snow drifts on the Blooms' shoulders and hoods as they make tracks in the parking lot after breakfast. It's a gentle snow, more snow globe than squall, and Rose appreciates how the camp looks when all the buildings are frosted with soft piles of white.

She walks by herself along the fence and watches the Diggers load building materials into an idling van on their way to Meyer's site. Over the past few weeks, Meyer has been working overtime, and has only stopped by the Millennium twice to see her. When he does visit, he's exhausted and excited, speaking in rapid-fire about how much better the building effort is going now, and that he feels confident the prototype will be completed very soon.

Every evening that Meyer doesn't appear, Rose has turned on the lamp in her window. Within an hour, the Barber usually stops by and hauls himself into her room to be with her. They've tried to keep their time together brief—a stolen half hour as they lose themselves in each other. Occasionally, their conversation lingers afterward, and they speak softly until late into the night.

She learns that the Barber is allergic to broccoli, and that he once saw a man lose a finger during an axe-throwing competition in the back of a bar called The Spur. That he'd been a decent student in school but didn't graduate because he had to work to help his mother with the bills when his father died. That he wants to open his own barbershop one day in a place where the cost of living is affordable enough that he can charge on a sliding scale. That he misses his mother and wishes he had said goodbye to her properly before leaving Dominion Lake behind.

The precision of his memory impresses her, and she wonders if it's because he was never implanted with a Flick. As she listens, she finds her own memories surface like flotsam riding along the edge of a wave. She tells him about the way the wind felt in her hair when she walked through the dunes, and how her mother would bring her breakfast in bed on her birthday. How she used to wonder what her father sounded like when he laughed, and when she read his paperbacks, she often imagined that he was reading aloud to her.

She tells him nothing about Damien, or the camp's true purpose, or what her work here is really for. She senses that he is withholding something from her, too, but she doesn't resent him for it. The elasticity of their intimacy is stretched out in such a way that sometimes she wonders if it is love he feels for her, or if she is merely offering him shelter. And perhaps there can be no other way, as the light of the hallway illuminates the frame of her door, and he quickly sneaks out the window into the night.

The van honks once as it drives by Rose and the mall. Through the fence, she sees a Digger looking out the passenger window, like he's staring into a portal to another world.

———

Later that evening, Rose sits on her bed and waits for the hour to turn. It is 8:55 p.m. Meyer never shows up past nine, which means that in five minutes she can put the lamp on in the window.

She looks up when she hears a knock at the door and thinks, *Meyer.*

When she answers the door, she finds the Foreman standing in the doorway.

"Good evening, sweetheart," he says. "Can I come in." It's not phrased as a question, but as a command. Before she can answer, he presses into the room and looks around. "Gloomy in here. I guess that's the way Meyer likes it."

He sits down on her bed and taps the spot next to him. "Come here. I want to talk to you. How are things with Meyer?"

She does so, reluctantly. "Meyer still suspects nothing. I was out with him at the shadow site, and he showed me the prototype he thinks he's working on."

"You're not being straight with me, Rose. I know that Meyer is losing it out here." The Foreman unclips the hunting knife from his belt and unsheathes it on his lap, the blade flashing silver. The knife is elaborately carved with a forest scene: swallows, and deer, and the tiny outlines of children weaving through the thick trees. He carefully places it next to him on the bed between them and says, "Reilly and the others have told me he is acting reckless. Wandering out in the cold without a proper jacket. Drinking alone in his trailer. He stays up all night working on his blueprints and says that the first citizens will be here soon. Did he mention any of this to you?"

"Isn't that what Damien wants? For Meyer to be fixated on his own project?"

"To an extent. But the larger he dreams, the more prone to disappointment and anguish he'll become, and we don't want our famous architect questioning why the supplies for his building project haven't arrived, or why the structural engineers we promised him are delayed once again. No, we want him to be docile. Not enraged. And he's become quite unhinged since arriving in camp. I warned Damien this might happen. Men who aren't used to this climate act out in erratic ways."

"Well, I'll do my best to calm him down. Is the survey complete?"

"It is. We'll be packing up and heading back south sooner than we expected. But I didn't drop by to only talk about Meyer." He picks up a glass with a cigarette butt submerged in an inch of watered-down whiskey off the nightstand. "This is the brand the Barber prefers, isn't it?" He looks into the glass. "Two red stripes around the filter. The Diggers only smoke filterless." He sets the glass down.

"The drink is mine," Rose says firmly. "I found the cigarettes in the gas station in the village."

"The stations have all been pillaged long ago." He waves a hand. "I don't give a shit if you're fucking the pretty boy. Camp nights are long, and lord knows Meyer isn't enough to satisfy any woman. But Damien will not be so open-minded. Gets a bit angry when something of his ends up in the hands of another, doesn't he?"

The Foreman's hand is on her knee now, a slab of flesh with thickets of hair on each finger. He squeezes her leg and leans into her. "Pretty thing," he says, and breathes heavily. "I can see why everyone is so smitten."

She pulls away from him as he grabs hold of her hair. A sharp pain streaks down her scalp. "Just lie back and relax." His breath in his ear. "Your secret is safe with me."

"I'm not working right now." She tries to push him off, but he pins her down.

"This won't take long." He drags her closer to him on the bed and rips the hem of her robe.

"Get the fuck off me." For the first time, she wishes the steady green glow of a surveillance camera was installed in the ceiling. If she were in the Loop, Avalon would have dispatched a battalion of security guards already. But no one is watching her.

"I thought your type like it like this." He clenches her jaw in one hand as his fingers press into her neck.

"I'll scream and report you."

"Who the fuck is going to believe someone like you?"

When she says nothing, he grins.

"That's right, little darling. You know what you're good for." He lets go of her to strip the robe off her body.

Why do men take so easily whatever they want? Because nothing will ever be enough, she realizes. The more a man possesses, the more he thinks he deserves.

The Barber's switchblade is under the mattress where she hid it. She feels for it until her fingers clutch its cool handle. She flicks open the blade and plunges it into the Foreman's stomach.

He yells and rolls off her, gripping one hand to the dark spot as it surges with blood. His other arm blindly reaches for his hunting knife that's fallen off the side of the bed. She kicks his arm, and he yells again, this time grabbing hold of her leg and throwing her onto the floor.

"Stupid cunt." The hunting knife is now in his hand as he looms above her, and he wipes it against the thigh of his fatigues. "I wasn't going to tell you, but Damien never intended for you to return to the Floating City. He told me to get rid of you in camp once the survey is complete. Looks like we're right on schedule."

She thrashes out, but it's no use. His boot is pressed against her cheek. She can taste the dirt of the work site on the boot's cleats, the rich sludge of the earth, the tang of precious minerals. Three round drops of his blood fall on her face.

Just as he edges the blade into the divot of her collarbone, the front door to the room bursts open and Judith runs in. The movement is so swift that the Foreman is momentarily surprised. But a moment is all she needs. Judith wrenches the knife from his hand and slashes it across his throat. The sound is unspeakable, but Rose will remember it for the rest of her life.

It is the sound of one world ending.

And another world begins.

The Foreman's body rests on the kitchen floor as the Blooms stand around him. In the dim fluorescent light, his corpse looks more like an animal than a man. Rivulets of blood stream off his body, forming red pools on the floor. Judith lifts up his arm and drops it. The sound is like a slab of meat slapping a butcher's block.

Judith wipes the blood off the Barber's knife with a cloth, and then examines it. She looks up at Rose and shakes her head. "And I used to pride myself on running a tight ship." She places the knife in her fanny pack. "We'll talk later. For now, someone get a mop." She drapes the bloodied cloth over the Foreman's face.

At first, the Blooms don't move, until Judith says, "He's dead, girls. He can't do anything now."

Fleur finds a mop in the closet in the kitchen and begins to clean up the blood. Violet fills a bucket with water, while Jasmine strips a tea towel into rags. Each Bloom picks up a rag and works in silence, until the trail of blood that leads from Rose's room down the hall to the kitchen is gone.

Rose sits at the kitchen table with a blanket wrapped around her shoulders. Her breath is irregular, and she doesn't speak when Iris sets a cup of tea on the table.

"Drink, darling," Iris says, and places her cool, powdery hand on Rose's face. "I know what you're going through, and you have to believe me that this will pass."

Rose leans her head against the older Bloom's shoulder. She looks at the Foreman's body and a flicker of rage grows in her as she thinks of his last words. Fucking Damien. She was a fool to trust him. And now she's lost all contact with him and, by extension, her mother.

Only Willow seems unshaken. She runs the Foreman's hunting knife under the kitchen faucet and hums as she works. When the water runs clear, she cleans it with a handkerchief and places it back in its leather sheath, and then clips it to her belt. Her back is turned when she speaks to Judith. "What should we do with him?"

Judith pins the Foreman's arms to his body with rope. "We'll get rid of him tonight."

Her hands move with an efficient purposefulness as she ratchets the knot tighter around the Foreman's arms. Judith seems at ease when she works, Rose notes. Confident and in control.

Willow looks over at Rose. "I told you not all men are harmless."

"I already knew he was a risk," Rose says. "In the bathroom during the New Year's party—"

"Yes, I know. Why else do you think I walked in?" Willow turns and looks at the Blooms standing with the bloody rags in their hands and calls out to Judith, "Do you think they'll help us?"

"They already have." Judith's voice softens as she speaks to the Blooms. "I know this must seem horrible to you. But I had no choice." She takes the blood-soaked rags gently from the Blooms and asks them to join Rose at the kitchen table. Willow remains standing at the door as Annie settles at her feet.

After Judith disposes of the rags in the trash, she says, "This was a necessary act." She gestures at the Foreman's corpse with a derisive wave. "This man hurt Rose. And who knows what he would have done to the rest of us once he had a taste of dominion."

Fleur starts to cry, and Iris reaches over to hold her. Jasmine and Violet's eyes are fixed on the table.

"Now," Judith says, "I want you each to hold the others' hands."

The Blooms look at each other, but don't move.

"You can do it," Judith says. "Just reach for your sister."

Fleur places her hand on Iris's, and soon a circle forms around the table, each Bloom clasping the hand of the next. Willow grasps Rose's hand firmly and whispers, "You're going to be all right. We'll take care of you."

Judith smiles. "There. That's better, isn't it?" She walks around the table and touches a hand to each of the Blooms' heads. "Sweet Blooms. Do you know there is a better life than the one you've been condemned to?" Her voice hardens. "Do you know what is happening right now? Men are killing women. Men are beating their wives. Men are paying sums of money to have their way with women, or no sums of money at all. Men are raping. Men are destroying. Men are consolidating power, as they have been since the beginning of time. The biological fact that men are stronger and larger than us was used as a tool for oppression, a way to keep us in the home to carry their brood and genetic line. No." Judith shakes her head. "Not anymore. Those days are finally over. And once you recognize this simple fact, you'll see the potential in life. One dead man is nothing compared to the destruction men have caused to this world." She gestures to the Foreman's body. "His life ended as it began. In a torrent of blood, midwifed by a woman."

Finally, Rose speaks. She steadies her voice. "Why don't we tell Meyer what happened? The Foreman attacked me. Meyer will understand it was an accident."

Judith looks at her sharply. "Will he, Rose? Or will he be angry that his sweet Bloom was hiding a knife in her room? I wouldn't want to see what Meyer's like when he's been crossed. Emancipated men are the most vicious. No. Meyer will believe what benefits him. A dead body in camp will not look good with his investors. We'll be shut down and sent home without pay. You and I will be tried for murder, and the rest of the Blooms as accomplices. But a man wandering out into the freeze after a night of drinking? That is hardly contentious."

Rose asks, "What are you saying?"

"Do as I say, and no one will know what happened. About the Foreman. About any of this. By tomorrow morning, you'll each wake up in your bedrooms and all of this will seem like an unpleasant dream. And next month, we'll be out of here with our contracts paid." Judith looks at each of the Blooms. "Are we all in?"

The Blooms keep their eyes fixed on the table. No one speaks.

Judith gestures at the Foreman. "No one will mourn him." She repeats loudly, "Are we all in?"

This time, the Blooms look up and slowly nod in agreement.

"Good." Judith turns to Willow. "Get a bedsheet."

Willow leaves the kitchen and returns with a floral bedsheet. She drapes it on the Foreman's corpse, so that only his filthy boots are exposed.

"Fleur, can you take a corner?" Judith asks. "That's right. And Iris, you take the other side. We're going to wrap him up nice and tight. That's good, girls. Think of it as wrapping a gift."

It is dark when they leave. Judith drives an orange camper van with tinted windows down the highway, while the Blooms sit crouched by the Foreman's body in the back. Willow is up front in the passenger seat and Rose sits cross-legged on the metal floor. Rose can feel the deadweight of the Foreman's arm against her leg, his cold body pressing against her when the van takes a corner. Fleur has been crying nonstop during the ride. She turns to Iris, who takes her in her arms.

"There, there," Iris says, and strokes Fleur's hair. "We're going to get through this, I promise."

When the van finally stops, the side door rolls open. The van's headlights illuminate the frozen lake.

"All hands on deck," Judith instructs, and tells the Blooms to unwrap the body. Willow walks out onto the ice with a flashlight and a long, serrated saw resting on her shoulder.

Not one of the Blooms move. They stand huddled close together with their arms around each other.

Willow calls out to them from the ice as Judith cuts the rope around the Foreman's body. "She's ready for us. Now, each of you take a limb, and pull."

Rose is the first to move. She grabs hold of the Foreman's cold hand. He is so heavy that it feels like she is pulling a block of ice. He doesn't budge. "I can't do this alone."

"I'm with you," Iris says, and takes the Foreman's other hand. Then Jasmine lifts one of his boots, while Violet takes the other. The last Bloom to join in is Fleur, who grabs hold of his head.

Judith nods. "Good, girls. Now, pull."

They drag the body across the ice until they reach Willow. She stands at the edge of a circle cut out of the ice, shining a flashlight into the dark, rippling water.

"Pretend you're tossing a coin into a fountain," Judith says.

Rose threads her fingers through the Foreman's hand. She can feel the strength of the Blooms as they push the body toward the hole, like a gale gathering force over water.

"On my count," Judith says. "One . . . two . . . three . . ."

Rose can feel her heartbeat in her chest. Yes, right there is where the knot of anger glows. Even out here in the cold, she can feel the heat through her skin, a soft, pulsing wave that reminds her that nothing is right in this world. Or has this tremor of hatred always been there and only grown with time?

She pushes with all her strength. The Foreman's body splashes into the dark water. Willow prods him with the saw until he disappears under the ice.

As the Blooms return to the camper van, the sun is rising over the dark crop of trees, casting orange and pink streaks on the ice. A hawk circles above, and for a moment, Rose imagines them from the perspective of a passing bird.

Seven bodies in formation.

Seven women walking away from a dark hole.

CHAPTER THIRTEEN

GRANT

When Grant walks into the cafeteria for breakfast, the Diggers are huddled together, whispering. They look up when they see him.

"The Foreman hasn't punched in," Wolfe says to Grant.

"Did you check his room?" Grant asks. "He might still be passed out."

"Swifty checked already, and he's nowhere to be found," Wolfe replies.

The Diggers eat their breakfast in silence, until someone suggests that maybe the Foreman headed out to the work site to get a head start. This seems to satisfy them, and by the time they're suiting up for work, their spirits have lifted.

Grant says goodbye and remains at the table, staring into his coffee cup. He should be preparing for the week's class, but his thoughts return again to winning the game and his conversation with Willow. His prize is still waiting, if he'd only work up the guts to cross over. But the moment he thinks this, he feels Jane's skin against his. Her breath in his ear. Jane squinting into the sun, her arm around his neck as she drinks a bottle of beer; Jane reading a paperback on the beach, then wading out into the Atlantic with her jeans hiked up around her beautiful, perfect knees. The quiet, controlled sex they had on a deflated air mattress once while camping, the pancakes they ate for dinner when they wanted to save money.

A dark sadness radiates from his chest, and he closes his eyes.

Don't cry, he thinks.

Don't fucking cry.

He opens his eyes. *Pull yourself together.* A brisk walk is what he needs. A morning to clear his head and think things through.

When Grant steps outside the warehouse, Meyer's black SUV is idling in the parking lot.

Meyer rolls down the passenger window. "Grant, can we talk?"

The last thing Grant wants to do right now is spend an hour with Meyer as he waxes poetic about a spruce tree.

"Can it wait?" Grant points to the highway. "I was just setting out on a walk."

"You shouldn't wander around outside by yourself. It's not safe," Meyer says. "Get in, and I'll explain why."

Seeing that he has no choice, Grant climbs into the passenger seat. The pointer in the backseat groggily lifts her head and opens one eye. When she sees Grant, she snuffles back to sleep. In comparison, Meyer looks like he hasn't slept. He unscrews the cap on his flask and takes a slug before saying, "The Foreman is gone. He wasn't in his bed this morning."

"Did he go back home?"

"No, that's impossible. No one can leave camp on their own. I'll ask the Diggers to keep searching, but I'm afraid the chances of finding him alive are low. It's not uncommon for men to lose their way back to camp if they've been drinking."

"You mean he's dead?" Grant asks in shock.

"Misplaced, Grant. The Foreman has been misplaced. Hopefully we'll find him when the snow melts and we can send his remains back to his family." Meyer takes another slug from the flask. "With our condolences, of course."

"You're being disturbingly calm about all of this."

"I'm being realistic. Besides, one death is nothing compared to what we will achieve here."

"Achieve?" Grant snaps. "There is nothing to achieve here." He's yell-ing, but he doesn't care. "I saw the Diggers' work site and it's a fucking hole. There is no campus. You lied to me, Meyer."

Meyer says nothing and pulls the SUV out of the parking lot. He starts to drive down the highway. "I told you what was necessary to get you here. When I saw your application, I had such high hopes for you. But you've disappointed me."

"You sound like my father," Grant says.

Meyer's tone turns flat. "I am nothing like your father."

The lake is now to their right, cool and blue. The spruce is thicker out here. Meyer parks the SUV in front of a silver Airstream trailer nestled in a copse of woods.

"Where are we?" Grant asks.

Meyer's voice mellows again. "Come inside and we'll share a meal. I need to talk to you about something important." He passes the flask to Grant. "Come on. As a favor."

Grant takes the flask and drinks. The whiskey softens his resolve. "Fine. But I'm not going to stay long."

"That's the spirit!" Meyer claps Grant on the back and leads him into the Airstream trailer. Inside, he gestures for him to sit at the small eat-in kitchen. The dog follows and paws at a cupboard door for food. A single bed with jumbled sheets is on one side of the trailer, next to a large drafting table installed under a small window. The trailer smells of dirty laundry, of meat on the edge of rot.

"How long have you been living here?" Grant asks, taking in the neglect of the trailer.

"A few months. It's not the most ideal habitat, but it's fine for now." He spears a dripping peach from a jar with a knife and then eats it. "You remind me of myself, you know. All those useless virtues. That Walden morality. When I first started working as an architect, I was around your age and thought I could change the world. But that altruism faded as I grew older and saw this world for what it is. What if I told you that I built dwellings for the wealthy? For the privileged minority to live free from catastrophe and misery? Would you be sitting in this trailer right now?"

Grant looks away with irritation. "I'm not sure. Maybe."

"No, you wouldn't, Grant. I know about your books, your supposed radical tendencies, what happened to your pretty, working-class girlfriend. I know it all and I remain sympathetic."

The reference to Jane makes Grant feel ill. He looks at Meyer and says, "You know nothing."

"Look, I shouldn't have to explain this to you. Books and poems and people standing together in protest and lighting the flag on fire doesn't matter one iota when we are dying of thirst, burning from the sun, sinking into the sea. Day Zero approaches us all. For some, it's earlier than others, but it's always there, a looming deadline for when we will expire. It's called death, Grant, and it's the only democratizing force we have left."

"I think it's called inequality," Grant snaps.

"No, no, you're wrong. You're still lost in a rhetoric that has no meaning up here." Meyer slaps the knife onto the table. "I want you to look at these while I prepare us something to eat. Maybe then you'll understand."

While Meyer stirs a pot of beans on the one-burner stove, Grant pages through the stack of blueprints on the drafting board. The blueprints are far more detailed than what the Foreman showed him at the site, sketching the settlement outside the perimeters of camp into the northern reaches of the region.

"This plan is large enough for a small country," Grant says, and looks at an aerial image of a cluster of settlements spread over the vast tundra. He examines the drawing of one settlement that shows each sector nested in a concentric circle. "This reminds me of the Floating City."

"Look closer. You'll see that this is far more ambitious than the Floating City."

In the blueprint, the largest ring is colored the green of the pastures and nature preserve, banded by the blues of the pleasure district. At the heart of the plan, a silver circle glitters.

"What's at the center?" Grant asks.

"The campus," Meyer says. "A monument to learning and knowledge acquisition." He sets two steaming bowls on the table and gestures for

Grant to bring the blueprint over. "What do you think is the biggest failure of the Floating City?"

"The citizens," Grant answers. "With their tech elitism and complete lack of democratic precedent."

"I agree," Meyer says. "The Floating City was initially conceptualized as a place for people from all backgrounds to coexist and forge a new future. But your father felt otherwise. He was the one who told me that the city would only be open to those who could buy their way in."

Grant sets down his spoon. "How do you know my father?"

Meyer's voice suddenly rises in pitch. "Do you really think you're here because of your brilliant thesis? Your father was keen to meet the city's chief architect when Grimley Corp came on as majority stakeholders. He was the one who told me all about his bright, precocious son. It was simple to learn all about you, Grant. Parents are easily flattered."

Grant looks at Meyer for a moment and feels the blood drain from his face. Of course. The chief architect who his father often complained about working with. At the time, Meyer had used his initials as his working name, so Grant hadn't made the connection.

Meyer grins, a rare, unbridled smile that shows off the top row of his cramped teeth. "We've nearly depleted our seed money, and we need to move forward. It will be a significant investment on your father's part, but I'm sure he'll be supportive of whatever project his son is a part of."

"You're on your own, Meyer. I'm leaving camp."

"Oh, so soon? But how do you expect to leave? It's not like you can hop on the next plane out of here."

Grant imagines Willow walking through the snow outside the Millennium with a pit bull by her side. "I'll find my own way out."

"Even your father can't find you here, Grant. The beauty and power of this place is that we've finally disconnected from the outside world." Meyer gestures at Grant's bowl. "Dig in before it gets cold. Our work is just beginning."

WHITE ALICE

The four rode for a full day through treaty territory, only stopping when we reached the tree line that indicated we had finally left the permafrost behind. In the distance, we saw black snowmobiles curve down a frozen road toward a cluster of aluminum-sided houses where the small figures of children played in the snow. The geographer briefed us that the Dene Nation who lived and hunted here had successfully protected their treaty land from the encroaching oil companies by road blockades and court injunctions. We pitched a tent under a scraggly pine on the outskirts of the reserve and ate the tinned meat we had brought with us.

"We'll camp here for the night, and then push on to Dominion Lake," Sal said. "We still have a full day's ride ahead."

We slept only four fitful hours that night in our subzero sleeping bags, knowing that if we slept a minute longer, we ran the risk of frostbite, which had crept into the engineer's left hand while driving the snowmobile. She assured us that she could still work with her right hand if the worst happened.

The worst wasn't the loss of a limb, like we feared, but the feeling of finally seeing Dominion Lake. We climbed a small hill north of the village and saw the modest settlement nestled around the lake. Small bungalows lined the plowed streets, and we could make out the metallic flash of trucks driving down the highway. The scene, in all its banality, broke something inside us. While we had been suffering in the station, racked with the possibility of freezing to death with our daughter, this little town had blithely continued on. It looked wholesome, quaint—*cute*, even, a word we loathed for its diminutive qualities. This nothing place would be our redemption?

"Look over there," Sal said, noticing the smokestacks funneling out of a dark patch of forest on the other side of the lake. We couldn't see where the smoke came from, but we sensed its purpose already. It was a refinery, evidence of the industry that made the region so prosperous.

We rode toward the plume of smoke, curving around the eastern boundary of the frozen lake. The smoke extended as far as we could see, obliterating the sky above it. As we drew closer, we finally smelled it, a rich tang of heat and exhaust. The smell of oil.

The man camp was the first structure we drove through. Hundreds of portable housing structures marked with the crown of Imperium, rectangular in shape, resembling the shipping containers that traveled from east to west delivering goods. The camp was mostly empty, with just a few cleaners and cooks weaving through the portables. The action, we soon learned, was at the site itself.

"Chasm" is a word often used to describe the absence of something. But as we saw the site for the first time, we didn't see a pit, or a ravine, or a crater. We saw the earth cut and torn open, a laceration so deep that it was impossible to see how far it bled. An annihilated species had been threaded through the sediment, layers and layers of prehistoric bones and vegetation now marked with a new utility. Millions of years of decomposition excavated in a dust mote of time.

We got off the snowmobiles and watched the men work. At the bottom of the pit, tiny orange blips of mechanical diggers were excavating the sludge, carving up paths to the dump trucks that lined the lip of the site. The engineer told us that the trucks would drive toward the smoke, to filter and process the bitumen in the refinery.

We didn't follow the trucks, knowing that our presence at the refinery would be unwelcome. We needed the crude in a more refined state, after it had been filtered and reprocessed and packed into barrels. We needed the pump.

The cartographer told us that only one highway existed in the region, running on a north/south direction. Dominion Lake was the last village on the highway, and she was certain we would find a gas station on the outskirts of town.

The EZ Gas was a small, two-pump station with a heated hut where a teenage boy sat staring at his phone. Sal tapped the window and the kid looked up, then opened the window a crack.

"Pumps take cards," he said.

"We don't have cards," Sal said apologetically.

He tapped on the window where a handwritten sign was taped: PAY AT THE PUMP.

We hadn't used a card in years. The last time we'd pulled out our wallets was back in basic training, when we had dinner at the roadside steakhouse before deployment. Home base had not equipped us with cards or Canadian dollars, and we hadn't questioned it at the time. What use did we have for money if there was nowhere to spend it?

"Can you give us an advance?" Sal asked, still smiling. "We just started working on the rigs, and our first payday is next week. We're good for it."

The kid pointed to a smaller sign taped below the larger one: ADVANCES ON PAYDAY CHECKS NOT ACCEPTED. "Sorry," he said, "company rules." He reached for his phone.

Sal slammed a hand against the window. The kid dropped his phone and backed away from the glass. "I'm calling my boss," he said.

"Forget it," Sal said. "We'll figure something out."

She looked at us, and we immediately understood the gravity of our situation. The engineer had estimated that the oil reserve in the station would last one week if rationed. We had just entered our fourth day, and it would take two full days for the return trip. If we didn't find a solution by the time the sun set, there would be no point in returning to White Alice.

Since we left the station, we had tried not to think of Aurora, but our minds finally turned to her as we drove away from the EZ Gas.

What was she doing right now as we tried not to imagine her heartbeat slowing, a dullness clouding her eyes? Does a child freeze to death faster than an adult? Or does their youth allow them to survive longer? We didn't know what was worse: watching her die or knowing she would die without us.

We drove for an hour before we found our first mark. An orange-and-beige camper van with the roof popped up was parked off the side of the road. We could tell that someone was in there by the dim glow behind the paisley curtains.

We hid the snowmobiles behind a stand of trees and followed Sal to the front door.

She knocked lightly. "Hello?"

No answer.

She knocked again, and we eventually heard a man's voice call out. "Be right there!"

The door swung open, and a man with bright eyes and a patchy beard stood there, dressed in stained jeans and a hooded sweatshirt. He was drinking a can of beer and had a half-smoked cigarette stuck behind his ear.

When he saw us, he didn't seem concerned or at all surprised, as if it was perfectly common for four women dressed in military fatigues to be standing at his camper van's door. "You lost?"

We nodded.

"Well, you may as well come in and warm up while you get oriented."

We entered the mayhem of the camper. The heat was cranked to ninety, and we soon saw for good reason. An enormous reptile tank was installed against the side of the camper's wall, with a glossy snake coiled on a bed of dirt.

"Severin's sleeping, but she should be up soon. She hasn't been feeling very good since we arrived in Dominion Lake." He plucked the cigarette out from behind his ear and lit it, while tapping on the glass of the tank. "I keep telling her that she'll feel better once we find work up here, but she hates the snow." He looked at us and shrugged. "That's a snake for you. Prefers their own habitat over one they're forced to endure."

Sal nodded, like she completely understood the challenges of reptiles living in the North. "I used to raise snakes," she lied. "Back when I lived in the Mojave."

"Did you now." The man grinned and settled down on a chair piled with dirty laundry. He pointed to the bed, also covered with laundry, and gestured for us to sit. "Severin would have loved it down there." He finished smoking the cigarette and dropped the butt into the can of beer, setting it under the table.

We sat and watched three white mice run on a rotating hoop in a small glass case on a tiny table. They ran and ran and ran, their red eyes focused on the middle distance. The man opened the top of the case and scooped one up in his hand. It wriggled and squeaked as it tried to squirm free.

"There, there," he said, stroking its quivering belly. His fist contracted and the mouse stopped moving. He opened the snake tank and dropped the white body onto the snake's sleeping form. "Severin won't kill her prey since we've come north, so I have to do the deed for her. I think she's depressed or something." He shook his head sadly.

We looked back at the mouse case and saw that the two remaining mice hadn't reacted in any way to their population being reduced by one-third. They continued to run on the rotating hoop.

"So you're headed out to the rigs, too?" the man asked.

"We are," Sal said brightly, "but we've lost our dog out in the woods."

"She a tracker dog?" the man asked.

"No, she's a mutt. Like Severin, she's not used to the cold, and we're hoping we can find her."

The man shook his head. "Dogs don't do well in the freeze unless they're habituated. How long has she been gone?"

"Just a few minutes before we found you. I'm sure she's close by."

"You might get lucky," the man said, now standing. "We may as well take a look."

Sal nodded. "Is it okay if they stay here and warm up while we go look?"

"Sounds fine. Severin doesn't like to be alone." He looked at us. "If she wakes, try to get her to eat. Poor thing hasn't eaten in days."

We said we would, and watched the man follow Sal out of the camper's door.

When they disappeared into the trees, we started unloading everything in the van. First the laundry, then the empties and cooking supplies, the milk crates filled with bits of scrap metal, then the sour bedding, and the mattress itself. We piled everything in the forest until the van was completely empty. By the time we were hauling out the snake tank, Sal walked back alone.

"I made sure it was quick and painless," she assured us. "He didn't suspect a thing." She surveyed the inside of the now-clean van. "Good work. We're halfway there." All that remained was the mouse house on the ground with the two white mice still running.

"For Aurora," we said. But we knew better. We kept the mice so we could leave with something still alive.

We parked the van and the two snowmobiles in the packed parking lot outside the Millennium Mall and drew straws as to who would complete the second half of our mission. Sal sat the round out, stating that she had already completed her service. The geographer drew the shortest straw and nodded. We escorted her into the mall and found the department store at the back of the building.

First, she stopped by the beauty counters and used a tissue and makeup remover to wipe the grime off her face. Then, she slathered the sweet-smelling creams on her skin, lining her eyelids with dark frost, curling her eyelashes. The transformation was immediate, and to us, hilarious. We laughed when she came back to us, looking like her head had been placed on a different body. She was still wearing her filthy fatigues, and the length of fur she had fashioned into a scarf.

"You look ridiculous," Sal said.

"Fuck you, Sal," the geographer said. "It's not my fault this is what men find attractive."

We followed her, still laughing, when she grabbed a black lace bra and a matching thong from the lingerie section, and then a red micro dress in satin, and a pair of gold heels. But when she came out of the dressing room, we stopped laughing.

"What?" she asked when she saw us. "Is it too much?"

The geographer looked completely and utterly transformed. Gone was the grit and sinew of the woman we knew and loved. In her place stood this specter of beauty. Where had the geographer gone? All we could see was the desire of others doubled over her, shadowing her face, her body, her voice.

"No," Sal said. "It's perfect." She took out a black marker from her jacket and handed it to the geographer. "There's just one last thing. Write our name."

"In the dressing room?" the geographer asked.

"Yes," Sal said. "Write 'White Alice.' I want us to leave our own mark."

The geographer shrugged and scribbled: WHITE ALICE IS HERE

We paid for the clothes with the cash we had scrounged from the camper van, and when we left the mall, we left as two separate entities. No one mistook the dirty trio as being with the beautiful woman who looked like she floated on air.

Our second mark was sitting in the lobby of the nicer of the two hotels in town. When the geographer walked in, he immediately noticed her. He was on a two-day site visit and had flown in the night before. The geographer sat at one of the tables next to him in the hotel bar and ordered a glass of white wine. She smiled at him when he looked over.

"Are you here working?" he asked.

"Yes," she said. "And yourself?"

He nodded and held up his name laminated on a lanyard. "For Imperium. I'm here with Accounts."

"Fascinating," she said, and leaned toward him.

He looked at her and laughed. "It is right now. We're having a hell of a time figuring out what to do about these prices." He rattled on for a few minutes about the astronomical costs in getting the bitumen out of the ground.

The geographer nodded in all the right places and drank her wine.

When he was finished talking, she asked, "Are you interested in tectonic plates?"

"No, not really. Geography wasn't my subject in school. I'm more of a finance guy. Why do you ask?"

"Oh, just checking." She had run out of things to talk to him about, but soon found out that it didn't really matter what she said. As long as she maintained eye contact and occasionally smiled, he kept talking.

And did he ever like to talk. First about the precarity of the oil industry, and how expensive it was getting the bitumen to market in such an extreme climate. And then about real estate prices in his hometown (Dallas? Houston? She didn't quite catch its name) now that interest rates were low, and then about an incredible burger he had during his layover in Minneapolis, and whether it was true that eating more than half a pound of meat in one sitting would exponentially lead to a heart attack.

It went like this for hours—two, to be exact—so that by the time the geographer was finishing off her third glass of wine, she had suddenly reached her limit. She would rather endure most things on earth than continue facilitating this one-sided conversation. Plunge a clogged toilet. Dredge a canal for a murdered body. Walk naked across a frozen lake. Even fuck this man on the flowered acrylic bedspread of his bland hotel room.

It was surprisingly easy to transition from the public space of the lobby bar to the private space of the hotel room. All she had to do was ask him if he wanted to head back to his room, and her meaning was instantly understood. He paid for their bar tab and continued talking all the way up the elevator, down the hallway, until he opened the room's door.

Inside his room, his manner suddenly turned professional, and she could see the finance side of him working.

"So, two hours in the bar, and then the service itself is, what?" He did some quick math in his head.

The figure he offered seemed like an accurate one, but it was nowhere near the amount we needed. "How much do you have in cash?" the geographer asked.

He pulled out his wallet and looked inside. "About that, maybe another thousand." He frowned. "That's quite high for an escort in these parts."

"I'm highly trained," she countered.

"I'm sure you are." He looked at her with renewed interest. "I can pay whatever you want."

"Good," she said. "We have a deal."

After he seemed satisfied, she turned to him in bed and asked if he was hungry. "Let's get a burger," she said in a light tone. "There's a drive-through across the street."

"It's late," he said, his voice already drowsy and near sleep. "Maybe tomorrow."

"No, now." She sat up and flicked on the bedside lamp.

"Okay, okay." He pulled on his clothes and then looked at her. "Kind of worked up an appetite, huh?" He laughed, but this time, she didn't join in.

In the parking lot outside, we were waiting while looking at the clock. The geographer was taking much longer than we had planned, and we knew that we would have to leave by dawn to return to White Alice in time.

When we saw her across the frozen parking lot with the second mark by her side, we felt a swell of relief. She was all right. And, more important, she had been successful.

As they walked past the van, Sal pushed the door open. This was our signal. We pulled the second mark inside the vehicle and clamped a hand over his mouth.

Sal put a gun to his temple and whispered, "Our request is very simple. We will drive you to the closest ATM, and you will withdraw the withdrawal limit. And then we will drive you to the next ATM, and you will do the same. When you are done, we will drop you back here, and you will return to your room safe and sound. That is it."

The second mark thrashed in the van, and Sal unceremoniously clipped him in the temple with the butt of the gun. A line of blood ran down his face.

"Will you do it?" Sal asked again.

The second mark nodded, tears mixing with his blood.

The geographer said, "He'll do it. You can let him speak."

"I have two children," he said in a rush. "Their photos are in my wallet. I need to get home to them."

"So do we," Sal said. She dragged the tip of her gloved finger through the man's blood.

The second mark did exactly as he was instructed and withdrew the maximum amount of cash that he could from the ATMs in town. The cartographer counted the bills and kept them stored in the glove compartment of the van. The amount was enough, she claimed.

After we visited the last ATM, Sal started driving away from the glow of the village.

"Where are we taking him?" the geographer asked.

"Remember what we always said," Sal said. "There can be no contingencies."

Sal had argued when the geographer was in the hotel that even if the second mark promised to keep quiet, we couldn't be 100 percent certain that he wouldn't immediately notify the police that a beige-and-orange camper van had thousands of dollars stored in its glove compartment. And if we bound and abandoned him somewhere while we secured the oil, the possibility of his escape before our getaway was always there.

The only reasonable decision was the simplest.

The sun was rising when we arrived at the frozen lake. We tied his limbs up with bungee cord, gagged his mouth, and put a plastic bag over his head. When we carried him out of the van, we saw that the edges of the lake were still frozen solid. Sal went ahead of us with the ice saw as we slowly dragged him behind us on the ice. When we reached her, she had just finished cutting the ice into a perfect circle.

"On the count of three," she said.

"One . . .

       Two . . .

              Three . . ."

We dropped the body into the hole.

CHAPTER FOURTEEN

GRANT

The Diggers are given two days off from work. One day to bury the Foreman's belongings, the second day to drink his memory away. The entire crew, plus Grant, drive out to a grove of spruce. It's an appropriately grim day for a memorial of a man no one really liked. No wind or snow. Just a stillness in the gray sky, interrupted by the occasional hawk that breaks away from the pines to dive-bomb its rodent prey.

Without a body to bury, the memorial takes on a peculiar sequence. Swifty and Wolfe dig a pit. A sealed plastic bag is lowered into the hole, marked with *The Foreman* in black marker. The objects in the bag are all that remains of the man—a silver chain with an allergy tag; a skull ring; a bronze flask.

The Diggers are quiet as they stare into the pit. Grant wonders what they're thinking. Are they mourning the loss of the Foreman? Are they relieved that he is gone? Or do they see his absence as a reminder that death is always there, reaching out its cold fingers?

Grant feels an emptiness as he looks into the hole. Meyer is right: books and poems don't matter. Nothing he did in camp will make a difference for these men. All of his teaching, his misguided belief in reading and writing, was an exercise in futility. The fact that he is being held as collateral for Meyer's colony makes him realize the excruciating truth. Even in the North, his family's power and influence still defines him.

He looks up to see Wolfe quietly weeping. Swifty puts an arm around Wolfe, who shrugs him off. Wolfe drags a hand across his face. "We're no better than animals," he shouts at the hole. "We're no better than dirt."

The Diggers each take a shovel and dig into the loose earth.

Grant can't bear to look at the grave any longer. He takes off a glove and fiddles with the class ring on his finger as the pit fills with dirt.

Jane, he thinks. *I'm so sorry.*

――――――

For Jane, the threat of catastrophe was the simple act of living. She had been raised in a town where fire season started every May and burned out by September. During the summer months, the sky filled with smoke so thick that the sun looked like a tiny pink dot. Summers were spent inside the house with the air filter on, and when it became impossible to see the neighbor's garage across the street, she would hitch a ride to the superstore where her father worked. The giant windowless warehouse never bore the wrath of the weather. The fluorescent lights were always on, the climate controlled by massive air purifiers. Wind, hail, fire, sleet, rain— none of it penetrated the monolithic box built out on the plains.

She once told Grant that her father thought himself a lucky man to have access to the coldest room in the region. Jane would often sit on a box of frozen chicken thighs as he stocked the humming meat freezers. When she couldn't feel the tips of her fingers, she would thaw out in the shopping aisles, inspecting the goods that had been manufactured in an eastern country she would never travel to.

It was Jane who immediately flew into action when the warnings sounded for Hurricane Xavier. Grant and Jane were beginning to cook dinner in their studio when they saw the forecast first on their Flicks. The churning spot on the Atlantic was expected to make landfall in New England, farther north than a hurricane had ever hit before.

"We need to prepare," Jane said. She filled their bathtub with water, stocked the kitchen with nonperishables, and duct-taped the windows. She bought candles and flashlights and an archaic battery-powered radio so that they could tap into the radio frequencies if the Flick's network went dark.

"If the storm is really that bad, my parents will bail us out," Grant promised.

"But what if they don't come for us?" she asked. Her voice faltered.

It was the first time Grant had seen her so scared, and her vulnerability deeply endeared her to him. He liked the feeling of being the one to take care of her. He kissed her. "Well, I'll be with you."

She nodded and buried her head in his chest.

Hurricane X arrived like a grudge Grant never knew existed. He had grown up with superstorms as the definitive season of the year, but this was different. They were just waking up when the storm arrived north of Boston. Sheets of rain poured down the windows, as the wind stripped the leaves off the maple trees on their street. One of the trees toppled over and crushed a car parked outside their apartment, the flat bleat of the car alarm an ominous harbinger of what was to come.

"We'll be okay," Grant said to comfort them both. "We're not in the mandatory evacuation zone." As if on cue, the power shut off and their studio sank into darkness.

"I think we should leave," Jane said, lighting a candle. "Doesn't Walden have generators on campus?"

"We're perfectly safe here. We have everything we need. Plus, it'll be romantic. Us versus the storm," Grant said, and held her close in the dim candlelight.

By the time they were washing that evening's dishes, their street was submerged, the waterline rapidly rising. First the sidewalk, then the front steps of the buildings.

When the water had reached the sill of the first-floor windows at the corner store across the street, Grant quickly logged on to his Flick when the power momentarily came back on. His feed was filled with increasingly desperate messages from his father:

Grant, let us know if you need anything. We're in the Floating City on standby and have space for you.

His messages grew in intensity and frequency:

Grant, just let us know if you have enough supplies.
Are you there? Send us a message.
Grant, if we don't hear from you in an hour, I'm coming for you.
I'm on my way.

When Grant logged off, he found Jane sitting in a cold bath in the dark, illuminated by the gray square of the skylight.

"What are you doing?" he asked, and ran a hand through her wet hair.

She told him that when she was a girl, it had been common to find the corpses of animals heaped in the wake of a fire, incinerated as they tried to escape. "I don't want to die like an animal."

"You're not going to die." He tried to kiss her, but she turned away from him.

"How can you be so certain?"

A whirring of mechanical blades announced his father's presence. He looked up to the skylight to see a helicopter hovering above the roof.

Jane looked up as well. "Your father?"

He nodded. "I'll go up and see what the deal is. Get ready and then I'll come back for you."

She stepped out of the bath.

Grant climbed the back staircase to the roof. The force of the wind was so strong that he had to use all his strength to wedge open the door. Through sheets of rain, he could barely make out the helicopter bobbing in the sky, marked with the glass spire of the Floating City.

He heard his father's voice but couldn't see him. "We can't land, Grant. Climb up the ladder!"

"Wait a minute," Grant yelled back. "I need to get Jane."

"We don't have a minute. Get in!"

The helicopter lurched closer, and Grant could now see his father leaning out the door. The image cracked something inside him; he had never before seen his father take a risk for him. A gale of wind blew the helicopter back, and for a moment, it looked like his father would fall out.

Grant rushed onto the roof and the door slammed behind him. He was soaked to the bone immediately.

"Follow my voice!" his father yelled.

Grant got down on all fours and crawled across the roof toward the sound of the rotor blades. When he heard his father yell for him to stop, he reached up for the swinging ladder and clung to the lowest rung. His father grabbed hold of him after he was pulled up into the cabin.

"Your mother will be so relieved to see you," his father said as he embraced Grant. It was the closest his father had ever come to saying he loved him, and he felt relieved that he was so wet his father couldn't tell he was crying.

"We have to go back for Jane," Grant said as the helicopter set off.

"She'll be okay, Grant," his father said. "We'll send another chopper for her."

Grant looked out the helicopter as the small roof of their building receded from view. As they flew farther away, he saw that all of Boston had gone dark except for the yellow glow of Walden's campus.

When they flew over the Floating City, it looked more stunning than it did from the mainland. Each of the concentric circles glimmered, and even in the storm Grant could make out the greenhouses and the wide pastures at the outer rim of the city. The knot of glass spires jutting out of the Second Sector were so high that Grant had the impression he could almost graze one of the buildings with his hand. The lights of the Third Sector were still on, shining neon blues onto the shops and restaurants. But the Fourth Sector was impossible to see clearly. From the sky, the very center of the Floating City looked like a dark hole.

The helicopter landed on the roof of his parents' tower. His mother was waiting for him in their penthouse that had views of the churning

Atlantic. When Grant walked in, she ran to him and took him into her arms. "My baby," she said. "We were so worried about you."

"Where's Jane? Has the helicopter picked her up yet?" Grant said, looking around the suite.

"She'll be here soon, darling. Now, you should sleep."

He allowed his mother to lead him to the bedroom that had been designed for him but that he had never spent a night in before. He took off his soaked clothes and climbed into the freshly made bed. Outside, far below, the storm surged on, but up here he felt blissfully separate from it. He would close his eyes for a moment, he thought, and then make coffee and wait for Jane in the kitchen. The wind rushing past the towers sounded like a lullaby sung by a ghost.

When he awoke, it was morning. The sun streamed through the window, offering a direct view of the bright blue Atlantic rippling below. For a moment, he forgot how he had gotten there, and took pleasure in seeing the ocean, how the light moved on the crests of waves as the tide gently rolled in.

Jane, he thought. His mother had laid out one of his father's crisp Oxford shirts and a pair of pleated khakis for him on the dresser. He quickly dressed and rushed out of the bedroom to find his parents eating soft-boiled eggs and drinking coffee in the dining room.

"Where is she?" he asked.

"Good morning to you, Grant," his father said.

"Come, sit with us. I fixed you a plate." His mother patted the chair next to her.

"Where is she?" he said again.

His father tapped a small silver spoon against the delicate shell of the egg. "We tried to dispatch another chopper, but the conditions were too rough."

"You didn't get her?" A taste surged in his mouth, like metal, like blood.

"She's fine, Grant. I had Pinson confirm the water level on her street, and the flooding is negligible. She'll understand what happened once you explain everything rationally to her."

"Egg?" his mother asked, and pointed to the chair again.

"I have to find her." Grant started walking toward the door as his father stood from the table.

"It's no use. The tunnel to the mainland is closed. It'll be at least a week before service is running again."

"And the fucking helicopters?" he asked.

"No need to be petulant. They're all dispatched to help those on the mainland who are actually in need. The devastation is widespread. Jane is one of the lucky ones." His father sat down and pointed at the plate. "You may as well join us for breakfast."

Grant sat at the table and stared at the silver cup holding the perfectly unblemished egg.

"There now, isn't that better?" his mother said, and smiled at him. "We're all back together where we belong."

His father nodded. "I can't believe the city fared so well in the storm." A note of pride rose in his voice.

Grant plucked the egg from its silver cup and held it in his palm. Without saying a word, he threw the egg as hard as he could. It splattered above the teak credenza and oozed yellow down the wall.

Neither of his parents reacted, and instead went back to excavating the gooey yolks on their plates. Within minutes, a maid emerged from a side door and wiped the wall clean.

The letter Jane wrote Grant detailed everything that had happened after he left her. She finished the bottled water, and then purified the bath water with the iodine tablets. She ate all the fresh fruits and vegetables first and stood at the window and watched the water level rise. After, she moved on to the tins of tuna for iron, and then cans of corn and peas for roughage. She siphoned the water out of the toilet tank and was shitting in a soup pot that she kept in the bathroom. On the fifth day, she burned down her last beeswax candle. And on the seventh day, she wrote, *I'm growing used to the way I sound when I cry in the dark.*

The letter to Grant occupied her. It gave her a task to work on and kept her hands busy. It was the longest letter she had ever written.

At first, the letter was filled with enraged epithets at Grant.

How dare you abandon me while you feast on filet mignon in your crystal penthouse, you motherfucker, you. You only loved me for the rebellion of it, for the principled edge it gave you. I was just something you thought would be amusing to play with and now that the world has gone to shit, you have left me where you found me.

Her letter-writing bore the brunt of her rage. She went deeper, darker, with more intent and malice. By the time she filled the pages, she wrote that she felt gutted inside. *Hating you has left me hollow.* So, she turned to despondence to remind herself what it was like to feel.

I should never have left and moved to a city that takes pride in its indifference to the needy. I should never have thought it acceptable to claim something more than what I was born into, to think that living here would give me a better life. I should have stayed in the scorched plains, watching the smoke roll in each summer. I should have gotten a job with Dad, taken over for him when his arthritis made it too hard for him to lift boxes. I should have stayed my father's daughter and never been possessed with this paroxysm of wanting more.

On the third day, when the burden of the past became too much to bear, she wrote that she was growing worried about Grant.

What if you haven't flown into the air with your father, and were pushed by a sudden gust of wind over the side of the building? What if you came back for me like you said you would, but the helicopter/boat/dinghy capsized in the storm? What if the Floating City sunk into the very bottom of the ocean?

She listed a number of dark, despairing outcomes for Grant, and eventually decided that she would believe that Grant was still alive.

You're too privileged not to die on your own terms.

Finally, she took to writing about the storm itself. How it felt to be alone for so many days with only the drift of her thoughts in the tomb-like studio. She started writing poetry again, a practice Grant knew she had given up years ago when she'd decided that poetry was only for the self-indulgent. At the very end of the letter, she confessed that she had started writing short poems on the walls.

in the dark spot
of morning
i asked myself
if misery can be solace

i wander down
a hallway
filled with the photographs
of strange families

once i dreamed of poison
now, i welcome it

She wrote that the poems were shit, but that she took refuge in the feeling of writing again, untethered, floating, dragging her hand against the terrible heat of the hallway wall.

Maybe this is the bright spot I'll salvage from the storm. The piece of me that hasn't drowned. A return to the world of words, a reckoning with my own consciousness.

The last line of the letter, and the line he returned to over and over, was simple:

The truth is: I still love you.

Grant's father was right. The tunnel between the Floating City and the mainland remained closed for a full week. When it finally opened, Grant immediately took the train to the Seaport District and walked the remaining two hours to Allston. He didn't recognize the city he had fled. Huge piles of debris and shrapnel lined the streets—the splintered hulls of boats dredged up from the marina, a smashed and upturned car that looked as flimsy as a child's toy. He threaded around the wreckage to Boston Common, where the uprooted willow trees lay drowned in the flooded lagoon, their massive root structures sticking up out of the sediment. He walked down a Public Alley in Back Bay, past the red-brick row houses with their darkened windows, until he arrived at the eroded riverbanks of the Charles River near the Walden Bridge. A family of geese swam in the river, the gray fluffy goslings ducking and splashing in the silty water. Grant felt a surge of resentment. How were they so oblivious to what had happened?

When Grant finally broke open the front door to their studio, he found Jane lying in the now-drained bathtub, the tips of her fingers stained blue with ink. She didn't open her eyes when he lifted her out of the tub.

"Jane," he said, and carried her to the futon. "I'm here. I'm right here."

He gently placed her on the bed and wrapped the duvet around her. Her body was cold to the touch. He held her hand and felt the limpness in her limbs.

"Jesus, Jane. Talk to me." He tapped his Flick on and connected to the emergency hotline.

"*Caller, you are one thousand and twenty-three,*" the robovoice said. "*Please hold, and an operative will be with you shortly.*"

He was sobbing now. "My girlfriend is unresponsive. She's twenty-one years old and lives in Allston. I need an ambulance immediately."

"*Caller, you are one thousand and twenty-two in line,*" the robovoice said. "*Please hold, and an operative will be with you shortly.*"

He lay down beside her as the robovoice methodically counted down. Her hair smelled like smoke and lavender, which filled him with a maniacal hope. Somehow, she still smelled like her.

He disconnected from the robovoice and dialed his father.

"Dad," he said when his father answered. It pained him to say it out loud, but he knew he had no choice. "I need your help."

In thirty minutes, an ambulance helicopter from the Floating City was hovering above their building. Two paramedics came down through the fire escape and carried Jane to the ambulance. "There isn't room for you,"

they said when Grant tried to follow. But Grant pushed past them anyway
and climbed to the roof. He stood and watched the helicopter take off and
fly away, a dark speck hovering above a drowned city. He felt so helpless,
so completely drained of purpose. Why hadn't he listened to Jane and
taken her to the dorms at Walden when she asked? Why had he been so
convinced he could take care of them?

When he returned to his parents' penthouse and his father told him
that Jane was dead, he cried out and fell to the floor. The sounds he made
were uncontrolled and guttural. He sobbed into the soft cream carpet of
his parents' living room, beating his fists against the floor until his knuckles were raw.

After he picked himself up, he calmly walked to the dining room and
slid open the door of the teak credenza. He broke every piece of the family heirloom china that was stored in there, all of it dating back to the first
Grimleys, who staked their name as merchants after the Revolutionary
War. His parents watched quietly as he threw a silver platter engraved
with the initials of a relative, against the shatterproof window. The platter
ricocheted off the window into a glass lamp, smashing it to pieces. A shard
of glass sliced Grant's cheek, and he yelled, pressing his fingers to his face.

"Let me find a cloth for you," his mother finally said, reaching for him
as blood streamed through his fingers.

"Don't you dare touch me." He threw his hand in the air, spraying blood
on the white carpet.

His father tried to reason, "We understand, Grant, that this is a painful
time for you."

Grant turned toward his father and snapped, "You're probably happy
she's dead. You never thought she was good enough to be a Grimley."

His father shook his head. "That's unfair to say. This was a terrible accident. An absolute tragedy. We'll do whatever we can to help you."

Grant looked up at them, his face smeared in blood. "Good." His smile
was crazed. "Stay away from me."

Jane had no will or estate, so Grant returned to the studio to pack up her possessions in cardboard boxes with a plan to drop them off at the Dispossession Estates, hoping that someone there would find a use for her books and her cast-iron pan, her mismatched cutlery and secondhand clothes. He kept a few of the things that mattered the most to him: a Polaroid of her standing in a dune near Crane Beach, a rabbit's foot on her key chain, her journals, and the prickliest of the cacti, potted in a vintage teacup. He would take these with him to remind him of her.

Before he left, he found the letter she wrote to him folded on the windowsill where they liked to drink coffee in the morning and read it in one sitting as the day turned to dusk. When it was evening and he could barely make out her words, he finally finished, and climbed onto the roof to look out at their neighborhood one last time.

The electrical grid was still off, so the neighborhood appeared softer in the dark. He could hear the sounds of night birds rustling in the bent and splintered trees, and the melodic fingerpicking of a neighbor playing acoustic guitar on their fire escape. Everything was black, except for the yellow glow of Walden and the distant blues and greens of the Floating City.

The truth is: I still love you.

The next month, he received the job posting in his Walden feed: *Seeking English Tutor for Innovative Campus in the Canadian North.* The province bordered the state where Jane had grown up, and it seemed like the exit he desperately needed. If he went up to Dominion Lake, he reasoned, and taught the same kind of working-class students as Jane's family, maybe, just maybe, he would feel closer to her again. He immediately applied for the job and was interviewed by video conference. One week later, he was hired.

Before he left Boston, he told his parents he never wanted to see them again. He told his professors that he wanted a different kind of teaching experience. He told his friends that he was desperate to get out of the country. But he told no one the real reason why he accepted the job in the North, upending all expectations on the trajectory of his life.

He did it to atone for Jane.

But being in camp has made him feel farther from Jane than he did in Boston, where each street corner bore a personal significance. Here, everything is foreign, and he feels the immediacy of her slipping away without his Flick to remind him. Archived in his Flick, Jane is still there, drinking tea by the window, laughing in bed, reaching for him in her sleep. A Jane without shadows, without scent, without taste. A facsimile of love.

After the Foreman's memorial, the Diggers drive Grant back to camp. Instead of going straight inside the warehouse, he lingers outside. Jane would want him to leave. To stand up for himself and find a place to call his own. To save himself and not wind up under a snowbank next to the Foreman's frozen body.

He starts walking across the highway. He'll pay the mall a visit and see if Willow can show him a new direction.

CHAPTER FIFTEEN

ROSE

At dinner, the topic of the Foreman sits as discreetly on the table as a severed head. Rose is the last to join, and quietly dishes a serving of pasta into a bowl. The Blooms are eerily silent, focused on finishing their meal as quickly as possible. Judith watches them eat.

"How is dinner, Jasmine?" Judith asks.

"Delicious, ma'am," Jasmine says, but doesn't look up.

Judith laughs. "Don't call me that. It makes me feel my age."

Rose has noticed that Judith's manner has changed since they dumped the Foreman's body in the lake. No longer is she their stern and wary Madam. She seems younger, lither, with a hint of humor shining through. Judith isn't the only one who is different. Willow's prickliness has disappeared. She is cheerier, more at ease. But she is also more watchful. During meals, she stands sentinel at the kitchen door with one of the pit bulls chained by her side, the Foreman's knife attached to her leather belt. Her right hand rests on the hilt.

The rest of the Blooms are in varying degrees of shock. Fleur barely speaks, her eyes fixed on the table whenever Judith or Willow is in the room. Jasmine and Violet are never apart, conspiring softly in each other's ear whenever they can. Iris talks in rambling bursts, and then quiets down and doesn't speak for hours.

Rose wonders if the Blooms are startled awake in the middle of the night with the image of the dark slash through the Foreman's throat. Or if they can still feel the leaden weight of his body as they dragged him across the ice. Of course they do.

They're accomplices now.

Sisters.

She has spent the nights since the Foreman's death reflecting on what she can do now that she knows everything Damien promised her is a lie. The condo in the Floating City, safety and citizenship for her mother, the false narrative that they could step into a life free from the threats of the world they abandoned.

She hates Damien for deceiving her and feels frustrated with herself for accepting the corruption he so lightly dealt out. That she somehow justified his actions as a routine method for gaining power when she knows now that power is never granted but seized. She never should have waited for it to be given to her. She should have taken it with her own hands and made it her own.

She thinks of what she could tell Meyer now in the wake of all this. How she can reframe the scene. How the Foreman came to her room uninvited. How he forced himself on her. How her only choice was to protect herself. Meyer will believe her. He'll even think it admirable that she lashed out. *Such bravery, Rose. I never liked that man in the first place.*

But to go to Meyer is to become beholden to him and the half-finished rooms of the prototype. If she asks for his help, he will only use her vulnerability as a way to twist her closer to him.

All she knows is that she can't bear to stay in camp a day longer. Waking to Meyer's breath on her skin, his hands in her hair, hoping he'll leave so she can put the black-lace lamp in the window. But Meyer has been with her every night, making it too risky to summon the Barber.

Suddenly, a phone rings:

B-r-i-n-g...

B-r-i-n-g...

B-r-i-n-g...

The ring is elongated and old-fashioned, echoing through the empty department store from the entrance of the mall. Someone is at the front gate. Someone who isn't a client, since Rose knows the clients have free access to the building.

"Go to your rooms, girls," Judith says. "I'll answer it."

"I'll come as backup," Willow says.

"No, back to your room with the others. We need to maintain some semblance of normality."

Rose leaves the kitchen with the rest of the Blooms and hurries to her room. She sits at the vanity, running a brush through her hair to give her hands something to do. She can hear Judith chatting with a man as they walk down the hallway. Judith's voice sounds fake and cheery, and Rose wonders who is important enough to cause her to speak so strangely. Rose opens her bedroom door, sits back at the vanity, and looks in the mirror as they pass by. The Walden student walks past her open bedroom. He pauses at her door and their eyes meet in the mirror. He looks less nervous than he did at the party. He nods at her once and keeps walking as Judith pulls him down the hall toward Willow's room. After a few muffled words are exchanged, Judith's footsteps retreat, and the mall is quiet again.

Rose tears a page from her notebook. This might be her only chance. She writes the note quickly without dwelling on each word:

No fiefdoms. No colonies. No floating cities.

Let's find our own utopia.

WHITE ALICE

The four returned to White Alice and told the rest of us what happened—they had no choice but to kill two men, and that the town of Dominion Lake was only good for its oil.

"We would never be content there," Sal assured us. "It's a backwater fixated on extraction. We'll be much happier here in the station."

After years of living in White Alice, we had grown wary of the outside. Not the outside of the natural world that briskly greeted us when we stepped beyond the station, but the outside populated by other humans. Even though life was curtailed in the station, it felt orderly and peaceful, completely ours to make our own. And whatever bickering or difficulties that occasionally spiked among our group had eroded with the addition of Aurora. Raising a child together had softened us in ways we hadn't expected. We were less divisive and more sentimental. More patient and hopeful. We thought less of our own pasts back in the South. We only keened for her future.

The meteorologist had concluded that the General's hypothesis was correct. The safest place to be in the future was precisely where we already were—the Far North. We tried to imagine Aurora at our age, living in this burning world, and even though it gutted us to see the future this way, it gave us solace to know that she would at least be in the best place possible, and that we would be here to protect her.

We used this reason to justify the deaths in Dominion Lake—to ourselves and one another. If we truly planned to provide for our daughter, we reasoned, then we would need to accept the brutal truth: survival required sacrifice.

Once we accepted this new narrative, it became easier and easier to take a life. Every few years, we raided the oil towns that pockmarked the northern region. Dominion Lake; Fort Principle; Minor Plains; St. Keg; Vandal; Ochre Valley. We targeted oil workers flush with payday cash. Party boys. Wild things. Men who snorted cocaine off the dashboards of their trucks on a Monday morning. Bruisers who fought in local bars as recreation before pushing on to the next job. Many of these men were drifters who had already severed ties from family and friends. The local authorities never raised an eyebrow if a rigger disappeared off the map. And we justified every death with the same dictum: every life we took was an act of protection for Aurora.

We still lived with the fear that we might be apprehended or killed. And because of this, Sal convinced us that Aurora needed to learn how to fight. Sal started training her at age five to hold and clean a gun, and by the time she was eight, she was proficient at throwing knives during target practice. She quickly became a skilled hunter and a hardy defender, strong and quick on her feet with an apathy toward blood. When our daughter turned thirteen, she started joining us on raids, riding down on the snowmobiles to secure oil.

Aurora, whose sweet face often made people stop on the street and smile, was the perfect alibi. No one suspected anything when this dreamy child was with us. She became adept at mapping out the journey south, precisely noting our stops for rest, for fuel, for money. Her inquisitive mind made her indispensable as a scout, and Sal began to send her into the towns to locate our next mark.

As a teenager, Aurora showed her abilities as a soldier with her shrewd mind for tactical engagement and a high threshold for pain. She dislocated her shoulder during training, and we only found out days later when she couldn't dress herself anymore. After this, Sal began training her in more advanced combat methods. The two often disappeared for a full day out on the permafrost, only returning at suppertime exhausted and depleted. It was Aurora who understood best the sacrifice at the heart of our survival. By the time she was fourteen, she'd cut a circle in the ice on the lake and helped us drown a man. At fifteen, she'd successfully led her first raid and secured more oil than any of us had.

Throughout this period, we sometimes asked Sal why home base never sent us a status update on our mission. She always responded with the same answer, "Home base will make contact when the moment is right." She argued that our mission had taken on larger consequences than she had the clearance to understand, and that all we could do was continue living as we saw fit.

We had grown accustomed to following Sal's orders and trusted her to know what was best for us as a group. So we gave up worrying why home base had stopped sending supplies, and focused on building our home in the station. The truth was we preferred it this way, cut off from the outside. As each year passed into the next, the programmer continued to transmit a weekly dispatch to home base, but we grew to believe that we were now truly alone.

Aurora's sixteenth birthday was the last year the oil rigs were still operating. We tattooed the station's coordinates as a birthday gift on her rib cage and brought out the bottles of champagne we had been saving for an occasion as special as this. She had finally grown old enough to have a drink, we said, laughing, as we poured the champagne into mugs and toasted her future.

But we all knew a change in our way of life was imminent. Now that our daughter had reached adolescence, we would have to look our future in the face. Recruitment to White Alice wasn't anything we had openly discussed, but it became clear that we would have to bring others to the station.

Our third generation could never exist without the introduction of a mate.

CHAPTER SIXTEEN

GRANT

The phone to the Blooms' compound is attached to the entrance of the locked gate. Grant picks up the receiver and presses 1 for the office. The phone rings three times before someone picks up.

"Hello?" a woman's voice says.

"Hello, are you open?" Grant asks.

No response. He can hear static, fuzz, echoing footsteps. More static. Fuzz. The crackling of distant conversation.

"Hello?" he says again.

The phone disconnects. The entrance of the mall suddenly swings open and Judith marches across the parking lot with a dog on a leash. When she arrives at the gate, she tosses a biscuit from her pocket to the dog, who devours the treat from the snow. She looks at Grant for a moment, and then breaks into a warm smile. "Grant, we've been expecting you. Willow has spoken so highly of you." She opens the latch on the gate and ushers him through the door. "Come on, I'll take you to her."

He follows Judith inside the mall, which feels vastly warmer and more welcoming than his home in the warehouse. The scent is part of it—something floral drifts in pleasant wafts. They walk down the hallway, past a red bedroom where a young woman dressed in a silk robe sits on a stool at a vanity mirror. She pulls a comb through her long black hair, and for a moment Grant's eyes meet hers in the mirror. He recognizes her from the party as Meyer's Bloom. She smiles at him, and he nods briskly.

"That's Rose. She's off-limits." Judith tugs at Grant's elbow and leads him away. "Willow is right down here." She pauses at a door painted with a tree. "Willow," she calls out in a soft voice. "Willow, dear. There is someone here to see you."

Willow answers the door also dressed in a silk robe. She takes Grant's hand, pulling him into the room and closing the door. A dark hedge of trees is painted on one wall, with the yellow eyes of an owl glowing above a branch.

Willow slips off the robe to reveal a set of black lingerie, showing her lean musculature as she walks to the bed.

"Do you want a drink?" she asks.

He nods yes and gestures at the room awkwardly. "Where should I sit? Sorry, I've never been in a situation like this before." He instinctively touches his beard. He still hasn't shaved since arriving at camp, and he hopes he doesn't look too scraggly.

"Right here is fine." She pats a spot on the bed and then goes to the dresser to fetch a bottle. He tries not to stare at her too directly but can't help but admire the way her legs move in her high heels, how she shows no shame or discomfort in being nearly nude in this room with him. A raw ache of desire ripples through him.

She brings him a glass of something amber. He drinks, grateful for the distraction, as his eyes flit around the room. The furniture is shabby and worn, and the woodland mural strikes him as amateurish and cartoony.

She sits down next to him on the bed. "So, I imagine you've heard the news?"

"About the Foreman? Yes, Meyer told me that he wandered drunk into the night and froze to death. I despised the man, but it's still an awful way to die." He shivers involuntarily. "But I'm not here to talk about the Foreman. Can you help me get out of here?"

"Out of camp?"

"Yes." He lowers his voice. "Is it safe to talk in here?"

"We should be quiet." She pulls him down to the bed where they lie next to each other. Her perfume smells like an orchid on the edge of decay. "The only route I know leads north," she whispers.

"North?" he repeats skeptically. "How far north?"

She takes his hand and places it on her skin, where a set of blue numbers are tattooed under her left rib cage. "If you follow these coordinates north, you'll end up where I was born. We live off-grid and are completely self-sustainable, with no allegiance to any country."

He traces his finger over the numbers. "Like a commune?"

"We prefer to think of ourselves as a family." She touches his face gently. "It's a special place where everyone is treated as an equal. We all have our duties, and you would have one too. The only currency is what we offer to each other in the community, and what we get in return."

"What kind of duties?" he asks. "I'm afraid I'm not very handy."

"Don't worry, we'll find something for you to do." She runs a finger along the inside of his forearm. Her touch is cool and soothing.

He blushes and looks away. "Does anyone know you live there?"

"No one. We've completely cut ties."

He thinks for a moment before saying, "And this is the only route you know of? Nothing else?"

"It's the only one I have access to. If you stay in camp long enough, you might find someone to take you south."

"No," Grant says firmly. "I can't go back south. Can you guarantee that my family will never find me where you are?"

"Yes," she says. "We'll protect you."

A feeling of relief cascades over him. Forget Walden and Boston and the Floating City. Forget Meyer and this wretched camp. Forget his father's expectations for him and Grimley Corp. Forget the fucking Grimleys. Forget Grant P. Grimley himself. Forget all of it. He can find a new name.

"I'll go," he says.

"You don't know how happy you've made me. I was worried that I was going to be all alone again." She smiles. "We'll leave tomorrow after the camp's deliveryman arrives with his supplies. Wait in front of the Diggers' warehouse and get the key from the driver."

"And then?"

"That's all you need to worry about. We'll come find you."

He sits up and begins to button his jacket.

"That's it?" she asks with surprise.

"Well, I don't want to impose."

"You're not an imposition." She tugs at him gently. "What do you want?"

"I want what you want," he says, and immediately wishes he hadn't. It sounds so mealymouthed, so tentative.

She pulls him on top of her. "That's not good enough. Tell me what you really want."

What he wants is to bury himself in her body. To obscure who he is and the terrible things he has done. To start a new life, severed from the one that came before.

He will be slow with her. Gentle. Soft. He kisses her neck. Her clavicle. The warm flesh between her thighs. He will make her feel good as a way to understand his own desires.

Grant slides her underwear off and places his mouth in there.

"You don't have to do that," she says, suddenly sounding far away.

"I want to." He folds her legs and grips the tops of her feet as he tunnels inside. As he investigates with his tongue, he wonders: What does his beard feel like to her? A tumbleweed. A horsetail brush. A knot of rope. A soaked sponge.

When he hopes she is finished, he sits up suddenly. She looks at him strangely, and then reaches for a tissue from the bedside table to dab his face. The tissue becomes splotched with red, and suddenly he is aware of the metallic tang in his mouth.

She looks at the blood spreading through the tissue, and frowns. "I'm early this month."

The mineral taste in his mouth mellows into something sweeter and more soothing. He wonders if his teeth are lined with blood.

"I should go," he says. "But I'll see you tomorrow."

"Yes, tomorrow." She touches a finger to his beard, and then withdraws it, admiring the dark red droplets.

No sound or light when he steps out of Willow's room. Everyone seems to be asleep. He feels his way down the hallway, trying to locate the exit.

Suddenly, one of the bedroom doors swings open. Grant looks over in surprise and see Meyer's Bloom framed in light.

"Hi," she says.

"Hi," he says back.

"You're the Walden student, aren't you? The Barber told me about you."

"He did?"

She nods. "He said you're a good man, and that you'd help me."

He feels a rush of pride to know the Barber was speaking so highly of him. "I'll do whatever I can."

She presses a note into his hand. "Can you give this to the Barber as soon as possible?"

"Of course. I'll give it to him tomorrow at breakfast." He places the note in his jacket pocket. "Who should I say it's from?"

She pauses for a moment before answering. "You can tell him it's from Nari."

CHAPTER SEVENTEEN

NARI

The name, Nari, was given to her by her mother, despite the fact her father's family protested.

"Name her something American, for god's sake," her grandmother said, but her mother would not relent. She felt she had already given up so much for her new husband's family; the name of her child was the only thing she could hold on to.

"I want to speak Korean whenever I call her name," her mother explained.

Now, when Nari thinks of her name, she longs to hear her mother say it. She remembers how her voice rolled over the dunes. *Nari!* They'd eat dinner seated on stools, her mother sitting with one leg tucked under her, expertly picking through the mackerel to find her daughter the juiciest piece. Nari was the sound of home, which was why she kept it siloed from her working life, preferring the flimsy pseudonyms she flitted through at the Loop that carried no personal freight or meaning.

She had always felt an implicit thrill using a pseudonym, the act of creating a character through a name and bringing her to life. The Rose in camp is flintier and more distant than Nari. She has to protect herself. Shedding Rose will feel like lifting a leaden blanket off her shoulders, walking around without the weight of all she has carried.

She's woken up early this morning, an hour before the Blooms usually rise. She'll pack her suitcase now and leave first thing tomorrow morning. Nari thinks of how good it will feel to hear the Barber call her by her real name, and wonders what his name is, too.

When she finishes packing, she steps out of her room to see Judith standing in the hallway with her arms crossed.

"Do you mind joining me for a cup of tea?" Judith asks.

She has been in camp long enough to know that Judith never makes requests, even if they're framed as one. The only option is to go.

"That would be lovely," she says.

"Good," Judith says crisply. "Follow me."

They walk down the hallway, past the kitchen, into the east wing of the mall. She can smell Judith's room as she approaches—chlorine, artificial lemon, the stringent scent of a room scrubbed with bleach.

The room is clean and bright. A ceiling of glass exposes the flat gray sky, casting light on the room's tiled turquoise floors. A hospital bed is set up in the corner, neatly made with white sheets and a floral comforter.

Judith directs her to a small folding table and pours them each a cup of tea from a teapot. "You take sugar, right?"

She nods.

Judith drops two cubes of sugar into each cup and waits for the crystals to dissolve before continuing. "You've been busy, Rose. How long have you been fucking the Barber?"

Judith's bluntness takes her by surprise. "Excuse me?"

"Oh, I'm sorry. *Making love.* He always was a sentimental one, wasn't he?" Judith stirs a spoon in her teacup. "One month? Two months? Since the very beginning of camp? I'd like a timeline on your deception."

"Deception to Meyer?"

"No," Judith says, and her voice turns grave. "To Willow."

Nari takes a sip of the tea. Too sweet. The tea is too sweet, and yet it still can't offset Judith's words. So she was right to suspect there was something between Willow and the Barber. "I didn't realize they were together."

"They had an arrangement," Judith says. "But the Barber's been cold to her since you arrived in camp, and now that understanding is threatened. I was always wary of you, but now I know why. You're not here just to pleasure men, are you? The Foreman was in your room for something else." Judith stands and retrieves a small black box from her desk. She sets it on the table in front of her. "Open it. You'll know what it is."

She opens the box carefully. A pile of silver ash is nestled inside.

"Dysprosium," Judith says. "A complicated name for a complicated commodity. But you know that already. Tell me, is this camp the only operation in the region?"

"Who told you about this?"

"The Foreman, of course. It didn't take much to get it out of him. Loose lips on that man after a few drinks." Judith laughs harshly. "But he told me that you know even more." She leans forward conspiratorially. "We can forget about what happened between you and the Barber if that helps. Just tell me what you know about the camp."

She looks at Judith carefully. "Why should I trust you?"

"Because I know what it's like to be cornered. We're the same, Rose." Judith's voice breaks. "Why else do you think I'm working in this wretched camp?"

She's never thought of Judith outside of the context of the Blooms. Never imagined what she thought or dreamed of. What she was leaving to work here, what she would be returning to. She only thought of Judith as a cog in a larger machine, merely there to urge the Blooms on.

"This is just the first camp," Nari says. "By next season, the entire region will be covered with mineral extraction camps."

She tells Judith that after the survey is complete, the project will continue without Meyer or the Diggers or the Blooms. The land will be parceled off, and the real extraction will begin. The highway will come alive with trucks and equipment and workers. The precious mineral will be pulled out of the ground and transported for processing back south, where it will be fabricated into the Flick 2.0. The cycle will continue until the region is nothing but a gaping pit.

A sadness passes over Judith's face. "It's even worse than I feared. Men will stop at nothing until everything is theirs." She reaches for her hand. "What if I told you that there is a place where you could be free from their tyranny?"

"That place doesn't exist."

"It does. Up north, not far from here." Judith's eyes are shining. She seems enlivened in a way she's never been before. "You've seen how I will protect you from any man who tries to harm you. And we never kill without reason. We work with respect, so the man has the clarity of mind to understand what is happening and why. I've already told the other Blooms the same. You'll never have to perform for a man's pleasure in White Alice."

A chill moves through her body. "I thought White Alice was a myth?"

"The villagers always wished we were a ghost story." Judith's eyes soften. "White Alice is aging. And we need to welcome a new generation."

That evening, Nari cooks one last dinner for the Blooms. The pantry is almost bare, but she finds a few cans of corn stacked in a cupboard, and a frozen trout in the freezer. She defrosts the fish and slits open its belly, emptying its guts into the sink, then seasons it with a dried bay leaf, onion flakes, and garlic powder before baking it in the oven. The canned corn is heated in a skillet with oil and salt and pepper. A simple meal, but it's the best she can do, given the limited supplies. Besides, the Blooms have other things on their minds to distract them from her cooking. Judith says they have until tomorrow to decide if they want to join White Alice.

The smell of cooked fish fills the kitchen as the Blooms gather for dinner.

"I'm not going," Violet says after Nari brings the platter of trout to the table. "I miss my family and friends. My own life."

Iris helps herself to a serving of fish. "But Judith says you can start a new life up there."

Violet shakes her head. "I'm good with the one I already have. And I don't love the idea of being trapped in another building with Judith."

Jasmine nods in agreement. "Judith thinks she can save us, but she doesn't even know we don't need to be saved. I'm heading back south with Violet."

"I wish I knew what to do," Fleur says quietly. She picks at a fish bone on her plate. "I'm curious about the station, but it doesn't feel totally right." She looks up from her plate at the other Blooms. "How is it any different than camp?"

"Well, you wouldn't have to work," Iris says. "Am I the only one who's considering Judith's offer?"

"You're going with her?" Jasmine asks in surprise.

Iris shrugs. "Maybe. I'm ready to take a break. Plus, I want to see more of the North. This might be my only chance."

As the Blooms eat, they go back and forth on what White Alice will be like. Iris argues that they can leave the station if they don't like it. Violet and Jasmine disagree. Neither Bloom wants to live longer in isolation, and they don't trust that Judith is telling them the entire truth.

"You saw what she did to the Foreman," Jasmine says. "She butchered him like an animal."

"She was protecting Rose," Iris justifies.

Violet crosses her arms. "No, she's a killer."

Willow speaks up for the first time during the dinner. "She did what she needed to survive."

"Survival doesn't mean you have to murder," Jasmine says. "There are other ways to get by."

"And how do you think you'll get back south?" Willow snaps. "Just by walking there?"

"Stop it," Fleur says. "I don't want us to fight on our last night together."

No one says anything until Nari breaks the silence. She points to the window, where the orange moon glows through the trees. "Look, it's finally a clear night. Why don't we take one last walk together?"

The Blooms leave the dishes on the table, zip on their parkas and boots, and step into the melting snow. They automatically pair off in the parking lot, reflecting their divided lines: Jasmine and Violet; Iris and Fleur.

Willow walks up to Nari. "Will you come to White Alice?"

"No," Nari says. "I'm going to find my own way."

Willow nods. "Judith already told me." They break off from the Blooms and walk by themselves for a few paces. "Take care of him out there. He's more vulnerable than he seems."

"You're not mad?"

"I'll miss him, but I'm glad that he'll be with you. He needs someone strong to lead the way."

"Don't you want to see the South still?"

"I do, but my family still needs me." Willow turns her face to the night sky. "Look," she says, and points. "The aurora borealis is starting."

Nari looks up. A lime-green haze streaks across the sky, sharpening the outlines of the spruce trees and making the forest appear starker and more alive. The light flickers and undulates, and momentarily fades away before glowing back again, crimson and lilac at its wavering edges. During her entire time in camp, Nari has never seen the northern lights, never thought to seek them out at night. She wonders why she has spent so much time looking at the ground instead of up at the sky.

The Blooms all stop in their tracks and look up, as their faces become illuminated by the otherworldly light.

"It's solar wind flowing back to our earth," Willow says. "The sun is reminding us that it's still there, even when we can't see it."

The Blooms are quiet as they watch the colors wax and wane across the sky. The light appears almost technological in its gradation and re- minds Nari of the way her Flick shimmered in iridescent colors after Ju- dith pulled it out. She touches the spot behind her ear, and hopes she'll remember this vision in the future.

A cloud passes, and the spectacle is over. The Blooms thread their arms together and trudge through the slush in the parking lot, back into the mall.

WHITE ALICE

We saw the boy first in the baking aisle of the Stop N Save in Dominion Lake while we were inspecting a can of chocolate frosting. We knew what we must have looked like to him. We wore parkas the color of pond scum, with the scraps of some tragic animal pinned around our hoods. Our boots were duct-taped around the toes. When we stood in line at the checkout, we made sure to speak in soft, lilting voices, occasionally breaking out into laughter. We could feel him watching us from behind the cash register.

Sal popped off her hood and rubbed her shaved head in the checkout line. "Do you accept gold?" she asked him as the conveyor belt jerked forward.

He looked at us like we had just stepped out of a chasm in the earth.

"Like a gold nugget?" he asked.

Sal pulled off her leather glove with her teeth and wrenched off the wedding ring she was given by her ex-husband, which she still wore as a reminder of what she had deserted. "Twenty-four karats," she said, and handed it to him. "We'll take all of this . . ." She pointed to the pile of canned corn and peas, zinc and vitamin C tablets, bottles of ibuprofen. She handed the can of frosting and a box of white cake mix to the boy directly. "Do you have any birthday candles?"

"Back in aisle nine," the boy said, and then added, "next to the sprinkles."

The botanist visibly brightened. "We'll take some of those, too." She returned quickly from aisle nine with the candles and sprinkles and added them to the pile. "It's my daughter's birthday."

The boy finally smiled. "Oh yeah? What's her name? I probably know her from school."

"She's homeschooled," Sal cut in, and then returned his smile.

"And we'll take all the oil you have ready in barrels," the engineer said, gesturing outside to the pumps.

"All of it?" the boy asked.

"He's a smart one," the biologist said to the engineer.

The boy looked outside the store's window to where our two black snowmobiles were parked. No one in Dominion Lake had seen snowmobiles like ours before. They looked more like beasts than machines, a pair of panthers encased in metal. When we turned them on, the engines roared and then settled into a hypnotic purr.

The boy took the gold ring, even though he was only allowed to accept the local currency. When he touched the ring, his fingers paused in Sal's hand for a moment. She noticed and squeezed his fingers. His face blushed red to his neck, and he quickly tossed the ring into the cash register and went outside to help us load the oil barrels into the camper van.

We had already stopped at the EZ Gas, the Super S, and the Green Owl. The camper was so crammed with oil that you could have detonated all of Dominion Lake if you had thrown a lit match in our direction.

But the boy didn't flinch or ask questions. He dragged barrel after barrel into the camper. We could tell he was a good worker. Methodical and diligent, never complaining about the labor. Only when he was done did he look at Sal and ask, "Where are you going now?"

"Back home," Sal replied simply.

"Where is that?" he asked.

"A place far from here, where we live according to our own desires," Sal explained.

We thanked the boy for his help, hitched the camper van to the back of one of the snowmobiles, and towed it away. When we looked back, we saw him still standing there, watching us drive the sleek snowmobiles north until we took a left at the lake, still frozen solid in spring.

The boy was still working the checkout at Stop N Save when we saw him again two years later. This time, we arrived with Aurora. He looked at her with interest when we walked in. She, too, was dressed in army rags and moved through the grocery store with a stilted nervousness, like a deer. She paused at the checkout to inspect the rows of glossy magazines celebrating a movie star's divorce while opening a package of gum.

"Hey, you have to pay for that first," he said.

Aurora looked up and quickly crammed a piece of gum into her mouth. She grinned.

The conveyor belt was already filled with nonperishables, zinc tablets and vitamin C, the heap of ibuprofen. He clunked it forward.

Sal's hair had grown longer since we'd last seen the boy and was now graying at the temples. She kept the sides shaved, but now braided the rest down her back.

"Oil's gone up," Sal said, and nodded outside at the gas price sign.

"Yeah, tripled in the last year since the rigs started shutting down." The boy shrugged. He was just repeating what everyone was saying. "No cake this time?"

Sal looked at him with a coolness in her eyes. "Excuse me?"

"Last time, you bought frosting and box cake," he said, and then added, "I was the one who checked you out."

"Oh," Sal said, and finally smiled. "I didn't recognize you now that you're a man."

"I'm trying," he said, and laughed self-consciously, noticing that Aurora was still staring at him. "I'm the manager now," he said.

"Are you?" Sal asked with amusement in her voice.

"Well, assistant manager for now, but I might be running this place in a couple of years."

"No rigs for you?"

"No one is hiring now that everything is shutting down for good. Half of the houses are empty, and people are moving away. I guess I'm lucky to have this job." He swiped everything through, and after he told us the total amount, he added, "And you'll pay in gold?"

Sal leaned forward and whispered, "Come with us instead."

"Excuse me?"

Sal repeated what she had said. "Come with us up north."

"Why would I do that?"

Sal tapped his mahogany clip-on bow tie. "The oil's not coming back, and you know it."

He looked out the window at the black snowmobiles parked outside, and then looked back at Aurora. Already, he could hear the engines purring. He tore off the clip-on bow tie and flung it on the conveyor belt.

Sal looked at him and smiled. "Good man."

At first it felt peculiar to live again with a man. His size, his voice, his smell were all uncomfortably foreign. But when he arrived in the station, we understood why he had been chosen. He was kind with Aurora, and deeply curious about our way of life. He immediately pitched in on helping us maintain the station, and we benefited from his good work ethic and inquisitive manner. And because he represented a future that extended beyond our own lives, we named him Genesis, and tattooed his new name above his heart.

Aurora quickly grew attached to our new recruit. She began to spend her days with him, not us, reading in the library, riding the snowmobiles beyond the station harvesting the vegetables and herbs in the greenhouse for our meals. One long summer night, we found them under the midnight sun, sitting at the edge of the radar shield with a bottle of stale wine between them. They were drunk and elated, and we wondered if they had already become intimate. Aurora was only eighteen, Genesis twenty. She seemed far too young to raise children of her own. We wanted her to have what we had—work, autonomy, a sense of herself beyond the perimeters of a man, and we worried her attachment to Genesis would prevent that from happening. Sal procured a box of condoms from the pharmacy on one of our raids and left them in her room, explaining to Aurora that it was necessary she take precautions. One day, Sal promised, she would be ready to start the next chapter of her life, and Genesis would be willing. But now was not that time.

By the time Aurora was nineteen, half of Dominion Lake had shuttered due to foreclosures and bankruptcies. When she was twenty-one, we rode down south to discover Dominion Lake had become a ghost town.

We spent those ghost years combing the abandoned stores and gas stations for nonperishables, leaving our name in writing on the walls after we took what we needed. With the villagers now gone, we felt an even greater desire to leave our mark to remind ourselves that we were still alive. White Alice had once been a legend in the oil region, often evoked as a curse, or a story parents told their children to keep them from misbehaving. A way to explain the economic downturn. A justification for the warming weather.

Better eat your turnips or White Alice will come and get you.

Oil prices are high—White Alice is angry.

Fire season again. White Alice must be on the move.

Some of the villagers alleged we were an actual demon who had fallen from the sky. Others thought us to be the ghost of a prostitute who had made her rounds at the man camp. Many believed we were made of ice, which was why no one saw us during the short summer. Whatever our origins were, White Alice was always depicted in the shape of a woman and embodied as a powerfully destructive figure.

The boys of the oil towns were raised to be fearful of us. Every year on "White Alice Day," the villagers hoisted a life-size doll soaked in oil up the village's flagpole. On their thirteenth birthday, each boy had the honor of shooting a fiery arrow into our cotton-batting heart.

For the girls, our role was more instructive. White Alice was the embodiment of what they should never become—mercurial, isolated, murderous. An icy woman who only lives in the winter and kills men for the heat of their blood.

As we walked through the pilfered aisles of the Stop N Save, we found ourselves missing the villagers of Dominion Lake. Their bodies. Their voices. Their humanity. It was surprising to suddenly feel something for a place we once saw as a compulsory burden. But now with the town empty, we felt our collective purpose shrink.

And there was the problem of oil. The last newspaper printed in Dominion Lake stated that the oil ban would devastate the extraction economy. The end of oil brought our life in White Alice into crisis. How could we survive if the energy source that allowed our survival no longer existed?

Our final trip down to the village offered a glimmer of a solution. A new camp was setting up in the strip mall. We dispatched Genesis to find out its purpose, knowing that as a former local, and as a man, he would appear more trustworthy than one of us. Genesis spent a few months living in his birth family's abandoned homestead, staking out the operation, and finally returned to White Alice to report that he had met the project's lead, an architect named Meyer, who claimed to be developing a new city in the region, powered by green energy.

"A city," Sal said skeptically. "But the land is gutted from extraction."

"That's what he said." Genesis shrugged. "He offered me a job, and anyone else who needs one."

Sal was the one to make the suggestion: What if we imbedded ourselves in the camp to find out more about this new operation?

We all agreed that we needed to adapt to green energy and find a new supply chain. Preparations for the mission began immediately. Genesis, Aurora, and Sal would travel to Dominion Lake and pose as workers in the camp.

A barber. An escort. A madam.

The remaining members of White Alice would remain in the station, and then caravan to the camp on the Equinox.

By then, the three insurgents would be ready.

We had never left the station at the same time and felt a surge of sadness as we prepared to leave for Dominion Lake. We stored food in the pantry, folded the linens in the bunkroom, swept the shelves of the library where we kept Aurora's keepsakes and toys—the threadbare dolls and wooden cars we had made many years ago, the books she'd written and illustrated. Before we left, we gathered in the greenhouse one last time.

Twenty-seven years. We had spent nearly three decades surviving in the station. The long winters, the raids, the hibernation, the light-filled summers had changed us. Gone were the visitations from a past life lived in the South. Gone were the memories of the people we once loved. Gone was the joy and electric pulse of our work. Gone was the specter of home base, even though we still tapped out the same message every week:

mission is operational

All we had was the station and our daughter.

When we looked at each other, we saw two versions of ourselves flickering. The curious, capable women who had once been dropped on this frozen piece of earth, and the hardened, resolute raiders we had grown into. We no longer thought of each other as the botanist, the engineer, the meteorologist, the cartographer, the geographer, the programmer, and the biologist. We had become like Sal, trapped and animated by a past that was larger than our professions.

We were given the code name White Alice by our sergeant, who claimed to read books as much as he claimed to see us as his equal. We suspected both claims were bullshit, but we liked the name because of the story he'd pickpocketed of a girl who fell through a hole and found herself in a place where nothing was like the world she'd left behind. The name was prim and proper, tinged with the boarding school etiquette that a few of us had undergone ourselves. It was the name of a nice girl in a pretty dress with a ribbon fixed daintily in her hair.

Even though Alice looked nothing like us, we respected her desire to contact a world that existed beyond the one she was born into. Alice wasn't afraid of visions, delusions, wild trips, or disorientating mazes. Her power was rooted in her curiosity, and she possessed just enough schoolgirl naïveté not to fear what she discovered.

This was what we saw as Alice's strength and weakness—she was blissfully unaware that the world she fell into could destroy her.

CHAPTER EIGHTEEN

GRANT

At dawn, Grant waits by the highway with his roller suitcase packed, squinting into the distance to see if he can make out any movement. Suddenly, he sees the glint of the delivery truck's headlights curl toward camp. When the truck pulls into the parking lot, Grant waves an arm in the air.

The door opens, and the driver climbs out and pulls his rucksack out from the front of the cab, then locks the door. "Is my ride back parked close by?" he asks.

Grant points to the snow-covered semi. "The Foreman asked you to give the keys to me."

The driver looks at him for a moment. "I was told to leave the keys in a box by the front door."

"Aren't we paying you enough not to ask questions?" Grant asks, adopting the indignant tone he heard his father use when speaking to his employees.

The driver shrugs and tosses the keys to Grant, shouldering the rucksack. "Well, I better push off to catch the first light." He looks up to see the pink streaks of dawn settling in the sky, and then trudges across the lot to the frozen semi. Grant watches him scrape the icy windshield while the cab heats up.

"Hey!" a voice shouts from across the highway. "Wait for us!"

Grant looks over and sees four Blooms run across the highway, dragging their suitcases with them. "Can we catch a ride?"

"Where are you headed?" the driver asks.

"As far south as you'll take us," one of the Blooms says.

"I can get you to the closest city, but that's as far as I'm going," he replies.

"That's fine," the Bloom says. "We'll find our own way home from there." She looks over at Grant. "Are you coming?"

"No, I'm waiting for someone," Grant responds.

She gives him a quizzical look. "Okay, suit yourself. We're getting the fuck out of here."

The Blooms quickly throw their suitcases into the back of the truck and pile into the cab.

The driver honks once as he backs out of the parking lot. Grant watches them drive away until the vehicle is just a dot in the distance.

When they are finally gone, he moves quickly. His fingers are shaking as he tries to fit one of the keys into the back of the truck. Finally, the lock clicks open.

Oil. Barrels and barrels of oil are stacked in the dark, piled as high as the ceiling. He shines his flashlight on the closest barrel and sees the markings of the company who once excavated the region. The name is the same as one of his classmates from Walden, a dopey blond kid from Texas who was blithe enough to not understand the politics of his family's name. Son of an oil baron, grandson of another, descended from one of the families who staked the land in shadow deals and court orders.

He won't have to deal with any of that from now on.

Grant sits at the back of the semi with his legs dangling off the ledge. He counts the specks of birds streaking across the sky. By the time he reaches one hundred, he sees the convoy in the distance. A copper station wagon is followed by a line of black snowmobiles and an orange camper van with the roof popped up. As the convoy gets closer, he sees that the van has a white rabbit painted on its sliding door.

The station wagon parks next to the semi as the vehicles idle in line behind it.

Willow steps out and tosses the car's keys to Grant. "Good work," she says. "You've earned your place with us."

"What now?"

"All you have to do is drive the car north to the exit out of Dominion Lake," Willow says. "We'll meet you there in an hour, and then we'll leave."

Grant nods toward the idling vehicles. "Who's with you?"

Willow smiles. "My family wanted to pay the camp a visit." Before she leaves, she kisses him on the cheek.

Grant slides onto the cream vinyl upholstery of the driver's seat. It's a beast of a car, with thick chains strapped to each tire. The interior smells of mildew and shoe polish, but the seat still has a nice spring to it, the coils surprisingly resistant after all these years. He catches a glimpse of himself in the rearview mirror. For a moment, he doesn't recognize himself. His face is streaked with grime, his beard scraggly and unkempt.

He inserts the key into the ignition and the dashboard lights up with a pleasant green glow. The glove compartment is filled with the miscellanea of an older, fastidious man. All the maps are sealed in plastic wrapping and stacked neatly in a pile next to a pine-scented air freshener tag and a bottle of Fireball whiskey.

With one hand on the steering wheel, Grant opens the bottle. The car fills with the stench of cinnamon hearts. He wonders what his duties will be in the commune. Perhaps he'll finish the novel he has been making brief and insistent notes on. Or learn how to build a post-and-beam house. Life will be lived more with his hands, he's certain of it. Up north, he will focus on the practical and the tactile—skills he never had the opportunity to cultivate in Boston. He takes a slug of the sweet whiskey and reverses the car out of the parking lot, heading north along the highway.

The pleasures of driving have long been dead to Grant. He and Jane only rented a car to escape the heat of the city a handful of times. The memory comes to him now with the clarity of a summons: he is driving a rental car to a stretch of beach north of Boston, while Jane sits in the front seat with her bare feet resting on the dashboard. The windows are open, and she is reading aloud a scene from *The Magic Mountain*, when young

Hans Castorp sees his skeleton for the first time during an X-ray. Hans notices the signet ring on his skeleton's finger, and suddenly becomes aware of the mortality of his own body.

"'He saw his own grave,'" Jane read out loud with a trace of awe and sadness in her voice. She put the book down and took Grant's right hand in hers, gently tugging on the Walden class ring he wore. "Take it off."

"Why?"

"I don't want this piece of metal to outlive you."

At the time, he laughed and said that he would probably lose the ring before he died. And yet, the ring is still with him now, while Jane is not.

He wrenches the ring off and then rolls down the window. The mild wind whips through his hair.

He slows down the car and throws the ring out his window. It arcs for a moment, fiery and gold in the sun. And then it's gone. He puts his hands back on the steering wheel and drives north toward the blankness of the melting snow.

Finally, a new direction.

WHITE ALICE

On the Equinox, we arrived in Dominion Lake. Every piece of weaponry and explosive was stockpiled in the camper van, and we were outfitted in tactical gear. When we rolled down the slushy highway, we didn't speak until we arrived in the parking lot. The geographer parked the camper in front of the hotel's cracked sliding glass doors.

We had agreed on the hotel in Dominion Lake as the site for our meeting. It seemed like a natural destination to convene, given how much time we had spent inside of its rooms extracting capital from men whom we did our best not to openly despise. The silver building looked blotchy and dull with the terrible purple curtains pulled shut. Vacated and diminutive, now stripped of its utility, the hotel was a husk of its former self.

The cartographer scouted the perimeter, and then indicated that the hotel was clear. The programmer took out a hatchet and nimbly cracked through the glass, shattering the door so we could step through.

The lobby smelled of mildew and rot, with a half foot of wet sediment on the floor. We sloshed through the muck and found our family seated in the lobby bar drinking cans of expired beer.

We rushed forward to embrace each one. Sal, with her wispy hair dyed brown and patches of rouge on her cheeks, looked like a high school drama teacher. We laughed when we saw her, and kissed her and Aurora on the cheek.

"How's life as a Madam?" we asked, and hoped Sal, too, would laugh. She didn't join in. Instead, she looked at Genesis with the dispassionate gaze used for roadkill.

"Genesis won't respond to his name anymore," she said.

We looked at him and asked, "What should we call you, then? Surely not 'the Barber.'"

He said the name pinned to his chest when we first found him in the Stop N Save. His birth name. A Dominion Lake name. A name that hadn't been uttered in ten years.

It was then we noticed the change in him. He didn't meet our gaze and pulled away from us when we reached for him.

"Are you all right?" we asked.

"I'm not coming back with you," he said. "I'm going south."

"South?" we asked. "But you've never been south."

"That's why I need to go," he said. "If I stay with you, all I'll ever know is the station."

"But what about Aurora?" we asked, and reached for her. "She needs you."

"As breeding stock?" He laughed bitterly. "That's all you think I'm good for."

"You're everything to us," we said. "Without you, we have no future."

He turned away from us and said, "This is your chance to imagine a different life."

"There's no point trying to convince him. He's defected from us," Sal said. "Besides, we don't need him anymore. We've found a replacement."

Sal briefed us on what the insurgents had learned while working. Aurora had posed as an escort and met the camp's Foreman, whom she knew exactly how to manipulate. He reminded Sal of our former sergeant back at home base. Same age. Same generation. Same deadened way of viewing the capacity of a woman. Aurora had gotten him drunk one night, and he had been happy to brag about the rare earth mineral the camp had discovered, and all the ways the extraction would continue. He told her that waves of men and money and infrastructure would spring up in the region, enlivening it once again. How the plan was to push northward, deep into the permafrost, farther into the region than had ever been mined before.

"Tell them what else," Sal urged.

"He knew about us by name," Aurora said.

The Foreman had told Aurora about a military station north of camp that had been maintaining American sovereignty for almost three decades. He said that they had intentionally been abandoned to see how they might survive in such hostile conditions. They'd been successful, and even given birth to a new generation, and their presence provided a legal loophole to continue an American-financed northward push. By summer, the company he worked for planned to arrive at the station and use it as a base for further exploration.

"We disposed of the Foreman as best we could," Sal said, "but he was a low-level hire and easily replaceable. If we don't do something with actual consequences, White Alice will be taken from us."

Twenty-seven years of living in the freeze, and we had never felt a cold so deep enter us. We were merely placeholders. Our work, our family, our lives were purely instrumental. All they needed were our bodies to live and breathe in the station to maintain it for their future.

All this time, we had thought survival was about the way we lived our lives and the choices we made. How we tried, as best we could, to raise our daughter with a morality that befitted the harsh life she had been born into:

Only take a life when it is absolutely necessary.
Love your family more than yourself.
Be reverent of your environment.
The sacrifice of one is worth the continuation of many.
Leave something behind for the future generation.

But we suddenly realized there, in the hotel lobby, that it didn't matter how we lived or how we conducted our lives.

All that mattered was that we remain alive.

Sal turned to us. "We'll caravan to the man camp and secure the delivery of the oil the camp uses to maintain the boilers."

"And after?" we asked.

"Remember what we've always said." Sal looked at each of us. "There can be no contingencies."

The sun is just rising over the trees when we leave for the man camp. Aurora leads us in an old station wagon that Genesis found parked in the barn of his birth family's homestead. The four pit bulls from the Blooms' camp sit at our feet with their muzzles tightly fastened.

When we arrive at the camp, we stay in our vehicles while Aurora speaks to our new recruit, a young man in glasses with a beard, who hands her the keys to the semi. We watch him get into the station wagon and then drive to the village, where he'll wait for us to lead him north. He looks young and earnest, the perfect benevolent father for our third generation and future partner to Aurora. We'll name him Exodus—the one who allowed us to leave everything behind.

When the car curves out of sight, we jump out of the van and start dragging the barrels out of the back of the truck. We work quickly, methodically, without speaking, until the van is filled with the oil.

We get back into our vehicles, and Sal leads the caravan north of Dominion Lake, around the lake itself, where the forest is wooded and thick. We park in a clearing where four Airstream trailers are camped. The Blooms' clients. Or, as Sal told us, the men who truly hold power in camp.

The pit bulls raise their heads when Sal calls for them softly by name. Turnkey, Blake, Spider, and Annie. She gently pulls off their muzzles and feeds them each a handful of kibble.

"Sweet darlings," she whispers, and pets each dog on the head. They wag their tails and nudge at her thigh for more treats. "They're ready," Sal says.

We break off into pairs. One of us holds a dog's leash, while the other stands ready at the trailer's door. Sal had warned us that timing is everything.

On Sal's command, we kick open the doors, and release the dogs inside the trailers.

With their muzzles off, each dog rockets into the air, a movement so sudden and fluid that we can't help but take pleasure in watching them move without constraint. They land in the entrance of each trailer, sniff the air, and then find what they're looking for—a man sleeping alone on a cot, cocooned in a burrow of blankets, chest rising and falling peacefully. The dogs lift their heads, sniff once again, and then lunge, dragging each man onto the linoleum floor.

We quickly shut the doors. The four trailers erupt into a cacophony of sound as the dogs do precisely what they've been trained for.

Once the trailers are silent, we open the doors carefully. Each of the dogs trots out, their mouths smeared with blood. They head straight to Sal, who rubs them behind their ears, and then rewards them with more kibble. She looks up. "Aurora, make sure the job is done."

We watch Aurora disappear inside each trailer. She finally emerges covered in blood. "It's done. I checked their pulses to make sure. But Meyer isn't here. He must have moved to the prototype already."

Sal shakes her head. "Meyer is irrelevant to us. He was always just a pawn."

"And the final mark?" Aurora asks.

"You know what to do," Sal says.

Aurora nods, and whistles once for Annie.

Sal is the first to crack a barrel. She begins to slosh the liquid around the edge of the trailers, leaving a slithering trail of liquid gold around each silver bullet. We overturn another barrel and then another, until the entire perimeter of the campsite is soaked in oil.

We stand together on a hill with our arms around each other.

This is it.

Sal lights a match, and the orange spark arcs onto the oil trail, erupting across the ground in a single breath. We watch the campsite become absorbed by flames.

When the trailers finally collapse, the sound is like something splintering under the earth.

CHAPTER NINETEEN

NARI

The walk to the yellow church takes less time than Nari remembers. Without a dog, or a man, or a Bloom, she feels untethered in a way she hasn't felt since arriving in camp. She walks quickly along the median of the highway with her suitcase, noticing tiny green shoots nudging out of the ground, and the first of the purple crocuses.

As she walks, she thinks of the long journey ahead of her, south to the border, and then east to the Atlantic. She hopes the Barber has enough fuel in his truck to get them to the United States. Once they've crossed into the US, she can access her bank account for the rest of their journey to the Northeast. Just one more week, and she'll finally be able to see her mother again.

When she arrives at the church, she pauses as she enters the front door.

"Hello?" she calls out. No answer.

She lets herself in and can barely make out the detritus of the Barber's home—tufts of dog hair, cigarette butts, and a mirror reflecting the church's emptiness. Once her eyes have adjusted to the dim light, she sees that all of the Barber's possessions are packed. His clothes are neatly folded in a duffel bag on a pew, and his combs and scissors are stashed away in a leather bag.

A rush of relief passes over her. He got her note in time.

Nari goes outside to look for him and picks her way through the church's yard. Turn left, then right, until she's back on the main street of the village, so close to the lake that she can see the fishing shack out on the ice. He must be there right now, packing up his tackle. She steps out onto the ice, bringing a flashlight with her. The lake is still blessedly solid, and she moves across it quickly until she reaches the building, then stoops through the door. The shack is dark and smells of old wood. A splintered dingy decomposes in the corner, and a bundle of fishing poles are heaped on the ice.

She traces the flashlight around the shack, and then aims it into the fishing hole. A hand floats toward her. Nari drops the flashlight, sending the light jumping across the ice. She forces herself to pick it up, then plunges her arm into the icy water and grasps the hand. She has to be sure. All the muscles in her arm seize up as she is dragged toward the hole. The hand feels like a block of cement attached to the weight of a whale. She pulls with all her strength and the Barber's face rises to the surface, eyes closed, mouth downturned.

She suddenly remembers kissing the sparrow tattoo on his neck. How she noticed it was inked in the precise place where the Flick is implanted. Such a delicate spot, she thought. One small bird trapped in flight.

She'll never know his name now. Never see him awash in sunlight. Never feel his warm skin or walk with him barefoot through the dunes.

She lets him go. His body sinks under the water and drifts away from her, to the bottom of the lake, to the center of the earth, to a place she can only see when she closes her eyes.

She runs out of the shack and across the lake. Through tears, she sees a flash of movement. A vehicle shines in the distance as it curls down the highway, the only point of acceleration in the still landscape. As it approaches, she recognizes it as Meyer's SUV. Her arm is so cold that it feels that it might shatter like glass.

Meyer parks the SUV and steps out. "Rose," he yells, running toward her.

She suddenly feels drowsy, like she might fall asleep on her feet. Hypo-thermia, she manages to think. She has to warm up immediately.

"Meyer," Nari calls out, and stumbles across the snow.

She lets Meyer take her in his arms and lead her to the passenger seat of the SUV, where the heat is blasting. He finds a blanket in the back as she pulls off her sodden parka. Her body shakes with the chill.

"You're safe now," Meyer says, and wraps the blanket around her tightly. "I'm here, and I'm going to take care of everything."

———————

They arrive at the prototype before dark. The building's glass panels form an elegant symmetry, capturing the sunset in triangles of blood orange and deep red. In the distance, the lake is visible through the trees.

Meyer leads her through the foyer into a sunken living room. On the wall hangs an aerial view of Dominion Lake with Meyer's settlements sketched into the thousands, extending as far as the plan will hold. She collapses onto a love seat in front of the fireplace. Here, in this living room with its calculated arrangement of furniture and art and forest views, she realizes that Meyer doesn't have the slightest clue as to how he was used in camp. He still believes curious and sensitive Americans will arrive by the electric carloads, unload their books and belongings, and take up pon-derous existences in these domes. The muddy precision of his ignorance horrifies her.

Meyer walks to the picture window and gazes out at the copse of aspen trees.

"I admit that we've had some setbacks," Meyer says. "There was a ter-rible accident at my colleagues' camp. An electrical outage in one of the trailers caused their camp to burn down. Luckily, I was here when it hap-pened." He shakes his head. "There were no survivors, and the rest of the camp has disbanded. Judith took off god knows where, and the Blooms and Diggers have all fled home now in the wake of the fire." He puts an arm around her shoulders. "It's just us now."

"Just us?"

"Yes, my dear. We're the very first citizens, but we'll stick it out, won't we?" Meyer points to a small dot on the aerial sketch, no bigger than a seed. "This is our new home now. We don't need all of the others. And if you're concerned about money and supplies, and all the rest, there's no need to fret. I've found a secure backer. Grimley Corp are coming on as partners. I was just speaking with the younger Grimley, and he was saying how thrilled they are to be a part of what we're doing." Meyer takes out a flask from his jacket and takes a generous swig. "We're really onto something, Rose. Here, let me show you the completed house."

He leads her upstairs to a room with a rose-colored door, pushes it open, and steps inside. "Darling, isn't it?"

She follows him into a small bedroom. A single bed with a ruffled bedspread is positioned in the corner of the room, and the walls are wallpapered with teddy bears. A white vanity with a plush pink seat rests against one wall, and a bookshelf filled with books and toys is against the other.

"This room is for a child," she says, and takes a step back.

"It was difficult to get the precise dimensions and décor, but I think it's a worthy duplicate of my daughter's room." Meyer picks up a heart-shaped pillow from the bed. "I brought everything up that I still had of hers."

A photo in a sparkly frame of a young girl who smiles with a gap in her front teeth, sits on the vanity. Nari picks up the photo. The girl's black hair is in a side braid and her nose is covered with freckles.

"This looks like me," she says.

Meyer squints his eyes. "I suppose there is a resemblance. I met her mother when I was working in Hong Kong, but we've long lost touch. My daughter hasn't spoken to me for ten years, either. But I'm hoping this will finally be my chance to start over." He gestures past the door. "There's a boy's room down the hall, just in case we end up having two."

"I'm not staying here, Meyer," she says, and pulls away from him.

"Oh yes you are." He kisses her on the head. "I can see it all so clearly. Why can't you?"

She closes her eyes and the image burns with a frightening intensity.

Trapped with Meyer in the woods. A lifetime spent stirring tomato sauce on the stove as Meyer looms behind her, his hands on her waist while he kisses her neck. A young girl with her face plays with eco wooden blocks in the sunken living room. Later, Meyer grunts on her in the Murphy bed, drunk on the home brew he's fermented in the root cellar, and when he comes, he says: *Rose, rose, rose, rose.* He laps the long syllable against her neck, reminding her of a Bloom in a dark room, her skin dry from the longest winter of her life.

She is not red sauce and the wet mouths of Meyer's children. She is not his wife, his daughter, his plaything, his mirror. She is not Rose. She is Nari.

She turns to him and says, "You don't know the first thing about me, do you?"

Meyer looks genuinely surprised. "Of course I do."

"Then tell me what I love."

Meyer pauses and considers before answering, "Vision. Community. An appreciation of the natural elements. Beauty. Grace." Meyer tries to kiss her, but she pulls away. "Am I right?"

"No."

"Then what do you love?"

She thinks of the Barber's face, frozen under the ice. "Nothing in your world."

"That's a pity." Meyer's voice darkens. "A man needs a worthy companion to survive." He reaches for her, but she pulls away again. "Come here, Rose. You must be exhausted. Let's go to sleep early. There's something I want to show you tomorrow."

She looks out the window and sees that it is dark. If she left now, she'd freeze again.

Just one more night, she thinks. And then she'll find a way out.

The next morning, Meyer drives Nari out into the tundra with a shotgun and the pointer nestled in the back seat.

"Where are we going?" she asks uneasily. They've been driving for an hour, much farther out than she's ever been before.

"Peak's Point," Meyer says. "The Barber showed it to me once. It's the best spot for hunting deer."

She flinches at the mention of the Barber.

"Are you okay, Rose?" Meyer asks. "You seem distracted this morning."

She looks out the window. "I'm just a little tired."

He pats her on the shoulder. "You'll buck up once we get into the fresh air."

Meyer parks the SUV in a clearing at the bottom of a hill. "We'll hike to the top and get the lay of the land before we start hunting."

The pointer sets the pace and trots ahead of them. Meyer picks his way through the bush with the shotgun resting over one shoulder and instructs her to follow closely behind. A dark V of geese flaps through the sky, and Meyer takes aim at the flock and shoots, scattering the birds into disparate points. They fly back into formation like magnets drawn together.

He takes in a deep breath of air. "Glorious, isn't it? This land offers so much, and yet we've treated it so poorly. Imagine what we can do now as collaborators."

"This land isn't yours," she says. "And it never will be."

"Well, technically it is." He rests the shotgun on his shoulder. "We bought a large parcel fair and square."

She looks at him and laughs. "Do you know why this land was bought?" She reaches down and grabs a handful of wet dirt. It feels cold and spongy in her fingers. "Minerals. What's buried under the earth. Your little project was just an excuse to get workers up here so they could dig down and find out how much this piece of land is worth." She drops the dirt and wipes her muddy hands on her parka.

"No, no." His face turns strained. "We're doing real work here. Ground-breaking work. You just can't see it."

"Look around. You're a smart man. Where are the engineers? The contractors? The investors?"

He shakes his head again, but she can tell his resolve is wavering. "They'll be here once we get more funding. Young Grimley promised me."

"He's gone, too, Meyer. He left with Judith. There's no one in camp but us and your dog."

"I refuse to believe it." He pauses, and then says, "You're just bitter because your boyfriend is dead."

She stops walking. The earth seems to contract. "It was you?"

"Do you think I'd lose you to a half-wit local?" He shoulders his rifle and aims it into the forest. "But who can really say? Men lose their way in the woods all the time."

They hike the rest of the hill in silence until they arrive at a craggy clearing. Meyer is nearly out of breath and rests against a boulder while the pointer pants beside him.

He brings out a pair of binoculars and scopes the frozen landscape, pausing at a cluster of trees. "A doe," he says, and hands the binoculars to her. Nari looks through the viewfinder and sees a deer move hesitantly through the trees, her spindly legs stepping through the snow. Her soft brown eyes blink in their direction. Two fawns follow closely behind.

Meyer puts a finger to his lips. The dog trots ahead and Meyer gestures for her to fall behind. "You keep the binoculars trained on the doe," he whispers, "and tell me when I'm in striking distance."

She takes the binoculars from him. This might be her only chance. "You go on ahead," she says. "I'll be right behind you."

"Good girl." He kisses her on the cheek. "Just let out a low whistle when she's in sight."

Nari nods and stands at the top of Peak's Point, training the binoculars on them. When they're out of sight, she starts to run in the opposite direction of the doe and her offspring, away from the murderous architect and his perfectly trained dog, his delusions of his own colony.

Down, down, down. She slides through the snow and dirt, jumps over toppled trees as the icy wind whips through her lungs. She takes in big, desperate gulps of air. She only stops running when she arrives at the SUV and sees with a leaping heart that the door is unlocked. She quickly slides into the driver's seat and turns the vehicle on.

Before she drives away, she looks through the binoculars one last time. In the distance, a man in a golden sheepskin jacket stumbles through the forest as he tracks an invisible animal.

CHAPTER TWENTY

NARI

The SUV takes each curve around the lake easily. Nari checks the energy gauge and sees that the battery is fully charged. She rolls down the window. The cool spring air whips her hair around her face. She speeds past the Millennium Mall, and only stops when she's miles away from Dominion Lake to search for a map of the region. She finds one in the glove compartment and spreads it flat on the passenger seat to trace the fastest route south, past Vandal, Fort Principle, Minor Plains. She'll blow right past them and keep driving.

She pulls back onto the highway and presses firmly on the acceleration pedal. The camp, White Alice, the prototype, all retreat farther and farther away as she drives into a sky larger and emptier than she ever imagined. The melting fields on either side lie fallow with a few rusted pieces of farming machinery and the splintered hulls of homesteads now collapsed under time and the weight of all that sky.

No traffic. No stop signs. Just the road as straight and secure as a line.

Night falls. She fiddles with the radio to stay awake. The stations flicker back and forth through thick static. She keeps the radio tuned to fuzz as she passes a black snowmobile abandoned on the side of the road. Is someone chasing her? She drives faster, the electric whirring of the vehicle an accompaniment to the radio's white noise.

In the distance, a woman and a dog walk down the center of the road. Nari flashes the high beams. She approaches slowly and sees Willow walking with Annie. Willow's parka is soaked with blood, and the knife tucked into her leather belt glints like a gutted fish. Willow and the dog turn their heads as the SUV approaches. Annie's eyes glitter green.

Seeing Willow brings the Barber back. Nari's tried not to think of him since she left camp, knowing that to do so will slow her down. But she suddenly remembers his face trapped under the ice, how he looked like he was lost in a moment of eternal supplication. A plea. Willow cared about him, too. If Nari doesn't stop, Willow and the dog will freeze to death.

Nari slows down and idles next to the pair. She lowers her window. "Get in."

Willow slides into the passenger seat and Annie settles by her feet. Blood is in her hair, on her face, on her parka. Willow wipes her hands on the seat without apology.

"What happened to you?" Nari asks.

"I had to leave my snowmobile because there's no more snow." Willow tries to squint outside. "I was going to hitchhike to the border."

"No, I mean the blood. Who did you kill?"

"Oh, no one. This is Annie's doing." The dog looks up when Willow says her name. "I mean, I guess I sort of assisted in the end." She looks in the back seat. "Where's the Barber?"

Nari accelerates again and keeps her eyes on the road. She'll tell Willow when they have the time and space to properly mourn. Right now, they need to keep moving. "He had to stay behind in camp."

"Why?" Willow asks. "I thought he was leaving with you."

"I'll tell you later. I promise."

Willow nods and digs around in her jeans. "They're here somewhere," she says, and frowns.

Nari flicks on the interior light as Willow rifles through her pockets.

"Aha!" Willow pulls out a handful of misshapen chunks. She cleans one with a handkerchief and then holds it up to the light. "I made sure to cut out the clients' prize morsels." A dozen gold teeth rest in her palm. They look small and benign, now separated from the mouths of the men. Just flecks of bone and mineral melded together.

Willow folds them back into the handkerchief. "I'll be adding some more to the collection soon. I'm on my way to the Floating City."

Nari looks over at her sharply. "You are? Why?"

"Judith trained me to always complete a mission, and one of our marks wasn't present in camp."

"And he's in the Floating City?"

"Yes. The Foreman told me that the CEO of the camp lives there. His name is Damien Mitchell. Do you know him?"

"I used to work for Damien. But you'll never get to him on your own. He's notoriously reclusive and well-protected."

Willow's voice remains resolute. "I have to protect White Alice."

"I'm warning you. Damien is ruthless." Nari pauses for a moment as a possibility clarifies. "But I can get you to him safely."

"You can?"

"Yes, he still thinks I know nothing. But only if you promise to do one thing."

Willow looks at her expectantly. "What is it?"

"Don't go back to White Alice right away. Stay in the South for a while and try to live your own life."

"Judith says White Alice is my family—"

"What mother raises her daughter to kill in her name?"

Willow's voice hardens. "You don't know what we've gone through. What we've had to do to survive."

Like a message traveling from a great distance, a voice cuts through the static and sings plaintively from the radio. It's a love ballad that sounds marooned between a prayer and an apology and reminds Nari of the songs her mother sang to fill the silence when she worked. Now, more than ever, Nari appreciates the low timbre of the singer's voice, how the words drag like a plow through mud. It's been so long since she's heard music that she'd forgotten how a song can take you into the bright light of the past. She's suddenly a child, sitting on the front stoop of one of the cottages, listening to her mother sing while she dips a rag into a soapy bucket and squeezes the suds out. Her mother looks up at Nari and smiles. She sings even louder, and her voice lifts up into the sky.

Willow tilts her head, listening intently. "Who is this?"

Nari says the singer's name. They're quiet as the music fills the vehicle.

After the song ends, Willow doesn't speak. She wipes her eyes with one blood-streaked hand, and then frantically fiddles with the knob of the radio.

"What are you doing?" Nari asks.

"I'm trying to find the song again," Willow says.

"It's over now," Nari says gently. "But there's a whole world of sad love songs out there waiting to be heard."

"But it's a shit world, isn't it?" Willow grabs Nari's hand. "I need to hear it from you."

"Of course it's shit." Nari squeezes her hand. "But it's the only world we have."

Willow relaxes under Nari's touch. She digs again in the pocket of her jeans and places the handkerchief filled with gold teeth on the dashboard. "How much do you think they're worth?"

Nari glances over at the bloody bundle. "Enough to get us to the Floating City."

"I've always wanted to see the ocean," Willow says.

"Good," Nari says, "because that's where we're headed. My mother lives near the ocean, and I promised to come back for her."

In an hour, Willow is asleep, slumped against the window. Her face looks peaceful, still, blank. Annie rustles at her feet, snorts, and then falls back into slumber.

A few hours later, Nari checks the energy gauge. Half-empty.

By the time Nari sees the lights shimmering on the horizon, Willow is awake. They look out the windshield in silence as they approach the border. The glow of the checkpoint appears ethereal and alien against the dark sky. They can't see anything yet, but Nari hopes that on the other side of that golden line, a future will bloom with people and light and love.

She checks the gauge again. A quarter full.

There's still enough time.

ACKNOWLEDGMENTS

My amazing editorial team, Amanda Betts, Natalie Hallak, and Jocasta Hamilton, and their colleagues at Knopf Canada, Atria, and John Murray. Thank you for your perceptiveness, diligence, and vision.

My steadfast and brilliant agents, Erin Harris at Folio Literary and Sophie Lambert at C&W, whose belief in my writing has been the guiding light of this book. Thank you to the foreign rights team at C&W—Matilda Ayris, Kate Burton, César Castañeda Gámez, and Jake Smith-Bosanquet, and Luke Speed at Curtis Brown.

My dear friends Saskya Jain and John Tormey, whose sharp and insightful comments were instrumental while revising, and for our discussions on writing and life.

For the conversations and community: Hadji Bakara, Mimi Cabell, Morgan Charles, Jenny Lee Craig, Katie Dutton, Adam Gollner, Marion Kadi, Adam Kaplan, Ana Isabel Keilson, Boaz Levin, Ret'sepile Makamane, Tracy Maurice, Hazel Meyer, Mark Polanzak, Lisa Rave, Alex Reynolds, Mayana Slobodian, Lisa Wilson, Tod Wodicka, Caroline Woods, Michael Young, and a special shout-out to my former writing group in Montréal: Anna Leventhal, Molly Lynch, Sean Michaels, Jeff Miller, and Camilla Wynne.

Page Richards and my former students in the MFA program at the University of Hong Kong. Xuefei Jin at Boston University and Stephanie Bolster at Concordia University, for mentorship and support.

My students in my "Reading the Future" course at Berklee College of Music, who helped me parse the texts I assigned about the end of the world and gave me the insight and optimism to imagine a different ending.

Endless gratitude to Akademie Schloss Solitude, where the first draft was written, and all the fellows I lived with next to the castle on the hill. A massive thank-you to the Banff Centre for Arts and Creativity, the Vermont Studio Center, the Virginia Center for the Creative Arts, and the Institute for Advanced Study at Central European University, for the gifts of writing time and space.

Thank you to everyone in my family for their love and unwavering support.

To Quinn, who is always next to me as confidante, discussant, co-explorer.

And to Yann, whose very existence makes me hope for a brighter future.